Ripple

Young Adult Version

E.L. Phoenix

Ripple

Young Adult Version

Second Edition
Copyright © E.L. Farris, 2013
Third Edition, Copyright © E.L. Phoenix
All rights reserved.

St. Mark's Publishing Company
Front Royal, Virginia and Jackson, Wyoming

Edited by Christina M. Frey
Cover Design by Brent Meske

ISBN: 978-0-9968478-1-0

Printed in the United States of America

Foreword

For weeks after I released *Ripple*, I felt a tinge of sadness and regret because my own daughter could not read it. "Mom," she would urge, her blue-gray eyes only partially hidden behind her girlish red eyeglasses, "can't you make a version of it just for me?"

I would laugh and smile without giving it too much thought. "Well, sure, darling. I could do that."

But she would persist. "Because I'd really like to read it now, and not have to wait until I'm—how old did you say I would have to be?"

"At least fourteen, but even then," I'd groan, "it would be dicey."

And then my youngest son asked me if I would come into his first grade class and speak to them about writing. Naturally I was overjoyed to comply, but first I had to run it past his teacher. I sent her a link to *Ripple*, and I could sense her cringing across the web. I followed up with a note in which I sent her a couple of funny chapters, ones that I'd read to all three of my children. "They laughed so hard they cried," I promised. She wrote back and gave me the all-clear to come in for a visit.

But all of this got me thinking. It isn't just adults who need a book like *Ripple*. Little girls, young women and even young men need a book they can read if they or someone they love is struggling with difficult issues like addiction and abuse. I wish there had been a book like this when I was a little girl. It would have helped me a lot.

As the mother of three and as someone who has been through many dark days myself, I want to assure the mothers and fathers who are reading this book that I think it's appropriate for young adults, and for even super-mature ten-year-olds like my daughter. However, I would encourage you to give this altered version a read yourself, or at a minimum, be available to listen to your kids when they come to you with questions.

This book is a condensed, abridged and cleaned-up version of *Ripple: A Tale of Hope and Redemption*. I have removed as much of the R-rated language as the story allows. However, most teenagers cuss; and in that respect and in so many others, Phoebe is like most teenagers. I also removed as much of the graphic description as possible. The fact is, my friends, many young adults and even children are treated—nay, forced to act—as adults, and so they must be spoken to as adults. While I realize that *Ripple* in both of its versions is intense and raw and in places hard reading, that is as it must be, because life can be intense and raw and hard.

The themes underlying *Ripple: Young Adult Version* are serious ones, but they are topics that we as a society must stop sweeping under the rug. In order for the afflicted to heal, we must be courageous and honest about what happens to more than twenty-five percent of our children.

More importantly, we must give these children and their friends coping tools and keys to healing. That is what this book offers, and I am hoping that its story of hope and healing will help the Phoebes of the world.

ACKNOWLEDGEMENTS

Writing a novel is a whole lot like running a marathon. Every time you think you're finished, you realize that there's another mile to run, and at times even one more mile can seem interminable. But just when you despair, another runner or a passerby cheers for you, and that's all you need to make it. It's lonely, but you're never really alone.

And once you do finish the marathon, and you've received your medal and your blanket, there they are, the family you love so very much. As you walk over to hug them, you know that they love you no more, and surely no less, for the 26.2 miles you just ran.

I owe so much gratitude to my family. My husband listened to me talk about the plot and the characters in this book for over a year. Often he counseled and advised, but mostly he just listened. When I got that faraway look in my eyes, he knew I was with Helen and Cass and Phoebe, and he understood. And just as he watches the children when I disappear for hours to complete a long run, so he watched our brood while I wrote at night and on weekends, and for that, too, I'm so very grateful.

Speaking of my children, they're everything to me. They inspire me in ways large and small, and it's my hope that in a few years my daughter and two sons can read this book and understand all of the things I simply cannot talk about with them directly. Madeline, Jim and Ben—I love each one of you so very much.

On a professional level, I've had the privilege of interacting almost daily with my incredible editor, Christina M. Frey. She helped me turn *Ripple* from a rambling wreck into what it is now, yet without "messing with my voice," as I often say.

I am also very much indebted to my dear friend and fellow author Deborah Bryan, who in addition to beta-reading *Ripple* is the first person I call whenever I want to talk about any and every aspect of writing.

On later drafts, I received great assistance from Astrea Baldwin, who taught me the subtleties of shifting points of view and encouraged me to "write better, because I know you can";

Douglas MacIlroy, an extraordinary writer in his own right; Karen Hartjen, who envisioned a future screenplay; and Karen Hackel, who provided a much-needed second eye on late-stage miscues and typos.

And for this revised edition, I am ever so grateful to Brent Meske, Stephanie Saye, and of course my editor, Christina M. Frey, for their advice, suggestions, and guidance. I owe a great deal to Brent Meske for his brilliant cover design work.

Any mistakes or errors in this book that have remained despite this generous assistance are mine and mine alone.

And to you, dear reader, thank you so very much for being a part of this journey, this long run of mine.

To my children.

CHAPTER 1

Helen Thompson slammed the glass door shut so hard the frame shimmered and vibrated. "The trial's in a week, Ashtray!" she thundered.

The young associate scurried out of the hotel's conference room, and Helen flung open the door and roared after him. "I needed that witness list two hours ago, Ashtray! If you can't get it to me in the next fifteen minutes, you might as well grab a cab to the airport and catch the redeye back to DC!" Helen glowered, imperious, her auburn hair and bellowing tone reminiscent of Queen Elizabeth I. If Queen Elizabeth could make a man move before finishing a sentence, Helen could make him run.

Helen's dark green eyes cut a slow arc around the conference room, searching for anyone or anything else not meeting her expectations. With one hand still on the gold-plated door handle, she made eye contact with her amused, dark-haired senior associate. Carl Hansen had worked with Helen long enough to know how to weather her frequent explosions. He shrugged, his eyes once again on the document in front of him.

Helen waved her hand. "Seriously, I don't give a crap what's going on in his personal life. These pimple-faced graduates don't pull their weight." She stomped across the room with one hand on her hip. A senior partner at the law firm Baker, Pitts, Kenzey & Moore, Helen stood astride the legal profession. She did not suffer fools, and within that category remained all new law school graduates until they had proved their mettle with years of hard-nosed toil.

Ashtray sprinted back into the conference room, shirt untucked and tie askew. Helen rolled her eyes as he barely missed colliding with a valet who stood at attention with a note in his hand. Second-year associates at Baker Pitts were not much good for anything other than emptying ashtrays; although the firm had long since outlawed indoor smoking, the nickname had remained too good to discard.

Helen nodded at Carl to take the note, her eyes fixed on the Impressionistic paintings that lined the walls of the Fairmont Heritage Place. She didn't like them; they were too undisciplined and amateurish. *I wonder if I should thank the valet?* Helen considered a moment, but shook aside the thought. At eight hundred dollars a night, she paid for top-notch service and expected to receive it.

With an impatient gesture, she dismissed Ashtray, then reached for the note and scanned it.

Judge's Chambers, U.S. District Court, Northern District of California.

Her eyes opened a little wider and she exchanged a glance with Carl. "Hey, would you mind taking notes so I can have my hands free?"

"That's what I'm here for, right?" He held up a yellow notepad.

Helen scoffed. "Those are going the way of the dodo bird. I'm going to spend part of your Christmas bonus on a MacBook Pro that you will learn how to use."

"Great," Carl groaned. "Beeping Blackberries. Messy crumbs from Internet cookies dripping all over the files that weave together our online lives. The blending of intrusive technology shadowing our interconnected existence . . . we live in the future already. And now you wanna add a Mac- whatever- Pro-book to the mix? Sheesh!"

Helen was barely conscious of what Carl was saying. It sounded like banter, and she wasn't fond of banter; nor did she have time for it. Helen rotated a pen in her hand while she paced. She had learned the trick from her husband, Richard Thompson, a Fairfax County, Virginia state court judge. The habit had annoyed her because she couldn't do it as well as he did, so one weekend she had practiced for hours until she was the best pen-flicker in the house. Pen flicking no longer annoyed her after that, and she found it useful in the courtroom. A rotating pen could hypnotize a witness.

Helen blinked and rubbed her eyes. "Okay, go ahead and dial."

Carl held his finger above the speaker button on the phone and paused. "I'm glad they're not Skyping us, you know?" He puffed out his cheeks and gave an exaggerated wink. "You never know when I might get caught making a funny face or some other crazy stuff."

Helen shook her head. Carl was almost thirty-five, and while he still acted like an irrepressible frat boy at times, he wrote better than any other associate at Baker Pitts. He never dropped the ball or missed a detail. Better still, Helen's female clients adored him. They wanted to help him meet a nice girl; they listened, rapt, to his engaging conversation over business lunches; and without exception, they respected his counsel as much as they loved him like a little brother.

The other thing Helen was planning to give Carl at the end of the year was a partner's stake in the law firm. With the number of hours he billed every year, the only thing blocking him from a stakeholder's share was his age; and for some reason, thirty-five was the magical demarcation between boy wonder and sober adult in the legal world. Not that she would know anything about how he acted outside the office, of course; aside from the occasional business dinner, Helen rarely socialized after hours.

Unlike most partners, she never escorted associates or clients to Redskins football games on the weekends. No one had ever invited her to a game. She didn't care. She wasn't there to make friends.

While Carl dialed, Helen rubbed the side of her index finger with her thumb. It was one of the only nervous mannerisms she allowed herself, and she figured it didn't count as a weakness because no one had ever noticed it. It reminded her of the perfect crime, if there was such a thing.

A voice boomed out over the speakerphone. "Judge Wilson's chambers. Fred McNamara speaking."

"Fred, Helen Thompson."

"Can I put you on hold?"

Helen shook her head. As a younger associate she would have added a trace of sugar to her tone, but she had learned very early in her career to save it for the jury. "Yes," she replied in an icy voice. "We'll wait." Helen unfolded her arms and stabbed at the mute button on the phone. "Unbelievable. Knee-deep in trial prep, and they put *us* on hold? Just once I'd like to put a judge on hold."

Carl puffed out his cheeks again, and when Helen relaxed a little, he added, "Yep. And it's not like one of us can duck out and grab a soda or take a leak or call an expert—"

"You call Dr. Wallace yet?"

Carl stopped doodling on the yellow notepad. "You've had me strapped to the freakin' conference table all morning tabulating compensatory damages. Now you're bugging me about hand-holding a long-talking, neurotic biology professor?"

Helen opened her mouth to respond and shut it as she realized that Carl had a point. The senior associate—her protégé—was a heavy hitter, almost a partner. At a billable rate of five hundred dollars an hour, he had more important uses of his time.

A subtle click announced Fred's arrival, and Helen nodded at Carl. As he leaned over and turned off the mute button, she observed the brisk cut of his trademark dapper gray suit with its matching tie and handkerchief. His biceps bulged as they pressed against his blue and white striped shirt. Helen sighed. She had no interest in Carl; indeed, he almost seemed uninterested in women, but being around him reminded her of what she did not have in her own marriage. Instead of a faithful husband, she had Judge Richard Thompson, who had chased around more secretaries and female clerks than any other judge within a five hundred-mile radius.

The pathetic thing, Helen thought, was that she still loved him. Even worse, she still wanted him, and she hated herself for this weakness even more than she hated him for his dalliances.

Fred cleared his throat. "Ms. Thompson, I am conferencing in Judge Wilson and counsel for the plaintiff."

Helen flicked her pen and spoke with cold precision. "We are standing by."

Plaintiff's counsel, Ray Ryan, came on the line with a perfunctory greeting. Helen liked trying cases with Ray because he never pretended to like opposing counsel. His legal practice centered on suing pharmaceutical companies in class action lawsuits, and he was a believer, a self-proclaimed avenger of all bodies corporate.

Judge Wilson was a different story. He was one of the old boys in a club that women and minorities were infiltrating all too slowly. "Helen, my dear, how is Richard enjoying the fairways of rolling Virginia?"

Helen took a deep breath. One of the best pieces of advice her mentor had ever given her was to remember that judges were more like big brothers or sisters than parents. *Treat them as equals and never beg for their respect.* "Judge Wilson, I am not a golf player. I cannot comment on my husband's fairway propensities at the risk of incriminating myself."

Judge Wilson laughed and Helen imagined his jowls shaking as he wiped the creases of his eyelids with his fat fingers. *I bet he's chewing on a cigar.*

"How is trial prep coming?"

"Fine. How is your ruling on our motion to dismiss?" Helen knew she was skating close to the edge of insolence, but she was losing patience.

"Actually, I was hoping to hear that trial prep was not coming so smoothly, Ms. Thompson."

"I'm not sure if I follow you, Judge." Helen overheard rustling papers and glanced at her watch. Richard had given it to her as a gift on her thirty-fifth birthday. It was simple and elegant, with large, clear numbers written on the face. The soft leather band felt comfortable except when she thought of her husband. *Who the heck is he screwing this week?*

"The thing is, we have a problem. I'm sure you've read about our case backlog, Ms. Thompson."

Helen nodded. The Northern District of California was notorious for its delays.

"Yes." Helen shifted her gaze across the room to the one piece of artwork that she liked: an oil painting of the Golden Gate Bridge, with its international orange color that had originally been intended as a primer. Buffeted by wind and rain and ocean waves, it still remained perfect in both form and function, and it would stand in the channel for many years to come. She felt solemn, as if staring at a stained glass window inside a cathedral.

The Judge was still speaking. As she waited for him to get to the point, Helen wondered why he was telling her all of this. She wanted to get home to her daughter and she needed to hustle to catch a plane. At this point, his angle, whatever it was, was taking too long for him to get to. She didn't grant or request favors. "So what you're saying is that our case is getting continued?"

"That's the gist—"

"Thank you. I'll advise my client accordingly."

Carl looked up from his notepad as the call ended. "What next?" The associate ran his hand through his hair. It didn't move a millimeter.

"According to my watch, it's almost five o'clock local time." Helen smoothed a few invisible wrinkles out of her skirt. "I assume you'd like to get home as early as possible to that beautiful woman of yours, right?"

Carl didn't answer right away. He licked his lips and stared at his smartphone, and while he appeared to be checking flights, Helen knew him well enough to sense he was avoiding eye contact. She shrugged. Helen didn't know what was bothering him, and she didn't want to know. She approved of a tight control of emotions and an iron will. The last thing she wanted from an associate, especially a male associate, was drama;

sometimes women cried when they were angry or tired, but a male litigator couldn't afford to seem soft. He'd get eaten alive.

Carl swung around in his chair, showing no sign of his initial discomfort. "You have five hours until you need to catch a flight. Shall I reserve it for you now?"

"No. Call the office and get one of our secretaries to book it."

"Ah, Helen. You know they'll screw something up."

Helen stared at him with a tinge of irritation, but before she could show it, Carl plowed ahead. "Anyway, it would take more time to call DC and have them book your ticket than to do it from my phone. Besides, if I call the office I'll have to explain why I'm not flying back until next week, and that could get a little awkward."

Helen studied Carl. "Why, what's going on?"

"You told me earlier this week that we were taking the weekend off, before it got really hairy, so I booked a flight for— well, it's been a while since we've had a long weekend, and—"

"And she's on her way?" Helen interrupted.

Carl started to speak, but Helen continued, "Of course. Go see her. I can get this figured out myself."

He grabbed his briefcase and put out his fist for one of his frat boy fist bumps. One side of Helen's mouth turned up despite her efforts to keep a straight face, and then she frowned. She didn't want to remember what it felt like to be young and in love.

"There you go," Carl said. "United Flight 355, leaving San Fran at 10:20 P.M., landing at Reagan National at 6:27 A.M." He waved without looking back as he headed off toward the bank of elevators, and Helen contemplated her schedule. Her daughter Phoebe, a high school sophomore, had an AP Chemistry test in the morning. She hoped Richard wouldn't stay out "networking" too late to make sure Phoebe got a decent night's sleep. Then again, as he always reminded her, she was the one who was always traveling. She, not Richard, was the absentee parent.

CHAPTER 2

Helen dialed the general counsel at Sintab as she stepped into the elevator. The gold buttons and gold-plated handles in the rear of the elevator shone bright with polish, and she got a glimpse of her hands in the reflection. If she inspected her hands, she could see the interwoven blue veins and wrinkles, but from far away her hands, like her face, showed little sign of her age. She had just turned fifty, but with her glorious head of wavy, auburn hair, she still turned men's heads. Yet they never stared at her for very long. Many of the partners at her firm called her the Dragon Lady behind her back, but the same men bowed and stood aside whenever she strode into a conference room.

"Mary?" Helen didn't waste any time on small talk once Sintab's general counsel came on the line. "Something has come up. And this may not be a bad thing." Helen spoke in her clipped Ivy League accent. "Remember Exxon? They delayed and delayed the Valdez plaintiffs from reaching a verdict for over a decade, and the longer they held that cash, the greater the return they got on their investments."

Mary was silent. Helen continued, unrushed, methodical and concise. "More cash means more money for R&D."

"The lifeblood of the business."

Helen heard a pen scratching on paper in the background.

"Good. Please send out an interim bill."

"Okay." The litigation team had already racked up more than half a million dollars in legal fees for the class-action lawsuit, which was the cost of doing business in the 21st century. "Consider it done."

Helen inserted the room card into the door of her suite and noted the fresh smell of Pine-sol, which made her think of the wood floors in her home back in Great Falls, Virginia. She tried the home number, Richard's cell and Richard's office, but each time she got the answering machine. Frustrated, she tried to figure out why his secretary wasn't picking up the phone. *Is he sleeping with her, too? Is he that reckless?*

Helen paced around her suite and then unlatched the balcony door. Once outside, she leaned against the metal railing, eyes closed, taking in the feel of San Francisco. If she could do it all over again she would live here, near Lombard Street. Or maybe in Half Moon Bay.

But would Phoebe like living here? There was much she didn't know about her brown-eyed teenager. She couldn't understand the point of most of the poetry or the short stories Phoebe wrote. Phoebe's gifts, riding horses and writing poetry and fiction, had little practical use and would never pay well. Pursuing your passion was great, right up until a woman couldn't support herself; no woman should ever rely on a man to pay her way. Helen never had, and thank God, for Richard wasted more money than he earned. Helen paused. Just because he was a mess of a man didn't mean her daughter would make the same mistake.

Helen surveyed the steep, flower-lined streets and the slanting rooftops. Off in the distance, dark blue waters swirled and slammed into the ramparts that held up the two bridges that crossed the white-capped bay. Helen wished she could like the Oakland Bay Bridge as much as the Golden Gate; it seemed shallow to prefer the one just because of the way the orange-red paint glinted off the dark blue, almost black waves. She shook her head. She really needed to hear Phoebe's voice.   Back inside the suite, with the balcony door open to capture the breeze from the bay, Helen dialed her daughter's cell phone. Guilt fueled her anger when it rang and rang without an answer. She felt displaced, nonessential, as if their lives sped along without her. She wasn't sure if she missed them or missed mattering to them.

Helen knit her brows as she typed a text message to Phoebe:

Darling daughter, I miss you terribly and will be home soon. My trial was postponed and I am taking the redeye into Reagan. Hugs and love. Mom.

Still formal even in a text message, Helen resisted proofreading but did it anyway. Once she hit the send button, she felt connected, no matter how loosely, to the creature she loved most in the world.

My Phoebe. Where is she now? Unlike most teenagers, Phoebe's social life did not begin and end with her cell phone, which Helen found both strange and strangely endearing. For her sixteenth birthday, Phoebe was requesting two things: a beaten-up old SUV and a partial share in a horse and stable. Phoebe was such a free spirit, and her mother had no idea whom she had inherited it from. Richard, except when drinking or golfing, was even more uptight than Helen. Helen found it even harder to comprehend Phoebe's love for horses. She would approve the purchase of the horse share, whatever that was, but she didn't understand her daughter's passion for something that could not be subjected to logical analysis.

Helen checked her watch. She had an hour to walk along the ocean, and she needed that time to unwind. She grabbed her room card and felt lighter as soon as she stepped through the hotel's revolving doors. The cool wind made the flags flap, and a fading, late-afternoon sun washed over her. Helen paused and breathed in the salty smell and the rich street odors, letting her senses absorb the thick, damp ocean air. In the distance, the glass lining the tall buildings in the business district reflected the vibrant colors of the row houses and the rustic, not quite industrial-looking streetcar lines. To her left the sidewalk slanted at an impossibly steep angle.

She headed briskly past several shops until she reached a cross street that sloped in the direction of the wharf. In the distance the towering orange-red spires of the Golden Gate Bridge rose toward the sky, and a surge of something like nostalgia rushed through her. It seemed impossible to feel wistful for something she was looking at, and yet Helen felt the loss of it—of the orange-red bridge and its delicately designed structures and the choppy waters rolling underneath—before she could even really enjoy it. The best things in her life were the ones she had to leave behind, she thought. Helen stopped herself. Phoebe was not a bridge or a faraway city.

Her eyes on the skyline, Helen almost bumped into two men who were holding hands. One of the men had dark hair that didn't move a millimeter. She knew that hair. "Carl?"

Helen searched for something to say, but for once found herself at a loss. What was it that her mother had always said? *Talk about the weather if nothing else comes to mind.* "Beautiful evening, isn't it?"

Carl froze, involuntarily letting go of the other man's hand. "Helen, this is Troy." Then he nodded and put an arm around his partner's shoulders. "The love of my life. Troy flew out here a couple days ago. We're engaged, and hoping to get married as soon as the laws catch up. I should have introduced you to him earlier. I'm really sorry for not saying anything. I just didn't know how you would take it."

Troy, a few inches taller than Carl, wore crisp khakis with a crease that ran all the way down to his black Italian loafers. His blue dress shirt opened to a bright white undershirt beneath.

With a sober nod of her head, Helen extended a hand to Troy. As she introduced herself, she wondered why he hadn't told her. She hadn't thought very much about gay marriage. In her mind the entire kerfuffle was more emotional than logical, and once she had figured out her views on the matter she had set it aside as yet one more thing that activists and politicians yelled about. Her brain was a neatly ordered one: questions asked, questions answered and questions left unresolved. As far as gay marriage went, if it didn't interfere with Carl's work performance, why should she care? If anything, attorneys took their work more seriously once they were married.

Helen quickly calculated Carl's billing rate, billable hours and the firm's bottom line. There was space in the budget. "Your two-week vacation starts now."

Carl looked down and cleared his throat, but he didn't speak. *He's trying not to cry. I have to keep talking until he collects himself.*

"And one other thing. You're up for partnership. No guarantees, but I think you're a shoe-in." Helen waited. She couldn't understand why Carl looked helpless.

Troy wrapped a reassuring arm around Carl. "I told you not to worry."

A faraway look entered Carl's eyes. "I'm overwhelmed, Helen. And as logical as you are, there must be a reason you're telling me this."

She took in both of them with a crinkle of her eyes. "I need you to remain happy. I would not be able to represent my clients nearly as effectively without a competent right-hand man. Or woman. It just happens that you're a man who loves another man. If I did not support you, would you keep working for me?"

Carl ran a hand through his hair. "Probably. For a while."

"Exactly," Helen said. "Until someone better offered you a position, and then it would be too late to treat you right. Meanwhile you'd be half with me, but with one foot out the door."

"So this is all about the firm?"

"Most of it, but I want you to be happy, too." She blushed a little. "I care about you, Carl. The firm is behind you. You have the firm's support. The two of you enjoy your vacation, bring me home some good chocolate from Ghirardelli's and come back ready to knuckle down and help me keep on top of our caseload." She tried to think of what else to say, and after a few uncomfortable moments of silence she nodded and began walking back toward the wharf.

Munching sourdough bread as she strolled along the bay, Helen kept sneaking peeks at the red-orange bridge she already missed. Maybe she could commission a photograph of it. Not a drawing; it was perfect as it was. She had read an article in the *Wall Street Journal* about needing healthy outlets. She could pay a therapist to help her find healthy coping mechanisms, or maybe she would pick this up as her new outlet: finding the right photographer for the Golden Gate Bridge.

Helen wrenched her eyes away from the water as she tossed the ends of the bread into a metal trash can. There was never enough time. She needed to get on an airplane in a few hours. She set her shoulders and remembered where she lived, and decided she would take pictures of the cascading water at Great Falls over the weekend. *And Phoebe can walk beside me.*

CHAPTER 3

A high-pitched shriek woke criminal defense attorney Cassandra White. Moments later, the telephone and the alarm clock began ringing at the same time, and Cassandra tried to shut out the dissonance. Her head throbbed.

"Mom! Ya gotta come quick! Zander barfed in the bathroom."

Cassandra pushed the tangled mess of silver-blonde hair out of her eyes and lifted her head off the pillow long enough to squint at the alarm clock. It was 6:03. "Aw, really?" she growled as she reached to switch it off. Her voice rose to puncture her noisy morning. "All right, I'm coming. Can you grab the phone? It's probably Dad." Cassandra's husband, a securities lawyer in DC, was trying a case in Florida and had been gone all week.

Her blonde ponytail waving behind her, Catherine ran into her parents' bedroom and picked up the handset on the seventh ring. "Hello? Is it you, Dad?" The teenager giggled and in a lilting voice added, "White residence. How may I help you?"

Cassandra lifted both hands to her head and ran them through her hair. Her Friday morning wasn't starting well. She swung her feet to the ground and winced as the tendons seized. She had run a hard ten-miler the night before, and at forty-eight years of age her body had already piled up a few thousand miles too many. After she got a shower, her aching joints would feel better. *Wait—darn. The barf is still waiting.*

She paused on her way to the children's bathroom and leaned into her son's doorway. "Zander, y'all right, sweetie?"

Her tiny, brown-skinned son lay on his side, his little blue-gray eyes open and alert. Zander was five years old, and on most mornings he would have been sprinting from one side of the house to the other. But today, his thumb in his mouth, Zander just lay quietly and blinked.

Cassandra surveyed his room, which was covered with toys and articles of clothing but not with vomit. *Thank goodness.* She took a deep breath. Her son took after her husband both in looks and in housekeeping, but she loved them both despite their messy ways. "Okay," she mustered, and turning, murmured, "You rest and let me figure out what's what and I'll be back, okay?"

With that, she walked into the children's bathroom.

"Whoa." Cassandra covered her mouth and tried not to breathe in the odor of last night's dinner. "Okay." She thought aloud. "This is gonna take a while."

She followed the sound of her daughter's voice and found Catherine sitting by the tall windows in the back of the study. With a gentle hand on the girl's shoulder she whispered, "I need to call the school and let them know Zander won't be there—can I have the phone?"

Catherine startled and then passed her mother the handset. "Here, Mom. It's Dad."

With a dramatic sigh, Cassandra opened the two-inch plantation blinds. "Hello, Frank?"

After he said a few words about the weather, she interrupted him. "No, I can't talk. There's vomit in the bathroom and I gotta call the school. Please tell me you're coming home tomorrow."

She heard her husband chuckle on the other end of the line. "As far as I know," he replied in a light way that made Cassandra want to hurl the phone across the room.

"Frank, seriously." Cassandra, a partner at her law firm, Brickman & White, tried to keep her voice even. "I have a jury trial next Friday, which means I have trial prep all weekend and next week. You're on call with the kids. We've *talked* about this."

His voice hardened. "Cass, I said I'd be there."

"No," she snapped. "You said you'd try, or something like that." Cassandra sighed. "I'm sorry, I don't mean to bark at you. It's been a heck of a morning already."

"Wish I was there to help you clean it up, darling." The hardness was gone from his voice. "I know you've never had a strong stomach."

She laughed. "No, you don't wanna be here. I better go. There isn't enough Lysol in America to clean up this mess." She paused and checked the clock, realizing that in twenty-four hours he'd be there. "See you tomorrow."

Fifteen minutes later, covered in *lemon-freakin' fresh Lysol* and dried-up vomit, she emerged from the bathroom carrying a trash bag, the laundry and all of the bathroom cups and toothbrushes. She tossed the clothes in the washer and the rest of it in the trash outside, pausing in the kitchen to wash her hands. Catherine sat at the kitchen table, flipping through a running magazine, while Zander, still in superhero pajamas, played with a matchbox car on the floor.

"Catherine, please drink your milk and get out to the bus stop." Cassandra shifted her attention to her son. "Zander, let's get you into the tub. Wait, Catherine, will you take the dog out for a quick walk?"

"Uh-huh." Catherine checked the position of her ponytail and, with one eye still on the magazine in her hand, reached for the leash while sipping a tall glass of milk.

Cassandra grabbed the phone and speed-dialed her secretary's home number.

"Morning, Cass."

Recognizing Janice's smooth voice, Cassandra rushed past pleasantries. "Hey, it's Cass. I'm going to be late this morning, or maybe I'm going to work from home."

"What's wrong?"

Cassandra opened the fridge door and sipped her water bottle. "Ah, Zander threw up in the bathroom and Frank's out of town. I can't take him to school and I can't imagine bringing him into the office. He might eat the goldfish, or something crazy like that."

"Is he sick?"

Cassandra thought for a second. "Nah, too many cookies. He must have dressed in his camos and conducted a late-night pantry raid."

Janice Rogers had been Cassandra's secretary for more than ten years. She thought of Zander as if he were one of her many grandchildren. "Bring him into the office and I'll set him up in the conference room with some movies and popcorn." She laughed through her nose. "No cookies."

Cassandra nodded and shut the fridge door. "Thanks, you're a godsend. Let me get cleaned up and I'll get on the road."

Freshly bathed, Zander sat in front of the television watching a cartoon in his mother's bedroom while Cassandra finished drying her hair. Her daughter burst into the room again.

"Mom!" Catherine was out of breath. "The bus is broken down and I can't be late! History exam!" A junior, Catherine had always been easy to parent. She rarely got in trouble or even argued, and sometimes Cassandra worried that her daughter didn't have enough fire in her belly. For the first eleven years of Catherine's life she had been the baby of the family, the center of her parents' adoring attention, and yet she was a responsible and loving big sister. *If only she took school as seriously as she took cross-country*, her mother thought, but all she said was, "How do you know the bus is broken down?"

Catherine rolled her eyes and threw a stuffed animal at Zander. "Mom, do you have to cross-examine me about everything?"

Cassandra thought about it and said nothing, so Catherine added, "Fine. Jason texted me."

Jason, a senior at Catherine's school, lived down the street and was a frequent source of irritation. Cassandra thought of him as a sort of oversized Dennis the Menace. She sat down to pull on her boots. "Jason texted you?"

"Come on, Mom. He's not that bad."

Cassandra raised an eyebrow.

"Mom! Stop!" Catherine placed a hand on her hip. "Anyway, Jason called his mom and his mom called the school and the secretary said that Bus Five was broken down in the middle of the parkway and it would take at least half an hour to get a new bus." With an innocent, open-eyed look, her daughter added, "Can I ride with Jason?"

"Jason? Um, I don't think so!"

"Why not?"

"Why *not?*"

Catherine shifted her feet. "Mom! I'm not five."

Zander jumped on the bed. "But I'm five!"

With a hand on Zander's shoulder to calm him down, Cassandra's expression took on a sober cast as she addressed her daughter. "No, you're not. So hear me. The word on the street is that Jason drives too fast. It's not just that he rides his Jeep across everyone's lawns. I've heard he even rolled his dad's car. So . . . no, no way, nada, never, heck freezes over before you ride with him."

"Mom!"

"Enough. I'll drive you." Cassandra's face, always expressive, grew impassive. She was done arguing.

Catherine stood still a moment, as if waiting for her mother to relent, but then shot a glance at Zander and shrugged. "Fine." She stuck her thumb in her backpack. "Can we hurry up and go already?"

Cassandra turned and brushed her hair one last time. "Thanks for walking the dog. Would you give Zander his milk and a Pop-Tart? I'll be ready to go in two minutes."

"Dad says Pop-Tarts aren't healthy," Zander announced.

"Uh-huh. They're not, they're junk food, but we don't have time for oatmeal, and I think you need to get something in that stomach to counteract the cookie bile. Go with Cat."

Zander grinned. "Cat? Cat! Make me fat."

Catherine took his hand and pulled him off the king-sized bed. "Downstairs, shrimp toast."

Cassandra picked up the hair dryer, which was still lying on the hamper, ticking, and wrapped her hair in a bun. She winked at the mirror and headed to the garage.

CHAPTER 4

Five days earlier.

He took a deep breath, cupping his hands in front of his face, and leaned into the back of the burgundy metal seats. "Deeee-fense . . . Deeee-fense!" As he exhaled he could see his breath, and he damn near laughed. *Autumn. Football. Pure joy.*

With a satisfied grunt, he looked around him at the bank of lights casting shadows on the spectators surrounding him. Burgundy and gold. *It doesn't get any better than this.* A whistle blew, and the crowd noise ebbed as Tony Romo took the snap. Romo drifted back, feinted once, backpedaled three steps and tossed it out of bounds right before the Redskins' hulking defensive end crashed in over left tackle. *Fourth and ten.*

As a breeze blew through the late night air, he felt the cold metal seatbacks under his fingers. With an almost shy smile, he turned around to his friend, Richard Thompson, and raised his left hand for a high five. Monday night football in the nation's capital, cheerleaders, season tickets on the fifty-yard line, and they were creaming Dallas, just creaming them. This was all a guy needed. *Almost.*

"Hey, Your Honor?" Bob waited for Richard to look away from the field with a wry smile. "Think Campbell's going to be any good this year?"

Richard took his baseball cap and turned it so that it sat on his head with a slant. He was trying to go street, chuckled Bob to himself, to match the look of the 'Skins quarterback. It was ridiculous looking, really, for a middle-aged white guy wearing khakis, a blue shirt, and a maroon and yellow tie, but funny. Richard wasn't getting any younger; *he just didn't realize it yet.*

Bob and Richard made a strange pair. A detective and a state court judge, they'd met years ago during a trial. Then still a prosecutor, Richard had made a series of jokes throughout the trial, jokes that had made Bob shake his head and laugh because they betrayed a total lack of understanding of what a hunt was really like. Richard had sounded so damn stupid that at a break, Bob had lit into him. But instead of whining or yelling back, Richard had folded his arms and roared with mirth. "Tell you what, Detective. I got some free time this Sunday. How about if I show you how a real man kills a deer?" He had, and they'd been friends ever since.

"Yep." Bob shoved his hands into the pockets of his old Wranglers and waved his hand toward the black kid selling beer. "Bud-WI-zer! Cold beer! Bud-WI-zer!" Kid had a hell of a voice, and it was a damn good time to grab another cold one.

"Hey, kid, over here." Bob's voice betrayed a Jersey accent.

"Damn, Bob, you still sound like you're on the Turnpike."

"Bugger off, Dicky." Bob grinned, and he reached over to hand the kid a twenty. "Two beers," Bob chanted, almost in a singsong voice. Sort of like the black kid talked. *No. That's crazy.*

Bob winced as he leaned over to grab his beer. Ever since he'd served his second tour, his neck had been killing him, but it had gotten worse lately, and now the first sign of one of his headaches was coming on. Seemed like they were getting worse. Maybe he needed to lay off the beer, but it was the only thing that helped. That, and . . . Bob felt his shoulders relaxing. And the girls. That helped, too.

"Richard, are you sure we're set? You know, for this weekend?"

Romo jogged off the field.

"That's right!" Bob got both lungs into it, yelling so hard that spittle flew out of his mouth. "You're a pussy, Tony!"

Richard laughed, and Bob shook his head, kind of pissed off, because Richard almost looked young again, at least in that moment. They'd been friends for years, and the fucking judge, at least with the lights dimmed, hadn't aged so much. A little belly fat, sure, but not so . . . unappetizing. Drank like a fish. Partied like a professional athlete. And he . . . *damn him*. Bob leaned his head back and swallowed a big gulp of Bud. And he got the girls. Unbelievable.

CHAPTER 5

A horse walked past Phoebe Thompson and tried to nuzzle her arm. Instinctively she reached into her pocket to find a carrot, but all she found was a string. A single string, loose and lost and out of place. Just like her. And it was dark inside that pocket, just like it was dark inside . . .

> *No. I don't want to see it. No! My eyes are closed. Dark. No! I feel it, I feel it, the image, and it cuts so hard, storming through me like a late-night train from nowhere. I feel it inside me and I want to disappear. To not be. Stop being.*

"Phoebe?"

Phoebe bent over and put her hands on her knees. Every cell in her body throbbed as she felt the soft surface of her riding breeches under her fingertips and tried to stop seeing it.

> *Fabric. A single thread, and then another one. Tight, knit tight, together, not loose, not lost. One. A series, a pattern of threads becoming one solid, firm, unyielding piece. If I feel the threads underneath, I can be here, not there, not feeling it—*

"Phoebe?"

Phoebe pushed herself to stand up straight and turned, her face expressionless. It was Sascha. A corn-fed Midwesterner, freckled and big-boned, Sascha had always seemed out of place at the elite McClintock School. Except for a few scholarship students, McClintock educated the children of the nation's senators and lobbyists and power brokers.   Sascha and Phoebe made an unlikely pair. They neither looked nor rode alike. Phoebe, although well-trained, rode with a simple grace, an intuitive flow, while Sascha excelled at riding as if it were a science. They had different, even opposite strengths, but worked well together and dominated county and state competitions.

Phoebe tried to shut out the shadowy sensations threading across her inner vision. *It can only hurt if I feel it.* She crossed her arms and leaned one hip against the fence. "Hey, Sasch. Ready to ride?" She tried to sound edgy but her words sounded flat, like an actress reading someone else's lines. Her mind drifted again as the other girl nodded.

I am a shadow. Part girl, part died. No one can share my sickness. No faces, no light. Eyes shut. I can't have friends. I tremble and feel the pieces tear, torn, ripped so long ago, and each breath makes it real. Am I real? What is real? How many times can I die inside?

Hey, Sasch, Phoebe thought, *I'm a whore.* She slouched and clasped her helmet, which felt odd in her hands as she rubbed her index finger over it and tried to calm herself. She took a few steps away from the fence, wishing that the swaying movement of the burnt grass beneath her would make her mind stop.

Kill her. I should kill her. I see a little girl and I am wrapping her in a warm blanket. I am carrying her to a safe place. I want to get her there, but there is nowhere safe and I don't care. It's not safe. It's an abandoned mansion rusting; falling cobwebs and rats and I can leave her behind and I will run so far and I'll be free of her and maybe my pain will die with her. If she dies will I have killed her or just taken her off life support? How can I think like that? I love her. I hate her. Can't I leave her bleeding in the mud? Hands and bodies drifting. I drift. He should have killed me.

Sascha was suddenly next to her, her hand on Phoebe's arm. Phoebe tried not to cringe involuntarily. A look entered her friend's eyes, a fragment of comprehension, a hint of knowing; and instead of removing her hand from Phoebe's arm, she patted her firmly but with the barest, the merest hint of tenderness. Together they walked toward their waiting horses.

"Hon, you're wearing the same shirt you wore yesterday."
Sascha made a dismissive gesture, and Phoebe thought that her
friend's eyes seemed as if lit from the inside. "Not that there's
anything wrong with that. But you're, you know, like, always so
well put together. Are you okay?"

Phoebe's legs felt funny. She willed them not to collapse
beneath her. *Colt legs.* Were the vultures circling overhead coming
for her? "Yep," she muttered.

"Are you okay to ride?" Sascha persisted.

*I first rode when I was five, and it wasn't a pony he put me on. He
told me I must not fear them because they look to us to know, and
he put his hand out, and he helped me up on the old Arabian
thoroughbred. And even though she measured fifteen hands, she was
so gentle, but he was not, was he?*

Phoebe gripped the reins and shook her head.

*No! Not here. Not now. Go away and let me ride. I was scared of
him, but when he told me not to be afraid of the horses he must have
scared me into believing.*

Teeth gritted, Phoebe used every last ounce of energy to
pull her mind back to Jupiter.

Riding is riding. Phoebe grabbed the reins and climbed on
Jupiter and let her mind drift back to the moment, the horse, the
wind and the sun, and for a few moments she rode free. She
processed a mental checklist without really even being aware of it.
Hands relaxed? Check. Heels? Right. Shoulders relaxed? Yup.
How is Jupe? Optimal. The saddle? Good.

*How do I separate him from the very thing he taught me to love
most?*

Sweat formed under her helmet and her feet itched inside
her long black riding boots. The smell of dung mixed with the
odor of falling leaves. Phoebe kept her hands on the reins, and
with the lightest of touches guided Jupiter toward the forest a
mile away.

That's what I told myself afterward. I dreamed I was dying and then I showered. He washed off me. He promised it was the last time and I knew it wasn't, but in part I didn't know if I wanted it to be.

Phoebe felt Sascha trotting in her direction by the slight shift in the breeze; she could sense the misshapen shadow of a horse with its rider before she spotted her sturdy friend heading out from under the tree line. Phoebe's back was to the sun. Sascha wrinkled her nose as she pulled her Quarter Horse up beside Jupiter. Phoebe nodded with unconscious approval. Sascha was a technician.

I love her, my sweet riding sister. If I told her . . . no. Sascha can't know. I can't have friends. No one can share my sickness. Look normal. Define normal? Who is? What is?

Sascha leaned over and slapped Jupiter's rump as both girls dismounted. "Jupe's a good egg, eh?"

Phoebe shifted her shoulders and tried to reply, but the words slipped away before she could touch them.

I am ice inside. And if someone touches what is inside, I will shatter like broken fragments of icicles. No one will touch me there.

"Phoebe?"

"Huh?"

"I'll help you muck today."

•••

Sweat dripped between Phoebe's breasts as she swatted away at the army of flies eating the horse manure. She grunted and let her mind float as she bent at the knees and tried to get through the mucking without complaining. Occasionally a horse whinnied or a tail thwacked at the wooden stall doors. Sascha hummed an old Methodist hymn and Phoebe, as much as she wanted to mock it, found it comforting. *Even if God hates me, I'm thinking this sounds all right.*

CHAPTER 6

Bob pulled into space 314, which wasn't really his space. That bugged him. Spaces were allotted to specific residents for a reason, and this departure from procedure went against every instinct in his ex-military brain. But one thing he'd learned from those years of service is that sometimes a man had to improvise. If the neighbor's hippie van was inhabiting his space, well, he'd have to borrow ol' lady Alice's spot for just long enough to change clothes. Then he was off to the range to teach ladies' firearms training. Some of those ladies brought it; at least they had the last time he'd taken care of raising a whole new generation of cute assassins.

Bob grinned. *As if.* Man, his ex was missing out. *I make a good salary. I'm funny. And charming.* At least that's what Richard's last hot thing had told him.

Too bad he couldn't have made it over to Richard's last weekend. But this one was going to make up for it.

It's gonna to be a hell of a weekend. JudgeandJury is setting up a thing at his house. Then on Sunday I have tickets to the Skins vs. Giants on the fifty-yard line. We might take the East this year. Fuckin' A.

Years ago, he hadn't minded the long hours. *But this last year or so, it was like he was losing his edge.* Bob shook his head. *Nah. Not me.* Then he chuckled. *Not I. See? I'm funny.*

A few tough breaks, a case they could not crack . . . a run of it. That was all. *If only* . . . Bob gritted his teeth as the late setting sun reflected into his eyes. He'd left his sunglasses on the dashboard of his Jeep Grand Cherokee, damn it. His head throbbed, and he'd already swallowed two handfuls of Motrin and a few Oxies. Maybe it was getting worse. Maybe he needed to see his internist.

Work really was killing him. He'd given his time to the military. It'd had been good, fair, honest time. Now he was looking at an early retirement from the FCPD. And his ex was gonna take half of it. *Life was a grind, man. All this, and for what?*

Bob ran his hand through his hair and paused. Hair? He used to have a full head of it, but now all he felt was bristles. He kept it shaved out of pride, out of a sense of esprit de corps. But it was getting a little pathetic, or that's what she'd said last time they spoke. "Where's all your hair, Bobby," she'd jeered. *She never understood. Ice queen. It's her fault, really. She wouldn't take care of my needs.* He deserved a break. He needed one.

He reached the white door of 455 Meeting Place and slid the key into the lock. He jiggled it twice until it engaged. He'd get some WD-40 on it this weekend, before the game. This weekend . . .This weekend he'd be sliding . . . he shook his head and felt his jaw hurting from smiling so wide.

CHAPTER 7

"Anything else you need, ma'am?"

Helen set her luggage on the stone walkway that wound from the stand of firs on the side of the garage up to the front door. She sighed as she breathed in the smell of the forest. It was good to be home. After shaking her head, she almost allowed herself to smile.

"Have a pleasant day, ma'am," the driver said, and without looking back he started up the Lincoln Town Car, pulled around the semicircular driveway and turned left onto the state road that ran alongside the Thompson family's white mansion.

Helen felt torn about the architectural design and layout of her home. Twenty years ago, she and Richard had purchased ten acres of land overlooking the Potomac River in Great Falls, Virginia. When the land values had skyrocketed a decade later, they had subdivided the plot, sold their original Frank Lloyd Wright-influenced home and used some of the profits to build Richard's dream house. Unquestionably the finished product, which they had moved into when Phoebe was five years old, was lovely: raised ceilings, circular staircases, aluminum appliances, wainscoting and chair rails in almost all of the rooms, bay windows, a hot tub and an indoor swimming pool. It had everything a man of "Richard's station," as he loved to say, would want.

But secretly Helen had never felt at home in Richard's monstrosity, which she called it in her darker moments. She found the sheer mass of the Thompson Mansion wasteful. A family of three did not need six thousand square feet of living space. Admittedly she appreciated the cherrywood floors and the views of the river from the back windows, but the thought of the wasted dollars spent on utilities bothered her enough to raise the issue with Richard several times a year. Their arguments would dissolve into long dissertations about learning to appreciate the finer things in life, until Helen would finally shrug, throw the bills on her husband's desk and retreat to her study.

Helen watched the light play off the pen oaks that towered over the sloping green lawn. Shadows danced across the pathway leading to the fenced-in backyard, and the smell of freshly-mowed grass mixed with spilled gasoline and decaying pine needles from a stand of fir trees lining the side yard.

The firs meant something special to Helen. Their scent brought back rich memories of the three years she had lived in Williamsburg, Virginia. Williamsburg is famous for its rich history, but all Helen remembered about it was the odor of firs and the sonorous beat of horses' feet clip-clopping along the august avenue that ran from the College of William and Mary to the Capitol building. The one stipulation Helen had insisted upon when she and Richard subdivided the land was that the firs remained within the Thompsons' property boundaries. Everything else she left up to Richard and their slightly shady realtor, Jim. *I did that too often. Left things up to Richard.*

Many nights, Helen had gotten home so late from work that she hadn't felt like arguing over the architectural plans or doing much of anything aside from playing with her little girl. *I wonder how she's doing,* Helen worried. The year had been crazy, and even when Helen was home Phoebe had seemed more and more silent, spending most of her time locked up in her room listening to Pink Floyd or writing more abstract poetry and experimental fiction. Was she sad or tense, or just a teenager? Over the last few months, Helen had started to read about horseback riding just so she could find something that would engage Phoebe enough to get her daughter to talk to her.

Helen sighed. Was it all worth it? The conversations lost, the memories not merely forgotten but never forged? Sometimes the price of her ambition combined with her unrelenting caseload felt too great. But she didn't know any other way.

Helen straightened her shoulders and gingerly stepped onto the slate stones that led to the doorway. The blue-gray stones had been laid in a winsome, mish-mash pattern that managed to appear unplanned, but the stonemason had received a tidy sum of money to make it all look "effortlessly elegant." Helen gazed from earth to sky. The leaves would start to change sometime this week, and the yellow and orange leaves would accentuate the blues and the fallen pine needles. She liked the way the blue-gray slates looked, especially in the fall.

Helen unlocked the front door and let her bags slide to the floor in the foyer. "Hello, I'm home?" she called out, hoping for, but not really expecting, someone to answer. Her voice echoed with a metallic note throughout the spacious foyer and up the winding staircase. The glass chandeliers tinkled as she slammed the door shut and leaned against it, breathing in the familiar smell of her home.

The mansion was less than ten years old, and Helen could never figure out if it was the glue on the floorboards or the soft wood lining the two main floors that made her house smell like home. But this morning it didn't look or feel or smell the same. Helen fumbled for the light switch. *Something is wrong. Stop and think.* A hint of cut wood and glue, but musky. *Food. Chinese?* Helen took off her shoes and flipped her hair out of her eyes.

She felt a little unsteady as she treaded slowly, hosed feet otherwise bare, into the kitchen. Chinese food cartons covered the black granite countertops and dishes piled out of the sink. Helen clenched her jaw and reached for the trash can, but before she could begin cleaning the stacks of dishes and food cartons, she glimpsed wine glasses. Two of them. *Darn it. Darn Richard with his golf game and his drinking and his cheating. Two wine glasses. Darn him.*

The smell jarred her again as she fingered the countertop. *Stale. What smells stale?* Acrid; strong. It smelled like failure. *Phoebe is too young, isn't she? Would she dare smoke weed inside the house? Where would she have gotten it? No. Could it be Richard?*

Darn him! He promised no more drugs, Helen thought, beginning to clear away the tiny white paper cartons. *But he is a lying bastard and so are all addicts.* Helen considered the irony of her husband's job. He sat on a bench sentencing drug users to long prison sentences, and though it was years ago, Helen knew he had smoked weed and dallied with cocaine in the early days of his legal practice. Never as a judge, though, or so she'd thought. *He has everything to lose*, she fumed, but Richard had always thought he was above the law. "I don't believe he'd do this," Helen whispered aloud. "I don't know what to do."

Helen thought back to the day she had lost the baby. Blood had covered the bathroom floor and she knew she was hemorrhaging and needed to get help. She had crawled to the bedroom and grabbed the phone and called Richard's office, but no one had answered. His cell had gone straight to voicemail. By this time, tears had flooded her vision and mixed with the pool of blood forming beneath her, and it had taken all of her fading strength to dial 911. She had known she had to crawl downstairs to open the door or else the paramedics would be delayed for precious minutes until the firemen could arrive and take an ax to the front door. She had slid down the stairs and got a finger on the lock and hit it, focusing on staring at the knob as the 911 operator yelled at her to "Stay awake, honey!" while she waited for the ambulance to arrive.

Richard had shown up to the hospital a few hours later, chastened, apologetic and barely sober. Helen had not asked what he'd been using; she had simply told him to leave and he had left. He had gone home and taken care of all the blood and paid for the carpets to be torn up and replaced, and it was all done before Helen had returned home three days later. They never had spoken of it again. Helen didn't know why.

Helen had always hated blood. Even so, the janitorial efficiency of Richard's cleanup had gotten under her skin. It felt as though with each spot of blood that had vanished, so too had her last chances of bearing a baby boy. She had never even gotten a chance to say goodbye to, let alone touch, her unborn son. She hadn't tried to explain any of this to Richard, who had long since stopped listening. Instead of trying to talk to him, Helen had immersed herself in her work.

She leaned over the counter and grabbed the metal-colored telephone. It bothered her how closely it matched the kitchen appliances. *Idiot decorators.* Her first priority was to make sure Phoebe was accounted for, since there was no telling whether Richard had been up to taking care of anyone last night. But she needed to ask without it sounding obvious that she didn't know where her daughter was or whether she had even made it to school in the morning. She glanced at her watch. 7:45 A.M. Homeroom began at 7:35. *Okay, this is like direct examining a hostile witness: Ask the questions without them knowing I am asking.* She dialed the front office for McClintock and waited for a secretary to come on the line.

"McClintock Upper School. How may I help you?"

Helen willed her voice to sound its most polished. "Good morning, Karen. This is Ms. Thompson, Phoebe's mom. I just got in on the redeye from California and realized that Phoebe may have left her science textbook at home. I wanted to leave a message for her just in case—also to let her know that I'm home and can drop by school with it if she needs me to."

Karen switched into efficient secretary mode. "Sure thing, Ms. Thompson." Helen heard papers rustling. "Looking at her schedule, it looks like she is in AP Chemistry right now. I'll send a student down to class to let her know that you are home and can bring her book in if she needs it."

Helen smiled into the phone. "Thank you so much, Karen."

Now Helen needed to figure out how to deal with Richard. She needed a clear mind, so she grabbed the teapot and filled it with water. She poured French Roast coffee beans in the coffee grinder and breathed in the invigorating aroma of fresh-ground coffee. Then she poured the grounds into the French press and, sorting through hazy thoughts as she leaned against the counter, she waited for the teapot to whistle. It didn't make sense to get Richard on the line when she was angry and tired. There really wasn't anything left to discuss anyway, and he'd be entering the courtroom in his stupid black robes any minute and wouldn't be able to take any calls. *He doesn't want to talk to me. He's got someone else; he's always had someone else, and the sooner I realize he will never change, the sooner I will be able to move on and start a life without him.*

Helen knew that she needed evidence for a case to make sure she banked maximum leverage at the negotiating table. Richard's lawyers would tear her apart, and that was fine; that is what lawyers do, but Helen worried. She needed to get full custody, and to do that she had to impeach his character.

With images of Richard rubbing up naked against a lithe young thing racing through her brain, Helen poured the boiling water into the French press. She stood there for a full three minutes, waiting for the coffee and the water to mix together as she replayed tedious fantastical shorts of Richard having sex over and over again in their bed. It was as if a movie screen were installed to her left and she controlled the projector, and each time he screwed a different woman he stared at her and grinned, refusing to look away until he grunted and came inside the other woman. *I need to get a grip*, Helen thought. She could cry later.

CHAPTER 8

Helen grasped the fridge door and swung it open, praying for half and half that hadn't spoiled. She sniffed the carton carefully and groaned. *Black coffee isn't the end of the world, is it?* She poured the carton down the drain, swirled some liquid soap on top of it and ran hot water for thirty seconds to kill the odor. *Be bold, Helen. Don't just drink it black; cherish every bittersweet sip and make the choice to enjoy it your own.* She nodded and sipped the witches' brew before quietly padding into Richard's study. *Time to read what he's been sending his latest mistress,* Helen thought as she braced for the words and images she knew she would find.

As she tapped the white mouse, the screen immediately lit up. Before she could enter any passwords, Helen realized that she wouldn't need them; he had left everything on. MySpace, e-mail, YouTube and several Safari windows appeared at the bottom right of the computer screen. A message flashed in the middle: Eject DVD.

Helen reflexively clicked OK and decided she would watch the video after she investigated Richard's e-mail and MySpace page. The camcorder was lying partially on its side, still connected to the computer via a white cable, and Helen tried hard not to think about what was on it. Hopefully it was innocuous: some video of the flowing water at the state park, caught on a father-daughter hike.

Helen tried to orient herself. She rarely had time to surf the Internet. She shook her head and stared at the blue and white screen on the iMac and tried to figure out where to start reading. Richard had chosen JudgeandJury for his alter ego. Helen rolled her eyes, which widened as she scanned his Information section:

Who says we Judges aren't above the law? I'm
tough on crime and even tougher on little girls.

Is that supposed to be a joke? She checked his friends count,
and was somewhat relieved to see only forty-three listed. There
was only one friend she recognized: his clerk, Paul Sanderson.
*Why would he include his clerk but none of his other friends? And why an
alter name?* Helen could understand that Richard might not want
any criminals he sentenced to access his personal information,
but the names of his friends were obviously false as well.

As Helen read through the list of friends, the hair on the
back of her neck stood up. Even worse, the entire list of friends
included photos that ranged from mildly obscene to beyond the
pale of raunchiness. And while the image of Phoebe on Richard's
profile at first seemed harmless enough, the company he kept in
his online world scared Helen, and she had not even read
anything he had actually written on his page or in any of his
groups.

Part of Helen wanted to run out of the room and stand
under a scalding shower to wash the filth of what she was seeing
off her, but she stayed in her chair and clicked through
JudgeandJury's life instead. She kept clicking, and then read faster
and faster until her mind spun and her body shook all over.

In another post, Luv2Watch had posted

If anyone has any hot videos, my supply is getting
a little thin. And if you want for me to market
your stuff, please send me a message.

But much worse, JudgeandJury had commented:

Might have something for you. It's hot.

Helen was horrified. *Is that what he was loading onto the computer?*
On the post from Luv2Watch, another man had added

Please, JudgeandJury . . . the stuff you described the other night made me HOT! That is one fine thing you got.

Helen felt tingly all over. The blood in her veins had frozen. She could not move. She watched and tried to think and felt lashed to the computer chair with invisible bands that would not release her. Almost against her will, she kept reading. Helen kept looking at her daughter's picture. *Phoebe! Why is Phoebe's picture on his profile?* She navigated back to JudgeandJury's page and clicked on Photos.

The first few photos were of other women. They looked like snakes. And then Helen saw the pictures of Phoebe and without realizing it, she had banged her coffee mug on the edge of the desk, sending warm liquid and shards of glass all over her lap and onto the floor.

There were pictures of Phoebe, but it was a Phoebe that Helen would not have recognized were it not for the prominent birthmark on her daughter's ankle. *Phoebe.* Her Phoebe. Helen tried to turn away but could not. She reached her arms out involuntarily to cover and protect the little girl she had birthed so many years ago, but the image stayed imprinted on the screen and paraded across her vision, blurring it.

Helen heard someone screaming. She tried to rise and run to help the woman who was in trouble, but then she was hitting herself in the head and it hurt, and she knew she was the woman. She screamed over and over again until she felt something warm. Helen stopped screaming. She pressed her hand against her forehead and realized that the warmth was her blood, and a voice inside of her screamed for more blood. She stood up and rubbed her arms, almost as if she were patting a child. She needed to think and to think, she needed to get control of herself, but for the first time in her life she had no idea how.

Time did not race past, nor did it drip slowly like a rusty old faucet. It simply lost all relevance. Time? For it to mean anything to us emotionally, beyond the setting of the sun and the turning of the calendar, we must be aware of its passing. Helen simply could not comprehend that she was standing *here*, staring at *this*.

Eventually she fell to her knees and whispered, "Oh please, God, help me." Tears ran down her cheeks and snot gushed from her nostrils and, as she wiped her face on her sleeve, she rested her head on the floor and curled up on her side and did not move until her eyes floated shut. Lights flashed in front of her closed eyelids until she gave into the relentless pounding of light and noise and pain and stopped thinking at all.

CHAPTER 9

Helen's cell phone jarred her awake. She didn't know where she was at first, and her eyes were almost swollen shut. She rolled up to a standing position too quickly, grabbing one of the bookcases in Richard's study to keep herself from collapsing. Her thoughts were jumbled. Everything felt foggy; even the bookcase seemed alien. *Where am I?* Then the realization hit her hard. *Home. Phoebe.* Helen heard herself screaming again. "Oh, no, no, no, no! Please let me be dreaming."

Who could be calling? She didn't want to talk to Richard. She wanted to kill the bastard. *Darn him!* She was a woman who operated according to reason's calm dictates, not someone who acted out of anger or passion, but *he hurt my baby*, she thought angrily. Blood churned and her mind roared.

Helen stumbled into the foyer and fished her cell phone out of her purse. *I shouldn't speak to anyone. Not making any sense.* She heard a hysterical giggle leave her body and she reached her hand up to cover her mouth. *No one must hear me when I'm like this.*

By the time she got her hand on her phone, it had stopped ringing. *Who is calling me?* She squinted at the register and wondered where she'd left her reading glasses, and then she felt the legs of the glasses pressing into her temples. It was Carl. Helen knew she should not call him back when she was in this state of mind, but she numbly pressed the return call button. The reasonable voice in the back of her head told her she needed to make arrangements for someone to watch her cases. *My clients need me and I cannot fail them.*

A male voice answered, but it wasn't Carl. "Hello, Carl Hansen's desk. How may I help you?"

Helen's mind raced. Carl wasn't at work. This had to be Carl's fiancé, Troy, covering Carl's phone just the way she would have covered Richard's phone back when they were in their late twenties, practicing law together in the same white-shoe law firm.

Before she could tighten her jaw muscles, Helen started to cry.

"Helen? What's wrong? Are you crying?" Troy's voice sounded gentle and rich, a modern Elvis.

Helen tried to speak but her words rolled up and over one another like a fast-moving waterfall. "Tell him I'm upset, okay, before he gets on the line. He's never seen me cry before, but I'm too tired to hold it together."

"I will. Give me a moment, please."

While Helen waited, she returned to Richard's study and grabbed the DVD out of his iMac and tossed it into the purse she was still carrying. She wasn't thinking about chain of custody and proof or anything lawyerly at this point. She just needed to get away from Richard and all of his things, and as much as she couldn't bear to watch the DVD, she knew she needed to. But if she was going to watch it, she knew she wouldn't be able to do it entirely alone.

Back in her own study, Helen noted how everything was right where she had left it. Her diplomas and law books and constitutional history books drew her into a warm, intellectual embrace, making her burden suddenly a little lighter. She felt strong and capable, surrounded by the tools of her profession. She kicked ass and always had. She could do this. *Whatever this is.* She could do this. But she couldn't watch the DVD alone. Not that.

A voice came on the line and her phone almost leaped out of her hand. *Please don't let me sound like Ophelia unwound when Carl gets on the line.*

"Helen?" Carl's voice was clear, controlled and without affectation. "It's Carl."

She nodded and then remembered that she had to speak. "Yes. Yes, Carl. I'm here."

"Can you talk now?"

"Yes."

"What happened?"

"Richard. It's him."

"Is he injured?"

"He has done very bad things and I am just finding out that . . ." Helen's voice wavered. She clenched her jaw and closed her eyes. She began speaking while it was still dark inside, black with pinpricks of pink light, but the darkness scared her because all she could see was Phoebe lying on her bed. "I found pictures and conversations on the Internet, on MySpace, of my daughter. He's bragging about it to his friends. And—" Helen was crying again and talking through the tears. "And he invited these sick friends to come over to our house to . . . my daughter, and . . ."

Helen's eyes shifted to the blue leather criminal procedure law book in her bookcase. Right next to it was a framed picture of a very young Phoebe in a royal blue soccer uniform. Phoebe had spent the entire time she was supposed to be chasing the ball counting daisies, and Helen had spent almost every soccer game sneaking peeks at her BlackBerry. If only she'd taken the time to get down on her knees and help Phoebe pick a daisy or—

Carl intruded on her thoughts. "Did you take screenshots?"

"I can't look at it again." Helen's voice rose until it sounded unnaturally high.

"I can do it. Give me his e-mail and his password."

Helen nodded. His password for everything, from bank accounts to computer programs, was the same: "Phoebe." Helen choked on her daughter's name and grabbed the edge of the desk to steady herself.

In a moment, Carl said he was in. He was quiet, and when he finally did say something it was not about Phoebe. "I never told you about Troy. I'm sorry about that. And I don't know all of the right things to say, but I will do everything in my power to help you. I need you to know that Troy is sitting right here following this, and I hope it's okay, Helen, because anything he hears will be protected by one or more privileges."

Helen tried to answer but she couldn't say anything. She didn't know why, but she had taken the DVD out of her purse and inserted it into her computer. Now she stared at it, too scared to hit the Play button and too curious not to.

Helen smiled through her pain. Somewhere, buried deep, she felt a fleeting sensation of joy. "Congratulations. You deserve a partner like that."

"Thanks. But that isn't the type of privilege I'm talking about exactly."

Helen picked up a ballpoint pen and, with an adept flip of her wrist and pinky, flicked it. "I don't follow and I am too tired to think, Carl."

"Troy is a therapist, and if it's okay with you, I am going to conference him into our call. He will know what to say when I don't, and he has contacts back home that can help. And anything you say to him will be—"

"Protected," Helen interrupted. "Okay. Thank you. I trust your judgment and I will take what help the two of you good men will give me." Helen teared up again as she spoke. The thought of there still being good men after what she'd seen on Richard's computer filled her with a mix of gratitude and pathos that felt nearly unbearable. *But nothing is unbearable, not truly, not when my daughter needs me.*

"Helen?" Troy's voice, smooth as butter, emerged on the line.

Helen nodded. "Yes. I'm gonna watch it. The DVD."

"Maybe you need to wait until someone is there with you."

He really does sound like Elvis. Just as convincing. Helen clicked Eject and put the DVD back into its jacket. She had seen enough to identify Phoebe and Richard, and Troy was right; she really shouldn't watch it alone.

"I am scanning over Carl's shoulder and we're taking screenshots of the statements, oh Helen, of the sick stuff we're seeing here. For one thing, he drugged her with gamma-hydroxybutyric acid, or GHB. Do you know what that is, Helen?"

"Oh God. Drugs? Rape?"

"Yeah. He's talking about that in here, and it looks like he mixed it and maybe something else with wine." His tone switched to a more businesslike one. "Before we talk too much, I need to get a few quick disclosures out of the way. I charge the standard $150 an hour and as you know, anything we discuss will be protected from disclosure. When I get back in town, I will send you a standard fee and disclaimer form. Got that, Counselor?"

Helen considered the standard fee and the disclosures. It was comfortable language to her. "Yes, I do. And thank you so much for talking to me. And on your honeymoon."

"Unfortunately, this is the sort of thing I do every day. And don't worry about me, Helen. I can take care of myself, okay?"

Helen frowned and then realized that he was right. She wasn't used to people talking to her like that, but in a way it felt good to let someone else take charge. "Okay, okay. I hear you."

"Helen," Carl interrupted. "Some of this is really scaring me as I read this. Where is Phoebe now?"

"She's at school."

"Did you see what your husband is saying about, uh, about . . . tomorrow night?" Carl kept his voice from rising, but Helen could tell he was fighting to tamper emotion.

Troy interjected, "After we finish talking, the first thing that I'm going to ask you to do is to go and pick her up. I understand how exhausted you must be right now, I do, but what is best for Phoebe is also best for you. And we need to get her to a safe house. Today."

"I have failed the one person I love most in the world. She deserved better." Helen did not realize she was speaking aloud until she heard Troy exclaim, "No. No. You did not fail her. We can talk through all of this later, and I promise we will, but you cannot fix what happened last night or last month or last year. It's done. It's gone. That moment, those times, are gone. But what is not gone is this moment, the here and now. And you can help this girl who needs you now. Okay?"

Helen rubbed her eyes. "I'm so tired, and I failed her." She started to cry again, and even as she kept mumbling, "I failed her" over and over, she knew she had to lay the blame aside. The knowledge of her failure and Phoebe's pain felt like a heavy weight wrapped around her neck, but right now Phoebe needed her to lay it down and focus.

"Helen?" Carl interrupted. "I'm sorry if I sound insensitive, but—"

"No, Carl, tell what it is. We don't have time for sugarcoating." Helen shook her head and thought about all the clients she had handled brusquely. Maybe she did need her hand held, but this wasn't the time for it. Besides, Carl wasn't one to hold hands. After all, he'd learned from her.

"Don't touch the glasses, okay? We will want the police to be able to run a drug screen on whatever is left in the glasses."

She nodded wordlessly, barely registering her actions.

"Helen, it's Troy again. Listen, I need to make a couple of phone calls. I have a partner, Cary Matterly. She helps out at this incredible place about an hour away from DC. It's a safe home for abused women and children and it's out in the country—and it has a reputation for top-notch security. I will text you Cary's number and she will be your emergency contact if you need to get in touch with someone local until we get you and Phoebe to the safe house."

Helen squirmed a little. Things were moving so fast. She didn't know Cary. She barely knew Troy.

"I know." Troy's voice felt soothing as he interpreted her silence. "This is a lot to handle. I know you can do this. Oh, and Cary is senior to me. She has more than thirty years of experience. Believe me, she can handle whatever you . . . whatever we throw at her. Are you comfortable with her being your local contact until I can get back to DC?"

"Thank you, yes. That'll work."

"Good. I will call her and fill her in on the back story. She'll help work out the logistics for getting you to the safe house within the next few hours. What time is it where you are? Around noon?"

Helen looked at her watch and a sharp, stabbing sensation rushed through her. *I wanna break this stupid watch. I hate him.* She blurted out, "I hate him. Richard. I want to kill him."

"You have every right to feel that anger, but for the next twenty-four hours, let's keep our eyes on the ball, okay, Helen?" He gave Helen his cell phone number and clicked off the call.

"Helen, it's Carl again. I am going to outline all of the crimes I find here in Richard's alter. Hopefully we can provide a neatly-wrapped case to the DA by COB next Monday."

"But Carl!" Helen gasped. "You're on vacation. You're supposed to be relaxing and enjoying . . ." Helen's voice trailed off. *So tired.*

"I'm a big boy. And I want to help you. You've done so much for me." Helen heard a strange note in Carl's voice.

Gratitude. It made sense. They'd been together for a decade, and she'd taught him almost everything he knew about the practice of law.

Helen thought for a moment. "Carl. Someone needs to completely take over my caseload for the time being, and you're the only attorney with both the competence and a personal connection to most of the clients. Job number one for me is taking care of Phoebe."

"I'll do my best."

"If anyone asks, please tell them I was called out of town on a—a family emergency, okay?" Helen stumbled over the words.

"Is it okay if we fly back Monday, Helen? I'm happy to come back on the first available plane if you need me."

Helen sighed. "Actually, Carl, it makes sense for you to stay in California at least until Monday. Sintab's General Counsel hasn't called me back yet to talk about Judge Wilson's ruling. She might need some handholding and she always liked you. Meet her on Monday after she gets in from Heathrow."

A hint of relief entered Carl's voice, and he didn't try too hard to hide it. "Thank you. What else should I be working on while I'm out here?"

"That's for you to figure out. Welcome to the partnership, you know?"

"Tossing me into the fire, eh?"

Helen paused. She needed to say something to bolster Carl's confidence, but cheerleading wasn't her sort of thing. She tried not to let her voice sound too wooden. "Given what I've seen of you over the years, I am confident you will rise to the challenge."

"Helen?"

"Yes?"

"We both will."

CHAPTER 10

Helen took a deep breath as she hung up the phone. And then another wave of grief struck, and she put her face in her hands and surrendered to it.

I'm falling again and I don't know where I will land. I gotta get it together and figure out what to do, but I'm sick inside. Why did work have to come first? I lied and I lied and I kept lying to myself that I was doing what I had to do for my daughter, but I wasn't. I was doing what I had to do to advance my career.

"What have I done?" Helen whispered aloud. *If I had been around, none of this would have happened to Phoebe.* An uncontrollable sensation boiled up inside Helen; a blind fury took hold of her. *If he walked into this house right now, I would kill him.*

The sound of the front door broke through her thoughts. But by the time the noise had stopped echoing in her head and Helen realized what it could mean, her anger had turned into fear. She had married a monster and now she was alone with him in the house. Helen looked around her office for potential weapons. Next to her computer was an expensive reproduction of Rodin's sculpture "The Kiss," and it was dense enough to do a lot of damage if she connected with it. *Too heavy.* Helen swiveled and spotted Richard's white golf bag.

How auspicious is this? she thought. *He must have dumped his crap in my office when I was gone and forgotten it.* Helen slid out of her chair, and with a delicate motion, removed a golf club from

Richard's bag. She slipped the titanium driver between two bookcases, waiting.

Helen heard him call her name, but she waited. She wanted him to come looking for her. She wanted him to look for the DVD and start to shake in fear when he realized it was missing. *I need him to feel scared or angry enough to come at me. And when he comes at me, I need to connect on my first swing.* Helen knew she was not very good at golf. But her target was Richard's head, and that would be a lot easier to hit than a tiny white ball.

Adrenaline gripped her chest, and she tried to breathe through it. She hoped he left before he confronted her. She didn't really know how to kill a man. But if she didn't kill him, he would kill her and then rape Phoebe. And his friends—*No!* she screamed, a silent scream. *No!* Richard had invited a whole group of men to gang-rape her daughter. What choice did she have? The courts could only do so much to protect her and Phoebe against him. Strangers, perverts, knew where they lived, and for as long as Richard drew breath there would always be the possibility that he could touch their daughter. *Her daughter. God.* How to protect her?

Her watch ticked and she tried not to stare at it as she waited for her husband's footsteps on the stairs. As much as she loved that watch, he had given it to her. She wanted nothing of his touching her skin. She turned her mind back to the legal case she would face if she killed him. What if all the evidence of Richard's online perversion got excluded at trial? They could argue that the evidence was tainted or that Helen had created the alter identity and written all of that stuff. And the video. Could they argue that it lacked evidentiary foundation? Could they claim that it wasn't Richard or that it wasn't Phoebe? She supposed they could. Helen had seen it all, and she didn't even practice criminal law, but she knew that the justice system did next to nothing to protect the victims of sexual assault. Helen shook her head and tried to clear her mind. There was nothing left to think about, except protecting her daughter from future harm. Her legal degree was not designed to protect her child.

"Helen, are you home?" Richard's voice rang from the hallway.

She didn't know what to say. What was taking him so long? She could feel her heart beating in her chest. His shadow preceded him. She stood there, arms akimbo, waiting, one finger tapping the other oh so gently, waiting.

As soon as he opened the door to her study and set eyes on her, all doubt left her mind. His eyes looked red and bloodshot and she realized how the handsome man he'd once been had been ravaged by years of drinking and bad living. When she had met Richard so many years ago, there had been something boyish and charming about the way he leaned toward a person when he was talking. She had loved him for it; but by the time she figured out that he treated every woman this way, it was too late. She was hooked on him, as if he was her drug. She should have kicked him out before it was too late. She had given up on fixing their marriage a decade ago and just endured him so that Phoebe could have two parents. *Now look where my blindness has gotten us.*

These days, Richard was red-faced and thirty pounds overweight. The veins in his face stood out and pulsated when he got angry. For all intents and purposes, Richard was already dead. He just wasn't awake enough to realize it yet.

"Helen," he said in a flat, almost dutiful voice. "When did you get in?"

"7:30, Richard."

"You've been home all day?"

Helen nodded. She could not stop thinking that the DVD was closer to her than it was to him. There was no way he would figure out that it was in her computer. Was there? Why would she insert it in her own hard drive? *That made no sense,* she thought. Now his lawyers could allege she had made it. *How did I manage to make such a mess of my own case?*

"Why didn't you call my office and let me know you were home?"

"Cut it out, Richard. I did call your office, several times, and no one answered the phone. What the heck is wrong with your staff, anyway? Are you all taking the same drugs?"

"What drugs, Helen?" Richard's facial muscles retracted and he looked almost feral. Helen did not answer right away and Richard moved a few steps closer. "What drugs, Helen?" She could tell he really wanted to ask her what she knew and how she knew it, but clearly he wasn't feeling reckless or desperate enough to tip his hand. Helen decided to tip it for him.

"I don't know, Richard. Marijuana isn't enough to knock out a little girl. I'm thinking that the movie of our daughter was taken while you doped her up on something stronger, but I'm sure the DA will test the wine glasses you left lying out on the counter. You're such a slob, Richard. You can't even molest your daughter cleanly and politely without leaving a trail of evidence from one side of our house to the other."

He shook his head and looked at the laptop. His eyes met hers and she whispered, "Looking for something? Maybe something you left on your computer?"

"Where is the DVD, Helen?" Richard looked ready to pounce. Helen tried to figure out what she could do to provoke him to try to hurt her. She only had one chance to get this right. *Hit him high, Helen.*

"Oh, I don't know that I should tell you, Richard. Or should I say, JudgeandJury?"

He moved a lot more quickly than she was expecting. In the split second that it took Richard to close the distance separating himself from Helen, she realized that she had grossly miscalculated her angle and the time she had. Before she got her hand securely wrapped around the golf club, he was within inches of her. He reached for her neck and she ducked. Richard's shoulder slammed into the bookcase but he still managed to get one hand on Helen's neck. Whimpering, she wrestled out of his grasp and, with her left hand holding the club, she pivoted to face him.

The head of the golf club hurtled through the air and connected with Richard's left temple. Helen heard a sickening crunch but felt nothing more than incompleteness, a void, a missing piece. Her arms tingled. Rage had been replaced by fear once he grabbed her neck, and the imperative to survive overcame any sense of regret or doubt.

Richard wobbled and threw a hand up to his head, moaning. He looked confused, and Helen almost set down the golf club, but then the image of Richard disrobing in front of Phoebe played out in her mind once again. Before she could shut down the images, another man moved into the frame. He was unbuckling his belt.

No you won't.

Helen pulled the club into a backward arc and, with every ounce of a mother's love, she sliced the club through the air.

Richard toppled sideways and slammed head first into the sharp corner of Helen's desk. The same left temple took the full brunt of the desk's corner. Blood flowed from Richard's head, and Helen realized that her ears were buzzing. She needed to sit down. She needed to sit down and put her head between her knees . . . *sit down, Helen.* She couldn't pass out again.

Helen backed away from Richard so that once again, her back was to the bookshelf. She knelt down where she was standing, letting the club fall limply from her hands. Then the buzzing in her head got louder and it got all dark around her. Bile rose in the back of her throat. She closed her eyes and started to pray.

Helen didn't know what to say to God, so she said the Lord's Prayer; and yet she didn't feel like it made sense to ask for God's forgiveness. She had done what a mother must do.

With one hand on the bookshelf, Helen pulled herself up, stepped over the puddle of blood and felt Richard's neck for a pulse. She felt his life beating on her fingertips. *Should I try to cover it up? Wipe my fingerprints off the golf club and just leave the house? Perhaps leave it up to the maids to find him?* In the end, she decided that this would only make her look guilty. She was in no condition to create the perfect scene. If she were caught spinning a web of lies, her credibility would be destroyed, and then where would Phoebe go?

I should wrap my sweater around his head, she thought. *There's always a sweater in here because I get cold.* Helen grabbed her off-white wool cardigan and wrapped it around Richard's head. At this point, she was covered in sticky, thick blood and she wanted to wash him off her. *I don't want to lie. But I can't tell anyone what happened until Phoebe is safe.*

Should she call 911? She did not want to wait for an ambulance. She wanted Richard to die and she didn't want to waste any time getting to Phoebe. But she couldn't help Phoebe from prison, and that was where Helen might well end up if she fled the scene now.

She fought the urge to call Carl or Troy and ask their opinion. Any advice they gave her at this point could get them in a whole lot of trouble, since anyone Helen spoke with could be charged with conspiracy to commit murder. Her hands trembled while she dialed 911 on her office phone.

An operator picked up the phone on the second ring and Helen recited her home address. *I'm so tired. I hope I gave the right house number.* She was shaking all over and her teeth chattered, making the words come out all jumbled. *Breathe, Helen.* Now was not the time to be strong; any woman would be upset if she walked into a room and saw her husband lying on the floor, bleeding. For once, it was not only okay to be weak, it was probably better. Sounding human would play better for the paramedics and make it less likely that they would be suspicious enough to call the police. Acting weak was being strong, for Phoebe. *Phoebe.*

•••

Helen sat next to Richard and waited. *I've got to get Phoebe to a safe place. I've got to get Phoebe to a safe place.* The paramedics arrived and Helen couldn't stop shaking while she watched them work. *Don't say too much. He fell and hit his head and for now, that's all anyone needs to know.*

While one paramedic removed his gloves and picked up his radio, the other checked Richard's neck and head before she, too, took off her gloves. "Ma'am, we're barely getting a pulse. How long has he been like this?"

Helen's eyes filled with tears. It didn't feel good to almost kill a man, even an evil man. "I was in the other room, and I heard a crash and came running. I think he might have been drinking again at lunch, but I hadn't even had a chance to say Hello to him, so I'm not sure."

"How long ago was this?" The female paramedic walked next to Helen and put a reassuring hand on Helen's shoulder.

"About fifteen minutes. There was blood and I tried to stop the bleeding with my sweater." Helen gestured at her bloodstained sweater and took a deep breath. "But I realized that he was bleeding way too much, too fast. So I called 911."

"Are you a doctor, ma'am?"

Helen shook her head. "No, but I know head wounds bleed a lot."

"What's your name, ma'am?" she asked gently.

"Helen. Helen Thompson."

"Helen, we're going to do all we can."

The other paramedic worked furiously on Richard, and Helen's eyes flickered back and forth as his hands flew across her husband's prone body.

"The thing is, when he fell and hit his head he may have suffered a subdural hematoma, or a brain bleed. We need to get him to a trauma I ER now."

Helen felt her temple throbbing and when she looked at the black-haired woman, her face was all blurred. "Trauma level I? Inova Fairfax, you mean?"

"Yes." She turned to grab one side of the stretcher. "Will you be riding with us, Helen?"

Helen tried to figure out what to do. *No. God, no. I don't want to ride with him.* She shook her head and tried to wipe the tears that were falling, but she felt something sticky and cringed. When Helen looked at her hands, she saw red across them. Richard's blood was covering her.

The female paramedic handed Helen a spare white cloth from her supply bag and hesitated. "Is there someone you can call, Helen? I know this is quite a shock."

Helen tried to wipe off Richard's blood, but it clung to her hands. "The thing is, I need to pick up my daughter from school. No one else can . . . in person." *As much as I hate him, it is still so hard to say he's gone. I am a killer.*

The male paramedic was writing on a brown clipboard. "Ma'am, I need for you to sign this form here, which basically says that we will be transporting your husband to the hospital. Since he is unconscious and may need surgical intervention, we need your okay."

Helen gripped the hard plastic pen. "I'll get out to the ER as soon as I pick up my daughter," she murmured, scrawling her signature in black ink on the permission form. She thought about it. This could look suspicious. *The truth will come out, Helen. But it will give me time to get Phoebe to a safe place.*

The paramedic continued, "I'm sorry, ma'am, but we gotta go now." He nodded and started moving before she could say she was sorry.

Helen clenched her jaw. She shouldn't say she was sorry. *That would make no sense. It was an accident. Think. Don't apologize. Thank God he's in a hurry and doesn't have more time, because in the back of his mind, he knows. He sees Richard's blood on my hands. My hands.*

Once they left, Helen tottered into the downstairs bathroom and tore off her blood-soaked clothing. With an involuntary shudder at the sight of his blood, she let the red-stained clothing drop into the aluminum trash bin. *Leave the clothes there. It can't look like a cover-up.* Desperate to wash his blood off her hands, she stepped into the clean shower stall and let the almost boiling water pour over her. She scrubbed so hard that her skin burned, and she waited for the hot water to turn lukewarm before shutting off the faucet.

She could still feel his blood on her. *No. Phoebe. I must.* Helen needed to select clean clothes out of her bedroom, and with one eye closed to avoid glimpsing the bed—*No, God, no!*— she removed slacks and a cardigan from her walk-in closet. *Hurry.* Phoebe's name was replaying in her head, calling her, begging her to leave that home. *Forever.*

CHAPTER 11

"Let's go, Cat, Zander! Throw your dishes in the dishwasher and get in the vehicle."

Catherine rolled her eyes and scoffed. "Can't you just call it the Volvo?"

Zander piped up, "It's a truck."

"No, it's a SUV." Cassandra's voice was crisp, not unkind. "Please buckle yourself in."

A few minutes later, Cassandra pulled up to a traffic light and glanced over at her daughter. "Cat, you have practice this afternoon, right? What time do you need a ride?"

"It's okay, Mom. I'll ride home with Jason."

Cassandra and Catherine exchanged a smirk. If Cat had been angry about Jason, and Cassandra doubted that, she wasn't anymore. The Volvo rolled forward and Catherine continued, "Our coach said—

"I'm a chick, Chickie," Zander hummed.

"—we're running intervals at the track, so I should be done at five."

"Intervals?" Cassandra groaned. "Argh. I don't miss them."

"You should come to the track and run them with us, Mom. You know you miss coaching."

"Yeah, I do. I'd like to come, but I don't think your coach would know what to do with the little chick in the back seat."

"Please, Cat! I wanna go with you!" Zander yelled, his feet jabbing the back of Cassandra's seat.

"Um, Zander, if you can't go to school, you can't attend your sister's cross-country practice."

A phone jangled and Cassandra felt confused for a moment. Usually calls rang through to her Volvo's Bluetooth device. "Oh," she exclaimed, eyes still on the road, "that's my work phone. It's in the glove box."

Catherine felt around for the phone and hit the speaker button. "Um, Hello, this is Catherine, White Family."

"Catherine. It's Miranda Brenner. Is your mom available?"

Miranda helped run the Bryson House, a well-funded safe house for battered women. Fifteen years ago, Cassandra had stood on the doorstep of the Bryson House in Middleburg, Virginia. She would take Miranda's call no matter what the circumstances.

"Cassandra, so good to hear your voice." Miranda sounded as unflappable as ever, and yet a little hurried to Cassandra. "I have a client and she needs immediate counsel. I know you are busy, but can you come?"

Cassandra frowned and switched the phone off speaker. "I have Zander with me, Miranda."

"We have people on staff who can watch him. Does he like to ride horses?" Fifteen years ago, the therapeutic riding program had been a mere dream. But with help from Cassandra's law firm and many of her friends, the Bryson House had raised enough capital to offer one of the most advanced programs in the country.

"Miranda, what are you getting me into?" Cassandra felt the muscles in her neck tighten. She looked over at her daughter, but Catherine was thumbing through her magazine again.

"I'm not entirely sure, but I think she may have killed her husband."

Cassandra didn't miss a beat. "Is he dead or not?"

Catherine raised her eyebrows, and Cassandra shot her a reassuring smile.

"Um. Not quite. Almost."

"Miranda, don't say anything else to anyone, and please give me her name so that we can make sure there aren't any warrants outstanding. That will buy us a little time."

Before Miranda could reply, Cassandra flicked on her turn signal and drove up the entrance road toward McClintock School. As she passed the gatehouse she nodded to the guard, who waved her in. Cassandra pressed the cell phone into her ear. "Before you tell me who this is, I need you to know there's no way I can do this kind of case pro bono. I'm going to need a pretty sizable retainer."

"Oh, I don't think that's going to be a problem."

Cassandra pulled up in front of the Upper School's entrance. "Can you hold on for a moment? I need to say goodbye to Cat." She looked at her daughter, a mirror of her younger self, and felt a familiar lump rise in her throat. "It doesn't look good for joining you for practice, sweetie. I will be there at five. Please text me if you need me sooner."

Catherine nodded. "Is everything all right?"

"I really can't talk about it." Catherine's hair looked even lighter under the sunbeam flooding through the moonroof. "I will be there tonight, I promise. And good luck with your exam—we're on time, right?"

"Yeah, we're close enough, Mom. I might squeeze into homeroom, and if I'm late I can blame it on the barf in the bathroom."

As Cassandra leaned over and hugged her daughter, Zander started to scream, "I wanna see Mrs. Roberts! Puh-leeze, Mama!"

Cassandra giggled. Her son's hair stuck up in one big, misarranged cowlick. "Zander, wanna go see some horses?"

"Horses?" Zander kicked the back of her seat again, making Cassandra wince. She sighed, threw the Volvo into Drive and picked up the cell phone again.

"Miranda? Sorry to keep you waiting. Where were we?"

"I think you were telling me about your retainer, and as I was starting to tell you, that shouldn't be a problem." She paused. "My client is Helen Thompson."

•••

Cassandra gripped the phone tightly. "Helen Thompson? Judge Thompson's wife?"

"Yes. That's the one."

Cassandra dropped her voice. "Doesn't her daughter go to the same school as my kids?"

Miranda did not respond for several seconds. "Yes, I think so."

Cassandra set that thought aside while she glanced at the rearview mirror to check on Zander, who was holding his matchbox car in one hand and a container of Tic Tacs in the other. The sound of crunching punctuated her sentences and annoyed her, but it created a sound barrier and a distraction for Zander.

"Okay. We'll figure this out once I get there." Cassandra realized she was pinching off blood flow to her fingers and relaxed her grip on the cell phone. "Can I pick you up a cup of coffee?"

"No, I'm fine. Maybe a doughnut if that's where you're headed."

"Still like the double chocolate?"

"Please." Miranda's flat voice sounded mellow. "And I will phone down to the guards and let them know you're on the way. 'William and Mary' is today's password."

After she called the office to let her secretary know of the change in plans, Cassandra rolled down the window and let the smells of the rolling hills waft into the SUV. It was late September and the early morning air held a chill that would soon fade. The road dipped and wove through the hills, and as they headed further west toward Middleburg, Cassandra noted the slight whiff of manure. Light dappled the great oaks and maples lining the curving two-lane road. Cassandra thought about the month of September and the memories it held: Catherine's birth, her first wedding . . .

She shook her head and tried to push away the thoughts of her first marriage, but heading toward the Bryson House brought back memories of her last night with her first husband. Her chest started to ache and her throat became heavy. Cassandra gripped the steering wheel and tried to remain rooted in the present. She didn't realize her palms were sweaty until a sweet voice from the back seat sang out, "Mama, I wanna doughnut!"

"Okay, Zander." Cassandra snapped back to the parking lot, where she coasted to a stop. "I can do that. You want a powdered one?"

"Yes, Mama."

"We need to be quick inside, okay?" Cassandra herded Zander into the Dunkin Donuts in Gainesville. "We'll eat the doughnuts once we get to my friend Ms. Miranda's."

"Can I eat by the horses?"

Cassandra nodded.

"Can I give doughnuts to horses?"

"I don't think that's such a good idea, Zander."

Cassandra plugged her iPod into its outlet and mindlessly flipped on Fleetwood Mac. "Go Your Own Way" played. It figured. She couldn't run from her feelings and she couldn't run from her past.

•••

I met Tim one night under the stars down at the old law school. I was walking back to my apartment with my friend Jen and we had been knocking some beers back at the main college bar in town, Paul's. Most nights dozens of 1Ls ended up at Paul's at around ten o'clock, but it wasn't really my kind of place. The law students were pompous and full of it, and the undergrads made me feel too old. Jen dragged me out that night. As usual, the beer took my nervous edge away . . . it was well into the night when we left Paul's.

"Hey, Jen?"

"Yeah?"

"Where's the Big Dipper?"

We paused and she looped her arm around my shoulder and tried to point up at the stars. We tripped on one another and fell in a heap, giggling.

"Aw, heck, Jen, now look what you've done! We'll never find the Big Dipper at this rate!"

We laughed so hard we cried, and when I paused to wipe the tears from my eyes, that was when I saw him. A smile tugged at the corner of his lips and a dimple cut across his left cheek. Thick hair ran up and down athletic legs. I imagined those legs wrapped around me.

"Hey, ladies," he drawled in a melodic voice. He wrapped his arms across his chest and spread his legs wide, and in my mind I imagined a Roman soldier patrolling outside the gates of his garrison. I smirked and glanced at Jen, who smoothed her hair back and tried to pull off arch and demure at the same time.

"May I give you a hand?" he asked, and I reached out and took the arm he extended. Before he could finish his pickup line, I reached over and grabbed Jen and yanked her up next to me. We giggled again, pretty much helpless in our mirth, and I looked into his eyes. "Can you help us find the Big Dipper?"

Still smiling, he leaned over so that his head almost touched mine. My body wanted to drift closer, and it wasn't the Sam Adams talking; it was this weird chemistry two bodies either share or don't share right from the start. Jen winked at me and drifted away back to the grad complex.

"If you look up right there, you can see the tail curving," he said, and he kept talking, but I wasn't listening as I fell into the twinkle of his blue-gray eyes.

"Oh, where did your friend go? Is she going to be okay?" He stopped staring at the stars and looked worried.

"Jen can take care of herself," I grinned. "She's from the Bronx."

"Are you sure? I should have walked her home." His brow furrowed and he turned in the direction of our apartment complex. "Does she live in the grad-plex?"

"Yeah, she's my roommate. Why? You live there?"

He nodded. "Yes. I'm a 2L. I thought I'd seen you around at school. Are you a first year?"

"Yeah. My name is Cass, by the way."

He looked at me again and a smile started in his eyes. "And I am Tim, not Timothy."

"Well, Tim-not-Timothy, how about buying me a beer?"

He laughed. "As long as we don't have to drink it at Paul's. Man, I hate that place."

"I hate it too! And it's so smoky in there, and you know what's worst of all?"

"What?"

"I quit smoking at the start of law school because I figured I'm an adult and like in that movie Dead Again, *I'm either a smoker or not one. But I swear, every time I have a beer I want a cigarette too."*

"You're a smoker?" He stared at me, incredulous. "But I thought you were this big-time runner?"

"You been keeping tabs on me?"

"Can't help noticing a gorgeous woman, I gotta admit it," he said, one hand reaching out to stroke my long blonde hair.

I sighed. *"Yeah, it's a weakness, one of many. Even now I am craving a smoke, and I got a ten-mile run first thing in the morning."*

"How about if we take a walk instead, and I can show you the Drunken Garden?"

"The what?"

We cracked up and he corrected himself. *"Sorry. The Sunken Garden is what they call it, but my best buddy calls it the Drunken Garden."*

"And why is that?"

"Come on and I'll tell you." He grabbed my hand and we walked and talked about property law and smoking and our favorite brand of scotch.

The flowering magnolias lined the old brick walkway as we wound through the dense southern foliage. I smelled pine needles; it's a smell I still associate with law school. *"Okay, so we go over this bridge just yonder, right over the pond there,"* Tim said. Halfway over the bridge, he stopped and looked at me solemnly. *"You know what they say, right?"*

I waited for him to tell me.

"Well, I'm not a superstitious man, but they say that if you walk across this bridge and are not kissed, you will remain forever more a spinster."

My heart beat a little faster and I tried to laugh. *"That's so cheesy!"*

"Maybe," he replied, and he pulled me close. Then he stopped and almost whispered, *"May I kiss you, Cass?"*

I reached up and held the back of his head, and his lips brushed against mine. The hair on the back of my neck stood up and I curled into him, trying to pull away, but pushing ever closer as his thick arms wrapped around me.

He let go of me and we laughed, but there was a serious tone to our laughter now. I wanted a lot more than a first kiss that night, but I wasn't that sort of girl.

"Come on, Cass, I promised to show you the Drunken Garden."

"So why do they call it the Drunken Garden, Tim?" I murmured as he led me to a bench.

"Cass, it's where drunks go to make out. Now come here, gorgeous," he ordered, and I followed.

•••

Catherine had been a toddler when they drove away in the dark that night, headed for the first time to the Bryson House. Cassandra had been so tired she couldn't even see straight, and she had left the house without grabbing a coat or shoes. All she had prayed for that night was to make it to a quiet place where she could rest and where her baby would be safe. She would never forget how, when she had stepped out of the car that night, Miranda had murmured, "Oh dear, look at this sweet creature!" Then she had scooped up a tiny Catherine and escorted them into their fresh-smelling temporary home.

"Mama?" Zander's voice drew her out of the past once again. "Mama, are we there yet? I see horses."

Cassandra looked off to her left and watched the light dance through the shadows cast by the trees. The land undulated and in the distance she spotted several horses milling about in a field of tall yellow-brown grass.

"Five minutes, buddy. You feeling all right?"

"Can I bring my Chickie with me to meet the horses?" Zander clutched his stuffed bird. She wanted to hold him as close and as tight as he was holding the toy.

"Sure you can. Maybe they will be friends."

CHAPTER 12

Jupiter startled and Phoebe glanced up across the field. A half-mile from the stables, a car skidded to a stop and the door slammed shut before the skidding noise had completely faded. Phoebe froze as Jupiter's nostrils flared and his ears moved back. *What the heck?*

There were a million BMWs shuttling classmates off campus at this hour, and even more than a few black M3s. But there was always something distinct, something purposeful, precise and powerful in the way her mother walked. Now, with her arms swinging at her side and her long legs swallowing ground faster than her shadow could keep pace, Helen looked like no one else.

Why is she here? I thought she was off in California for the month on some darn trial. That's unfair of me. I missed her. But why is work so important to her? Phoebe stacked her pitchfork and waited, with an effort to seem blasé, for her mom to cover the remaining hundred yards that separated them.

"Holy moly," Phoebe mumbled to herself. "She isn't wearing a suit!" As she stifled a grin, she felt an unexpected surge of love for the woman who always seemed too well put together to be her mom. *And yet . . .*

Phoebe inspected her mother a little more carefully. Something looked off, but she couldn't decide what was wrong. Helen wore makeup. Her cardigan was gaily tied around her shoulders just so and her slacks showed off her figure, but not too much. Her auburn hair was swept up and off her face and . . . *wait.* A wisp of hair, unbidden, had escaped from the casual clip that usually held it. It was the first time Phoebe had ever seen her mother's hair appear with even a single lock out of place.

Helen was twenty-five yards away from Phoebe and closing in fast. *Why is she here?*

There was a faraway look in Helen's eyes. *Why does she look lost? What is she thinking about?* Phoebe felt a jolt in her stomach as Helen stopped and stood in front of her. *Does she—could she—how would she know?*

For a moment they stood and looked at one another and said nothing. Sascha had given Helen one look, but words of greeting never made it out of her mouth. She had seen the fire in Helen's eyes and had turned, with a discreet nod, to resume mucking.

Helen reached out a hand and brushed the sweaty bangs away from her daughter's face. Phoebe felt the subtlest of vibrations as her mother's hand shook, and she knew that Helen was doing her best to control whatever it was that was making her shake.

"Mom?" Phoebe's brash loudness melted away as she surrendered her relentlessly upheld, uncaring facade. Silent tears began to fall.

Helen nodded and put her hands on her daughter's shoulders, though she could say nothing more than her name because she was sobbing and shaking. She looked at her daughter with a glance so stern and so fierce that almost anyone else would have thought she was furious, but Phoebe knew better.

"I got back too late, Phoebe. I am so sorry."

Phoebe didn't want to let go at first. To release her grip would unleash it, this avalanche of pain. It would expose everything that hurt to human touch. But this was Mom. Mom was finally there.

If she would hold me like a little girl. And then . . . please. Just a few minutes ago I wished I had a knife, but I don't want to cut it all out of me right now. I just want her to cover me so it will stop bleeding inside. Hold me. Please. Please hold me.

Phoebe held it all in as long as she could, and then she fell into her mother's strong arms and stayed there for a moment that stretched into a seeming eternity. Helen leaned against the split-rail fence as she grasped Phoebe firmly, tucking her daughter in against her.

She used to hold me just like this. I never knew how much I needed her when she was gone. The late nights and trials and client dinners all resulted in promises that she didn't so much break as fail to keep. I remember being five, and she was picking me up early from school because I was sick. I was waiting in the office, and then I saw her and the world stood still for a moment. And we measure time just as much as time measures us, but some moments occur outside of time and that was one of them. I saw her and she smiled at me, and as awful as I felt, it was like her, my mother, brought the sunshine into my heart as she entered the office, and for that moment, in that moment, I knew everything would always be all right. Oh Mommy, I love you.

Helen removed her cardigan and wrapped it around Phoebe's shoulders. "I kept calling last night, and texting, and you didn't pick up."

That's because I was with him. Him and the shadows on the ceiling, or the shadows on the ceiling and him. I watched him and . . . some kid. A girl. She stared back at me and I could see her eyes and I told her, with my own eyes, not speaking, to hold still and it would be over soon.

"Sorry. I was, um, not—" Phoebe squirmed and looked down. She couldn't say it, but more lies? She was so tired of them. But she couldn't tell. He'd told her that no one would believe her.

Phoebe willed herself to stay silent. If she spoke, she would tell. She couldn't tell.

Helen patted Phoebe's shoulder and pulled her closer. "Don't say anything. It's okay." At first Phoebe shivered so hard that her entire body shook, and then all the muscles released their grip, one by one, until she slumped, exhausted, against her mother.

Helen kissed her on the head. "I'm here now. I'm going to take care of you. I promise, if it's the last thing I do, I'm going to take care of you."

Phoebe was too tired to figure out what any of this meant. She leaned against Helen. "Okay."

"Listen, we gotta go, okay? But I need to talk to Sascha."

Phoebe shot her a quizzical look.

Helen dipped her head in Sascha's direction. "Is that your friend Sascha?"

Phoebe nodded.

"I need to speak with her for a moment. Can you ask her if she can step on over here?"

Phoebe realized that the shadows had lengthened considerably and she wondered how late it was. She disentangled herself from her mother, and at first her legs buckled underneath her like a foal stumbling around for the first time. Helen reached out to steady her daughter.

Phoebe found Sascha scrubbing a saddle with a brush. She could tell that Sascha had been trying assiduously not to listen to Phoebe's conversation with Helen. Concern was etched across her friend's brow.

"Are you okay?"

Phoebe nodded and suddenly realized that her eyes were swollen and red-rimmed from crying. No one at school had ever seen Phoebe cry. "My mom wants to talk with you." Her voice clanged with a dissonant note and she wondered whether it sounded weird to Sascha, too. *Or is my hearing all messed up from crying?*

Sascha methodically set the saddle soap brush where it belonged and Phoebe tried to contain her impatience.

Darn it, she always takes her time, even when she is supposed to be rushing; she never runs, just walks a tad faster. What happens when she is late for the bus? That makes no sense. She doesn't have to take the bus, but if she did, would she run to catch it if she were late? Is Sascha ever late?

"What is it, Phoebe? Is that who you were talking to outside?"

Phoebe shuddered as Sascha's comment hit her. Sascha had never met her mom because her mom was always working.

But she loves me. I can tell she loves me when she looks at me and when she holds me in her arms and tells me everything is gonna be all right. So why was she never there? Am I angry? No? Shouldn't I be? I cannot bear it now. I need her. I need my mom.

"Yes," Phoebe said aloud. "Will you please talk to her? I don't know what she wants, but don't be intimidated. She's not even wearing a suit."

"Okay," smiled her blue-eyed friend. "I guess this is clean enough."

Usually Phoebe would have snickered and joked with her quieter friend, but the brash words just felt tired when she rehearsed them in her mind. "Thanks." It hurt Phoebe to say "Thanks," but she had no idea why.

"Ms. Thompson, did you need me for something?"

Helen nodded and put an arm around her daughter, who was shivering again. "Yes, Sascha. I need to call your parents and talk to them. It's important. May I have your mom's cell number?"

Sascha nodded and surveyed the traffic circle that led into the lot where Helen had parked. "Yes, ma'am." She dutifully repeated her mom's number and added, "But I think that's her car up there."

Helen paused as she punched in Mrs. Meincraft's number. "Oh, you mean the minivan that just pulled in next to my car?" Phoebe and Sascha cringed as they watched Sascha's little brother bounce out of the Honda Odyssey and bang into the BMW with his toy baseball bat. Even from a distance, the girls could hear the impact.

Sascha nodded and Phoebe spoke for her friend. "That's it, Mom. That's Mrs. Meincraft and Sascha's little brother."

Sascha started to answer, but Helen ignored the girls and started walking quickly toward the parking lot. Over her shoulder she replied, "Let's go talk to her now." She didn't wait for Phoebe and Sascha to catch up to her.

Sascha's eyes grew even wider than usual. "Phoebe, is everything all right?"

Phoebe searched for the right words. "No. It's not okay, Sasch. Things have been really messed up for a long time at home, and . . ." Phoebe stared at her hands, which were shaking. She willed them to hold still.

"You can tell me, Phoebe."

Phoebe looked over at Sascha. Coldness seized her from within and froze the words before they formed in her brain.

I wouldn't know where to start. You will hate me and never wanna talk to me again, so sick, so ugly. I hate the words that would come out; I hate the images that press up against my eyelids when I close my eyes. How could I tell this innocent girl who's never been touched like that? She will, they will think I wanted it, asked for it, begged for it. I don't know. I said the words. But did I mean them?

"Phoebe?" Sascha halted and Phoebe fell into place next to her. Sascha had donned her hand-knit sweater, the one that she seemed content to wear every day after she rode.

What would it be like to pull on the same cozy sweater day after day and not worry about the threads coming unwound? Sascha could knit her own sweater, so if this one lost even a single thread, she could knit a new one. Everything I have will unravel. And I am afraid of the unraveling and of nothing remaining, and if I tell Sascha, will the unraveling sickness spread? And yet Sascha is so comfortable. Keeping it from her protects her. I can't tell her yet, but I can tell her something.

"Sascha, I can't tell you what happened, but I will try to tell you someday."

Phoebe tried to wipe away her tears, but before she could, Sascha removed her only hand-knit sweater and handed it to Phoebe. "It works pretty well as a Kleenex," she cracked. "But that's between you and me. Why don't you hold onto it for the ride home?"

Phoebe nodded and started to cry all over again. *She's so kind to me and I'm so dirty.*

Helen was talking with Sascha's mom, and usually Phoebe would have left the adults alone. But today she felt an aching need to move in Helen's orbit and under her mother's protection, so she curled into Helen, who did not stop talking even as she wrapped an arm around her daughter and pulled her close.

> *Mom is here. I can breathe. She will know what to do. She takes on corporations and eats their CEOs for breakfast, lunch and dinner, or so I heard Dad bragging at dinner once. He said I reminded him of her before she got busy and old, and only I could help him bear it when she was gone. Stop. I can't be like this around her. Maybe she knows already. Mrs. Meincraft doesn't know, but if she stares at me long enough my sins, my sins will pour out of me like water.*

As Phoebe stood in her mother's embrace, Sascha grabbed her little brother, who had darted around to the other side of Helen's sports sedan and was about to swing at the rearview mirror. "Hey Sascha," he urged. "Race ya!"

Sascha took off across the freshly mown fields of green, not looking over her shoulder. Phoebe followed them with her eyes, each step they took making her ache just a little more.

CHAPTER 13

"Carol?" Helen's voice was clipped, measured and feminine, and she had been mesmerizing juries with it for twenty-five years. She was a specialist in an ever narrowing profession. A century ago, attorneys would throw up a shack, hammer a shingle to it and handle whatever legal business walked through the door; but over the decades, as the economy grew more complex, the legal profession had expanded and changed to meet the tasks required of it. The profession had split and kept subdividing and multiplying, sort of like a single cell reproduces into a complex microorganism. What once had been an all-around generalist subdivided into commercial and corporate and ever narrowing fields of study. Eventually there would be as many law specialties as there were ice cream flavors.

Helen had savored the courtroom too much to take on the firm's Department Head position that was hers for the taking. With a $50 million book of clients built from a small but tight coterie of law school friends who ran the legal departments for several Fortune 500 companies, Helen held power, yet she was able to cultivate her own practice with little interference from the other partners. If they called her the Dragon Lady behind her back, so much the better for her reputation.

Despite her New England upbringing and Ivy League undergraduate degree, Helen was an old-fashioned, barn-burning trial attorney. In the courtroom she became animated, even fiery, and this, mixed with her supreme confidence, made her opposing counsel's worst nightmare. She had successfully defended billion-dollar lawsuits involving the pharmaceutical, healthcare and banking industries and no experienced lawyer celebrated when seeing her distinctive signature underneath her name on a pleading. Any case involving Helen Thompson would feature a cavalcade of motions, crisply argued pleadings and creatively constructed, often unassailable legal arguments.

Despite her skill in the courtroom, however, Helen could not think of how to start this conversation. She cleared her throat and glanced at the marshmallow clouds turning peach in the distance. It bothered her that she didn't know what to say. Even talking about the weather felt impossible. "Carol?" Helen said again, speaking with solemnity. "Good evening." She paused and waited for Carol to say something, and Carol nodded, her eyes not quite twinkling, but somehow making it easier for Helen to keep on talking.

"Well, gratitude is . . ." Helen swallowed back tears and straightened her shoulders. *What's wrong with me? If the other partners at the firm saw me now, they'd go in for the kill.* Helen shook off the thought and instead of finishing her sentence, watched Sascha and her brother running across a soccer field.

Carol wrapped her hands around her elbows and swayed for a moment. "Well. It really is lovely to see you. I know Phoebe missed you very much these last few weeks. How is your trial going?"

Helen had no script, and in court that wasn't so unusual because she was always prepared. Now, standing in the mud-covered grass parking lot, she was at a loss for words. She made a gesture, as if to speak again, but her eyes filled with tears and she merely waved her hand at Carol.

"I take it you had to fly back unexpectedly, then?"

Helen nodded.

"How was your flight home?"

"Uneventful." Helen tried to summon a smile.

With an amiable nod, Carol stated more than asked, "And I am sure you were happy to see your husband—or should I call him Your Honor?"

A look of exquisite agony wracked Helen's entire body. Helen shivered and her teeth chattered. Carol grabbed Helen by the shoulders and ordered Sascha, who had meandered over to the van to drop off her backpack, to get the emergency blanket. Next Carol handed one end of the blanket to Phoebe, who had never left her mother's side. "Go right ahead and wrap it around your mama, hon." With a brisk movement, Carol tucked the other end of it around Helen. *So this is how good people act when you're hurt.*

Carol sat down next to Helen and it was as if she had created a sacred space right there, in the trunk of her minivan, where Helen could rest for a minute. Carol kept speaking in a quiet voice, something about the clouds moving overhead and a lot of other things that didn't register. When Helen still did not respond, Carol spoke in a matter of fact tone. "Helen? What can we do to help you?"

Helen looked up at the sky and watched a flock of geese fly overhead. She gathered up all of her energy and, in a voice just above a whisper, explained, "Phoebe and I are in danger. We need to get to a safe house and no one can know where we are."

Carol gave Helen an appraising look. "What about your husband?"

Helen gulped and whispered, "He can't help."

Carol's eyes narrowed. "He can't help? Isn't he a judge?"

Helen wrapped her arms around her legs and winced, as if the thought of her husband spread pain to all of her nerve endings. "He *was* a judge." Helen tried not to show how unsure she felt. The truth was that Helen had no idea what she was doing. For once in her life, she was flying by the seat of her pants.

"Your husband's not available?" Carol took a sip from a water bottle as slowly as if she had all the time in the world.

"No."

"Does he know you're in danger?"

Helen laughed once, a harsh laugh that cut through the twilight. "I think not." Her face turned a starker shade of white. "There are some things I can't tell you. We're in danger and need to get to a safe house, and no one can know where we are."

"Not even your husband?"

Phoebe stirred as Helen shook her head. "Mom? Why not him?"

Helen didn't answer.

"Why not, Mom?"

Helen bit her lip and willed herself to stop talking. She really couldn't get Carol involved.

"Mom, can I still ride in this weekend's show?"

Helen opened her mouth and then closed it. She turned to Carol, who shook her head with a wan smile.

"Mom, please?"

"We will have to see," and enough of an edge entered Helen's voice that Phoebe stopped asking.

Carol examined her hands carefully and said, not looking up, "Whatever you and Phoebe need from us, please ask."

"Thank you." Helen fought hard to smile for Phoebe's sake.

Carol tilted her head. "What about you? Are you okay?"

Helen tried to issue a brisk nod, but instead found herself collapsing. Covering the space between them, Carol gathered Helen into her arms and Helen allowed herself to shut her eyes for a few moments.

As Carol patted her back, Helen raised her head, turned to her daughter and tried to sound confident. "We're going to be okay. We'll grab a cup of coffee and a snack and then we'll be on our way, okay?"

Phoebe inclined her head, a vague, unfocused look hiding whatever she was feeling.

Meanwhile Sascha, after buckling her little brother into his Britax car seat, strolled over and stood in front of Phoebe. As Phoebe shrugged as if to turn away and then stumbled, Sascha reached out and wrapped her in a tight hug. Phoebe shuddered, her body moving one way, her hands thrown up for momentary protection, dropping almost as quickly as she surrendered to Sascha's hold on her.

Both Carol and Helen saw the gesture, and Carol grabbed Helen by the arm and pulled her out of earshot. "Did he make her that way?" she hissed.

Helen folded in on herself like a Raggedy Ann doll that a dog had torn apart and left in shreds. She inclined her head at Carol but did not speak.

"Then good for you for whatever you did. Now you go do whatever thing it is you need to do, and whatever you need, whenever you need it, you know where to reach us." Carol hugged Helen again and watched, a protective arm wrapped around Sascha's shoulder, as Helen backed the black M3 sports sedan out and headed down the winding hill into something unknown.

CHAPTER 14

At a traffic light, Helen reached out and gently pushed a strand of hair out of her daughter's eyes. Phoebe shifted so that she sat a little closer to her mother. Then she leaned over and grabbed a stack of CDs that were inside the console.

"Sheesh, Mom, what did you do? Don't you have any bands or singers whose names don't start with P? Pink, Pink Floyd, Pearl Jam, Patsy Cline, Patty Griffin, Pat Benatar, wow, Mom, what do you wanna hear?" Phoebe chuckled, and Helen noted how her daughter sounded so old and so young at the same time. It was like nothing had happened in the field; or maybe she felt safe, or needed to feel safe, just for a moment.

"Come on, darlin', I need something quiet so that we can talk. How about Patty Griffin?"

They drove in silence for a few minutes as the music played. Helen had long ago stopped trying to be a perfect role model for her daughter. She expected Phoebe to accept her sharp edges just like she accepted Phoebe's artistic indulgence. *No*, reflected Helen, *Phoebe isn't self-indulgent when she pens poetry or writes short stories. I just don't understand it because she won't make any money off it.*

Air from the heat vent sent Helen's scarf fluttering past her left eye. With an absentminded sigh, she removed her scarf and set it next to her on the armrest. To her surprise Phoebe stroked the scarf, almost as if it were the soft part above a horse's nose. *Darn it. Darn my eyes. I have not been here for her.* The well-bolstered racing seats pressed into her lower back, and Helen frowned and reached her right hand behind her to massage her sore muscles. Nothing felt right, but she knew it wasn't the fault of her M3.

"Phoebe," Helen began, "I have so many things to say to you."

"Am I in trouble, Mom?"

"No, of course not!" Helen placed her hand on Phoebe's. The silk scarf under Phoebe's fingers was fluttering again.

"But I did things," Phoebe said in a strangled voice.

"No, sweetheart. *He* did things." Helen's voice sounded harsh as she thought of her husband parading in front of the camcorder, so she tried to temper it by squeezing her daughter's hand again. "Don't think for a moment that what happened was in any way your fault. Don't ever—"

"But Mom, I ended up in bed with my own father. You know that, right?" Phoebe's words packed blunt force and Helen tried not to flinch.

"Yes, Phoebe. He made a video." One of her eyes went into a spasm. "And he left it on his desk. I know what happened. I know what he did."

"What about what I did, Mom?" Phoebe persisted. "You saw it, right?"

"Yeah. I saw a kid drunk or drugged and staring at the ceiling; that's what I saw. It wasn't your fault. I can't say that enough to you. It was *not* your fault."

"Is this a bad time to talk about horses?" Phoebe cringed as soon as she said it.

Helen sighed as she downshifted into third gear before her car attacked the apex of a curve. The M3 was the equivalent of more than three hundred horses. *How screwed up is that math, anyway?*

"I feel like the worst mother ever and would do just about anything to make it up to you, but we have some really serious things to talk about. If it makes you feel any better, I had been thinking about buying you a horse. Before all of this." Helen stumbled on her words and then added, without taking a breath, "And this, this changes none of that."

"Really?" Phoebe stammered. "I mean—I didn't mean I wanted you to buy me one."

"Yes, really. I know you didn't ask, but I was thinking about it in San Francisco. We'll talk about this at length, later."

Phoebe didn't answer.

Helen rubbed her thumb on the steering wheel and then leaned into another curve. She grimaced. Pain shot through her left elbow, a not-so-subtle reminder of Richard. An image of the blood seeping out of his temple passed across her field of vision, and beneath the sound of the wheels rolling on the road she could hear the golf club crunching his skull. Helen shivered and tried to dismiss it. *Him.*

"Just not right now," she added. "We have too much to talk about." Helen tried to sort through all the topics they needed to cover and how she should go about it, and then she realized that certain things just needed to be said. "It's going to be rough the next few weeks. We are driving out to a place called the Bryson House." A choking sensation made it hard for Helen to talk. She felt ashamed, somehow. *How in the world did I go from a $50 million book to ending up in a safe house?* "It's a secure, guarded place for survivors of domestic or sexual abuse. We are going to stay there until it's safe."

"Why, Mom? Why would we have to go away?" Phoebe rotated her hips so that she faced Helen. "Are we running?"

"Yes, we're running."

"From Dad?"

"No." Helen took a deep breath. "He's in the hospital. He came in and I was already home. I found everything, and. . ." Helen paused, and she felt every muscle in her body seize up again as she felt Richard's hands on her neck. "He knew I knew, and tried to come at me. I don't know how else to say this, so I'm just gonna say it. I smashed his head in with his golf club."

Phoebe's eyes filled with tears, and she shook her head. "Mom."

Helen tried to grip the steering wheel to keep her hands from shaking.

"Why do we have to go away, Mom? And are you in trouble?" Phoebe leaned forward and turned in her seat, trembling.

"I'm not sure. I'll be meeting with an attorney tomorrow. If he wakes up from his coma, I could be in trouble. But if he dies—" Helen's voice cracked. "If he dies, and they do an autopsy, there's no way they will overlook the shreds of golf club stuck in his skull."

Phoebe tightened the muscles around her eyes as horizontal lines sketched across her brow, and Helen remembered too late that her daughter was still a kid. "It's important that we don't lie to each other, so I need to tell you that there is a chance I might end up in jail if your father dies."

Phoebe stared, but Helen continued. "There's something else. The problem, honey, is that your father gave out our address to some men online. And he invited them to come and . . ." She could hardly breathe. *It's just a word, Helen. And you need to tell her.*

Phoebe drummed her fingers on the dashboard. "To do what, Mom?"

Helen flicked on her turn signal and did not answer.

As they continued west on the interstate, Phoebe sat up in alarm, as if she had only just heard the words "go to jail." She turned to face her mother, straining against the seat belt. "Wait! You said jail! No! Mom! Where would I go?"

"Phoebe, sweetheart, when I said a chance, I meant a slight chance. He hit me first. I hit him back in self-defense. I am going to meet with an attorney tomorrow and I will promise you that I will do everything in my power to stay out of jail. And if I can't, I will make sure you're taken care of."

"Taken care of? What do you mean, Mom?" Her daughter's voice had risen to a near shriek.

Helen took a deep breath. Phoebe was right. She couldn't go to jail. Richard's parents were dead and so were her parents, which was just as well. Her parents had not aged easily and both of them had died too young. She needed to choose a guardian for Phoebe, and she needed to choose one as soon as she could. And she needed to explain all of this in a way that wouldn't scare her little girl to death.

"You're right to be upset, Phoebe. I don't mean to seem insensitive. I don't think I will go to jail, but sometimes we can't predict how cases are decided." *I will pretend I am preparing her for a tough deposition and guide her with care through the process.* "I don't think that a prosecutor will even press charges, but they will investigate me. There will be a time where we just don't know how things are going to go. The problem is that we're at the mercy of a legal system rather than a justice system."

Helen paused and glanced over at her daughter. Was she making this more complicated than necessary? Shaking off her self-doubt, Helen continued, "I will do everything in my power to hire the best counsel I can find."

"That shouldn't be hard, right? Someone from your firm?"

"My firm doesn't specialize in criminal law. I need to talk to a couple of people tonight." Helen needed air. *There was no air. No air.* "Please don't worry. I know a lot of attorneys, and I will find a top-notch one who did not appear before your father."

Phoebe and Helen sat next to one another in silence for a few minutes. Helen's mind raced through all the things she needed to get done; one detail, one tiny nuance or fact unmeasured, would leave both of them falling through the cracks. *I can't afford to be tired or to forget anything. Not now.*

"Phoebe. We need to talk about a guardian. How about Carol Meincraft?"

Phoebe didn't hesitate. "Yes. I love her, Mom."

"I need to make some arrangements and talk to her this weekend."

"Maybe you can ask her Saturday, at the Show?"

Helen tried to hide her annoyance. Really it was guilt, because this was unfair, even cruel, that her daughter couldn't do the one thing she enjoyed. *So much of this is my own fault. I want to make it all better for her.* Helen took another deep breath. "I'm so sorry. But no. The problem is that it may not be safe for us to go out in public. And until the police place your father's friends into custody, I have to keep you at the Bryson House."

Phoebe was quiet.

"They have a world-class therapeutic riding program." Helen held her breath a little. It would have to be, not because she was spoiled, but because that was what Phoebe was used to. That was, after all, what McClintock was all about.

"What does that mean, Mom? Will the horses really be any good?" Phoebe tapped her fingers on the dashboard again, and Helen knew her daughter was trying to act grown-up. It had grown dark inside the car, but she suspected that Phoebe was biting her lip and trying not to pout.

Helen sighed. "I'm willing to bet they have some thoroughbreds and a decent trainer."

"I need to be able to ride and train, Mom. It's all I want to do; it's the only thing I really care about." Helen caught the whites of Phoebe's eyes flashing and she understood not so much the words Phoebe was using as the passionate glow in her daughter's eyes.

Helen's hands again pulled tighter on the wheel. When Phoebe gripped a horse's reins, it was probably the only time she felt in control. *Was that the only time my little girl could forget what he did to her?* The truth was, she didn't really know what else he had done to her. Or when it had started. *It's my fault. It's his fault. But I should have been home more.*

Helen pulled off I-66 and took the exit for Route 234. She brought the car to a full stop at a Shell station and surveyed the landscape as she stepped outside her sedan. The gas station was situated in another strip mall in Manassas, where northern Virginia shifts from blue state to red. All of a sudden the BMW, at home in Fairfax, looked out of place surrounded by pickup trucks and American-built SUVs. Helen gazed off into the distance at the line of green mountaintops in the distance. The Shenandoah Mountains were a little more than an hour's drive away. Before the miscarriage, Richard and Helen had hiked there with Phoebe many weekends.

Phoebe, meanwhile, had grabbed the squeegee and was cleaning all the windows. Helen felt nostalgic. This had always been Phoebe's job as a little girl.

"Thanks, dear. I need a cup of coffee. Do you want to grab something over at the Starbucks?" Helen inclined her head toward the strip mall and Phoebe, clearing the last bit of clear fluid from the windshield, didn't answer right away.

Helen repeated her question until finally Phoebe, shaking the squeegee, murmured, "Uh-huh."

Does Phoebe drink coffee? It kills me that I don't even know whether she likes coffee. I don't even really know what her favorite music is, or who she has a crush on, or what kind of horse she wants. And it's time, way past time, for me to fix all of that.

The gas pump clicked loudly and Helen twisted the gas cap shut, wrinkling her nose at the fumes. She nodded in the direction of Starbucks.

"Frappacino?"

Her daughter shrugged, her shoulders betraying annoyance. "That's junk. But a coffee would be great." Helen hid her pleasure. She knew it was silly, but it made her want to smile to know that she shared something, anything, with her only daughter.

Helen poured half-and-half into Phoebe's coffee, stirring until the brew turned mocha, and handed the cup to her daughter. As Phoebe cradled it in her left hand, Helen marveled at how strong her daughter's hands had gotten.

All the things I've been missing. Those long, strong fingers used to curl up into my hands and she would hold on until both our hands would get all warm and sweaty, and she'd keep on holding past the time I'd want to let go. The tiny toddler hands would grow a little each year, but at some point along the way I stopped noticing how she was changing.

Helen put an arm around her daughter's shoulder and hoped it wasn't too late. "Ready, hon? We need to get out there before it gets totally dark. I'm not exactly sure I know where this place is."

An unmarked police car pulled in behind Helen and a nondescript cop slammed his car door shut. His face was red and weathered, even pockmarked, and it looked like his shirt was a size too small. The officer glanced at Helen's windshield and fingered his black-backed book of tickets.

"Evening, ma'am," he said. His tone was not exactly condescending or arrogant, but clearly he was accustomed to being in charge.

A chill ran up Helen's spine. *He is here to arrest me. For sure.* "Good evening, detective," she replied in an even voice.

Then he smiled, but the smile did not go to his eyes. He looked at Phoebe more than Helen while he asked, "Did you gals realize that your registration has expired?"

Helen sighed. It was nothing. Just a technicality, and she wasn't going to jail. *Not today, anyway.* In Virginia you had to get your vehicle's emissions inspected every year, no matter how old the car was. Like so many things in her busy life, this chore had fallen through the cracks. "I apologize, Officer. I was on a business trip and I just got home and, oh shoot, I forgot." Helen used her most persuasive courtroom voice and willed innocent thoughts into her mind.

The officer rotated the toothpick that hung out of his mouth and tapped the hood of the car. Then he slammed his black book shut and inclined his head. "Just promise me you will get that taken care of, okay, little ladies?"

Helen tried to keep her mouth from turning downward at the police officer while she thanked him. No one had called her a "little lady" in a long time.

As she turned the key in the ignition and merged back onto Route 234, she thought about Phoebe. *In a few months she will start driving lessons, but she doesn't even want a car. Will I be in jail when she turns sixteen?*

Helen added another item to her already long mental list. She needed to get a trust drawn up in Phoebe's name, just in case. *I need to tell her about the trust and why she needs it. I need to tell her about the rape kit and the safe house, and oh God—where do I begin?*

Helen had never been known for having a soft touch, and in some ways it had defined her as a high-powered litigator. She was known for tearing apart witnesses with clinical precision and for destroying the reputations of witnesses who testified for fortune-hunting plaintiffs. Helen had worked so hard to perfect this outward image that she had lost touch with the gentler side she needed now.

Just pretend you've got to put one of the corporation's witnesses on the stand, and they're all messed up, and you gotta prep them for trial, and you gotta proceed just right without scaring the heck out of them. So you go real slowly.

"Are you okay, Pheebes?" Helen asked, using an old nickname.

Phoebe didn't answer; instead, her eyes followed the mountain range moving toward them.

And no matter what, you must look confident for the witness, because they are a hair's breadth from crumbling under the stress of it all. Phoebe is like that shaky witness, and she needs me to handle everything; she needs to feel like everything is going to be okay.

Helen grimaced in the darkness. How could she make her daughter think everything was going to be okay if she wasn't sure herself?

"Are they going to feed us at the house?" Phoebe asked. "I would do anything for a warm meal."

"I never thought to ask, but I assume they'll feed us. I know it's crazy and weird and maybe scary, but the future, our future, starts now." Helen tried to read a road sign. She didn't even recognize the name of the town they were in. The last hint of light faded into advancing nighttime shadows and Helen's eyes strained to glimpse the numbers on the mailboxes. "But one thing I know is that we're starting over together. Everything is going to be okay."

But it won't be okay, not for a little while. Should I tell Phoebe we need to get her examined? I guess we don't have a choice. Not so much from the standpoint of my case, although it might help if they find physical evidence.

Helen sighed. "Phoebe, there's something else that we are going to have to do tomorrow."

"Besides checking out the horses?"

"Yep. Besides checking out the horses." When Phoebe didn't answer, Helen explained, trying to stay clinical and straightforward. "And of course, my darling, I'll be right there holding your hand."

Phoebe tightened her jaw and pulled her knees up to her chin. "As long as you're there with me. I guess we need to do what we need to do." The girl wrapped her arms even more tightly around her knees, and Helen gripped the steering wheel in her left hand and opened and closed her right hand, trying to ground herself in the moment.

Phoebe stared out the window at the darkening sky and was silent. Helen felt her own heart beating faster and faster. She felt like she needed to pray but, like so many times today already, she didn't know how to begin.

CHAPTER 15

The phone had been ringing off the hook all afternoon. Each time he answered it, his heart raced a little. *Anticipation is just killin' me.* He swiveled around on his chair. It was going to be a pretty sick weekend . . . if Richard would return his call. It wasn't like the judge to blow off his calls. *Second thoughts? Maybe?*

Bob chewed on the end of his ballpoint pen. He could hear his mom railing at him, "Bobby, don't put foreign substances in your mouth."

And then his pop would chime in, "Goddamn fag. Just practicing for sucking—"

He'd always just walked to the fridge and tuned out the rest of it. Best way to deal with his dad had always been to hand him another can of Schlitz.

The pen snapped between his fingers, and ink spurted all over his desk. It was weird. Part of his brain was cussing, the way it usually would, but he just sort of sat there, watching the ink spread, thinking about his own fluid spreading seeds inside a girl, making something, but he shook his head, and closed his eyes.

What the hell is wrong with me, anyway? I was never a warrior-poet. That guy always takes a bullet to the head in movies.

Bob put his head in his hands and shivered a little. He'd seen a lot, and now—now he needed a break from it all. A break from the blood and the gore. A break.

Answer your phone, Richard. He had even called the judge's home number a few times. Stupid, careless, maybe, but he'd rerouted the calls. Well, not exactly. He'd bought one of those disposable telephone . . . *what? Things.* Bob shook his head. It wasn't like him to forget words. It was that girl's fault. And soon, he'd be done just staring at screens. He'd be getting some.

CHAPTER 16

Cassandra dialed her office on the Bluetooth and started speaking before her secretary finished reciting the firm's name. "It's Cass. I'm almost at the Bryson House. I just thought of something—the trial next Friday. Is Nadia in yet?" Nadia was Cassandra's rock-solid fifth-year associate.

"No, but she usually gets into the office at nine."

Cassandra checked the digital clock. It was five minutes before eight. "Okay, as soon as she walks through the door, I would like for you to hand her directions to the Bryson House." Cassandra rattled off the address from memory and relayed the password. Then she added a list of supplies she would need, and instructions for Nadia.

"You're not wearing jeans, are you?"

"Yeah."

She imagined her secretary gazing with disapproving eyes cast down over half-rimmed granny glasses. "Really? How about if I send Nadia out with your emergency suit?"

"Nope. It wouldn't look right with my boots. And she's not hiring me for my sartorial choices, is she?"

Cassandra could hear Janice making a clucking sound. Janice made her want to laugh, but there was no time. "Thanks, love." After she hung up, she drove west on Route 29, toward Middleburg, Virginia.

It had been fifteen years since Cassandra had been to the Bryson House. When she first visited the Bryson House, she had been a desperate, battered woman with a small child in tow. Cassandra tried not to think about it, but her mind, with inexorable force, replayed the memory and she stopped fighting it.

She gripped the steering wheel and shook her head with a touch of shame. *It's hard to explain to someone who hasn't been hit. You don't get married thinking you're going to be one of those pathetic statistics. How the heck had it happened?* That wasn't the first time Tim hit Cassandra, but it was the last.

The entrance road for the Bryson House appeared after several sharp turns, its only marking a brown mailbox with the numbers printed in white reflective tape. The grass in Middleburg looked greener than the grass on the golf courses back home in Fairfax. Bales of hay waited for transport, their dark yellow rectangles standing out against the lush fields that surrounded the unpaved road.

Cassandra braked as she approached the guards' house. Two armed, well-muscled men approached her. "Good morning, ma'am. May we see some identification?"

Zander asked, "Are you getting a ticket, Mama?"

"Not this time, love." Cassandra nodded at the guards and handed over her driver's license.

The guard cleared his throat and returned her driver's license. "Thank you, Ms. White. Ms. Harrington called down and said that you should swing by the stables on the way to see her."

Cassandra nodded. A lump in her throat made it hard to speak. As she followed nondescript signs that directed her toward the stables, it felt like she was coming home. The undulating hills, the overgrown wildflowers and the brown fences that demarcated meadows: a quiet place in the country where troubled minds could rest. The road branched off toward the stables before it extended at a steeper angle to the top of the hill.

From there, Cassandra steered her SUV around a circular driveway and parking lot made of grayish-blue brick laid in a herringbone pattern. Inside the grounds of the Bryson House she felt utterly safe, and yet this feeling of security touched on the mess that had first led her there. That memory felt decidedly unsafe.

Clad in jeans and a button-down shirt, her usual outfit when she didn't have a court appearance, Cassandra jumped out of the driver's side of the SUV and landed on two feet. She smiled at her choice of footwear. Her handmade, chestnut leather riding boots were one of her oldest and most beloved possessions, although admittedly she wasn't much of a horseback rider.

"All right, Zander, hop on out of there, buddy!"

Clinging to his stuffed chicken and matchbox car, he looked wee, scruffy and intimidated yet excited as he jumped beside her into the only puddle within a hundred yards of their SUV. Mud splashed on both of them and Cassandra grinned with amusement. Zander grinned back at her.

"Well, I'll be!" Mimi Harrington had a voice that could fill an auditorium and a body wide enough to block an aisle. In two short strides she had covered the remaining distance and enveloped Cassandra in a comforting hug. Mimi, along with Miranda, managed the Bryson House and had been there from the beginning.

Mimi's long, thick gray hair smelled like shampoo, and Cassandra's thoughts drifted. It was funny how someone's smell could be such a distinct piece of them, like a man's aftershave or a baby's gentle soap. When Cassandra thought of Mimi Harrington, she thought of clean soap and shampoo.

Mimi, her long skirt flowing in the breeze, patted Cassandra's shoulder and turned to Zander. "Hey, young man. You brought me breakfast. I like you already."

Cassandra took the box, handed Zander a doughnut and passed the box to Mimi. "Zander, this is my friend, Ms. Mimi. She knew Cat when she was smaller than you."

Zander shifted his feet and hopped again, his eyes focused on something in the distance, clearly waiting for his mother to dismiss him. Cassandra bent over and kissed his forehead. "Okay, run ahead to the horses, but do not go past the fence. I'll be right behind you."

As Zander scampered off, Mimi cradled the box of doughnuts in one arm and clasped Cassandra with her other. "You look well, honey. The running agrees with you. And by the way, you ran another marathon, yes?"

Cassandra blushed and laid her head on Mimi's broad shoulder. Mimi hugged Cassandra a little closer. "Miranda and I are grateful for all the clients you've helped over the years. I wish we got to thank you in person more often."

Cassandra nodded and to her surprise, admitted, "I'm sorry, Mimi. I mean to come back and . . . and then I get caught up . . . with work and the kids, but really, being here brings it all back. It's hard." Cassandra took a deep breath. She fought back a nervous giggle, or perhaps it was a sob. Mimi squeezed Cassandra but didn't say anything. The two women walked side by side in silence down the sloping, shaded side yard.

"Mimi?"

"Yes, Cass?"

Cassandra smiled broadly. "This place is pretty freaking bucolic!"

Mimi burst out laughing. "Wait until you see the barn and the ponds and the greenhouse."

Mimi unlatched the gate and approached the double-fenced paddocks, nodding in the direction of the white brick barn. "If you'd like to take Zander in to see the horses, you'll run into our riding instructor. She's expecting Zander. Don't worry, she can handle him."

Cassandra raised her eyebrows. "You sure?"

"Yep. Hurry inside. Helen is waiting."

Cassandra tried not to frown. "Mimi, that's fine, but if Zander wigs out I want someone to come get me."

Mimi looked for Cassandra's eyes and held eye contact for an extra second. "You've got it," and the way Mimi spoke made Cassandra feel affirmed. Mimi always had a way of doing that, of seeing everything about a person and knowing what to say, even the hard things. Cassandra hoped that when the time came, she'd be able to do the same.

CHAPTER 17

"Yes. I'll be by later. Thank you, doctor." Helen hung up the phone and stared at the wall.

A knock on her bedroom door startled her.

"Yes? Come in, please."

Mimi opened the door and took a long look at Helen. "You look pale. Is everything okay?" Mimi leaned on the round door handle.

Helen brought both hands up in the air and held them next to her head, then rubbed both temples slowly. Part of her wanted to cry, but she had no tears left for him. "The hospital called. They're taking him off life support."

Mimi let go of the door handle and crossed the room. "I'm so sorry. Whatever we can do to help."

Helen tried to say something, but Mimi hugged her. Helen hugged her back and then stepped backward, moving her hand up to her head and lifting her arms with a confused look, almost one of consternation. "Are you coming up to let me know that Cassandra White is here?"

"Yes. You ready? Cassandra is just now driving up past the guardhouse. She'll be up in a few minutes."

•••

"Ms. White?" A voice interrupted Cassandra from her thoughts.

"Call me Cass. You must be Jamie, the riding instructor." Cassandra craned her head and shook hands with the woman, a towering presence who with riding boots stood more than six feet tall.

"Yes, ma'am. And is this your son?"

Zander bounded up to Jamie and shoved the last piece of powdered doughnut into his mouth. Cassandra leaned over and wiped the powder off his face with her sleeve, while Zander howled in protest. Grimacing, he bounced over to the fence and started to climb it.

"Young man, no, we don't climb fences," Jamie announced in a soft, authoritative voice. Cassandra suppressed a smile and put a hand on Zander to help him climb down.

"Zander, this is Ms. Jamie, and she's going to teach you about horses. And I need you to listen to her, okay?"

"Can I take Chickie on a ride with me?"

"It's up to Ms. Jamie."

Zander allowed Cassandra to hug him. She turned and, hooking her thumbs through her belt loops, walked back to the Volvo. As she started to think through what the case would look like, she saw a girl leaning on the fence, watching a horse canter. The girl wore riding pants and black riding boots and was carrying a riding hat in one hand. She appeared too young to be an instructor, but she seemed thoroughly comfortable around the stable and riding rings. Cassandra stopped a few feet away and hesitated. The girl looked familiar, but she walked away toward the stable before Cassandra could say a word.

Cassandra watched the girl's shadow grow smaller and remembered how a long time ago, she had been that young. She shook her head and tried to throw aside all her emotions and memories so that she could process the facts of the case objectively. She needed to focus before the memories of a nightmare long since gone knocked her off her A-game.

●●●

Cassandra wiped the muddy bottoms of her boots on the brown and dark green doormat. Before she stepped inside, she inhaled the morning air. She smelled the horses and the manure and she hoped that Zander would stay away from the mud, off the top of the barn and away from sharp fence posts while she met with her new client. Cassandra chuckled to herself. She gave it even odds.

Cassandra hadn't moved more than a foot from the entrance when Miranda glided around the kitchen corner, as quiet as she was neat. "Hello Cass, darling. I cannot thank you enough for driving out here on such short notice, and with a sick kid in tow, from what I understand."

Miranda's hair was, as always, folded gracefully on top of her head in a deftly-crafted French twist, and her tasteful (but probably secondhand) outfit began and ended with a well-maintained French manicure. In fact the only thing that had changed about Miranda was that her black hair had a white streak running down the middle of her scalp. Cassandra smiled as she imagined Mimi needling her about it. Mimi and Miranda had been running the Bryson House together for more than twenty-five years, and they shared a dark sense of humor if nothing else.

Mimi and Helen Thompson emerged from the other wing of the house, and though they seemed deep in conversation, Cassandra could tell that Helen was looking her over. It figured she was wearing jeans and boots. *I am what I am.*

Helen shifted her eyes, and she inspected Cassandra with a mixture of respect and gratitude and relief. "Ah, the cavalry has arrived. And it almost looks like you rode a horse to get here this morning." Helen nodded at Cassandra's leather boots and continued, "But Mimi here tells me that you brought your son, so I'm thinking you drove." Helen spoke in a clipped accent, and Cassandra liked the way it sounded. *Someone who talks as fast as I do. We'll get through this interview at lightning speed.*

Cassandra inclined her head. "To the extent that I am the cavalry, I'm glad to be here. I have heard that you're a heck of a trial attorney and I'm so pleased to finally meet you, but I do wish it were under different circumstances."

"I never thought I would be in this type of situation."

Cassandra looked into Helen's eyes and read sadness and uncertainty, both cloaked in a shaky bravado. When Helen looked away, as if at a loss for words, Cassandra thought about trying to put an arm around her client, but it didn't feel right. She might pull back a stump.

Mimi and Miranda drifted away in another direction as Cassandra guided Helen into the study. "I can only imagine how difficult this must be, Helen," Cassandra began as she turned to face her client, but Helen interrupted.

"I feel like I failed my daughter," Helen blurted out, looking surprised that she'd voiced the thought.

She sounds so vulnerable, Cassandra thought. *I need to connect with her, so I have to take a chance.* "I felt the same way when I was here so many years ago," she confessed. It was a risky thing to tell a client at an intake interview; then again, this wasn't the run-of-the-mill client interview, or the run-of-the-mill client, for that matter. She couldn't be afraid to tell her own story. *Not if it will help my client.*

A shocked look flitted across Helen's face. "You were here? I know you volunteered here and got the word out for the Bryson House in the community and represented a lot of women pro bono, but . . ." Her voice trailed off.

"Yes." Cassandra glanced at her hands and then more words tumbled out. "Yes. Me. It's not as rare as you'd think. But as I was driving here today, I remembered how awful I felt about myself before I left my first husband."

"I'm so sorry. I just feel, I don't know, overwhelmed. How did you get it all figured out, if you don't mind my asking?"

"Mimi and Miranda helped me get back on my feet, and they helped me see I was a lot stronger than I thought. And I knew I needed to do what was best for my child. At the time, Catherine was a toddler and I was pregnant with . . ."

Cassandra's voice trailed off and she gasped and held her hand up to her mouth. Helen moved closer, and then shifted from one foot to the other, unsure what to say or how to react. With a faraway look in her eye, Cassandra whispered, "I lost that baby. And we started over."

"I am so sorry, Cass. I lost . . . one . . ." Helen couldn't finish her sentence. She reached out and grasped the polished surface of the table, sinking down into one of the leather desk chairs. Helen rubbed her face, her eyes welling up with tears.

As Cassandra pulled up another burgundy chair beside her, Helen continued, "Thank you, Cassandra. I didn't mean to ask such personal questions. I don't usually."

"Please call me Cass."

Helen rubbed her index finger with her thumb, one eye falling on the layers and layers of books lined up on the bookshelves.

"So why did you think to contact me?" Cassandra tried to diffuse the tension in the room. "I'm not a big firm lawyer anymore. And there are a number of very high-powered defense attorneys downtown. Don't get me wrong. I am confident I can represent you competently, but I am curious."

"Two different people recommended you."

"Who, may I ask?" Cassandra folded one leg on top of the other and glanced down at the muddy heel of her boot.

"The first was Carl, my senior associate. He will be taking over all my cases while I'm gone. He heard you speak at a domestic violence seminar and he said that he respected the way you wove your own background and cases into what you were teaching. Oh, and," chuckled Helen, "he also said, and I quote, 'Cass kicks ass.'"

"Ah yes," Cassandra said, suddenly laughing. "Wise man."

Helen looked out the window next to the fireplace. A wood log burned and the bookcases gave the study a homey feel. "Yes, he has been a tremendous asset at work for years, and I don't know what I would have done without him and his partner yesterday."

Cassandra followed Helen's gaze through the bay windows and wondered whether Phoebe was out there riding with Zander. The idea of it warmed her inside. "His partner? I thought he was a senior associate."

Helen folded her fingers together in the shape of a temple. "His life partner, Cass, is a man named Troy. And Troy is not only a very fine man, he's also a licensed therapist. He talked me through this yesterday, and . . ." Helen's voice again trailed off before she finished her sentence.

Cassandra waited for her client to go on. *It must be so hard for her to be a client, and she's a handful.* But maybe this wasn't a disadvantage. It would be nice not to have to tiptoe around a client so much. *To a certain extent, I will have to let her guide me through this at her pace, and when I need to knock her in the kneecap, she will understand and won't get all wimpy about it.*

"Who else recommended me?" Cassandra shifted her hips and thought about the late evening run she had taken last night. She was still stiff from it and now she was regretting the stretching she hadn't done.

"You remember Troy? Carl's partner?"

Cassandra nodded.

"Troy and Carl were in San Francisco yesterday, so when all of this . . ." Helen made an opaque gesture before continuing. "When everything happened yesterday, I spoke with both Troy, in his capacity as a therapist, and Carl, in his capacity as my attorney, until I could secure counsel to represent me. Troy had me speak with his business partner, Cary Matterly." She paused, uncertain.

"I know Cary!" Cassandra exclaimed. Cary had been Cassandra's therapist many years ago. "Small world! So she recommended me?"

"Yes, Cass, she sure did."

Out of the corner of her eye, Cassandra noticed a blue sedan winding around the circular driveway that led to the front of the Bryson House. A young woman in a gray suit stepped out from the driver's side and slammed the door shut with her foot. It was Nadia, and as always, she was right on time.

Nadia was a fifth-year associate at Brickman & White. She'd taken a cut in pay and left a big firm in DC to work for Cassandra in exchange for more trial experience and what the younger attorneys lovingly called a better "quality of life." Unlike most name partners in modern law firms, Cassandra was both loved and respected by the attorneys who worked for her. Nadia, for one, seemed to appreciate that she didn't work crazy hours or have to "show face" on the weekends.

"You know how Carl is your right-hand man? Well, my own indispensable associate just arrived. Will you excuse me for a moment?" Cassandra gestured toward the window. "She looks a little lost."

"Go right ahead."

Nadia did not have the typical brash personality of a trial attorney. In some ways, she looked more like an English professor than a lawyer. A jumbled mass of thick black curls sat on her wide shoulders and her dark blue eyes lit her brow line. Although she was only thirty, she already bore sharply creased, vertical thinking lines on her forehead.

After a quick tap on the door, Nadia let herself into the study, thanking Mimi and greeting Cassandra all in the same breath. Cassandra looked over Nadia's shoulder at Mimi, who ambled off with a genial wave.

•••

"As I was saying, Helen, Nadia is my indispensable and effective associate, and she almost always takes second chair for me."

Helen made eye contact with the young woman. "Good to meet you, Nadia. I do appreciate indispensable and effective young attorneys." The corners of Helen's mouth lifted slightly and Nadia set her computer bag and brown leather tote down on the round table next to the window. Cassandra waited a few beats for Nadia to turn on her laptop. She and Helen sat side by side around the conference table with Nadia flanking her boss.

"Nadia, Helen and I were talking shop until you arrived. I assume you know that Helen is a partner at Baker, Pitts, Kenzey & Moore, and she needs legal counsel in relation to her husband, Judge Thompson."

Nadia's fingers moved over the keyboard with precision and she didn't stop typing as she said "Yes" without inflection.

Cassandra leaned over and poured a glass of water from a pitcher that Miranda had left on the desk. "Helen, take it from the top. Start wherever you want and I will ask questions as you talk. And Nadia: please chip in anytime, too. The more minds we have working on this, the better."

"Okay, Cass. In one sentence: I confronted my husband when I realized that he had abused our daughter Phoebe and had invited several online friends over to our house to participate in something awful he was organizing."

An uncomfortable silence hovered in the air. The only sound was of Nadia's fingers tapping the keyboard. A bird began singing outside the window.

"What did he do?"

"Strangled me." Helen, Cassandra thought, sounded like his hands were still wrapped around her throat. "I broke free and hit him on the head with one of his golf clubs. Always hated those golf clubs." Helen hesitated, and then a ragged laugh, a single staccato sound, rolled off her tongue and she glared at her hands. "Now he's in a coma and they've taken him off life support per his advance directive. He'll be gone any day and then, well, I may have some explaining to do."

Cassandra took all of this in. *I really could use a smoke*, she thought, but still she did not allow her facial muscles to betray her thoughts. "You mentioned he was organizing something. What's that about?"

"Richard was bragging about how he'd . . . hurt . . . Phoebe and he asked other group members to private message him if they wanted to get in on the action."

The muscles around Cassandra's eyes tightened but her voice remained level. "And did other members PM him?"

"Yes," Helen said. "They were arranging something for tomorrow night." Tears filled Helen's eyes and she trembled as she finished her sentence.

Nadia handed Helen a box of tissues and Cassandra followed her instincts and grabbed one of Helen's hands.

Cassandra knew she had to reach out to Helen before the older attorney got lost in the fog of her grief. "Phoebe is safe now," she murmured in a deep, low voice. "We're going to get through this together, Counselor, okay?" Then she added a little more loudly, "Is this when you found the DVD, Helen?"

Helen moved almost convulsively, as if casting aside an invisible cobweb. She nodded.

"What was on it?"

Helen wrung her hands and whispered, "Terrible things."

Cassandra, realizing the other woman was afraid, pulled her chair closer to Helen. "Please let me do the worrying about your case. Your job is to tell me the truth. That is all I ever will ask of you."

"You're assuming I'm going to hire you."

Cassandra ignored the sarcastic tone in Helen's voice and gave her client an appraising stare. "We don't have time to go over all that. I'm sure you've already transferred funds into an account to pay for my retainer, right?" Cassandra leaned back in her chair and folded her arms.

Helen was amused rather than chastened. "Of course, Counselor. And yes, you are hired."

Cassandra inclined her head. "Good. So, the truth."

Helen picked up a pen from the table and twirled it. "So you're not one of those defense lawyers who doesn't want to know if their client committed the murder?"

Cassandra shook her head. "First, I don't want you to ever use the word 'murder' again, either in my presence or to anyone else, got it?" She waited for Helen to make eye contact, and then repeated herself. "Got it?"

Helen pressed one hand into her temples, and with one eye closed as if in pain, nodded.

"Good. Now help me piece together what happened— before we get into a philosophical discussion about criminal law."

"Or figure out the truth."

"Yes! Exactly. Then we need to determine how to tell your story in the most advantageous light possible. That's my job: with your help, to tell your story. Not your job. My job. You have enough to deal with right now. That's why you hired me." Cassandra didn't look away while she spoke to Helen, and she could read the respect in Helen's eyes as she finished speaking. "I know how hard it must be to sit on the other side of the table, but now that you're there, you need to trust me."

Helen looked at her hands, and then stood up. She removed her ring and, without a word, walked over to the trash can and let the ring slip through her fingers.

Cassandra reached over and took hold of a white DVD file cover. "Okay, Counselor. I'm so sorry, but we need to take a look at that video together. The prosecutor's going to need to see it, and we need to know exactly what's on there before we have that meeting."

Cassandra held the DVD and Helen sucked in her breath, knowing what was next.

Cassandra waited for Helen to sit down. "Nadia, can we watch the video on your laptop?" Cassandra handed Nadia the DVD and steeled herself for what she knew she had to watch. She knew it wasn't going to be easy for any of the women in the room.

Nadia's computer whirred and the images flashed in front of them. *I need a cigarette,* Cassandra thought as she watched the video. You could tell it was a girl; anyone could tell.

"Helen? Can you confirm for me who that is?" Cassandra hated to ask this question, but it was necessary.

"It's Phoebe. Birthmark, right ankle." Helen sounded sick.

Cassandra grimaced. *I hope it isn't too much to make her watch this again, but I need to assess how she reacts to it to get a read on her. This is when I hate being an attorney. To get to the truth, we can be so cruel.*

By the end of the eight-minute video, Cassandra was shaking and about to cry. All of this had made her so fearful for Catherine, but now she needed to comfort her client. "Thank you, Nadia. Please turn that off now."

"Ms. Thompson," Nadia started, her voice just above a whisper, "I'm so sorry. I'll do whatever I can to help you and Phoebe." She pushed away from the table and put a hand on Helen's shoulder. Helen reached up and patted Nadia's hand.

And it all looked and felt awkward to Cassandra, but she reached out for Helen's right hand. The three of them didn't say anything. There was nothing to say.

CHAPTER 18

Phoebe held her riding helmet under her arm and sat on a fence post, waiting for Jamie to get out of her way. Phoebe's brown hair appeared lighter as the sunbeams flickered behind her, and she kicked her feet against the wooden post as she studied the scenery. She didn't mind waiting.

Aside from eating breakfast and dinner with the rest of the Bryson House occupants, Phoebe had spent all of her waking moments by the stables. She had been around horses her entire life and wanted to get to know the horses and to give them the chance to know her before she saddled up.

I don't wanna ride one of the dumb Quarter Horses. I wish they had a few thoroughbreds, even aging thoroughbreds. Even a draft cross would be wicked. Might need a mounting block to get on one of those gentle beasts. I've seen one that was nineteen hands high.

Some people thought that draft horses were ugly, but draft crosses could be pretty good at dressage. And they weren't bad looking, either. *Clydesdales dress up pretty darn good on TV*, Phoebe thought.

She sighed, wishing. The wind blew leaves across the fields. A few leaves floated until they reached the fence, where they settled into the soft Virginia clay. Phoebe thought about colors. When she closed her eyes at night, the last thing she usually saw in her mind was the color brown, mixed with red and black.

Reddish-brown clay. Tack. Tack is always brown. Trees are brown. Stables are black. Reins are black. Except for white fences, which must take forever to paint, fences are brown. I don't dream or think in Technicolor. I dream and think in brown and black.

"Are you riding or are you watching?"

Phoebe looked around, and from fifty yards away she caught a glimpse of an aging woman wearing the oldest, best-polished pair of dressage boots that she had ever seen. Distracted by the boots, Phoebe jumped off the fence and sauntered over to the barn, helmet still tucked under her elbow. *Ah, I forgot. The best boots are black. I love a fine pair of dressage boots. I wonder how old those are.*

For a split second, Phoebe noticed the woman giving her a close inspection. Then the girl turned away and stared harder at the dressage boots, which seemed to be the type usually worn at the highest levels of competition. Dressage boots have a stiffened shaft at the back of the boot to prevent it from sagging at the ankle, and often they are custom-made. Either the woman wearing the boots was an idiot riding impostor or the real deal.

"Are you riding or watching?" the woman repeated. She sounded annoyed, but her eyes twinkled. Phoebe swung her arms behind her and cocked her head to the side. Given the multitude of creases and the fine sheen on the leather on the boots, it was likely that the stranger was a serious equestrian.

"I reckon that depends, ma'am."

"Please don't call me ma'am. That's what they called my Mama, and we buried her ten years ago. My name's Anne McCaffrey. And you're old enough to call me Anne."

"I'm Phoebe." Phoebe reached out and offered her hand, and Anne took it with a vice-like grip. *Good grief, she's strong—would hardly guess she's old enough to be my grandmother!*

"Ah, Phoebe. You're named after the goddess of light." Anne nodded at Phoebe as the girl continued to study Anne's boots.

Anne wore tan riding breeches. A hint of white hair, neatly tucked in under a sturdy but high-quality riding helmet, showed at the nape of her neck. A white blouse appeared under what seemed to be a navy blue dressage coat. Phoebe felt like she was gaping, but she had never seen such a gorgeous coat. It was every bit as formal and functional as the boots Anne wore.

"So, are you riding or are you watching, Phoebe?" Anne asked again. Phoebe couldn't tell whether the woman was mocking her; this time, Anne's brown eyes were not giving away her thoughts.

She's testing me, the girl thought. *I'd say "Game on" but an old Quarter Horse is gonna bore me.*

Phoebe twirled her riding helmet, holding it by the strap. "That depends," she replied, maintaining eye contact with the older woman. Her posture seemed to announce that she was neither afraid to ride nor to spend the entire day perched on the fence post, watching everyone else.

Anne bent over and grabbed an errant rock, which she deposited in her coat pocket. "Depends on what?"

"The type of horse," Phoebe replied, enunciating each syllable carefully.

"Why does that matter?" Anne asked.

"I'm training for dressage shows, and certain horses aren't going to be able to pull off the moves I need to perform. I don't want to pick up any bad habits. And with the wrong type of horse or even the wrong saddle, I might get lazy or lose my focus."

Anne raised her eyebrows. "I like the way you think," she said. "But even as a dressage-only rider, it would still benefit you to get time in the saddle. It makes it feel like you belong there. So take as much experience as you can, especially with some of the warmbloods." Anne grinned and nodded toward the stables. "However, that won't be necessary, because I have three Iberians which are very well-suited for your type of riding."

Phoebe's eyes widened. "You have Iberians?"

"Two of them are Lusitanos; the other is Lipizzaner." Anne turned and started to walk into the stable. "Follow me."

Phoebe followed Anne so eagerly that she almost tripped on Anne's heels. "So, do you work here?"

Anne laughed. "I guess you could say that. In a way I do work here, if you consider raising horses work."

"Do you live in the main house?" Phoebe persisted.

Anne shook her head. "No, but I used to, back when my husband was alive." As she answered Phoebe's questions, Anne grabbed a dressage saddle and shifted her eyes toward an almost identical one stacked beside it. "I think you will find that meets your needs, child," Anne murmured.

"Anne?" Phoebe tried to think before she blurted out what she was thinking, and then her curiosity got the better of her. "Were you an abused woman?"

Anne shook her head. "No, I wasn't. You're wondering why I lived in the house, I suppose."

Anne paused to open the padlocked door in front of a smaller stable next to the main one, and Phoebe felt a blush start around her ears and spread down to her fingertips. Why had she asked such a personal question? Couldn't she have asked something about the Iberians? "Yes, ma'am," she stuttered.

"I own the house, the stables . . ." Anne made a sweeping gesture with her arm. "The land . . . everything," she explained. "I rent it to the charitable organization that runs the Bryson House."

Phoebe searched for a response, but the only thing she could manage was a quiet "Oh."

Anne moved inside the stable and opened the first door. "Here," she instructed Phoebe, changing the subject. "Help me get this saddle strapped on while I grab a mounting step, please."

Phoebe had never used a mounting step before; then again, she was young, and she felt this with a note of melancholy. She tried not to stare. Anne was arranging the dressage saddle on the Lusitano horse. A buckskin-colored horse, he bore white markings on his head and feet. Phoebe grinned at a stray thought; he was like a cup of cappuccino with white foam on top.

Anne finished saddling up and grasped the reins. "If you don't mind, would you carry the mounting step outside for me? And then you can grab the horse you're going to ride. She's named Ginger, by the way."

Phoebe did as she was told and Anne continued speaking. "This is my fifteen-year old. I named him Lusitania, after—"

"The British liner in World War I," Phoebe interrupted, finishing Anne's sentence.

"Good, so you like history? Now if you still want to ride, Ginger is waiting in the barn. I'll wait for you out here."

Phoebe hoisted the second saddle and reminded herself to slow down as she approached the other Lusitano. As the girl went about readying the saddle and the reins, Ginger stood patiently.

"*Phoebe, horses are herd animals. You need to establish that you're in charge and to be confident at all times. Never show fear or hesitation. That means you are deliberate. Never, ever let it smell your fear.*" Phoebe's stomach churned a little, remembering her father's words from so long ago.

"What do you mean, 'smell your fear'?" she had asked.

"Every animal sweats out fear and other animals can smell it," he had said. "It's a strange smell, not clean like sweat, but dirty, like fear. A horse will know what it is, even before you do. Do you understand, Phoebe?"

She did understand, but it bothered her that his words still echoed inside, ricocheting like ghastly phantoms.

He was so good to me then. How could he have taught me so many of the lessons I most needed to learn, and then did that to me? He said it was love. But if that's love, then love hurts.

Phoebe realized that she was crying. She leaned against Ginger's body and patted her neck. Ginger nuzzled her hand as the girl stared into the horse's brown eyes and took a deep breath.

•••

For the first few minutes Anne and Phoebe rode side by side, warming up their horses, and, in Anne's case, stiff muscles and joints. Phoebe hid her red eyes behind her dark shades. She didn't think the older woman could see that she had been crying, and yet in a way, she wasn't afraid to share her pain; sometimes it is easier to tell a stranger that you're falling to pieces than to tell a friend. Phoebe almost hoped Anne would ask her—

"What's hurting you?"

"It's messy." Phoebe's voice was barely above a whisper.

"I've lived through a whole lot of messiness," Anne replied, applying gentle pressure on the bit. "Messy does not scare me."

Phoebe rubbed her index finger against the reins. It was a nervous habit she had inherited from Helen. "My father's in a coma."

Anne sat tall in her saddle and listened as Phoebe haltingly groped her way through a string of words. "He's the one who taught me to ride. He taught me all about horses and it's the one thing I can really do, the one thing I really love. It's like he's here. He can't be! I can't get away from him, not even here. But I will not give this up just because . . ." Phoebe struggled to go on, but the words hurt so much to say.

Anne asked, "What happened to your father?"

Phoebe inspected her reins and kept her eyes on her hands. "My mom had something to do with it. I'm probably not supposed to talk about it."

"Is your mom here too, Phoebe?"

Phoebe looked at Anne out of the corner of her eye. "Yeah. She's inside meeting with a lawyer. I need to go in later. They need to examine me." Phoebe found it hard to stop talking. There was something calming about riding next to this woman, this expert rider who was two generations her senior. Anne listened to her. Most adults just talked *at* her, not really hearing.

"Examine you?" Anne prompted.

"Rape kit," Phoebe answered. She swallowed after she said it. Would Anne know what that was? *Why did I have to say that? Will she think it was my fault? That I'm dirty?*

But Anne did not bat an eye. Instead she murmured, "Ah. Those aren't fun, but they don't last too long. And your mom will be there with you, I imagine."

Phoebe wanted to ask Anne more questions. She wanted to talk to Anne the rest of the morning and well into the afternoon. She wanted it like she needed a cold glass of water and a light summer blanket. *Who is this crack rider with the thoroughbred Iberians and a background, it would seem, in counseling?* She felt a strange connection with her.

Phoebe felt Anne observing her and shifted her gaze. With an edge of swagger, she tossed her head back. "What? You're thinking how well I ride and you're wanting to know where I learned all these slick moves?" Phoebe's smile was more exuberant than obnoxious.

Anne laughed. Vertical lines ran up and down her cheeks and forehead. "Are you asking for blind affirmation, or do you want to improve, Phoebe?"

Phoebe's jaw tightened and her inner child bristled. "Well, that depends on who is talking," she finally replied. "Exactly what are your qualifications?"

Anne's gray eyes looked a shade lighter in the bright sunshine. It softened the effect of her words. "When I was your age, I didn't really care about someone's reputation. What I really wanted to know was whether they could help make me a better rider. You have talent. A lot of it. But you have a lot to learn. For example, you are pulling Ginger's bit too often, and each time you regrip your reins or tap your index finger—which is a nervous tic—you knock off your balance by a degree or two. Over time, that will stress out your upper back muscles, which are really tight right now as we speak. It will also force your horse to bear more of the job than she ought. Good riders demand the least from their horses. Does that make sense?"

Phoebe was speechless. *What the heck?* Her feelings were hurt, and that had never happened in the ring or at the stables. *Since when is a little criticism going to make me cry? Why am I so anxious to please this old crone?* She dismounted and sprung, catlike, to her feet. Without asking for direction or permission, she removed Ginger's saddle and began grooming the mare. She was crying again as she worked the brush over Ginger's coat.

> *I'm such an idiot. I'm mediocre and just didn't realize it. Everything Anne told me was right. I do need to get better, but there's no one at McClintock who can coach me to the next level.*

"Phoebe?" Anne had followed her and now stopped a few feet from the younger rider. "I should have told you who I am. I am semi-retired now, and I've trained many riders, so if you are willing to work with me, I would love to train you." Anne put one arm around Phoebe's thin shoulders. "So with that in mind, well, I hope what I said doesn't hurt so much."

Phoebe wanted to lean into the older woman, but pride or shame or something else made her pull away. She craved Anne's approval and based on how well Anne handled Lusitania, she already had a serious case of hero-worship.

"Come on," Anne urged, almost as if she were coaxing a jumpy warmblood onto a van. "I need to go up to the main house and grab my mail. How about if we walk up there together?" Wordless and still shaking, Phoebe walked beside Anne, her shoulders back and her eyes searching the tree lines again. A blue heron flapped its large wings twice; the sound was like a flag flapping in the wind. The heron glided out of sight, and Phoebe wondered where the graceful bird was headed and whether she would see it again.

CHAPTER 19

Cassandra paced outside, and as her hands shook she gave in and snagged a near-empty pack of Marlboro Reds from Mimi. This case was going to tax her. *I'd better call Cary at the next break. Seventeen years sober and this case has already got me hanging on by a fingernail.*

Helen laughed as she strolled over. "I didn't take you for a smoker, Cass."

Cassandra surrendered a half-smile. "I was more of a drunk, actually, until I quit, but I smoke when I'm on the job sometimes. And I run marathons." Cassandra pulled out a lighter. "Go figure." "More of a drunk" was a bit of an understatement, of course. She had hit bottom eighteen years ago, and it hadn't been pretty.

Helen contemplated the pack of cigarettes. "I was trying so hard not to hammer Phoebe about smoking and God knows what else, but I'm a mediocre role model myself." Helen reached her hand out for the cigarettes.

Cassandra inhaled deeply, and even as the smoke entered her lungs and moved through her bloodstream, inner peace met with guilt. *So long as Zander doesn't see me, it's okay.* The paper crinkled in Helen's hands as she removed a cigarette. Helen looked like a sophisticated actress from an old black and white movie when she inhaled, and Cassandra realized that she had never smoked with a client during a break. Yet with this client, this fellow attorney, it somehow felt okay—perhaps because representing Helen was going to require some blurring of roles.

Cassandra exhaled. "Back when I first came here, I hoped I'd never see my husband again. I don't know if I was more scared or angry, to tell you the truth. All I knew was that I'd had enough."

"Is that why you came here? That night?"

"Yep." Cassandra now paused, her eyes unfocused and looking off into the distance. "I kept thinking that there was no way I could even tell my own mother, but she had died years ago. And then I wanted to kill him."

"Your husband?"

"Yeah. It was a mess, and for so long. He was drinking; I was drinking. We were both working, but he was gone more and more. And no matter how hard I tried, I couldn't bill enough hours and still be a good mom. The stress of it all was tearing me up inside, and it was destroying Tim. His drinking just got worse every day, and when he wasn't sitting in front of the television with a beer in his hand, he was at the office, working later and later. So when he said that—"

"That you were a bad mom?"

"Yeah, when he said that, I knew he was being cruel. I knew it was the beer, but it didn't stop there." Cassandra paused and collected herself. "Then he hit me, and he threatened to hit my daughter, and that's when I left. And when I got here, I was pretty hysterical. I kept saying I couldn't do it alone."

Helen moved another few inches closer to Cassandra, and Cassandra sensed that the older attorney wanted to offer comfort but didn't know how. She gently put an arm around the dragon-slaying senior partner and kept talking. "You know what Mimi said to me when I got here?"

Cassandra kept an arm loosely draped around Helen, almost as if they were in a football huddle, and waited for Helen to shake her head.

"I curled up on the sofa in the rec room and kept asking, 'How'd I mess this up so badly, Mimi?' She told me that my husband failed me and he failed my child and that this wasn't about me. And that I had to be strong for my child."

"Really?"

"Yeah." Cassandra allowed her eyes to crinkle. "I was so tired. She told me exactly what we needed to do in the morning. Stuff I knew, or should have known, but it seemed impossible. File a police report. Call a lawyer. Get a restraining order. But I kept saying, over and over again, that I couldn't do it. So Mimi got up, which was a production even then, and ripped the mirror off of the wall." Cassandra chuckled as she described it. "The wires were dangling back and forth when she put the mirror in my hands. She made me look inside it."

Cassandra had peeled her fingers away from her eyes and looked in the mirror. Lines knotted her face like ropes cast out to the water from ship's edge. Her grayish-blue eyes had lost the blue tones and her gaze wavered in and out of focus. The pallor of grief had stained her. High cheekbones ran like rafters to her temples and brown hues bracketed the skin around her eyes. Her countenance seemed far, far away and for once, she looked every day her age, if not older.

"What did you see?"

Cassandra wrinkled her nose. "When I looked in the mirror, I thought I looked like hell. Broken. No one else would have me. But then Mimi had sat down next to me and in that slow way of hers, she'd said, 'There is a strong, beautiful woman inside that mirror. I believe in her. You need to reach out and grab hold of her and believe in her, too.'"

"Wow."

"Yeah." Cassandra turned her eyes to Helen and didn't try to hide the pain in her eyes. "But I whined that I couldn't do it. So she sent me to bed. 'You will have a clearer head after you get a few hours of sleep,' she said. Or something like that."

Cassandra wiped away a stray tear. "When I climbed up the circular staircase and into bed next to my sleeping daughter, I heard Cat breathing quietly and smelled Downy on the sheets. And it didn't seem all better, but it seemed safe enough. My little girl, and she's big now, a senior at McClintock, but she was tiny then, and she wrapped her tiny body around me and I whispered over and over again, 'It's gonna be okay, we're gonna be okay.'"

Helen's eyes crinkled. "And you were. You were okay, right?"

Cassandra nodded, and then turned to face her client. "But it wasn't easy at first. Especially court. I've been on the witness stand before and it can be a lonely place, Helen."

"The divorce?"

Cassandra turned to face her client. "Yep. Divorce. That's why I started telling you this story. In court, they tore into my past and shredded me. So when we go back inside, I want to make sure that we go over everything they can use against you."

•••

May 5, 1991. Maryland. Rockville Circuit Court.

Cassandra filed into the wood-paneled courtroom. She wore a crisp navy business suit and stockings and polished shoes that were killing her feet. She leaned forward and bounced on the balls of her feet with hands clasped behind her, and then she remembered, *I'm not about to toss a ball over to first. Once a ballplayer, always a ballplayer, I guess.* Her tangled mess of hair tumbled over the edges of her white silk blouse. Cassandra took a deep breath and looked around for her ex.

He stood next to his attorney, an expensively-coiffed partner with rimless glasses and hair swept back into a bun. Cassandra stifled a nervous half-smile as Tim spotted her. His legs rose and he began to stand, but then he must have remembered, because he repositioned the back of his suit jacket. Somewhere deep inside, she wanted to rush over to him and beg him to hold her one last time. *Stand straight. Shoulders back.* She waited.

With a brisk movement of his head, Cassandra's attorney nodded at the bailiff, and the words "Please rise" cut through the quiet hum of the nearly empty courtroom. Cassandra recalled the judge from a recent trial, and a glint of recognition entered the judge's eyes. *What does she remember me for? Everyone's been talking about me.* The American flag and the yellow, black and red state flag of Maryland framed the judge's black robes as she nodded to Cassandra. "Morning, Ms. White. Counselors, do you have any motions for me?"

At the last moment, Cassandra closed her mouth and let her attorney approach the bench. She tuned out the quiet discussion in front of the bench and focused on the silver thread hanging from her attorney's sleek Armani suit. Kyle Anson was attractive, and his square jaw and gray temples make her feel a little weak in the knees. *I'm not single yet*, she admonished herself. *Anyway, I couldn't get any breakfast down, so it's low blood sugar and not an aging lacrosse player's bulging calves that are making me feel ill.*

Kyle's suit pants flicked, one leg rubbing against the other, as he returned from the bench. He put his hand on her arm as he glanced at the denied motion to exclude prior substance use from evidentiary consideration. "Cass, I'm sorry, but we'll do our best to limit their use of it," he whispered, and the muscles in his face tightened and flexed as he cleared his throat and sat beside her. He had warned her during witness prep that all of it was probably going to come into evidence, but the full reality of the words "addiction" and "recovery" only now hit her. *Things could get nasty in a hurry.*

"You allege that my client refused to seek help for drug use, but isn't it true that you yourself spent four weeks in a rehabilitation center in January of this year?"

Cassandra waited for her attorney to register his objection for the record. He rose. "Objection, Your Honor."

"On what grounds, Counselor?"

"Relevance, Your Honor."

Cassandra swallowed and tried not to crave a cigarette. It had been a year since she last inhaled, but she knew she was going to bum one off Kyle at the next break. Smoking was an old habit she took up every time she tried a case in court, and she was as expert in quitting as she was at starting again. She sighed and tried not to bite her nails as she waited.

"Ms. White? You may answer the question."

Cassandra tried to imagine a cigarette between her index and middle fingers. "Yes."

"And what substance did you seek treatment for?"

She could smell the scotch. "I drank too much."

"Isn't it true, Ms. White, that you also received treatment for drug use?"

The color left Kyle's face. "Objection, Your Honor!"

"I'll allow it. Ms. White, answer the question."

"I did not go in for rehab for drug use." The fact that she had used drugs had come up in therapy, but scotch and gin, not coke and marijuana, had been her downfall. The words sounded metallic and she tasted the harsh flavor of a Dunhill as she licked her lips.

Tim's attorney frowned at Cassandra as if she were trying to explain something to an uncooperative child. "Isn't it true, Ms.

White, that you were arrested when you were seventeen for using and driving under the influence—"

"Objection, Your Honor," Kyle exclaimed. "Not only has Counsel for Mr. Garrett failed to lay a foundation for this line of questioning, but anything my client may or may not have done as a teenager is clearly irrelevant to this case."

"Your Honor," Tim's attorney argued, "Ms. White is alleging that my client . . ."

Cassandra couldn't stand to listen anymore.

Eyes closed, joint in hand. Marijuana had relaxed her as a teenager when her parents fought. It had been ten years since she last constructed a bowl, but if she happened across a dime bag of it now, she didn't know what she would do.

Cassandra squirmed on the witness bench and watched the stenographer tapping away.

Hearing after hearing, all she does is sit and listen and type her 150 words a minute. She rarely even looks up at the people speaking the words she's copying into their machines, and yet whatever she types is accepted as truth. What does a stenographer think of it all? Is she the proverbial fly on the wall, or is she a public servant of some sort, paid to get it right the first time and only noticed when she makes a mistake? By recording what everyone else says, is she trying to capture some sort of truth? Or are the words she types into her black machine a disorganized, bleak fragment of our reality, out of order, mixed up, partially obscured and forever wanting?

Tim's attorney appeared out of the corner of Cassandra's eye and interrupted her daydream.

"Ms. White, for how long have you been taking medication to treat depression?"

"About three years."

"And when did you start taking Xanax?"

"Right after I stopped drinking."

"When was that, Ms. White?"

"Christmas of last year."

"And you've taken antidepressants and anti-anxiety medication every day?"

Cassandra shook her head. "Not every day." The attorney paused and Cassandra wondered where she was going with this.

Will she suggest that I'd grown dependent on anti-anxiety medications? Will she delve into the causes of the depression and attack me for needing help? I guess they think I'm a screw-up for taking meds.

A heaviness pressed on her chest, but she waited.

Tim's attorney fingered a document and Cassandra caught a hint of recklessness in the way she frowned, one hand theatrically placed on her hip.

"Ms. White, why did you stop drinking and go into rehab?"

Cassandra pushed her fear back and replied, "It was affecting my work and my relationships."

"I'll say."

"Objection, Your Honor!"

"Counselor, really!"

Opposing counsel held up her hands more in supplication than acknowledgment. Then, after the judge raised an eyebrow, Tim's attorney went on: "But Ms. White, isn't it true that you were found in a compromising position with another man at your firm's Christmas party?"

"No!"

"So you're saying that you weren't found unconscious in the ladies bathroom, half-naked?"

Tears rose to Cassandra's eyes and she did not wipe them away as she replied, "It is true I had too much to drink. It is true I passed out. But I was not the one who took off my clothes."

"What are you saying, Ms. White? That you were assaulted?"

"Yes."

"Did you contact the police?"

"No."

"Why not, Ms. White? Wouldn't that have been the sober, responsible thing to do? Wait, I remembered. You weren't so sober, were you?" After a brief pause, the attorney shook her paper. "Withdrawn, Your Honor."

•••

Cassandra looked at Helen intently. "I don't care what you've done, whether to Richard or in your past. Whatever it is, you need to tell me the whole story. That's the only way I can protect you. Okay?"

Helen flicked her ashes over her shoulder and coughed. "This is an unusual conversation. To be frank, I'm not accustomed to women who talk about first marriages and domestic abuse the first time I meet them, but . . ." She paused and smiled awkwardly. "A few days ago, this might have given me pause. But this has been . . . helpful, and I'm grateful."

Cassandra felt her neck turning red again, and for a split second she regretted revealing so much. *Aw, shoot. If it helps one woman.* She shrugged, tapped her Garmin and scratched the ground with her boots. "Right. Shall we get back to work, Counselor?"

Helen remained rooted to the spot and Cassandra noticed a shade of black shadowing her client's irises. Helen's eyes were boring into her own, but without seeing her. *I understand. It's going to take time.*

Suddenly Helen's phone beeped, and Helen, glancing at it, swayed as though about to fall. As Cassandra rushed to get an arm underneath her, Helen murmured, "Hospital. I think he's dead now."

CHAPTER 20

Back inside the study, Helen, slumping against the table, spoke into the telephone just loudly enough for Cassandra to overhear. "Yes. Thank you. Yes, please conduct the autopsy. Yes." Helen didn't cry as she turned to Cassandra, but her voice shook as she whispered, "He's gone, Cass. He's gone."

Cassandra sent Nadia into the kitchen to ask for tea, then folded her client into a brief, almost athletic hug. "I'm so sorry for your loss, Helen."

Helen pulled away from Cassandra but gripped the younger woman above her elbows. "Please keep me out of jail," she barked. "Please." Helen sounded more like she was demanding than begging, and her eyes were lit with a fierce intensity.

"I'll do my best. That, I promise." Pausing to fill her voice with confidence and force, Cassandra added, "And that starts now. Please sit down. I have a few questions."

Cassandra wasted no time getting to the gist of the case. She asked hard questions, guiding Helen through the scene right up until the moment the ambulance took Richard away. Helen struggled to describe the sequence of events leading up to Richard's collapse.

"It was a huge break he didn't die at the scene," Cassandra said. "Because it's standard operating procedure for the EMTs to call the police."

As Helen sipped from the light blue teacup Mimi had wordlessly brought a few minutes earlier, Cassandra continued with quiet strength. "It's good that you didn't try to cover anything up." She paused. "You didn't conceal anything or try to hide anything, right?"

"I thought of all of that, and no, I didn't even throw out my clothes or wash off the golf club," Helen said. "I showered and left the clothes in the kitchen trash can, along with the evidence Richard left all over the house of the crimes he committed."

"Good! Helen, all of this is good," Cassandra exclaimed, grabbing Helen's hand. "I think we can make this work, absolutely, Helen. It's messy, but you did well by not covering your tracks, for sure."

"Well, yeah, we all grew up reading about cover-ups, didn't we, Cass?" Helen remarked with a touch of irony.

Cassandra folded her hands together and contemplated the case. "Okay, here's the deal. I do think this is a fairly open and shut case of self-defense. The mere thought that at some point you felt angry enough to kill him doesn't create the requisite motive for murder. Your motive here, clearly enough, was to protect your daughter from a predator—from several predators, really. And your story, that he came at you with the intent to inflict bodily harm, should easily be supported by the physical evidence. What we need to do, as far as I am concerned, is to go on the offensive and report the pedophile ring to the authorities. I am sure that this is what you were planning on doing anyway. His death does not change the need to put these other pedophiles away, does it, Helen?"

Helen shook her head. "No. It doesn't. And we're not safe until we know they are behind bars."

"Exactly," Cassandra agreed. "Richard may be gone, but he can still reach you from the grave by means of the men he invited to your home."

Cassandra ignored the sickened look that crossed Helen's face. At this point, the younger attorney had a job to do; Helen's emotional state was really a therapist's job. "In the course of questioning you," continued Cassandra, "Richard's death may come to the surface organically. When we go to the prosecutor with the sex crimes, the facts surrounding Richard's death will come up and we'll deal with them carefully. And of course I will be at your side during any questioning. How does this sound?"

"That makes sense. Do you think I am going on trial?"

Cassandra shook her head. "My best guess is no. I'm not making any promises, and I fully intend to make use of the media to confuse the jury pool, but I don't think they will charge you with a crime. And tactically, I strongly recommend that we meet with a DA as soon as Monday."

Helen had opened her mouth to answer her attorney when she heard her daughter's voice carrying from down the hallway. "Okay, Cass. This afternoon we need to get a rape kit for Phoebe." Helen put her hand on the right side of her head as she spoke, almost as if a jolt of pain had shaken her.

While Helen clenched her jaw muscles and massaged her temples, Cassandra sat there, impassive, and replied, "That would be helpful."

Waiting for Cassandra to continue, Helen gave a subtle wave of her hand.

Cassandra pushed aside the thought of her own daughter and went on, "I am going to need to talk with Phoebe and get her version of things, and the sooner the better."

"Is that something I need to be there for?"

Cassandra shook her head. "It would be better if I talked to her one-on-one, I think, as long as you're comfortable with that."

Helen nodded and Cassandra noticed that the folds on Helen's skin looked wider and deeper than even an hour ago. The sound of people talking permeated the silence in the study.

"If you don't mind, Cassandra," murmured Helen. She stood up and walked away from the conference table.

•••

One of the services the Bryson House provided for its temporary inhabitants was free medical care. When Mimi and Miranda had started the domestic abuse safe house twenty years ago, they had cobbled together services from surrounding businesses; from nurses and doctors to handymen to lawyers, an army of professionals had donated their time on an as-needed basis. Later, as the Bryson House grew more and more viable through donations, it had been able to hire many of these professionals either full or part-time.

From the very beginning, Anne McCaffrey, an ex-Olympian, had closely supervised the therapeutic riding program. It was only recently that Anne, convalescing from a serious car accident, had handed over the responsibility for running the program to her much younger niece, Jamie.

Anne was deeply engaged in conversation with Phoebe when the two equestrians rounded the walkway and strolled into the foyer of the mansion. Anne almost bumped into Mimi, Miranda and Helen before she could remove her boots.

"Well, shucks now," boomed Mimi, who was searching through the folds of her long skirt for a receipt Miranda had asked for. "How many times do I need to remind you to take your boots off before you streak manure all over my floors, Anne?"

Still distracted, Anne leaned over to unzip her boots before grasping Miranda's arm. "Oh hi, Miranda! Mimi, so sorry. Beautiful day for riding isn't it?"

With a sideways glance, Phoebe unzipped her own boots and handed them to her mother.

"Hey Mom, I want you to meet Anne." Phoebe waved her arm in Anne's direction and slouched.

Miranda took over at this point, and with her usual reserve and formality, she inclined her head. "Helen Thompson, this is Anne McCaffrey. She owns the Bryson House and the land surrounding it. Without Anne, we could never have made the Bryson House a reality."

Anne smiled at Miranda with an affection that came from years of friendship, and she leaned over to shake Helen's hand. "Your Phoebe is a very talented rider, Ms. Thompson. I am hoping I can work with her."

Mimi rubbed her hands together. "That's great news, Anne. I knew you weren't ready to retire."

Anne continued speaking to Helen as she adjusted her socks and breeches. She managed to appear dignified even without her boots. "Helen, I've seen many riders over the years. I don't know where Phoebe is riding now, but if she wants to train with me full-time and works hard enough at it, I foresee a future in the sport."

Phoebe stood up straighter.

"Just so you know," Mimi added, "Anne rode in the Olympics, and she has trained three other Olympians. So if Anne says Phoebe has potential, well, trust her."

Recognition flooded into Phoebe's eyes. She turned and, with a star-struck look, gasped, "You're *that* Anne McCaffrey?"

"Yes, I'm that Anne McCaffrey." Anne removed her riding helmet and pivoted to the left, heading down the hallway toward the industrial-sized kitchen. "I will see you tomorrow morning at 5:00 A.M.," she tossed over her shoulder,

"Mom?"

"Yes?"

"I don't think I need to go to the Show tomorrow."

Helen folded her arms. "I wasn't going to let you off the grounds tomorrow. For now, we will be staying here."

Phoebe bit her lip. Mimi, realizing that Phoebe was feeling reality's harsh tug, broke in. "Hot apple pie for dessert tonight!"

Phoebe tried to smile, but her shoulders sagged a little. To the surprise of both, however, Helen seemed to know what to do; she walked over and gave her daughter a big hug and whispered, "We'll figure this out, darlin'. It's going to be all right."

Phoebe hugged her mother back and closed her eyes. As she opened them, she sighed. "I just want to get this over with. When are we going to do it?"

Without flinching, Miranda told Helen and Phoebe to follow her, and she led the way up the winding staircase to the infirmary. As they headed upstairs, Phoebe trailing a step behind, Miranda explained the process to Helen. "A nurse practitioner works here full-time. She is trained to administer these kits."

Helen breathed in her daughter's horse smell and felt soothed by its familiarity. "Does the nurse really have a lot of experience with this sort of thing?"

Miranda removed a fleck of dust from the wooden banister. "More than you might think."

Helen waited for Phoebe to catch up to her once she reached the top of the stairs. Phoebe's face was expressionless, and Helen's stomach churned. "Are you okay, sweetie?"

"I just wanna get this over with, Mom. I've been through worse." Phoebe sounded like she was older when she said this, and the contrast between the world-weary words and the youthful set to Phoebe's face pained her mother.

Helen threw her arm around her daughter's shoulders. Phoebe was almost as tall as Helen, and with a lump in her throat the attorney remembered when Phoebe could barely reach up high enough to hold her mom's hand. "I love you, Phoebe," Helen whispered with a sad smile.

Phoebe leaned against her mother and closed her eyes. "I love you too, Mom."

Helen and Phoebe linked arms and marched into the infirmary. Phoebe listened as Helen told her about Sintab and San Francisco and Ashtray the associate. She talked as Phoebe disrobed and kept talking as the nurse removed tissue samples. Phoebe stared into her mother's eyes through the entire examination. When the nurse finished she removed her white rubber gloves, and the sound of the rubber snapping together echoed in the exam room as she placed them into the garbage can. Then the woman scribbled chain of custody information on the slides.

While Phoebe had squeezed her mother's hand with a death-grip, it had taken all of Helen's energy to continue telling work stories. She hoped that the sound of her voice would resonate in Phoebe's mind, its rhythm rolling like a brook flowing over all else that Phoebe could, would . . . otherwise see. Helen imagined herself talking away at the phantoms she felt must be fighting inside her daughter's mind, not knowing if Phoebe could hear her, and trying not to picture her now-dead husband doing things, terrible things, to the little creature that connected them all. Everything the nurse did was a blur to Helen. All she wanted to remember was the gentle warmth of her daughter's hand wrapped in her own.

CHAPTER 21

At Mimi's invitation, Cassandra swung into the kitchen and picked up a fresh baguette, a package of lunchmeat and a couple of sodas, and then headed through the winding hallways on her way to eat lunch with Zander. Cassandra marveled at the unaffected, cozy country beauty of the mansion's enormous kitchen. The décor was rustic but high-end, the walls painted a cheerful red that mixed beautifully with the dark wood floors and white chair molding. She briefly peeked into the dining room, which contained a table large enough to sit twenty people.

As she had passed by the study earlier, Cassandra had assigned Nadia the task of researching the head of the federal sex crimes unit in northern Virginia. "Because the deceased communicated with individuals in other states," Cassandra had explained, "I think we might need to get the Feds involved from a jurisdictional standpoint, even if we take the case to the Commonwealth's Attorney over in Fairfax. Please call Helen's associate, Carl, and coordinate with him. We need to get whatever he's assembled to the Commonwealth's Attorney on Monday. Oh, and grab yourself something to eat from the kitchen," she'd added. "I'm going to check on Zander."

Cassandra hooked one finger into her belt loop and strode down the grassy hill toward the stables. She tried to set Helen's problems aside. One of the coping mechanisms she had learned many years ago as a young lawyer fresh out of rehab was to compartmentalize her work; as her therapist had explained to her, if you wouldn't bring a client home to dinner, why would you bring your client's problems home to dinner? This didn't mean that Cassandra never thought about her clients when she was away from the office or the courtroom, but simply that she tried not to worry about her clients or her caseload when she spent time with her family. Sometimes this worked. Months or even years passed while she set work's endless time pressures on the back burner and took an active role in her children's lives. Now, since Cassandra was one of the name partners in her law firm, she had been able to step back her hours and work an almost strictly forty-hour week.

Cassandra sighed. All of that would be changing, and she was scared, not of the case, but of the way it made her crave two of her old vices: smoking and drinking. She bit her lip. It made her sad, the minutes she would not be able to spend with her youngest child. Or scared. But of what? *Remember to smile, Cass. Man, I need a drink. Darn. Once a drunk, always a drunk, darling.*

•••

The sunshine appeared between shadows cast by the pine trees near the stables. Cassandra spotted Zander sitting astride a black pony and headed in his direction. Zander wore a black riding helmet that fit him well, and Cassandra paused to reflect on how far her temporary home had come. Back when she had stayed at Mimi and Miranda's, the place ran on a tiny budget, was staffed by volunteers and stayed in a perennial state of near-disrepair. Cassandra wagered that Zander would get to keep the riding helmet. A decade later, the Bryson House and its renowned therapeutic riding program were very well funded.

Zander caught sight of his mother and grinned at her from under his helmet as he started to wriggle in his saddle. For a moment, Cassandra thought he might tumble off the side of the black pony, but Jamie reached up with her hand and steadied the young rider. Cassandra couldn't hear exactly what Jamie told Zander, but she discerned the instructor's tone and liked it. Jamie spoke firmly but calmly, and Zander sat still and held the pony's reins, shooting his mother a proud smile.

Jamie helped Zander clamber down off the pony and held its reins as the boy raced off through the mud toward the fence where Cassandra stood. "Mama, I ride horses!" he yelled happily. Without waiting for her help, he scrambled up and over the fence and jumped into her arms. She laughed and almost fell backward as she caught him.

"Gosh, Zander!" she exclaimed. "Gimme a little warning next time before you leap!" Cassandra raised her voice so that Jamie could hear her. "And please don't climb on the fence again."

"Okay." Zander studied her face with his blue-gray eyes. He had his father's eyes, and Cassandra thought about her husband. She pictured him holding Zander high up in the air, and she felt happy and sad at the same time.

"Mama!" howled Zander, breaking into her thoughts. "Ms. Jamie said I could ride more after lunch!" As Zander waved his arms and tried to tell Cassandra ten things at once, Jamie walked up beside the fence and nodded at them both.

"Right, Ms. Jamie?" Zander called out. By now he was standing next to his mother, but hopping in place.

Cassandra turned her attention to Jamie and spoke in her most gracious tone. "Zander seems to be having a great time. I am most grateful to you for looking after him."

Jamie waved her hand, her attention split between Zander and what Cassandra imagined were inchoate worries. "I don't know if I would call it looking after, Ms. White. It's my job to instruct riders, and I'm just doing my job."

Cassandra tried to figure out what the younger woman thought of her son, and then decided that it didn't matter. Jamie's standoffish attitude annoyed her, but she was doing her job and Zander seemed happy. *Perhaps*, Cassandra thought, *maybe Jamie was an acquired taste; or maybe she was just prickly*. Cassandra tried not to glare. She knew it was not personal. "Well," she murmured, "thank you for doing your job and instructing my son. What time shall we meet back up with you?"

Jamie barely made eye contact with Cassandra and shifted one shoulder, a movement that turned into an almost full-body shrug. It wasn't exactly a rude gesture, but Cassandra felt the burn of annoyance until she realized that Jamie's eyes twinkled when she looked at her son.

"Friday afternoons around the Bryson House are for chores," the instructor said. "I'll be working in the barn and walking the grounds making spot repairs. So whenever he's ready, walk him over to the barn and I'll find a way to put him to work."

Zander bounced off Cassandra's legs and blew kisses to Jamie, but she was already moving away.

Cassandra knelt down and rested her arms on his shoulders, waiting for him to stop wriggling. He tried to squeeze under her arms and race under the fence and back to the pony. "Zander," Cassandra said firmly. He kept bouncing around until she repeated his name, much more loudly, and then he settled down and hugged his mother a little too tightly.

"Mama, you're wearing red lips today," he whispered, eyes sparkling.

Cassandra nodded. "Yes, I am wearing red lipstick."

"I like it when you wear red lips."

Cassandra giggled and picked her son up, carrying him over her shoulder fireman-style as he squealed and laughed. She found a bench on the other side of the smallest riding ring and deposited Zander, still talking nonstop, onto the seat.

"Ooh, Mama, I like when I ride you," he said. "Can I have soda?" He smiled in a charming way and thanked her when she handed him the can of diet soda that she had brought down from Mimi's kitchen. They sat on the bench side by side until eventually, after devouring most of a can of soda, several ripped-off slices of the baguette and an impressive amount of salami, Zander curled up in Cassandra's lap and began sucking his thumb. For several full minutes he stayed cuddled with Cassandra; the only sign that he was still awake was the way he kept patting her with the gentlest of touches. She hugged him and smelled horse and little boy. Then she thought about her older child and smiled with contentment.

After Cassandra had hugged Zander one last time and left him to help out in the barn and around the grounds, she retraced her footsteps back up the grassy hill that led to the side of the Bryson House. The next interview was going to take a lot out of her, and before finding Phoebe she needed to sit and think without distractions. Cassandra opened the trunk of her Volvo and hopped up on the tailgate, which was one of her favorite thinking spots. Swinging her legs off the edge, she stared at the sky and the geese flying overhead.

I need to talk to Phoebe about what her father did to her. And I need to go about it right, and I have almost no idea how to do that, at least as a lawyer. All I know is how my therapist talked to me after I was raped.

Cassandra shifted her body until she was leaning on her other hip and contemplated what Cary had said that day so many years ago.

•••

August 1991

It was a Friday morning. Usually Cassandra worked on Friday mornings, but after the "incident" in the women's bathroom, the law firm had placed their promising associate on medical leave. In the harsh words of one of the female litigation partners, "You had better get that drinking problem under control—and let's just hope all of this doesn't get out, or your future here and in this city is done." Cassandra had spent a month in a treatment center in Bethesda, Maryland, around the same time that she had begun seeing Cary for biweekly therapy sessions. It had taken a few meetings for Cary to gain Cassandra's trust.

Now it was their fifth session, and Cassandra was perched on Cary's green sofa in the therapist's tenth-floor office. She glanced around the room and pulled her sweatshirt close. She was wearing gray sweatpants that were three sizes too large and a black fleece sweatshirt that her ex-husband had given up on getting back from her. Warily, Cassandra watched her therapist. Right from the first meeting, Cary had surprised Cassandra with her tough speech patterns, which seemed a contradiction when combined with her long, silver hair and predilection for flowery skirts and Birkenstocks. In many ways, they were each other's mirror image: Cassandra's tough exterior disguised a sensitive, easily injured psyche, while Cary appeared as gentle as a flower child but underneath was steely and firm.

After surveying her younger client, Cary tapped her notepad, her gaze impassive. "How are you?" she asked.

Distracted, Cassandra patted the arm of the sofa. "I keep thinking that I'm dreaming. That I just made it all up. Do you understand?"

Cary nodded.

"I can't see it, not all of it, so how do I know it was real?"

"You were raped, Cass."

The words felt like a slap, a blast, and Cassandra gasped. Her hands shook and she kept shaking her head, over and over.

"Cass. Look at me."

Cassandra's eyes blurred, but she tried to focus on Cary.

"Do you know who did it?"

"It doesn't matter. It doesn't. It doesn't."

Cary wrote something down on her notepad, her gentle eyes belying her stern tone. "Yes, it matters. Who was it? Do you know who it was?"

"I think so," Cassandra whispered, and she stopped and thought about holding a cigarette between her fingers. "I can feel it sometimes. Someone's there. He's touching me. It hurts. It hurts so much, Cary." Cassandra's voice rose until she was shrieking. "I can feel it there. It feels like . . ." Cassandra gulped, and the words froze, suspended, and she wanted them out of her, just like she wanted him out of her.

"What does it feel like?"

"It hurts. I want it to stop. Or maybe I don't . . ." Cassandra leaned over and felt the bile rising. I can feel it. My body remembers."

"Who did this to you, Cass?"

"I don't know!" Cassandra held onto the sofa as the scene from the Christmas party buffeted her. Her mind swam in and out of the pattern on Cary's skirt.

"What do you mean?"

"It hurts so bad, I'm in pieces. I'm like a spaceship falling, hurtling through the air. The engines have exploded and the pilot is dead and I can't steer or figure out how to land. I want to die. I don't. I want to hurt myself. No." Cassandra sighed. She was so tired. "It's embarrassing, always feeling like this. Why am I so weak?" She gave Cary a broken, beseeching look.

Cary stopped writing and exclaimed, "Weak? You're not weak. Not at all. If you could stop blaming yourself for going to the bathroom at the wrong time for a few moments, I see a very strong woman."

Cassandra blushed. She thought about the scotch and the beer and the drugs, which was what she and Cary had talked about the most. And then she asked, "Then what is wrong with me? Why am I always thinking like this?"

"Cass, you were assaulted. You wouldn't be normal if you didn't feel like this."

Cassandra nodded and tried to hold on so that she wouldn't let out the sobs.

"Are you breathing?"

"No," Cassandra choked.

Cary waited for Cassandra to take a deep breath, and then went on asking questions. "What does it feel like when your body remembers?"

Cassandra felt the room spinning out of control, and she gripped onto the arm of the sofa so that she wouldn't fall. "Like something is inside of me."

"What does it feel like?" Cary asked.

"It's hard. It will break me," Cassandra breathed.

"Why?" Cary continued asking questions rapid-fire and Cassandra knew it was a therapist's technique to recreate the scene, and yet she was losing power to resist the flow.

"It's so hard," Cassandra repeated.

"Why are you shaking?" Again, Cary managed to use a comforting tone even as she took Cassandra deep into the trauma.

"What you must be thinking." Cassandra's eyes filled with tears. Cary would get overwhelmed and wouldn't want to listen to her story.

"This is not about me."

Cassandra couldn't let it go. "Am I making you sick?"

"No. *Cass.*" Cary paused and set her notepad down. She shifted forward and put out her hand, which Cassandra held onto with relief. Once Cassandra had started to breathe again, Cary said, "You were saying that it's hard and you're shaking. Why?"

"I don't want to cry," mumbled Cassandra.

"Why not?"

"It makes it seem real." Cassandra's entire body was shaking from the effort to hold her tears inside.

"You can cry now or you can cry later," stated Cary matter-of-factly. "It doesn't matter when. You've got to face it sometime. You gotta stop hiding."

Cassandra was exhausted; she wanted to curl up and close her eyes and turn her mind off. "Stop hiding?"

"You can't hide from it, Cass. It's there and you gotta stop and face it. How much more can you put your body through? How many more drinks to make the pain go away? How many more nights are you going to lose? Days? Years?" Cary's voice rose but did not sound shrill. And yet it held enough starch to calm Cassandra down.

After she wiped her forehead on her sleeve, Cassandra continued, "I don't know. What if I stop and rest and can't get back up? What if I face it and cannot go on any further?"

"Then you wait until you can move again."

"What if I wanna hurt myself?"

"Don't, Cass!" Cary's voice landed hard. In a gentler tone she added, "No, Cass. It won't help you. "

"Why do you care?" Cassandra didn't mean to sound angry, but it didn't register with Cary.

"Cass. Stop. This isn't about me."

"I'm such a mess-up." Cassandra felt her heart thundering in her chest. "I hate myself. There, I said it! I'm not even human. I can't cry. I'm numb to everything."

"I don't think you are. You're holding so tight, but when you let go, you'll feel. And in feeling, you will begin to heal."

"When I look inside, when I feel, it's all ugly. I'm ugly. I hate what I see."

"No." Cary shook her head. "I think you're a beautiful human."

"But . . . look at me!" Cassandra pointed at her black polar fleece. "I close my eyes and I hear . . ." Cassandra made a sound, something akin to a dog being strangled.

Cary passed a tissue box but wouldn't stop asking questions. "What do you hear?"

"A man's voice," cried Cassandra.

"What's he saying?"

"Bad things." Cassandra grabbed her hair, frantic, willing the pain to end and the voice to go away. "Why is he saying that? What does he know? He did this to me—did he do this to me? I gotta know it's real and I can't even have that. I can't even have a coherent memory. He ripped that out of me. I want more than a confused snapshot of it." Cassandra cried and held her head in her hands, and still Cary kept asking questions.

"Cass, what are you seeing?"

"Bright lights. Patchwork, cold floor. Vomit. What happened to me? Why did it happen?" Cassandra looked at her therapist with wounded eyes. "Are you sick yet?"

Cary shook her head.

"Why not?" Cassandra cried.

Cary shrugged. "Seriously? Cass, I've heard worse."

Cassandra glanced at her hands, which were going numb.

"Who raped you?"

"I don't remember his name."

"Did he rape you?" Cary spoke in a no-nonsense tone and Cassandra found herself wishing for, wanting and needing her mother. She needed her mother to hold her and comfort her, but her mother was dead. Cassandra felt the blanket on Cary's sofa and mentally sorted and arranged the pattern in it until her mind began to numb out and fade into black.

"Cass? Did he?"

Tears welled up in Cassandra's eyes and rolled down her cheeks. Cassandra nodded. Cary nodded back but did not speak.

"It hurts," Cassandra gasped. "I can't breathe."

Cary pulled her chair closer to Cassandra. "You keep speaking of bright lights and a cold floor. Why did you go into the bathroom that night? Did you go in there to have intercourse with one of the clients?"

Cassandra felt as if Cary had slapped her. She curled up even more tightly and what she yelled came out much louder than she had intended. "No! I'd sooner die than dishonor myself and my marriage."

"Cass, why did you go into the bathroom that night at the party?"

"What do you mean why? Why am I the one on trial?" Cassandra's voice spiraled higher and higher. "I don't remember, I don't remember! To go to the bathroom, I guess. It's not my fault I was raped."

Cary nodded, as if satisfied that she had made Cassandra say it aloud. Now the healing could begin, but the hardest part of it was over.

•••

Cassandra touched the cold metal lining of her trunk and listened to the sounds of the Virginia countryside around her. Sparrows hummed and the breeze shook the trees until they made as much noise as tambourines. A flock of geese flew in a V-formation overhead, honking as they passed across the sky. Cassandra remembered the time Cat had asked why the V-formation wasn't named after the number seven instead. And how did the birds know which one to follow, and why there was always a front runner? *The ironic thing*, Cassandra thought, *is that Cat has turned into a front runner in cross-country.* The hardest thing to change in a runner was that instinct to lead the pack no matter how much the oncoming breeze took out of the runner—or the goose, for that matter.

Cassandra smiled in a melancholy way and thought about how Phoebe was just a few years younger than Cat. Cassandra had held hard discussions with her daughter about sex and drinking and drugs, but she had never had to interview her daughter about something like this. Yet this was exactly what she needed to do once she went inside, and Cassandra shivered once. She felt like she was flying outside of formation, without any guidance.

If Cassandra rushed through the interview or asked too many questions, she could do more harm than good. *More than anything, I need to establish a rapport with her, but I don't need to even talk about the assault. In fact, I don't need to talk much. Really, I need to listen. That's what Cary did.*

With easy athleticism, Cassandra jumped down from the tailgate, wincing when she landed on her tender right foot. For years her foot had been dogging her and she had almost given up running in frustration, but running was the only thing that kept her from falling off the wagon. Cassandra gritted her teeth and shook off the pain. Then she walked into the Bryson House to talk with Phoebe.

CHAPTER 22

Cassandra passed by Nadia and waved from the opening to the study. Nadia was talking on her cell phone and typing on her laptop, and Cassandra resisted the urge to ask for a status update. It had annoyed her when she was Nadia's age and older attorneys had micromanaged her. Nadia waved back, even her wave holding a note of confidence. Nadia was growing into an even more formidable attorney than Cassandra had expected when she had hired her from a big firm two years ago.

Mimi and Miranda shuffled past, arguing over the finances, and almost bumped into Cassandra as she turned to climb the stairs.

"Ladies," Cassandra drawled with exaggeration, and Mimi laughed, but then again, Mimi laughed all the time.

Hands on hips, Miranda mumbled something about "lost receipts" under her breath. After twenty-five years of working to build and maintain a complicated and often heartbreaking charity, Mimi and Miranda loved each other like sisters. They also griped at each other like sisters. Mimi winked at Cassandra. "Look, Miranda," Mimi said with mischief in her voice. "Cass has her boots on!"

Cassandra pretended to glare at Mimi as Miranda exclaimed, "Cass, you know better than to wear those dusty, messy things inside!"

Cassandra smiled and sat down on the second step of the stairs to take off one of her boots. "Like my socks?" she asked, waving her rainbow-colored foot in front of Miranda.

Mimi leaned in. "It's got unicorns!"

"Frank calls these my hippie stockings." Cassandra wrinkled her nose and chuckled. "They're great for running."

"Oh dear," mumbled Miranda.

"Maybe she should keep her boots on, Miranda." Mimi poked her friend in the elbow.

"But they're my lucky socks!" Cassandra pretended that her feelings were hurt and the three women laughed until Helen and Phoebe appeared at the top of the stairs.

Helen's sober demeanor cast a sudden silence over the women waiting at the bottom of the steps. Phoebe stared at her feet as she descended the curved staircase, and Helen rested a protective arm on the railing next to her. Helen's face was a tight-knit mask

Cassandra removed her second boot in silence, then stood up and handed them to Miranda. "Sorry about wearing these inside."

Overhearing the banter about the socks, Helen forced a smile as she said hello. Then she added, "I suppose luck plays a role in all legal cases, at least the ones I've tried in court. What do you think, Cass?"

Cassandra nodded. "For every case I predicted would go a certain way and did, many more of my cases veered off course and hewed to a path I couldn't have predicted."

Helen's eyes were red; the makeup around them, smudged. Cassandra hoped she wasn't pushing too far and too hard, but in her estimation there was no other way. She needed to compile as many facts as possible, figure out a strategy for handling the case and reach out to the Commonwealth's Attorney no later than Monday. There simply was no getting around the fact that it was going to be a long weekend here at the Bryson House, which would have to serve as her part-time mobile office for as long as Helen and Phoebe remained in hiding.

Crap, Cassandra thought, her maternal instincts kicking in. *I need to make sure Frank will be home in time to cover Zander. Cat can look after herself, but it's unfair to ask her to watch her brother all day.* She made a mental note to check in with Frank later in the day.

She then turned her attention to Phoebe, and for the first time caught a glimpse of the girl's eyes. Phoebe looked away quickly, but not before Cassandra could read fear and even a touch of disdain. Cassandra wondered whether it was the socks. She tried not to feel self-conscious.

Miranda and Mimi drifted out of the way. It was no surprise that the slender Miranda always moved out of a conversation at exactly the right time, but Mimi, bustling and booming as she was, possessed the same knack. Both women were tactful and gracious and Cassandra sometimes wished she could take a course to learn the same social qualities; then again, trial attorneys rarely needed grace and tact. They needed lion-hearts, and that—that, Cassandra owned.

Cassandra waited an extra beat for Phoebe to finish walking down the stairs. From a tactical standpoint, she wanted to carry on a conversation with Phoebe at eye level. Sometimes Cassandra hated the way her mind broke everything into winner and loser, dominator and dominated, top and bottom; but in this case, for Phoebe's good, Cassandra needed to hold the reins.

> *Helen's attitude, as odd as it might seem to almost anyone else, makes sense. Law school changes you forever. It makes you harder, tougher, like a boot camp for logic and persuasion and toughness.*

"Would now be a good time for me to speak with Phoebe?" Cassandra put her hand on the banister and waited.

Helen's jaw stiffened. She stood up straighter, as if she did not want Phoebe to know how much watching the exam had hurt her. In Helen's posture, Cassandra could see that Helen felt it was her job to be strong enough for both of them.

"Phoebe, now would be a good chance for you to talk to Ms. White."

"I recognize you," Phoebe said. "You're Cat's mom, right? I've seen her when she's running and I'm riding."

Cassandra darted a glance at her Garmin. "Yes, I am."

"She is also my attorney, Phoebe. Our attorney. And she will be handling my defense." Helen spoke in an authoritative voice. Cassandra almost expected Phoebe to cringe, but Phoebe had grown up with a mom who issued orders like a warship's captain heading into battle.

The girl shifted her shoulders from right to left without shrugging, and then, as if Cassandra weren't in the room, demanded, "Is she experienced in this kind of case?" Phoebe stood stock-still, a horse that would not be ridden.

Cassandra felt her neck getting hot under her now-wrinkled button-down shirt. Phoebe was rubbing her the wrong way, but Cassandra had a job to do. And, Cassandra reminded herself, maybe it was good that Phoebe felt safe enough to act like a typical teenager. *This isn't about how she talks to me. It's about getting her story down so that I can help her mom. Even her healing isn't about me. We don't have time for that. But it will come.*

Helen put an arm around her daughter and spoke in a quiet, yet slightly outraged tone of voice. "First of all, I'm the one writing the checks, and I wrote one addressed to Ms. White for an amount that would buy you a few thoroughbreds." Helen tilted in toward her daughter. "Second, I, too, am an attorney, and you need to trust that I know my job well enough to hire the best attorney for us. And third, even if you don't get the first two things I told you, you owe Ms. White some respect. She is a well-respected attorney and her job is to help us. It is your job, Phoebe, to help her help us. Got it?"

Phoebe didn't answer right away. She stared at her nails. Cassandra imagined that the fifteen-year old was searching her mind for the most unpleasant thing she could get away with saying that wouldn't result in a correction from her mother.

"Phoebe?" Helen prompted.

"Yes, ma'am," Phoebe answered.

Cassandra suppressed a sigh. Catherine was so easy, but this kid? *Darn.* On the other hand, Phoebe had been through so much. *Like me, so hard, so tough, even if my trouble began later. So much like me.*

"Did you hear what I said?" Helen demanded.

"Yeah, Mom, I get it. Right. But seriously, did you have to pick out an attorney with such ugly socks?"

The teenager smirked, and Cassandra took a breath. *It's not personal.*

"Will it make you feel better if I take my socks off and talk to you barefoot?" Cassandra said evenly.

At this point even Helen laughed.

Phoebe looked over Cassandra again. With an effort, she made eye contact and acknowledged Cassandra in a way that suggested tacit cooperation, but she didn't smile or nod or apologize. "Okay then, where do we go? I'm following orders today, apparently."

Cassandra gestured toward a smaller study on the opposite end of the hallway from the main study and library, and the three women headed toward its double doors. In contrast to the main study, this one felt intimate, dark and cozy, with its forest-green walls, black leather furniture and standard-sized windows. "Helen." Cassandra turned toward the older attorney. "May I speak with Phoebe alone? Would you consent to that?"

"Of course." Helen took a breath and then drew herself up to her full height, appearing as imperious and authoritative as though she were about to approach a jury box. "I think I will go take a walk down to the stables and look at the horses."

Phoebe's face lit up momentarily. "If you wanna borrow my boots, they're on the front porch."

Helen waved and managed a weak smile.

•••

Cassandra was aware of her heartbeat. It wasn't exactly racing, but neither was it at her usual resting pulse of forty-four. She had worked hard to get to such a low resting pulse, yet even after years of therapy, her body still betrayed her when she was anxious. Talking to Phoebe was going to take a lot out of her. *Slow down. She is safe and so am I, and everything is going to be all right.* Cassandra silently repeated her calm-down mantra, the one Cary had taught her. She used it before she entered the courtroom or began a difficult deposition, or even before the gun fired in the marathons she ran. Sometimes it slowed her racing heart. This time, it didn't.

"As you know, Phoebe, your mom has retained me to protect her interests."

"Yes, ma'am." Phoebe spoke in a flat, expressionless tone.

"I'm so sorry about what happened, Phoebe. And I'm so sorry for your loss."

"Why are you sorry?" the girl demanded. Phoebe's hair flipped in front of her eyes and she didn't bother to move it. She lifted her chin and glared.

"It's not easy to lose a dad." Cassandra curled her toes, feeling the floor underneath her, and prayed for strength. *I have no idea what I'm doing.*

"He had it coming to him." Phoebe spoke through the brown hair.

"Yes, I reckon he had it coming to him." Cassandra sighed, and a long silence followed. The room felt cold. It must have felt colder to Phoebe during the exam upstairs.

"Not that I would expect you to understand," Phoebe grumbled. "You've got a normal family."

"I didn't always. I'm on my second marriage." Cassandra talked faster than she could think. "It hasn't always been an easy ride."

Phoebe's hands gripped and released the arms of the chair. Her brown eyes turned on Cassandra. "Is my mom going to jail for what she did?"

Cassandra shook her head. "I can't make any promises, but I doubt it. I think we have a few good arguments that she was acting in self-defense and in your defense, which is why I need to talk to you. It's why I need to ask you about what happened."

Phoebe stood up and walked over to the window and stared into the distance. "The birds are flying in formation," she said. Her eyes remained on the thick gray clouds layered off in the distance, out where the sky met the mountains.

Cassandra got up from her chair and leaned against another window, about three feet away from Phoebe. "Yes. I always wonder where they're going and how they decide how to get there."

Phoebe followed the birds with her eyes, and then she stared at Cassandra's feet. "Did Mom tell you what he did to me?" Phoebe's voice had changed inflection. It was no longer lifeless, but contained a note of exhaustion and anguish; and it was aged, as though it were the voice of a much older woman.

"Yes." Cassandra hesitated, then she decided Phoebe could handle the truth. She'd heard enough lies and half-truths and evasions. "I saw the video."

Phoebe brought her hands up to her face. Cassandra couldn't tell if Phoebe was ducking from embarrassment and the pain it brought or wanted to smash her fists into her face.

Probably a little of both. The blue veins in Phoebe's hands stood out from her light skin and her hands and wrists appeared strong for such a wan, slender creature. Cassandra could not get the images out of her mind even when she closed her eyes.

> *There's no escaping what she's been through. There is never any escape. There's just time, and it passes and eventually it heals.*

Cassandra pushed aside her dark thoughts. She needed to appear in control for Phoebe, and she could see that the girl was done trying to sound tough. The attorney spoke gently, as though she were talking to her own daughter. The thought pained her.

"Phoebe, honey, it's going to be okay," Cassandra said. "Not today, not tomorrow, not for a long time. But after a while, it will hurt a little less."

Phoebe looked dazed. "How?" She pressed her hand to her head. "How?" she demanded, her voice rising.

"It just does, sweetheart," Cassandra murmured, simply and without adornment. "It does and it will."

"You think it was my fault."

"No. It was not your fault." Cassandra looked Phoebe in the eyes. "I am sick about what he did to you. And it's my job to figure out how to protect you and your mom."

Phoebe wiped her sweaty arm across her forehead. She tried to breathe, but every time she took a breath it felt like a sob was going to escape. "What do you need me to do?"

Cassandra crossed the room, picked up a box of tissues, and sat back down on the window ledge she had claimed. She knew what it was like to both crave and fear physical comfort. She had read Phoebe's fear of being touched, and as much as she wanted to comfort the teenager, she didn't want to spook her. After the assault, it had taken Cassandra years to get used to people hugging her. She handed Phoebe the tissue box without saying a word.

It was quiet in the room. Cassandra stroked the rubber wristband of her Garmin and closed her eyes as she listened to the second hand ticking. That sound had always soothed her. What would comfort this child? She opened her eyes. *Horses.*

"Phoebe, maybe you're sitting there thinking I don't understand. And that's okay. So what I'm about to tell you is no secret or anything like that. I've gotten to the point in my life and in my career where I'm okay with what I've done and what has happened to me in the past. I'm not telling you this so that you feel bad for me. I just want you to know that there are people who survive this, and not only survive it, but go on to thrive. Are you following me?"

Phoebe examined her hard-bitten fingers and then raised her chin. "Yeah, I guess so. Are you trying to tell me something?"

"I was beaten. I was raped. I thought my life was over. I was desperate and broken. But I got the help I needed, Phoebe. It wasn't easy. I ended up divorced and working at a different law firm at a much lower rate of pay because the first law firm lost faith in me."

Phoebe clutched a couple of tissues in her left hand. "How . . . how did you ever stop hating yourself?"

Cassandra flexed her hand, which was starting to cramp. She needed to drink more water and relax her tight muscles; more than anything, she needed to go out for a run to release all the tension. "I focused on understanding and then accepting myself, and at some point the self-hatred fell away. It was like shedding a lizard's skin."

"That's sort of weird." Phoebe smiled for the first time since they'd begun talking.

Cassandra took this in without comment. "I went through a lot of therapy after the rape. I didn't do this alone."

"Holy crap, you mean you saw a shrink?"

"A therapist. And listen, hon, there's nothing wrong with getting the help you need. You'd be surprised how many people need therapy, and how beneficial it can be."

Phoebe took all of this in, then she allowed her eyes to drift until they almost met the older woman's. "Why are you telling me all this, Ms. White?"

Cassandra knew what Phoebe meant to say. It really boiled down to figuring out what Cassandra stood to gain and whether it was going to be at Phoebe's expense. Phoebe needed to know what she was expected to give, and until Cassandra said it aloud, Phoebe wouldn't, couldn't . . . really, *shouldn't* answer.

Cassandra kept her tone non-threatening, gentle but confident. "Because I might need you to testify, and I *am* going to need you to talk to the authorities. No, let me say that in a different way. My job is to protect your mom's interests. And you are the one thing in the world your mother really cares about." Cassandra felt her eyes welling with tears as she thought of her own daughter. "So we need to keep her out of jail. In order to do that, you're going to need to tell other people what happened. Maybe as soon as next week."

"What do you want from me?" Phoebe folded her arms and glared at the attorney.

"We need to get this info to the prosecutor and the detectives as soon as possible." Cassandra avoided making eye contact by pretending to adjust a button on her shirt. *Surely the little girl would be crumbling inside.*

"Why? So we can go to trial sooner?"

"No." Cassandra paused. "We need to tell the authorities about the people your father already invited to the house, to join in when he . . . hurt you."

Phoebe slipped down from the window seat and slumped into a sobbing heap on the floor. Cassandra moved away from the ledge and knelt down in front of Phoebe. As she wept, Phoebe pushed her head into Cassandra's knee. Cassandra didn't say anything at first. She waited. Then she glanced at her watch. A lot of time had passed. Too much, and she realized that she might have pushed Phoebe too far.

"Phoebe," Cassandra murmured. "No, no, he shouldn't have; yes, yes, you are good enough. You didn't ask for this. But it is over. You are safe now." Cassandra placed a guiding hand on Phoebe's shoulder and kept it there.

Phoebe put her head on top of Cassandra's hand and for a moment it felt like Phoebe was nuzzling Cassandra. It made Cassandra think of a frail colt, searching for warmth on a cold, dark night.

CHAPTER 23

While waiting for Cassandra to finish interviewing Phoebe, Helen transferred her pacing to the side lawn. The zigzagging line of pine trees reminded her of law school and of home, and she wasn't sure how this made her feel. She shrugged off the thought. Her currency had always been logic; she had never dealt primarily in emotions. The last thirty-six hours had been surreal.

She needed to make a few phone calls, and none of them were going to be easy or enjoyable. She needed to call Sascha Meincraft's mother to ask about making Carol a backup guardian. She thought of several excuses for not making the call. When she caught herself reusing excuses, she took a deep breath and dialed before she could stop herself.

A voice with a Minnesotan accent answered. Words tumbled out of Helen's mouth in a disordered pattern.

"Whoa, Helen, let's take it from the top, okay?" Carol murmured. "Where are you calling from?"

"From a safe house about forty-five minutes away."

"How is Phoebe? How are you?"

Helen forced herself to say something positive. She didn't have any female friends, but she remembered how Carol had talked to her. The pine needles felt soft underfoot as she paced back and forth. "We're hanging on. It's not been easy on Phoebe. My lawyer is here and there's a lot that we need to get done. It's been exhausting."

"Can you tell me what happened? I don't mean to pry, but is your husband dead?"

"He is now, yes. I don't think I am supposed to say anything else until we notify the authorities. I'm sorry. I'm tired."

"I'm sure you are." Carol sounded calm. "The one thing I don't understand, and I hope you don't mind my asking, is why you're in a safe house."

"I wish I could tell you. You'll know everything soon enough."

"Please tell me what you need us to do. Start with what you need right now and give me the list."

Helen flexed her toes inside Phoebe's boots and realized that they fit her as if made for her. For a few painful moments the line was silent. Helen hated feeling vulnerable; worse, she detested needing anyone. It hurt to contemplate asking for help and not receiving it. "The most important thing is that I need to designate a guardian in case things don't turn out well."

Carol's voice, measured and kind, came back on the line. "And do you have someone in mind? To act as guardian?"

"No." Helen tried to breathe. *Why couldn't she just ask the question?*

"Well, if you are calling to ask if we're available, the answer is that of course my husband and I would be honored to act as guardians for Phoebe if it ever comes to that. Phoebe is already like a sister to Sascha."

Helen scuffed the toe of her daughter's boots and wished that she could have given Phoebe a sister.

"You still there?"

It took a moment before Helen could respond. "Oh yes. I'm just overcome, that's all. To be honest, I was scared to ask, but I trust you. And Phoebe trusts you, so it—you—I mean, you were the only choice that made sense."

"We'll be praying for you. Hoping that all will be well." The words washed over Helen; all she really heard was the compassion in Carol's tone.

"What are you doing for funeral arrangements?"

"I don't know." Helen paused, and her voice grew hard. "I don't really care how it looks. I can't imagine standing in line and accepting condolences." She gasped as Richard's bloody face flashed before her eyes. Helen rubbed her temple and went on, "I guess I will tell them to cremate him and just do what they want with his remains. Maybe that is harsh, but I can't do a memorial service. And I am so tired . . ." She paused, stuck again in exhaustion and confusion. There was no rulebook for how to bury a husband who had done what he'd done.

"Will you let me help? If you would like, you could sign over a limited power of attorney, and I could then arrange a very quiet service. That way people, including Phoebe, could say goodbye to him. People wouldn't ask as many questions, and yet you wouldn't have to deal with it."

"That's too much! How could I possibly ask someone to do that for me?" Helen envisioned wearing a black dress and a black hat, but then she saw a darkness seeping into her as if her heart were turning black. *Is this guilt?* She had no idea how to fight it, so she took a deep breath and stared at the white clouds overhead.

Helen didn't know how to grieve for Richard or whether she even should, but a part of her longed to go to church and fall on her knees in front of the altar. She shook it off quickly. As an attorney, she had gotten ahead through reason rather than emotion, and she had reached the top without help from others. In her calculations, when someone did something for you, then you owed them something in return. She didn't have the emotional capital to help anyone else right now.

Carol seemed to misunderstand the silence. "Hey! This is what friends are for. Please let us help you!"

"How could I ever repay you?" Helen wondered aloud. "I specialize in complex commercial litigation and I suck at everything else."

"Well, if it is worrying you that much," chuckled Carol, "then you can put a good word in for Sascha at your undergraduate institution, which was, if I remember correctly, one of the Ivy Leagues, right?"

"Okay," said Helen, and she nodded. Now she felt at ease, as if on equal footing. She could do something to pay off her debt to the Meincraft family.

"Great, so it is settled. How about if Sascha and I come visit you and Phoebe tomorrow? Sascha's already said she isn't going to the Show if Phoebe isn't. I can sign whatever documents you need me to sign, and the girls can hang out?"

"Yeah." Helen's temple still throbbed, but she added, "Make sure you bring your little guy, too. My attorney is going to bring her son tomorrow and let him ride horses and run around the grounds. I will e-mail you with the directions."

Carol hung up the phone, and as soon as she heard the silence on the other end, Helen tapped the End Call button. She adjusted her collar and tried not to worry about going to prison or talking to detectives. The thought of spending time in prison filled her with an anxiety and sadness that she could hardly bear contemplating. Prison may as well have been the end of the world: lunch trays made out of hard plastic; ugly cotton uniforms in drab colors; hardened, wild-haired women. A tiny cell and a hard bed. Helen had never been to prison, not even for work. Not yet, at least.

She took a deep breath and told herself to hold it together, but it was becoming harder and harder. Phoebe, so long so far away, was close, and Helen never wanted to let go of her again. Prison would take her far away from her only child.

Helen tried to tune out the noise of the crows overhead as she dialed Carl's cell phone.

Her associate answered on the second ring. To Helen's relief, he wasted little time with what she would call trivialities. "Have you spoken with a lawyer yet?"

"Yes, and thanks for the recommendation. She's competent." After a brief pause, she added, "Great, really. I told her associate, Nadia, that she should contact you with follow-up questions."

"I think she already has. I got a message from a Nadia, and she mentioned you. I wanted to make sure it was okay."

"Yes. Give her anything she asks for. Like you, Cass wants to prepare something for the federal or state sex crimes investigators and hand it over next week." Their words overlapped one another, rapid-fire, and Helen appreciated how little time they wasted.

"So you're going on the offensive. I like it." Carl paused. "Oh, and by the way, we're going to fly back Sunday."

"Not for me, I hope," grumbled Helen.

"Well, boss, I got a lot of work to do and one of us needs to man the phones in town. Anyway, Troy has a few emergencies to put out."

"Really?"

"No, but it sounded good." He laughed. "Actually, he wants to meet with you as soon as possible. He thinks that Cary should talk with Phoebe and that it would be a good idea for you to talk to him."

Helen sighed and nodded. "That makes sense. Phoebe does need to talk to someone. Thank you. Perhaps I do need to talk to someone, too."

"I'll tell him. Is that all for now?"

"For now." Helen hung up the phone and looked at her watch again, the one Richard had given her. The leather band suddenly made her fingers itch, and before she knew what she was doing she had thrown it on the ground and crushed it under the heel of Phoebe's boots. The glass face shattered underfoot but the band, almost the color of the Virginia clay, lay intact. Helen strode away without looking back at the watch. It had come from him, and it belonged where she had left it.

Helen tucked her phone into her cardigan and resumed her pacing. She realized, with a quiet chuckle, that she was overdressed; maybe she needed to buy a pair of jeans after all. She hadn't worn jeans since college, and even then she had ironed them. When she drove to law school for the first time, she had left behind her jeans and her cigarettes, deeming both child's play. Now, as she clomped around the grassy land in Phoebe's boots, she realized that tailored slacks and dry-clean-only fabrics were pretty darn uncomfortable. Maybe she needed to snag more than one pair of jeans. And wouldn't it make sense for her to also purchase a few warmer shirts made of washable fabrics? Helen inspected Phoebe's boots. They were darn good ones—she had paid the bill—but what she really wanted was a pair like Cassandra's. Burgundy or brown, maybe even black. She could wear those anywhere, and not just when she walked down with Phoebe to the stables in the morning. Their life was changing so quickly.

Helen turned, hands clasped behind her, and she almost tripped over a wild-haired, mud-covered boy who was sprinting past. Reacting on impulse, Helen reached her hands out to catch the little creature. He flashed a winsome smile at her.

"Why do you laugh?" he asked.

She realized, as she started to answer his question, that he had left muddy handprints all over her white slacks. Helen thought of attempting to rub off the stains, but reconsidered as she realized that tailored slacks had no place in the middle of a grassy field textured with red clay. She pointed to her dirty slacks and said, "I was laughing about how silly it was to be wearing fancy pants around the stables."

The boy nodded and took a hopping step in the direction of the house. Then he stopped and asked, "Do you know where my Mommy is?"

Helen felt her chest tighten, but forced herself to relax. *We're not in the middle of an airport or a shopping center. He's not lost. Everything is okay. We'll find his mother.* "Well, what is your mother's name?"

"Mama," said the boy as he hopped up and down again and shoved his thumb in his mouth.

"What does your dad call your mom?"

"Cats," he murmured. It was hard for Helen to understand him. She hadn't been around a little child in a long time.

"And what is your name?"

"Sander. And my sister is Cat. Kit Kat never fat," he hummed. Helen thought about it and realized that she was talking to Zander, Cassandra's son.

"Well," she said, "in that case, I do know where your mother is. She's inside the big house. How about if we go find her together?" Zander grunted and shoved his grimy hand in hers. Helen noticed that Zander had a funny way of walking. He hopped twice, ran two steps, walked a stride and stopped, still holding onto Helen's hand and reciting nursery rhymes as they walked up the hill toward the front porch. *Perhaps this is what holding a son's hand would feel like,* she thought, and she found herself smiling until they ran into Cassandra in the foyer of the mansion.

"Mama!" The boy let go of Helen's hand and slammed his little body into his mother's leg. Cassandra knelt down and picked up her son. Once she was standing again, she whirled around with him and closed her eyes for a moment. "Where did you come from?" she asked, a note of concern in her voice.

Zander shoved his thumb back in his mouth. "Out there," he mumbled.

Helen added, "I was outside making some phone calls, and he literally ran into me." She gestured at her muddy white pants.

"Oh! Oh no, I'm so sorry!"

Helen waved her hand. "It's nothing. In fact, I was thinking that I needed to buy some new jeans and some more casual clothing, and that's when I met this cute little guy."

Cassandra said to her son, "Look at me, Zander." Zander looked at Helen. Cassandra took two of her fingers, pointed at her son, and then pointed at her eyes. "Zander, look at *me*. Not at Ms. Thompson. At me." Cassandra sighed to herself. Zander was a different creature than Cat; she had only had to say something once, and Cat had listened. With Zander, Cassandra needed to repeat herself often; and if she didn't tell him not to do something, he could be relied upon to do it. Zander didn't look for trouble. He flew straight into it like a jet airplane.

"Who is Ms. Thompson?"

Helen spoke up. "That's me."

"Whose Mommy are you?"

As Zander was firing off his questions, Phoebe appeared around the corner.

"She's my mom." Phoebe glanced at Zander and almost smiled.

Zander grinned at Phoebe, but it was a strange-looking grin because he was still sucking his thumb. His eyes were slightly closed and almost had a lazy look about them, like a dog curled up next to a fire. "I saw you riding horses," he said.

Phoebe sidled up next to Helen and waited for her mother to put an arm around her, too. "I bet you did. Why aren't you down there helping clean the stables? I heard your instructor telling you that's what your job was going to be this afternoon."

Zander hugged Cassandra. "Mama. I missed Mama."

Meanwhile, Helen shot Phoebe an appraising glance. Phoebe never had showed an inkling of responsibility or even interest in what anyone else did; then again, Helen had never observed her daughter at work or at play, or even around horses. *Maybe that's where she learns what she needs to know; maybe her love of horses is bigger than I realized. If that is the case, I'd better stop thinking about hopping on this bandwagon and take charge of it.* Helen made a mental note to have a talk with the woman who had spoken well of Phoebe's riding ability earlier in the morning.

"So, Zander," added Phoebe, "how about if I walk you back down to the stables and show you how to muck a stall?"

Helen nodded her approval, and Phoebe grinned. "Oh, and Mom . . . I heard you talking about your wardrobe. Let's get you some jeans. Maybe we can go shopping tonight. For now, may I please have my boots back?"

Helen shook her head. There was no way they could go to the mall, but she didn't want to embarrass Phoebe in front of anyone else. As she returned her daughter's dusty boots, Helen whispered, "We'll see."

Cassandra set Zander down just as he wriggled and tried to jump out of her arms in order to run off back to the horses. Helen and Cassandra watched their children run side by side down the hill and toward the stables.

•••

In the main study, Helen stood by the window. Cassandra came over beside her, and without saying a word, she followed her gaze through the windows which framed the mountains behind them. Nadia, who had been flipping through evidentiary documents stored on her laptop, excused herself with a circumspect nod.

"Hey?" Cassandra said as she kept her eyes on her son.

Helen wrapped her arms around her elbows and absentmindedly patted herself. The room seemed chilly; she wished she were wearing a thick sweatshirt rather than her lightweight sweater.

"Yes?" Helen realized that she felt at ease with Cassandra. It felt strange, but good.

"I'm glad your daughter is taking charge of my little maniac. He's a handful."

Helen yawned. "Gosh, so is she. Being with him is good for her." She tugged at an invisible string. "Oh, I need to call Cary. My therapist thinks Phoebe needs to talk to someone."

"I already called Cary. She's on her way now." Cassandra lowered her chin. "I'm afraid I pushed Phoebe too hard. She started to cry, and she blames herself. I wish we didn't have to put her through this, but I see no way around it. She's been through so much, yet still we're asking her to go through even more."

Helen gripped her shoulders tighter and worked it all out in her head. If Phoebe testified, it would traumatize her. But she had to testify, because if she didn't, Helen could end up in prison, which would be even worse. "Just do your job." Helen flexed her fingers, which she'd been gripping in a fist. "And I'll do mine." *Finally. Finally I'll take care of my child.*

Cassandra glanced at her watch. "Cary's on her way. She'll probably be here at about four, which is when I need to leave to pick up Catherine from practice."

At that moment Nadia returned, holding a thick stack of documents. She paused and stood by her boss, waiting for an opening.

"Is that what Carl sent you?" Helen pulled at the invisible thread again.

"Yes, Ms. Thompson. I just pulled it off the fax machine."

"So what's our next move?" Helen acknowledged Nadia with the barest of nods, directing her question to Cassandra.

"I'll be here most of the day Saturday to prep you for our meeting with the Commonwealth's Attorney on Monday."

"You mean the state prosecutor," Helen stated more than asked.

Cassandra nodded. "I've got a good relationship with a friend who worked out of the Fairfax office, and I hope she can work us in; meanwhile, Nadia is working with Carl. Right, Nadia?"

"Yes." Nadia's black curls shone as the sun hit them, turning them almost blue. "In fact, he's already sent me a well-written compendium, with on-point analysis and case law of everything Mr. Thompson and his conspirators were up to. Really, there's not nearly as much work as I would have expected left for us. Uh, I mean, for me," Nadia laughed. "And I will be working all weekend on trial prep anyway, so what I meant was . . . oh, you know what I mean?"

Helen waved her hand in Nadia's direction and tried to soften her voice. "Great. Carl said he would draft a memo. I would expect nothing short of excellence from him." She turned away so that only Cassandra noticed the tears welling up in the older woman's eyes. "I'm going to go and watch my kid down by the stables. I need to get some fresh air."

Cassandra put a hand on Helen's arm. "I know it's been a hard day. We'll go over more tomorrow. I will be down there in about fifteen minutes. Oh, and I forgot to ask you if there was anything you needed from town?"

"Well, I can't get anything from my house, but I think I will order some things online. We don't have enough clothing."

"Call me if you need anything. Even if you want to borrow a pair of jeans," she added, and Helen smiled over her shoulder as she walked out of the study.

•••

"Are you ready for your marching orders?" Cassandra spoke in a quiet, authoritative tone that didn't seem to bother Nadia. Cassandra always worked at least as hard as she expected her associates to do, and they respected her for it. In all her years of practicing law Cassandra had never raised her voice to anyone in the office.

"Yeah. But I was hoping to have a quiet evening with my fiancé tonight, if that's okay," Nadia replied.

Friday nights were sacred in the White household, and Nadia knew that Cassandra would never ask an associate to work on a Friday night. Cassandra said nothing while she peeked at her Garmin. It was three o'clock. If she left now, she could catch the last hour of Cat's cross-country practice and still have the chance to catch up on all her reading after the children had gone to bed.

"Have a good night with your fiancé." Cassandra waved over her shoulder on her way into the kitchen.

Mimi, in the midst of preparing dinner, greeted her warmly, and Cassandra wished she had more time to stop and chat with the woman. "We serve brunch from eight to ten in the morning," Mimi said. "So if you come early enough tomorrow, just come right in and grab a plate."

"How did you know I'd be here tomorrow?" Cassandra leaned one hand on the white doorframe and peeked at the modern fixtures, massive ovens and the cook shuttling back and forth between baking projects.

Mimi removed her apron and, wrapping one arm around Cassandra's waist, walked her to the front door. "Because your client needs you, and I imagine you have a lot of ground to cover. Besides, this is a fun place to bring your children on a Saturday."

Cassandra reminded herself how intuitive Mimi was; nothing that happened at the mansion escaped her attention. "Thanks, hon. You're right, and I appreciate that you and Miranda made my kid feel so welcome. I'm sure he'll beg all night to return, and you know what? It will feel good to be able say yes." Cassandra hugged Mimi and jogged down the hill.

Inside the ring, working right next to Phoebe, Zander stood holding a huge rake in his hands. Phoebe was speaking to him in a quiet tone that reminded Cassandra of the way Cat talked to her brother.

When Phoebe spotted Cassandra, she stood up and leaned on the pitchfork she was using to spread hay. "Hi, Ms. White. You got one helpful little guy here," she said, winking at Zander. Zander grinned at Phoebe; then he dropped his rake and raced off to climb the fence and jump into his mother's arms.

Cassandra shook her head at how fast things seemed to have changed with the teenager. Rather than question it, she would just flow with it. She laughed. "Thanks for putting him to work."

"Anytime, Ms. White. I hope to see him back here soon."

"Careful what you wish for," Cassandra quipped. "It just might come true."

CHAPTER 24

As Cassandra drove out past the gatehouse, she noticed a dark blue American car pulled over to the side. One of the guards was displaying his gun; the other stood there holding a radio. A shiver ran down her spine and she wondered what had happened to make Mimi and Miranda hire such an aggressive security team. Cassandra hoped that Zander hadn't seen the gun. Through her rearview mirror, she watched as the sedan turned around and, with a burst of acceleration, passed her Volvo and peeled out onto the main road.

Zander had nodded off to sleep as soon as he assembled his Chickie and his matchbox car in his lap. Cassandra checked on him and watched his chest rise and fall as she tried to absorb the present, the here and now of her first and last son's existence. Zander was more than eleven years younger than Catherine, and while she detested the term "oops baby" almost as much as she disliked categorizing her son by race, Cassandra had to admit that he hadn't been strictly planned for either. In so many of his facial features Zander resembled his mother, but his lanky frame and medium-brown skin color marked him as his father's son.

Cassandra listened to Fleetwood Mac as she drove back through the rolling hills of northern Virginia. She stroked her left quad and her tight iliotibial band and hoped she could keep up with her daughter at cross-country practice. She frowned. A few years ago she could have outrun anyone on the team, but Zander's complicated pregnancy had knocked her from 3:25 marathons to a race time of 3:40. For the last three years she had battled injuries and slowing times so much that her "decreased fitness," as the athletic director at McClintock termed it, had led the school to hire a young man to replace Cassandra as the head coach of the girls' cross-country team. Although she had been offered a position as an assistant coach, Cassandra had turned it down. Still, she tried to show up at practice to run with her daughter as often as work and her wounded pride allowed.

Cassandra kneaded the soft leather steering wheel and thought more about what a long day it had been. *It's going to be a long weekend, too.* The interview with Phoebe had left Cassandra in pieces and she really wanted to process it, but she needed to hold it together until after Cat's practice. *It's going to be a rough night and I am going to want to drink to help me sleep.*

She needed to think about how she would get through another one of these nights alone. It had been more than fifteen years since she'd had anything to drink. She was strong enough. She had to be.

•••

March 5, 1990, Fairfax, Virginia

It was time to get dressed for her first outpatient group meeting. Cassandra waded into her closet and slowly removed a black suit from the rack. Usually she wore black suits when she delivered closing arguments; it gave her that last bit of confidence she was always lacking. She laughed and ran her hand through her barely-controlled blonde hair. Even as she laughed harder and harder, she knew she was closer to crying. What did it matter what she wore to a four-hour outpatient meeting? Whom was she trying to impress or please or even mislead? Just by entering that door and saying those pseudo-magic words of greeting, she would brand herself as just another mess. No one went to these meeting unless they had to go. She was like a freak show and she wasn't even that interesting.

Cassandra rummaged in her closet some more. She could wear baggy gray sweats that announced her inner slob.

Gray sweats two or three sizes too big proclaim a few truths that should be self-evident: I don't like what's underneath the sweats; I'm uncomfortable; I've got no pride left; and I'm too far gone to give a crap what they think. Who is "they," anyway? They're all a bunch of losers, too. I don't care what they think. And gray sweats sure would feel cozy.

And yet Cassandra just couldn't do cozy in front of the world. Strangers snagged her cozy feeling and turned it on its head and made the fleece inside the sweatshirt feel like scratchy winter wool. Cassandra shook her head and put the black suit back on the rack.

If I can't pull off the power suit and I can't fall as low as gray sweats, what am I left with? Do clothes make the woman, do they really? Jen used to tell me in law school that I could make anything I wore work for me if I walked with a sassy swagger, so you know what? It's going to be jeans and my boots.

Cassandra tried to practice walking without tripping on the dog's toy as she rounded the corner and swung around the banister. "Jeez, Cassie," her ex would have screamed, "you're going to break it if you keep doing that! It's an expensive repair." Silently she answered, *Shut up Tim.* She poured coffee into an aluminum mug, and, with a glance at the clock on the microwave, sipped it. Cassandra took one last look around the house and tried to remember what she had forgotten. She leaned over and rubbed Barrister's ears and headed out to start up the Audi and drive into the city. *I guess I'll fit right in drinking coffee with a bunch of drunks, but no matter how much of a drunk I am, I won't sink to drinking joe out of a styrofoam cup."*

She checked behind her left shoulder and slammed on the accelerator as she merged onto the interstate. *Will anyone know me there? What do I care, anyway? The rumors are true.* Cassandra imagined she could see Jen shaking her head with frustration. "No, Cass, you really aren't more fun when you're drinking. Really. You should try having fun without it sometimes, hon, before it's too late." Cassandra had smirked at her closest friend and exclaimed, "Aw, Jen, c'mon, it will be fun tonight, I promise!" And it had been fun.

And it kept on being fun even after Jen stopped coming. A lump formed in Cassandra's throat. *If I called Jen, would she pick up the phone? Would she let it ring and make me talk to the answering machine?*

Cassandra glanced in the rearview mirror and tried to stop thinking about her friend. The coffee smelled good. It always tasted good after a long, hard night of drinking. She pulled up to the abandoned building on the southeast side of the city and took another halting step toward sobriety.

•••

Cassandra rested her head on her hand for a moment and realized that she really needed to talk to her therapist. Not now, while driving in the country with a sleeping child in the back seat, but she could and would call tonight, right before she called Jen. One of the many great things that had come out of her sobriety was a rekindled friendship with her best friend; Cassandra could call Jen any time and never had to fear whether Jen would be impatient or frustrated with her. Cassandra nodded. Sobriety had its advantages.

Fifteen minutes later, Cassandra pulled through the gatehouse at McClintock for the second time that day. She drove down past the soccer fields and ball fields and parked about a quarter mile from the stadium, which was big enough to seat several thousand fans and fancy enough to host district and state track meets. Before she woke Zander, she stripped off her jeans and slipped into unlined soccer shorts, which she often preferred to running shorts. Particularly around teenagers, four inches of coverage seemed insufficient. Cassandra double-laced her orange and white trail running shoes. They were not exactly the right shoes for running intervals on a track, but they would have to do.

"Hey Zander," she cooed to her son, who rubbed his eyes and looked confused.

"Hey Mama, horses?"

"That was this morning," Cassandra smiled. "We're here to see Cat. And you get to run around the bleachers and look for treasures." On the weekends she would often take Zander with her to the track for a workout. He would spend the time crawling around under the bleachers in search of lost items, which he'd be allowed to shove into his pockets. Zander's eyes lit up and he skipped ahead of Cassandra toward the stadium.

Cassandra set aside a few nervous twitches in her stomach. From a distance, she could see a group of several girls running from one side of the soccer fields and into the stadium.

She nodded. It was four o'clock, which meant that an hour remained for the main workout, a ten-minute cool-down jog and five minutes for halfhearted stretching. The newbie girls never listened to her when she lectured them about stretching and injury prevention.

Cassandra waved her arms and tried to limber up before she stepped through the black gate leading into the long straightaway on the track. Her nerves fluttered like angry butterflies in her stomach, and she told herself that she had nothing left to prove, not to herself and certainly not to Coach J.T. As the girls' cross-country coach, Cassandra had led the team to three district titles and developed several solid collegiate runners. Now that he wore the whistle, J.T. bore the pressure to win. While Cassandra missed coaching, she certainly didn't miss the burden of all those expectations.

"Mama! Can I find treasures?" Zander asked.

"Go ahead, but Zander . . ." Cassandra knelt down and spoke sternly to her curly-haired, muddy boy. "Do not go past the black fence, okay?"

"Okay, Mama!" Zander raced off to the bleachers and Cassandra hoped he wouldn't dash back onto the track in the middle of intervals.

Out of the corner of her eye she noticed a smiling man wearing dark green running shorts and a white tech t-shirt with "Oregon" printed in green. "Coach, how are you?"

To Cassandra's surprise, J.T. rubbed his hand over his prematurely thinning hair and exclaimed in frustration, "Ugh! The girls are killing me with their crap today. I am so glad you showed up to run with us. You are going to run, right? They need someone to give them a kick in the butt, and you're just the weapon I didn't know I had in my arsenal."

Cassandra couldn't help smiling. Maybe she hadn't been fair to him when she had met him last year. It wasn't his fault he was young and fast and full of new ideas about how to run a cross-country and track program. Anyways, she wanted him to succeed, if only for Catherine's sake. "The girls often get goofy on Friday afternoons. I found that by the seventh or eighth quarter run at 5K race pace, they stop giggling and get a little more serious."

A quarter in cross-country parlance was a quarter- mile sprint around the track, followed by a quarter-mile recovery jog. After the last runner finished the recovery jog, the next quarter would begin. Cassandra would have her girls run at least ten quarters, or five miles, with warm-up and cool-down miles forming the bread for the quarters, the meat in the sandwich. She had believed in old-fashioned quantity, and even her girls without natural talent had made up for it by running more miles than most private school teams. This had made her controversial among other local coaches; some had thought that the girls would be permanently damaged from running too much, too soon. Then again, a lot of the same coaches had copied her training programs after they grew tired of losing to McClintock's cross-country and track teams.

J.T. grinned. He was cocky, and for good reason. "Do you want to blow the whistle while I run laps with them? That way we can really tire them out."

"Nah. You don't want me to share your whistle. God knows what kind of germs I'm carrying."

He made a face. He didn't have children yet, or even a serious girlfriend, and the idea of snot-nosed, sick kids freaked him out in a way that amused the mother of a young child. He ignored Cassandra's remark, rubbed his hands together and jogged off in the direction of the gang of girls bearing down on the stadium.

Catherine led the pack into the stadium, and Cassandra watched her long-legged, blonde-haired child hurdle the sand trap laid out for the long jump and lope along the middle lane of the slightly banked track. Catherine braked to a stop in front of her mother and gave her a not-quite-crushing fist bump, which Cassandra turned into a quick hug. She let go of her daughter and they grinned at one another.

"Mom, you made it!"

"I did, and now I'm going to show you how a quarter's run."

"Come on, Mama Slow, who are you kidding? You'll be running in my red dust," teased Catherine as they approached the starting line and waited for the team to line up next to them. Several of the girls gave Cassandra shy smiles. Five seniors had graduated in the spring, and the team was composed of more freshmen and sophomores than juniors and seniors. Cassandra was respected, even revered, by the younger runners.

Cassandra smiled and bellowed, in her voice that carried across ball fields, "Lots of new faces! Let's see who can run down an old lady!" The girls waited for their coach to blow his whistle.

Cassandra lost a half step while she messed around with the bevel on her Garmin, and she silently cursed it as she took after her not-so-little girl. After they rounded the first turn, she slowed down and realized that she couldn't take her daughter in the first few quarters. *Young legs.* She decided to conserve her energy so that she could whip Catherine on the second half of the quarters. Cassandra hated to lose, but she wanted to teach her daughter an important lesson about front-running. The senior had developed a bad habit of front-running and not leaving anything for her finishing kick. If Catherine wanted to place in the state finals this year, she needed to learn to hold back during the first mile.

Cassandra issued instructions and advice as she ran a few strides behind her daughter and the lead pack. As she passed the bleachers, Cassandra checked on Zander; even from fifty yards away, she could see that his hands and face were now streaked with yet another layer of dirt. She grimaced as she watched him take a handful of dirt and shove it in his mouth.

Before Coach J.T. blew the whistle for another quarter, Cassandra whispered in her daughter's ear, "Save some in your tank for the last few laps." Catherine ignored her and raced after the coach, who now ran with the girls. Cassandra watched her daughter run, and with pride she realized that Catherine ran with her body aligned in a perfect T. With a veteran coach's practiced eye, Cassandra reckoned that if Catherine worked hard, she could win states. If she won states, or even placed, she might get recruited to run for the University of Oregon.

After the fifth quarter, Cassandra felt limbered up and decided it was time to get serious. She stopped talking and giving pointers and tucked in right behind J.T.

Focus. Ninety-second quarter; then eighty-eight, then eighty-five. And darn it, the last two quarters in seventy-eight seconds, even if it

*kills me. She needs to learn to dig deep and find nothing, and dig
even deeper.*

Cassandra matched the younger version of herself stride
for stride as they both drafted off J.T. They passed the finish line
together, and Cassandra felt as though she could take off like a
military jet. *Four quarters left.* She noticed, as they ran two more
negative splits—at faster speeds each successive quarter—that
Catherine had set her jaw. *Maybe there is no quitting,* thought
Cassandra. She nodded to J.T., and the coach blew the whistle.

This time Cassandra ran flat-out, nothing left in reserve.
It was time to see what her daughter really had. She cleared her
mind of all thoughts and let loose, muscles tight but not straining,
feet churning at 180 beats per minute, arms in perfect sync. *It
hurts, it doesn't, I'm flying. I'm free.* She didn't look at Catherine but
felt her daughter matching her, and she knew that two jawlines
were set. They crossed the line at the same time.

"Mom, how fast was that?" Catherine panted.

"Seventy-nine flat. And if you want states, you need to
run seventy-seven. Right here, right now." Cassandra spoke with
a hurried intensity that would have sounded angry, were it not for
the glimmer of excitement in her eyes.

"States? You think?"

"Yeah. States."

•••

J.T. stood aside for the last lap, and when he blew the
whistle, Cassandra saw that he was watching Catherine. *Good. He
knows she's got it. He can coach her up to it.* They rounded the first
curve and Catherine took charge. Cassandra tried to draft, and
her body cried, *I hurt.* And she replied without speaking, *I'm flying,
I'm free.* But her legs did not respond. Catherine opened up a five-
yard lead and blasted across the finish line two seconds ahead of
her mother. And then Cassandra realized, as she slowed to a walk,
that Catherine was ready now.

Cassandra overheard the young coach gasp, "That was a
75.9! Holy cow, what a workout!" Catherine nodded and
stumbled over to the bench, spent.

Cassandra caught her daughter and wrapped an arm
around her. "No, no, no. Keep walkin', darling. Keep walkin'."

Catherine leaned against her mother and whispered, "I can go faster, Mama."

"I know. But not today. Soon." Cassandra let go of her daughter and shouted, "Zander! Come run a victory lap with your sister!"

Catherine rolled her eyes but waited for her dirt-encrusted, whirling dervish of a little brother to climb the black fence and leap into her arms.

Cassandra remained a few feet behind her two children and watched as they zigzagged across the white lines separating the eight lanes of track. She tried to relax, but an unbidden image of Phoebe intruded. This time, rather than force the image out of her mind, Cassandra imagined that she was there with Phoebe and covering her with a thick white blanket. *I could not help her then, but I can help her now.*

CHAPTER 25

Cassandra hit the button to open the garage door and a reflection of dark metal caught her attention.

Zander squealed, "Daddy's home!"

Cassandra pulled into the garage. Before she could depress the emergency brake, Zander had jumped out of the car and was tearing up the steps. He yanked at the handle to the door and ran into the laundry room. Catherine kicked off her running shoes as she sauntered slowly into the kitchen. The teenager grabbed a red Gatorade from the fridge and handed another one to Cassandra, and they both leaned against the counter, too tired to talk, while they waited for Zander and his father.

Cassandra groaned as she took in her kitchen. Crumbs decorated the floor. Tomato sauce from last night's spaghetti dinner splattered the blinds and the white trim around the windows. And she had thought she'd left the house clean that morning! Paintings hung askew on walls that bore innumerable smudges. Her brown leather sofa and matching loveseat bore pencil-inflicted puncture wounds and no longer hinted of luster or even a tiny layer of polish. Cassandra felt her shoulders and neck tightening, but she released the tension and reminded herself that her children's happiness mattered more than a mess-free house.

Frank walked around the corner, Zander sitting on his shoulders. Father and son smiled identical smiles and Cassandra felt her tension suddenly melt away. She wanted to run across the room and leap into Frank's arms, but with the children around, casual comings and goings were exchanged without real romance. She was at peace with this most of the time, for the children's sake, but tonight she yearned to collapse into Frank. With a hint of sultry swagger, she merely winked at him. Then she glanced at Catherine. "Tell your father how fast you ran that last quarter."

Catherine took one more swig of Gatorade before she grinned at the only father she knew. "Guess."

"Wasn't 80.0 your previous best?" Frank grabbed Zander's hands and swung him to the floor, but Zander started to whimper and clutch his father's leg. Frank picked his son back up, and as they cuddled, he sat down on the arm of the sofa.

"Faster." Catherine suppressed a smile.

"78.5?"

Catherine tried as hard as she could not to look too proud, and the overall effect made her look much younger. "75.9, Dad!"

"No!" Frank exclaimed.

Cassandra stopped calculating splits while she stared at her husband.

Frank Worthington had entered Cassandra's life the same day her ex-husband left it for good, seventeen years earlier. She had just heard the judge's verdict granting her full custody of Catherine and a restraining order against Tim. The judge's words still rang in her ears: "I am not inclined to grant even partial custody to a man who has battered his pregnant wife. A man like that has shown that he cannot be trusted around children. This Court will not give him the opportunity to inflict more harm." Cassandra was shaking when she stepped into the elevator; she hadn't noticed the man standing next to her.

"Rough day, ma'am?" His voice was so kind, so sweet, even comforting. She had looked up and gazed somberly into his dark eyes.

Then, as now, Frank appeared taller than his athletic six-foot-two. Cassandra noticed his brown hands as he leaned over to touch the ground floor button. His fingers were long but finely proportioned. That day he was wearing a custom gray suit with white pinstripes and a purple and white-striped tie that looked elegant rather than garish. To her surprise, Cassandra found herself nodding at this stranger and starting to cry.

"You wouldn't believe how bad of a day. I just got put on trial in my divorce proceedings. He beat me when I was pregnant, I lost the baby and I was the one who got put on trial. It was so unfair. And on top of it all, they ran my past through the mud." The words tumbled out of Cassandra faster than she expected.

He had listened to her quietly, then handed her his purple silk handkerchief.

She took it, and as she wiped her eyes with it, asked him his name. They had kept talking and never stopped talking, really, until one minute had become seventeen years of talking.

Cassandra smiled.

She sent a surreptitious wink at Frank and she closed her eyes and imagined herself running her hands over his smooth head. She had missed him.

And then a fleeting image of Phoebe played like a scene from a movie in her mind. Cassandra put her hand to her mouth. With a quiet wave to Frank, she walked out of the room and into her study. She shut the painted wood door behind her and turned the lock to make sure she had privacy. She would call Jen. Or Cary. She couldn't decide whom to call first, so she pulled a blue and white crocheted blanket to the desk to cover her knees and sat there, thinking. The video of Phoebe had brought the trauma from her own rape back to her. *I need a drink.*

Cassandra knew alcohol and its siren call all too well. She needed help and she needed it now, before she was too weak to ask for it. If she called her best friend, would she be supportive? Or would Jen get frustrated? Maybe, finally, she would crack and explain that she could not bear to hold Cassandra's hand through another relapse?

As Cassandra imagined Jen's rejection, she started shaking. She couldn't risk it. She gripped her pencil but couldn't remember why she was holding it. Her feet hurt and her knee ached. To distract herself from the pain, she observed the pattern on her grandmother's old blanket and got lost in the matrix of colors. It had been five years since Cassandra had seen Cary the last time, and she wondered if she would sound any different if Cassandra called her now. Then she remembered that she didn't have Cary's phone number handy. Gritting her teeth, she typed her therapist's name into Google.

Darn, darn, darn! Cassandra took a deep breath. She hated calling, but she knew that if she didn't get help, she might end up in a convenience store, buying a bottle of gin. That could not happen. Her clients needed, her kids needed . . . no, *she* needed. *I can't.* She dialed. *I have to.* It hurt, somehow, that her therapist's phone number no longer was on speed dial. *We should all have our therapists' phone numbers on speed dial, especially loser drunks like—*

"Hello?" Cary answered the phone herself, which caught Cassandra off-guard. She kneaded the blanket and tried to let it soothe her.

"Uh, Cary?"

"Yes?"

"This is Cassandra White." Cassandra could not get any other words out; the standard greetings, given her state of mind, felt insufficient or stilted.

"Cass! It's good to hear your voice." Cassandra remembered how much she had adored this not-quite mother figure. Her own mother had passed away when Cassandra was still in college, which was about the time she had started to drink.

She smiled. She had missed Cary, and she felt a tremendous gratitude toward her. "Wow, have I missed you!"

"Well, I know you're not calling me just to tell me that." Cassandra heard a burble of laughter on the line. "I imagine this has something to do with Phoebe and Helen. Is that right?"

Cassandra rested her head on her hand, contemplating. She couldn't figure out if Cary was allowed to talk about Phoebe with Cassandra, and she hated to think that she would overstep her clients' privacy limits. "Kind of," she began. "This case is hurting me. It's bringing up so much. It's like an exhumation of memories I thought had long since been buried. That's why I'm calling. Oh, and I totally messed up the interview with Phoebe today, but I bet you already know that. It's just, I feel so bad about all of it."

Cassandra tried to wait for Cary to formulate an answer. She needed to shut up and stop talking, but she had a bad habit of interrupting people and finishing their sentences for them.

"It's good you called me, then. And we need to set up a plan so that you can decompress when things feel intense."

Cassandra rolled her eyes a little. Cary loved plans. She solved problems methodically, and sometimes Cassandra really wanted to wallow. She knew it got her nowhere, but right now she felt weary and she didn't want to plan anything.

"Hell with making a plan. I feel like hell and I need a drink," Cassandra exclaimed, and they both laughed.

"Well, all right. I'll put my plan-making aside for now. Talk to me."

"I watched the video of this little girl, and that's what she is. She's a kid. And I wanted to rescue her. So bad." Cassandra kept going, even as her voice shook. "It brought me right back to feeling helpless and defenseless and I might as well be that drugged, drunk little girl. And it hurts, the pain, it hurts, and all of that hurt is connected to the bottle of gin, because it's what got me there, in the bathroom all those years ago. I feel ashamed and guilty all over again. Like I deserved to be raped because I'm just a drunk, so I should drink again because I deserve no better." Cassandra's voice dropped to a whisper and she shook so hard that she could scarcely hold the phone. "But I don't want to lift that bottle again, Cary."

Cary made a sympathetic sound but did not answer right away. Cassandra knew the therapist was listening and thinking. "The fact that you're feeling a psychological compulsion to drink is not bad in and of itself. In fact, it is a testament to how strong you are, that you recognized it and reached out for help rather than reaching for the bottle. Right?"

Cassandra traced the lines on her chair, and the more she did so the straighter they appeared. She stopped shaking so violently. "Yeah, I guess."

"I'm sure of it, if that helps. How bad is it for you?"

Cassandra tried to speak. She felt like something had a vice-grip around her chest or her heart. "I see her every time I close my eyes. And she's naked. And that animal is . . . and I can feel it."

"I imagine that is scary and painful for you."

"Yeah, and I haven't even told Frank about it yet. Maybe I can."

"This case is going to be a challenging one, isn't it?"

"Yes, but I still need to represent Helen."

"I would never tell you not to represent a client. Let's talk planning. Are you ready?" Cassandra imagined Cary giving her a serious but respectful stare. She nodded.

"As far as Phoebe goes, from now on when you need to interview her, I want to be in the room. Or at a minimum, Helen should be there."

"Did I mess up with her?"

"No, I don't think so, not under the circumstances. She trusts you. But we need to handle her with care, okay?"

Cassandra felt relieved.

"Also, you need to build your support system. Call your best friend. Tell Frank. Find time to go to AA meetings. Are you still running? Does this make sense?"

Cassandra groaned. It sounded like a lot of work. "Okay, Cary. Yes, I am still running. Not as fast, and my legs are killing me, but I run, even with my daughter."

"Good. I'm sorry about your legs. Aging sucks." Cary laughed, then got more serious. "And I am here to support you. Can you meet me next week, say Tuesday at nine in the morning?"

"Yeah." After she hung up the phone, Cassandra rested her head on her hand again and thought about calling Jen. Her friend would be awake, but what if she was busy? Instead of calling, she tapped out a quick e-mail:

> Dear Jen: I'm struggling. Hard case involving rape and a little girl. Makes me want to drink. I'm okay; I mean, I'm not, but I talked to my therapist and I won't drink tonight. But can I call you if I need to? Tomorrow?

Cassandra was surprised when the computer pinged back a minute later:

> Cass, you know you can call me ANYTIME. Please. Pick up the phone before you pick up a bottle. Please write back and promise me you will call me first. Love you.

Cassandra felt secure and safe and proud. She had Frank. She had Cary. She had Jen. She had her children. Every day that she wanted to drink and did not do it made her feel like a warrior.

After reading Jen's message, she pushed up from her chair and overheard the clanging of dishes and pots and pans. With a sigh, she unlocked the door and tried to make her face look expressionless.

"Hon," she murmured, "have you got things under control for fifteen minutes? I really need a shower."

His eyes twinkled. "Sure. God, I missed you, gorgeous." He crossed over and hugged her from behind.

As soon as she sensed his chest pressing against her back, she felt her body tingling. Cassandra grinned and tried not to blush. She was way too old to blush, but somehow Frank's voice made her feel like he was undressing her already. She forced herself not to respond because nothing appropriate would come to mind. The kids were still around.

Cassandra padded upstairs, taking one step at a time, every muscle and tendon and ligament protesting vigorously. She groaned and cursed the not-so-subtle effects of aging.

In the bedroom she paused for a moment and gasped at the dirty laundry, mini-bottles of deodorant and plastic baggies containing the detritus of Frank's trip, spread out from bed to hamper to closet. Willing her blood pressure to remain steady, she leaned over to grab some clothing and instantly regretted it. Her lower back ached and she wished, as she wished every day, that her husband would pick up after himself. *Not my mess. Not my problem.* Instead of holding the angry thought, she released it and let go of the boxers she held. She tried to envision Frank wearing that gray suit with the purple tie, and after she placed her own clothing in the hamper, she stepped into the scalding shower.

As the water beat down on her, she took a few deep breaths and tried not to think. But whenever she closed her eyes, all she saw was Phoebe, so she kept her eyes open. And then she heard the bathroom door open.

"Frank!" Cassandra giggled. "Where are the kids?"

He kissed her neck and chills ran from head to toe. "I sent them out to walk the dog, gorgeous."

She laughed, and as she stepped out of the shower, she wrapped a towel around herself. And as she laughed, her voice was as sultry as his handkerchief had been silky.

"Did you lock the bedroom door?" she whispered.

"Yes. Any other questions, Counselor?" he whispered.

Frank kissed Cassandra on the lips and she nuzzled his shoulder. "Wow, good plan, sexy man," she smiled.

•••

He touched her cheek with the back of his hand and she thought to herself, *I could ask him for a new motorcycle right now and he'd buy it for me.*

Frank said over his shoulder, "I don't like that look in your eye."

She howled with mirth. "Darn. You know all my tricks."

"Reckon so, gorgeous. I've been paying the bank for all of your toys all of these years," he teased. Frank leaned his head back into the bathroom. "And the answer, of course, is yes. Better just to buy it first and ask forgiveness second. Isn't that what you always tell your friends?"

She couldn't stop laughing. "Okay, good, I really need a new Harley. Thanks, darling." He shook his head and shut the bathroom door behind him, and Cassandra smiled.

•••

After Frank had fallen asleep, she went outside to get a breath of air. When she couldn't sleep, Cassandra liked to stand outside and look at the stars. The night sky lifted her up inside; it didn't make her feel small or meaningless, but spoke to her of possibilities, of rising and reaching higher. It made her want to run faster and grab hold of the moment and live in it. She breathed in and felt the crisp night air ruffle her plaid pajama pants, and this time when she closed her eyes she did not see a tiny girl being raped. She saw an empty red track and a setting sun and a lone runner, and that lone runner looked like her, but she was younger, and she was faster, and her mind and her body felt free on the track and free in the night sky.

CHAPTER 26

Bob switched off the light in his basement rec room and paced back and forth, holding a football that had been signed by his favorite Redskins player, *John Riggins*. Now that was a man who played hard, partied harder. He remembered the time Riggo had told Sandra Day O'Connor she was too tight. "You need to loosen up, Sandy."

Bob patted the football and felt his jaw clicking again. He was the one who needed to loosen up, but for the past week he'd been out of his mind. Seriously, this wasn't like him. Deeper and deeper he was getting into her, and he couldn't let her go. Not after seeing her standing there, in public, of all places.

Check, double-check . . . crap. He was so tired. Tracking them down was becoming a job in itself. Or an obsession? He was getting careless. Him, of all people. He should have Googled it or run the owners at work, but he'd driven out there in an unmarked sedan to get a read. Gatehouse. Two guards. Nothing he couldn't handle. The guards were old. Pretty well-equipped, not bad for civvies, but a mere obstacle, to be assessed, calculated and eventually overcome.

They were targets A and B. Obstructions between him and his brown-eyed girl. He was growing hard again, but he wanted to wait. Wait for her. It would make it feel more special, almost like his first, his beautiful Janie. She had the same brown eyes.

The slap-on was working great. He knew where they were, but he couldn't get a read on who lived at the address on the GPS. It listed Anne McCaffrey as one of the principals, and then it seemed to refer to a fund or a charity called the Bryson House, or Bryson's House. He needed to double-check it once he grabbed the tax records. Maybe the owners had forgotten to file something with the county, or had violated some arcane regulation. All he needed was a tiny reason to get past the guards without bloodshed.

Or better, he needed a way to get his girl away from The Bryson House. Interview her, lock the door, and she'd be his.

CHAPTER 27

For years, Cary had acted as the on-call therapist for the Bryson House. She had first met Miranda when they were both just out of grad school. Miranda and Cary, then in their mid-twenties, had worked at a suicide line together back when both 800-numbers and suicide lines were new. Between the two of them they had staffed the night shift on weekends, and they'd spent many nights talking outside and sharing a smoke after hours of white-knuckling their way through sessions of desperation and consolation. Cary came from California, and Miranda, an East-Coaster with a semi-permanent, tightly wound bun, never tired of calling her friend a "wild-haired hippie," but in some ways their friendship proved the law of opposites. As close as Miranda and Mimi had become over the years, no one knew Miranda the way Cary did. And Miranda respected and loved Cary in a way that no one else could quite understand. They had grown even closer when Miranda's husband had passed away after a sudden stroke.

Cary wheeled her silver Lexus SUV up to the front door of the main house and stepped out, trying to look organized and not to drop too many things. Her spacey, southern California look got her in trouble all the time, and it bothered her today until she reminded herself that she wasn't standing in her office talking to a client. Besides, her messiness never hurt anyone. Messy and soft-edged on the outside, the plain-speaking therapist was a practitioner of cognitive behavioral therapy. She took an organized, often hard-nosed approach to helping clients solve their own problems. Initially many therapists had frowned at her style, which sometimes seemed harsh and unyielding, but throughout the years Cary had become a well-respected, even admired therapist. Besides, after thirty years of serving clients, she wasn't changing the way she practiced without good reason.

•••

Inside the light-drenched study, Cary asked Helen to sit down. After shutting the double wood-paneled doors behind her, the therapist fixed her gaze on Helen. "Before I talk to Phoebe, I need to touch base with you about Phoebe. How're you holding up?" Cary whipped out her notebook and waited for Helen to respond.

Helen studied her hands and rubbed her finger, tracing the indentation that remained even after the ring was gone. She spoke even faster than usual. "I killed my husband. Now I can't get him out of my mind. I know what he did and I can't stop replaying the video in my mind. And it isn't just prison I'm worried about. I'm worried that I'm going to hell. I don't even know if hell is real. I think it probably is, and I think that if it is real, he's there now. And if I see him there, will I keep having to kill him over and over again to keep him from raping my daughter?" She did not start crying but sat there, eyes moving rapidly as though searching for answers to questions both formed and unformed.

"I'm so sorry. So sorry for your losses. For all of them."

Helen took a deep breath. "But this is not about me. This is about helping Phoebe. That's why you're here. You're here to help my kid."

Cary wrote and looked at Helen while she scribbled in her notebook. Helen found it both distracting and impressive. She made a mental note to practice this blind writing trick; it would make a good tool for her practice. *Oh my God, I haven't checked all of my e-mail yet.*

Cary frowned. "I can't help Phoebe without helping you, too. More than anything, Phoebe needs you now. So part of my job is going to be to help Troy support you, as you help her through this process. You need a support system just as much as she does."

"Will this take time away from the time Phoebe receives in therapy?"

Cary shook her head and scratched out another blind note on her yellow legal pad. "No. The way I will do this is that I will meet with you sometimes separately, and while I can't tell you what she tells me in session, I can teach you some coping mechanisms that will help Phoebe, and help you as a mother. Naturally, there is an exception to her confidentiality."

Helen's eyes welled up with tears. "Suicide threats?"

Cary gave a brisk, matter-of-fact nod. "Yes. She is still a minor, and if I fear that she is at risk of harming herself, I will tell you. And I will never promise her that everything she tells me will be kept secret."

Helen looked down at the floor. *If only there were a way to make all of this pain and hurt disappear.* "Please tell me she is going to be okay, Cary. *Please.*"

"Helen, I promise you that we will do everything in our power to help your daughter. In my book, what you did took great strength. It's a mess, but it's my job to help sweep up the broken pieces. I brought you a couple of books to start reading." Cary leaned over, reached into her fabric-covered floral briefcase and put two books into Helen's hands.

Helen looked uncertain. "Are these my copies?"

Cary set her briefcase down. "Yes. Go ahead. Take notes. Make them your own. I will add them to your bill." As Helen nodded, Cary said, "Helen, I need your permission to meet with Phoebe now."

•••

Phoebe knocked on the door and pushed it open with the slightest of touches.

Cary stood up and shook hands. "Please sit down wherever you feel comfortable."

The thing is, Phoebe thought, *I don't feel comfortable anywhere.* She did not sit down right away; instead, she froze and hugged her arms around her body.

"Or you can stand," added Cary. "If that makes you feel better."

Phoebe surveyed Cary and looked at the bookcases, but she didn't focus on any of the titles. The colors of the books merged into a mélange of shades and hues, and then she leaned back against the conference table. She crossed her legs and kept her arms wrapped around her body. "What? Some false illusion of choice? Give me a break."

"What do you mean by illusion of choice?" Cary spoke with precision and a suggestion of authority.

"There is no such thing as choice. It is a lie. An illusion. What choice?" Phoebe's eyes flashed, and then she turned them on Cary. "Don't tell me about choices."

Cary nodded. "What is it about choices that makes you angry?"

Phoebe examined her hard-bitten fingers, so used to wrapping themselves around brown leather reins. At least in the saddle she was something. *Somebody. Someone.* "Come on. We both know why I am here."

Still scribbling on her pad, Cary replied, "Yes, perhaps. We both choose to be here. What is it about choices? What were you saying?"

Phoebe was far too accustomed to adults taking what they needed from her. Nothing, not love, nor comfort, nor even a roof over her head and rules to abide by seemed to come without strings attached. It came down to whether Phoebe could trust this woman.

What currency were they trading in? She knew it wasn't sex, but the unknown was scary. No adult cared about her enough to take care of her, not without demanding something in return. Phoebe wasn't accustomed to adults caring about her. She found it scary. She trusted no one except her mother, and even she had let Phoebe down by being gone all of the time. Phoebe sauntered toward the door. "Who says I choose to be here?"

Cary didn't move. "I am asking you to be here. Will you please talk with me?"

"Fine. But don't tell me about choices. I have no choice, not really. No one does."

"How so?"

Phoebe slid down in one of the desk chairs and for thirty seconds she remained silent. Cary set her notepad on the end table next to her and cocked her head, waiting for a response.

Phoebe swung her dangling foot from the edge of the chair. "I still can't figure out what I chose and what I didn't choose." With a faraway look in her eyes, she leaned toward Cary. "Who says I didn't choose what happened? How the heck do I know that I didn't want it?"

"Is that what he said, Phoebe? Is that what someone said to you?"

Phoebe's body recoiled as though she'd been slammed in the chest with a heavy bag. She tried to keep her expression blank, but the effort was strangling her. Cary was not betraying a reaction, and it confused Phoebe.

What is she thinking? If she doesn't care, then can I trust her? Why is she here and why am I here and when, when is she gonna hurt me? They always do, and maybe they always will. Or will they?

Something even stronger screamed inside the girl and she couldn't tune it out. *Please, if you can help me. Help me. Please help me.*

Lower lip trembling, Phoebe demanded, "What do you care? You don't know me. What if I'm lying? How do you know if I am lying?"

Cary still showed no sign of her thoughts, but she followed Phoebe's eyes until the girl gave in and made eye contact. "Did he say you wanted it?"

Phoebe looked down at a darker brown section of wood on the floor. "Yes."

"Did you want it? And before you answer that, I want you to know that a lot of rape and incest victims report conflicting responses. It is not unusual for a woman's body to respond to physical stimulus." The ticking of the grandfather clock punctuated the bustling sounds of dinner preparation coming from the kitchen.

"It's not?"

"No, not at all. The mere fact that your body may have felt aroused does not mean that you wanted it or even chose it."

Confusion knotted Phoebe's brow. "I hate my body for liking it. I hate him for making me want it. I'm such a slut, you know?"

"No. I don't think you're a slut. Being the victim does not make you a slut. It doesn't make you anything. This isn't about you. It's about your father. It was never about you."

Phoebe tried to shut out the images that flooded into her mind.

"I want to cut every piece of him out of me, and I don't care if it makes me bleed." The words hurt to say, or at least she thought that they should; she knew how it would feel when they did. And then she realized that Cary had flinched, and Phoebe spotted a touch of sadness in her therapist's eyes. The girl stopped speaking.

"No, Phoebe, no! You must not hurt yourself."

"Why not?" Phoebe challenged, a defiant look in her eyes.

"Enough harm has been done. You have no control over that. But you can control what happens now."

The teenager pushed her hands against the desk and lifted herself up so that she sat on the edge of the table, her feet hanging down. In her fluffy tan moccasins, she seemed to flip between awkward girlhood and something older, a young woman in the bloom of her beauty.

Cary nodded again, which Phoebe thought was either a pronounced nervous tic or an early sign of Parkinson's Disease. In a more nurturing voice, the therapist repeated, "Enough harm has been done. And what happened in the past, while it affects who you are, does not dictate your future."

"Why did it happen if it wasn't meant to be? He said it was God's will and that it had to be because he needed me so bad. He said God put me there to take care of him. He said he had no choice, and that I had no choice, and that it was fate and destiny was fate and . . ." Phoebe's voice rushed on like a tsunami. "So I was born just so I could have no choice. Freakin' perfect!" she cried, throwing her words into Cary like daggers.

"It was not about sex."

"Then why did I enjoy it? Why did my body, why did my body, why did my body?!" Phoebe shrieked.

Cary held eye contact. "You have to understand that you have no control over your body's response. I've seen this so many times with molested boys. When stimulated, they sustained erections and even ejaculated. Do you think this means they were participating voluntarily?"

Phoebe bristled at the question. "Probably."

Cary waited her out.

Phoebe tapped her foot in frustration. "Well, no, I guess they weren't, not if they were young."

Cary nodded again. "So the boys who actually ejaculated weren't voluntarily participating in their rape. Even if they were manipulated into asking for it, do you think any of them really wanted it, as in consciously, with full knowledge of what everything meant, choosing to have sex with their molester?"

Phoebe's features froze as she tried to suss this out. "Are you telling me I was born to become an incest victim? That's why he had me?"

"No. You weren't born so that you could become a victim. Your father chose to make you a victim. As far as why you were born . . . honestly, who knows why anyone is born; you had nothing to do with that original choice. But each day, you choose in the moment, each moment, how and why and what you are fighting for—as do all of us." Cary re-crossed her legs. The gentle lines in her face lent weight to her words.

"He stood beside me in the stall and, with his big hand wrapped around her fingers—"

"Whose fingers?" Cary interrupted.

"My fingers." Phoebe closed her eyes as if watching a movie that only she could see. "He curled his fingers around the brush and showed me how to clean the old mare's coat. He reassured me and I relaxed." Phoebe opened her eyes and coughed again. "And then the same hands are wrapped around me, caressing my back, and I feel only his palms, and I smell the old mare, and above me are these shadows, and they're moving on the ceiling, and . . ." Phoebe closed her eyes again and whispered, "And I feel him, but it's not me, because I'm gone now. I can see him, and her, and her body feels pleasure, but my heart, her heart, we're screaming, 'No, please, no!'" Phoebe wiped away the tears that streamed down her cheeks.

"This was not consensual sex. It cannot be. It simply cannot be. Not between a grown man and a girl."

"But he said he couldn't resist me. He said he couldn't help it and that if I didn't want it, he wouldn't give it to me. And he called me beautiful. His. And I liked it when he called me beautiful." Her face turned wistful as she spoke.

"Even if it felt good, it doesn't mean you chose it." Phoebe opened and shut her mouth, her words buried now; but she was listening, so Cary continued, "Our bodies are designed this way. We can't always stop our bodies from reacting, but it does not make it your fault. Not ever."

"I feel like you're saying my body betrayed me."

"Your body did what it is supposed to do." Cary slapped her notebook with her hand for emphasis. "You weren't betrayed by your body. You were betrayed by the father who used your body and abused you."

"How do you know this, anyway?" Phoebe's mood changed abruptly, now more defiant than broken. Cary's expression remained the same.

"I've been doing this for thirty-five years. I've seen it all. I have counseled many young women and they all share some common responses."

One of Phoebe's shoulders rose slightly in a not-quite shrug, and she tried to sound dismissive. "Really? Like what?"

"Like shame. Everyone feels ashamed, no matter what the details of the abuse. Everyone feels shame." Cary peered at Phoebe. "Am I right?"

Phoebe couldn't speak the words. *Every minute of every day. All the time.*

•••

Cary headed up the stairs in search of her old friend Miranda, thinking about her young client. It wasn't always easy, but the habit of bearing witness to acts that barely stood the weight of the words used to describe them had taught her, only after many troubled nights, to remain a safe distance from her clients. She cared about them, but she could not let any of them get too close. It was too exhausting, too painful; and ultimately, paralyzing.

And yet now, with a sinking feeling, Cary started picturing her own college-aged daughter wrapped around a man Cary had never met. *Don't tie this painful memory to your session with Phoebe,* she cautioned herself, but she realized, with a pang in her heart, that this young client was going to get under her skin.

Maybe Miranda can help, she thought. She figured that she might find her friend watching the sunset from the upstairs balcony, and sure enough, Miranda was leaning against the railing that looked out over the rolling countryside that surrounded the Bryson House. Miranda took a sip from her coffee mug and waved to Cary, who moved her mug to her other hand and slid the heavy door shut.

Cary made it out to the Bryson House most Friday evenings, and she always ventured up to the second floor balcony to share a cup of coffee with her old friend. Every once in a while their talk extended through dinner and into the morning hours, and sometimes the divorced woman spent the night. Some of the women who stayed at the Bryson House wondered about the two, but there had never been anything but a close friendship between them.

In some ways Miranda was not only a best friend to Cary, she was also her therapist; although the therapeutic relationship remained loosely defined. A licensed counselor as well, Miranda could hear about Cary's clients without Cary breaching client confidentiality. In a sense, they had served as one another's psychological clearinghouse for more than thirty years. Being able to rely on each other for open-ended professional advice and support had made both more effective therapists.

Cary handed Miranda a box of dark chocolate caramels. "I missed you when I was on vacation."

"My favorites! You know I'm going to eat the whole box tonight!" Miranda exclaimed.

Cary shook her head. "It beats me how you stay so thin."

Miranda tried to open the package and winced a little. Her arthritic fingers ached after a long day working on the books.

Without a word, Cary took the box from her dear friend and opened it, passing it back after removing a chocolate herself. The women never talked about Miranda's aches and pains. Miranda preferred it that way.

After eating one of the caramels, Miranda set the box down on a glass table beside her and began talking as if their last conversation had never really ended. "It's been a zoo around here, and my gosh, this poor kid and her mother. They both amaze me." Miranda sipped her coffee and a smile curled around the edges of the coffee cup.

Cary reached into her pocket with a smile. "I found something else for you while I was out walking in Point Lobos, in Carmel. There were all these seals flopping on rocks, and the waves were pounding, and the water was green and blue and white, kind of otherworldly, you know?" Cary paused and waited for Miranda to nod.

"Go on, yes, I remember the pictures you e-mailed me." Miranda ate another caramel.

"Well," Cary continued, "there was this bird. Some sort of seagull, I think, but different than seagulls on the East Coast. I meant to look it up, but . . ." She paused and waved her hand. "Anyway, it landed in the water near the seals, in a place where the water was still. And with the splash of its feet on the water, a ripple went off, and it spread and kept going until I couldn't see how much further it went. And Miranda. It's been such a hard year. A tough year. But all through it, I've had my work. Our work. And we help each other, and then we help other women, and then, like Cassandra, they go on to help other women, you know what I mean?"

Miranda rubbed her elbow and looked up to the right, as if searching the sky for an answer. "Each time we help someone, it creates a ripple? Is that what you mean?"

Cary pulled her hand out of her pocket and showed Miranda the seashell she was cradling. "Yeah. One woman at a time. That's what I wrote on this shell I found right on the shore near where the bird landed in the water. I wrote it with a Sharpie," Cary giggled. "Funny that I had a Sharpie, but that was all I had, and I wanted to write it down before I forgot it. We help one woman at a time. And that's enough, you know?"

Miranda hugged Cary and rubbed her back. "Yes, love, I do know. That is so wonderful. I'll cherish this and think of you whenever I see it."

Both women looked off into the distance and surveyed the rising stars and the dim outline of the moon. Beyond the tree line, the sun had already dipped below the horizon, leaving a red triangle just above the trees. Cary took a deep breath and felt content until she suddenly thought of Phoebe. She gasped involuntarily.

"What's troubling you, Cary?" Miranda touched Cary's elbow. "You're in pain."

Cary nodded as she tried to get control of her breathing. Sessions with rape survivors had never been easy, but working with Phoebe reminded her of her own daughter's rape. "It's my daughter. And it's Phoebe. And it's the millions that we could not help." Cary's tough accent belied the softness behind her words. "And this girl, she's shattered. She is totally shattered. And before she gets better, she's going to get worse."

Miranda watched the last piece of the red triangle fade to dark blue, and then she wrapped an arm around Cary. "It's a heck of job, but you've done it many times before, and you're going to be fine. Just work the process, and even if you speed it up because she needs more intensive work, remember that she needs your experience, not so much your broken heart. You know you're still grieving for your daughter, right?"

Cary nodded.

"But she's moved on. And you need to find a way to let it go and move past it as well. There is nothing you could have done to prevent that rape, your daughter's rape."

Cary shivered. Miranda used the word rape when talking about her daughter in exactly the same way Cary had used it when counseling Cassandra and many other rape victims, and it was an effective therapeutic strategy. It also hurt, unbearably sometimes, to hear the word used to describe something that had happened to her own daughter. *Words have meaning*, Cary thought.

Miranda paused. "It's okay to cry, Cary." She sipped her coffee and nibbled another caramel.

Cary grasped the railing with one hand, as though leaning on a crutch or a cane.

"Why don't you spend the night and drive back when you're fresh?" Miranda suggested. "Maybe you can work with Phoebe tomorrow, and if you can't get with her, a couple of the other women?"

Cary checked her watch. "That makes sense. I should spend a couple of days here. Anyway, no one is waiting home for me." Cary couldn't keep all the bitterness out of her voice as she continued, "There are other women who could use an ear, correct?"

"Always. No one has taken an easy path to get here; besides, Phoebe will be riding for most of the morning with Anne."

"With Anne?" Cary's eyes widened. "I thought she had retired."

"She had. Apparently the girl has a real talent in the ring, and Anne wants to train her."

Cary held her still-warm coffee mug against her chest and watched the full moon rise. For a few minutes, neither woman spoke, then Cary shot a look at her companion. "Don't tell me we have a future Olympian on our hands?"

Miranda's glasses reflected the light of the moon and she pulled her black knit sweater tighter before grabbing her own mug and turning to go inside. "If Anne is training and Phoebe is talented, there is no saying how far that girl could go, you know?"

"Yes, I do know," replied Cary, and she followed Miranda inside.

CHAPTER 28

One of the customs honored at the Bryson House was that every resident could eat dinner between six and eight in the evening. Mimi or Miranda would pull up a chair at the massive dining room table and take the pulse of the women and children staying at the home. At the moment, though, Helen and Phoebe were the only residents seated in the dining room.

Helen was flipping between articles in the business and legal sections of the newspaper, unable to focus long enough to complete more than a paragraph of a story. Next to her, Phoebe paged through her favorite equestrian magazine, but her eyes were not really following the words, either. Anne arrived at half past seven and chatted with Mimi at the other end of the table. The equestrian looked elegant and orderly in a black A-line skirt, polished black dress boots and a frilly white shirt with a lace collar that buttoned up almost to her chin.

Phoebe hardly noticed that anyone else was in the room. Her mind cycled from visions of her father to images of horses cantering across an open prairie, and then back to her father; and the images blurred faster and faster in her mind until Helen tapped her arm. Phoebe, realizing that she had started shaking, moved her head toward her mother as if to ask for guidance. *I want her to grab the reins and I don't get why she won't.*

Helen simply put an arm around Phoebe and spoke directly to Anne. "So I hear that you rode in the Olympics. What type of riding?"

Anne stared at the delicate patterns on her glass of Coke and watched the colors change as the light from the crystal chandeliers bounced off the rust-colored liquid. In a genial tone, she replied, "Dressage."

"I suppose that is very different from jumping and steeplechase." Helen rested a hand on her water glass.

Anne nodded. "Yes. There are three different types of Olympic sports. They are show jumping, cross country jumping—that's the steeplechase you mentioned—and dressage. And a three day eventing combines all three types of riding."

Helen opened her mouth to ask another question, but Phoebe spoke for the first time since she had sat down at the table. "Which event, Anne?" the girl blurted out, and when Helen started to correct Phoebe, Anne held up her hand and murmured, "It's okay, Ms. Thompson. I already told her to call me Anne. It makes me forget, just for a second, how old I really am now."

"I'm not sure that I'm comfortable with that, Anne. But in my case, please call me Helen. None of this Ms. Thompson nonsense." The two women smiled at one another and Mimi laughed as she gathered up several dishes and carried them to the kitchen.

"Phoebe, what was your question?" Anne's strong hands grasped her glass and Phoebe realized that Anne had to be really old, what with all of her blue veins and liver spots.

The girl tried to gather her thoughts this time before she spoke. "Which event did you ride in, Anne?" Her voice didn't sound timid, but Helen noticed that it shook a little.

"I rode in the three day eventing. That way, if I had a bad day I could pick up points on one of the other two days, which kept the pressure on me more manageable. Besides, I loved jumping." Anne rubbed her hands together just once, and then folded them under her chin for a moment.

"Isn't it more pressure to have to perform all three days?"

Anne shook her head with a rueful glance at her hands. "I suppose you could see it like that. But that is a darn good way to lose—to try to look for ways not to lose, you know?"

Mimi leaned over and tapped her knee. "Yes, well-said, Anne!" As usual, the tall woman's voice was a hair too loud. "Fearing failure is a guaranteed path to defeat."

Phoebe took all of this in but didn't know what to say. She was feeling a little overpowered by Anne's philosophical adages. Changing the subject, she asked, "Where did you place in the Olympics?"

Helen gritted her teeth, but Anne didn't flinch. "I did not make the podium, Phoebe. But that's not the only thing that matters."

"Why not?"

"Because there is only so much you can control on any given day. What if the wind changes direction right before your final jump? And it causes a subtle shift in the angle you need to take, and you and your horse get it wrong? What if your horse comes down with something on the long trip overseas?" Anne's gray eyes took on a youthful cast, and she looked off as if gazing into the past as she continued. "How about if you eat the wrong thing the night before, or drink tap water even when your coach told you not to, and you get food poisoning? The point is, you're human, the horse is fallible, and you simply never know how things are going to go on a particular day."

"We used to always say after a case went to court that the results were out of our hands." Helen leaned forward in Anne's direction. "On any given day, a ruling from a cranky judge, an inattentive jury, too much rain, a bad performance by an expert witness . . . any number of factors can affect the disposition of a case, yes? Much like your horses, judges and juries are human, and sometimes there's just no telling how things are going to go during a given day."

Anne gave an approving look, and for the second time that day, Phoebe watched as her mother treated another woman with great respect. *But what was Anne thinking?* "Anne?" Phoebe began.

"Yes, Phoebe?"

"Why didn't you make it to the podium?"

"Phoebe!" Helen exclaimed. "That's none of your business."

"Mom," Phoebe replied crisply, "it probably *is* relevant if Anne is going to be my trainer." Phoebe almost rolled her eyes, but thought better of it when she caught Anne staring her down.

An uncomfortable silence gripped the room until Anne spoke. "It doesn't really matter how good of a rider I was,

Phoebe. I suppose you think you'll listen to me if you observe that I know my way with horses, but you already get that, correct?"

Phoebe nodded.

"And," continued Anne, "my position a step away or on the podium thirty years ago tells you much less about my relative abilities as a trainer than does the performance of the riders I trained. If I were looking for a trainer, as you most certainly are, then I would ask, 'Who did you train and how did they fare at the highest levels of equestrian competition?'"

Phoebe was nonplussed, but she recovered quickly. "That makes sense, yes. So how did they do, Anne?"

Phoebe knew she was out of bounds from the look on her mother's face. She waited for Helen to rebuke her; instead, Anne spoke in a gentle but authoritative voice, "Very well indeed."

Anne folded her thick cloth napkin and laid it down next to her plate. With a glance at Helen, she continued, "Perhaps tomorrow we can take a stroll and talk about Phoebe's training method." The older woman winced and placed a hand on her hip, and Phoebe almost winced in sympathy. "For now, I'm wanting to grab an ice pack and lie down in flannel pajamas on my most comfortable sofa and read until bedtime." She paused. "Phoebe, if you are ready to start training with me, you can find me tomorrow morning in the stables. Assuming your mother assents."

Phoebe tried not to look too excited as Anne continued, "First light. If you really do have dreams of competing at the highest equestrian levels, we have a lot of work to do. That was one of the main secrets to my success as a rider and as a trainer: We rode more hours, in more diverse conditions and places than our competitors rode. As long as proper technique is followed, there is simply no substitute for time spent in the saddle."

"Helen, do you mind if Phoebe works with me?" Anne lifted her chin. "I must warn you, I expect a serious commitment from both the rider and the rider's parents, or else conflicts will arise later on down the road. I'd like to ascertain we're on the same page."

"Yes, we are." Helen spoke firmly and gave Phoebe an appraising glance. "I am honored that you would think of my daughter in this way. We can work on that whole first-name basis thing." Helen glanced over at her daughter and then added, "And she has never lacked for a serious work ethic."

Phoebe bristled with irritation. "How would you know about my work ethic? When is the last time you watched me ride?"

Anne glanced at Mimi, repeating, "First light." With a slight limp, she headed out into the foyer as Mimi vanished into the kitchen.

• • •

Helen rested her head on her hand and sighed. It seemed dimmer in the dining room, as though someone had turned the lights down. The candles flickered and sent shadows moving on the walls. She knew what was coming. She had been expecting it. Phoebe felt betrayed and unprotected, almost like all those hours Helen had spent at the office were an insult to her daughter's very being. Worse, the simple fact, the unrelenting reality of it, was that if Helen had been around more, Richard would not have been alone with Phoebe as much. Could lack of opportunity have prevented the rape? Helen felt sick. *Phoebe must hate me*, she thought. And she secretly felt hatred and a burning loathing for herself, too.

Helen smelled the burnt-out ends of the ham served at dinner and caressed the tablecloth with her fingers. In her mind she saw a tiny version of Phoebe riding a white horse that stood sixteen hands high, and she tried to focus on how Phoebe's black felt helmet was awkwardly perched on top of her head. Her daughter had grinned at her and made a clicking sound with her tongue, and the horse had taken off in an easy canter. Helen had marveled at how such a little creature had been able to control a living, breathing giant. Even then, her daughter had been such a competent, even powerful being, and Helen had smiled so wide, with so much pride, that her cheeks had hurt.

"Too long. Too long."

Phoebe sat up in her chair and her eyes flashed. "Is that all you have to say about it? Or are you going to come up with some line about how the firm needed you? And the great work you were doing protecting some corporation's bottom line?" Her daughter's mood had turned very dark, a hurricane of hatred.

Helen resigned herself to it. She knew she deserved the better share of Phoebe's anger; she really did. Cases flowed into more cases, and clients begot more clients. She envisioned lawsuits with their signature first page, Plaintiff vs. Defendant, and thought of how the final page of each lawsuit bore her signature. At first her name was listed second or third under a partner's name, but now each pleading, even the ones she barely glanced at, bore her name and her fancy scrawl. And it had made her proud. It had made her too darn proud.

Phoebe didn't stop talking even when Helen tried to apologize. Her words fell like bullets, rat-a-tat-tat in the now-empty dining room, and suddenly the room looked bigger, even cavernous to Helen. Wishing she could sit one last time in the first house she and Richard had owned when Phoebe was a baby, Helen felt swallowed by a gloom that she could not escape as she held Phoebe's frantic, searching glare. She collected herself and, with her eyes on Phoebe, took a sip from her water glass and waited. Phoebe had things to say, and Helen would not be able to say the right thing, but at least she could show her daughter how much she was hurting, too. At some point, someday, Phoebe might forgive her.

"What do you mean it's all true, Mom? If you knew it was wrong, why did you keep working more and more and more and more? What was ever going to be enough?" Phoebe's voice rose higher and higher, echoing off the walls and the varnished wood floors, and Helen's head roared with pain.

"You're right, Phoebe. I should have been home more." Helen leaned toward her daughter, as if to hold her, but Phoebe pulled away with a scowl.

"Why weren't you home more?" She scratched her hand on the tablecloth; the sound of it bore into Helen's head.

"I don't know."

"Why was work so important to you?" Her daughter's anger was like a thing of its own, alive, throbbing and dangerous. The walls looked to Helen as though they were vibrating and shifting, but it was because she was shaking. *Phoebe mustn't see me shake*, she thought, but even if she was in control, it didn't matter. Phoebe wasn't focused on the Helen who sat beside her. A decade of hurt feelings and disappointments and worse had coalesced in this moment, and the smell in the air, the warm, yellow light from the chandelier . . . none of it was reaching her daughter. She had become an elemental force and the rage inside her drowned out everything else in the room.

When Helen didn't respond right away, Phoebe continued shouting. "You don't know why you worked so much, but I know one thing: You weren't there. You weren't there the long nights I spent with him. You weren't there." Her voice seemed to roar louder and louder, and the words drilled into Helen like hot nails. Phoebe stood up from the table and looked down on her mother. "What was so important, Mom, that kept you from being home? Where in the hell were you? Why? Mom? Why? Why didn't I fucking matter?"

Tears streamed down Phoebe's face. Helen felt like she had been electrocuted. *I am dead. Everything is dead. I am dead inside; I am nothing and no one and it was not . . . what have I done? What have I done? I failed my Phoebe, my Phoebe, my daughter.* Helen opened her mouth to scream, but she was sobbing too hard to make any sound. An icy sensation entered her heart and she crumpled to the ground by her chair.

Shoes squeaked on the polished hardwood floors and Cary and Miranda rushed into the dining room. Helen lay curled up on the floor, and Phoebe was staring at her mother in shock. Miranda and Cary exchanged a glance, and Miranda, with an arm on Phoebe's elbow, murmured, "Come on, love, let's get you up to bed."

The staircase creaked as Miranda guided Phoebe out through the entrance to the foyer and walked her up the steps and to her room. Speaking in her firm, competent way, Miranda set Phoebe down on the edge of the bed and pulled the covers back while she kept one hand on the girl's shoulder. Somewhere in the distance an owl hooted and broke the still silence of the night. Still too shocked to speak, Phoebe crawled under the covers and turned a helpless, frightened face toward the aging woman.

"Everything is going to be okay, sweet child," Miranda whispered, and she sat beside what was really just a sad little girl, keeping a protective arm around her shoulder until Phoebe drifted off to sleep.

•••

Back in the dining room, Cary knelt beside Helen and placed an arm on the attorney's shoulder, waiting for her to open her eyes. Helen's eyes rolled backward and her jaw remained locked in a silent scream. Cary quickly calculated whether she should treat mother or daughter, and realized that she didn't have a choice. This was an emergency. Helen, already suffering from shock, was close to having a psychological breakdown. And Phoebe needed a mother, so Cary was going to have to figure out a way to get Helen back on her feet emotionally as well as physically.

Cary could feel Helen shaking under her hand. Any mother would feel guilty in this situation. The guilt could be addressed in treatment, but it could never be erased; the key thing was to help Helen find the possibility of redemption. Cary needed to instill in her some hope that she could find a bridge to peace, and she needed to start now.

Helen's hair was a mess and her eyes focused on everything and nothing. Cary got all the way down on the floor so that her face rested six inches from Helen's, and she tried to find a piece of Helen in the attorney's gray-blue eyes. Nothing. Helen's body was there, but her mind seemed to have abandoned her.

Cary reached out and grabbed Helen's hand. "Helen, if you can understand me, please squeeze my hand."

The attorney's long, thin fingers depressed the skin on Cary's hand, and the therapist sighed with relief. At least her patient wasn't catatonic.

"Are you feeling guilty for what happened to Phoebe?"

Helen's eyes searched for Cary's and she opened her mouth to speak, and this time the word "Yes" mixed with a sob. Helen's chest heaved.

"You feel like you should have done more to protect her, Helen?" Cary spoke in a soothing voice. Helen gripped Cary's hand and finally, as tears fell, great sobs rushed from Helen's throat.

For a few minutes the attorney lay on her side next to Cary, and Cary took in all of Helen's pain until it felt like her own. For Cary, there was something tragic in watching the fall of one of the country's top-ranked female attorneys, seeing this competent, confident, almost royal woman, now broken.

And then Cary was crying, too. She didn't quite understand why she was crying, but she had no other response, no clinically detached advice to offer this woman who had fallen so far.

Finally Helen sighed and pulled herself off the floor. Cary kept a hand on her elbow as Helen gripped the polished, dark wood banister and climbed the stairs. Once, Helen fell into Cary's arms and allowed the therapist to support her for a few moments. Cary patted Helen on the back and did not let go until Helen did. Then, with a weak smile, Helen waved and headed down the hallway to her own room.

•••

On her way to her room, Helen paused outside Phoebe's door and knocked on it twice. Hearing nothing, she turned the old-fashioned metal doorknob and tiptoed across the creaky wood floor. Helen knelt beside the bed and rested her chin on the cold white sheet. She whispered, "I am so sorry, Phoebe. None of this was your fault. Please forgive me," and her voice cracked.

CHAPTER 29

Cassandra opened one eye and took in the luxurious feel of sleeping late on Saturday. She stretched and felt for Frank, but his side of the bed was vacant. Alarm gave way to relief. Of course. Frank, an early riser, got up with Zander most weekend mornings and let Cassandra sleep a bit later. Birds in the maple tree next to her bedroom window twittered, and Cassandra tuned out their too-cheerful melodies. She hated mornings and wanted to curl up and sleep more, but she needed to leave for the Bryson House in an hour.

Cassandra felt old as she crept down the stairs and waited for her arthritic feet to stop burning and aching with each landing. Getting old made her feel annoyed. She gritted her teeth and forced a neutral expression onto her face as she rounded the corner and limped into the kitchen.

"Mama!" Zander screamed at rocket launch decibel. Cassandra winced and smiled at the same time, bracing herself as Zander launched all of his forty pounds like a linebacker at her legs. Frank laughed.

Cassandra chuckled and picked her son up and hugged him. "Good morning, darling," she murmured, kissing his curly hair and cheeks.

Cassandra looked at Frank over Zander's head. "Coffee, please. Now." Frank nodded with a good-natured smile and handed Cassandra her favorite white mug, the largest one in the house. She had taken her coffee from the same mug for almost a decade, and the writing on the side of it had nearly worn off from thousands of dishwasher cycles. Still, it was her favorite mug; and as she held the handle and closed her eyes, she took her first sip of black coffee and felt a little better.

As Cassandra contemplated coffee and its role in sobriety, Zander tapped her arm and interrupted her. "Horses, Mama? We will go see horses? *Puh-leeze?* And doughnuts? I want a doughnut and I wanna see horses!"

Cassandra leaned against the counter, where she could see Frank and also keep an eye on the clock above the front wall of the kitchen. It was a quarter of eight, and she could feel the time ticking by.

"Frank, I need to work at the Bryson House most of this weekend. I meant to tell you about this last night, but you fell asleep right after Zander."

Cassandra tried to force a gentler tone into her voice and to smile at Frank, but it was no use. She was on a case, as her father—a police officer—would have said, and she was dialed in and serious. Frank had a demanding practice and he understood Cassandra's focused expression, but she knew he worried about her whenever she worked a difficult case. She tended to internalize her clients' concerns and work the fine details of a case out in her head at all hours of the night. While this made her a heck of a lawyer, it also turned her into a ghost for weeks on end.

Still, Frank couldn't change the woman he loved. He'd learned this several years ago the hard way, when he scheduled a romantic getaway that conflicted with one of her trial dates. Without a moment's hesitation, she had refused to go to Hawaii with him; and when he had threatened to go on the vacation alone, Cassandra had glared back at him and retorted, "Suit yourself. I have a client to represent." Frank had taken that vacation alone. They never spoke of it, but from then on, Frank always checked her calendar before he planned anything for the family.

Frank sighed, and Cassandra felt a tug of loneliness and frustration. He'd been gone for two weeks. She knew she wanted to spend time with her, to spend time with all of them as a family. And while Cassandra the wife cared, Cassandra the lawyer did not. She could not afford to worry about Frank. He'd always said he was a big boy and could take care of himself. Cassandra tried again, this time with an even softer tone. "I am so sorry, Frank. I'll be back in time for dinner. And I'll take Zander with me, if that's okay with you. That should give you some free time."

"It's okay. I'm a big boy," he grinned. "Anyway, it's been a long time since I've spent time with just Cat. I'm sure we can amuse ourselves." An image of Phoebe flashed through Cassandra's mind, and before she could stop herself she pictured Catherine in Phoebe's place. For a moment, the briefest of moments, her mind switched Frank for Richard, and she grabbed the edge of the counter and counted to ten, very slowly, in her head.

Frank is safe. I am safe. Cat is safe. Zander is safe.

Cassandra let go of the countertop and, after smiling at Zander, she turned on a *Thomas & Friends* DVD and asked Frank to come and talk with her upstairs.

Up in their bedroom, Frank hugged Cassandra and began kissing her on the neck, which made her tremble a little. She almost resented how weak his kisses made her feel, how much they made her desire him. But she was working the case now, and after a brief hesitation she engaged what felt like a shield. "Frank, this case, it's going to heat up and be really hard," Cassandra said, putting her hands on Frank's chest and pushing him back a little. "I need to get out there and talk to my client."

"What's it about?"

She sat on the edge of the bed and stretched her hamstrings before she answered her husband. "You know Helen Thompson? The attorney."

"Yes. I met her husband, Judge Thompson, at a legal function." Frank yawned and did not look at the pile of his clothing on the floor at the foot of their bed. Cassandra wanted to pick the clothes up; even more, she wanted to burn each article of junk and leave it outside for the garbage truck to collect.

Instead of continuing, she waved her arm at the laundry and lifted one eyebrow.

He glanced at the laundry. "I'll get it later."

Cassandra hated when Frank promised to get to things later, because she had no control over when later would happen. This was making her anxious. If she lost her temper now, they would fight and not make up until that night, and her anger would make her feel even more shattered and sad inside. She counted to ten a second time. "Please pick your laundry off the floor. It might seem small to you, but it bothers me and I feel like I'm going to yell at you. And if I yell at you, we will argue and we will both feel like crap all day, and I really, really need things to be okay between us because this case is tearing me apart."

While talking, Cassandra had moved closer to Frank, placing her head on his shoulder. He stroked her hair and lay down, bringing her down onto the bed with him. For a few minutes he just held her. She knew he was waiting for her to tell him what was really bothering her, but she wasn't sure herself. It wasn't the laundry. They both knew that.

Cassandra ran her hand along his arm and breathed her husband's smell. She tried to organize her thoughts about Helen and Phoebe as she gave Frank a rough outline of the case. Frank listened quietly and did not ask any questions until Cassandra had finished talking.

"You've got your hands full for sure. Do you think this will go to trial?"

Cassandra glanced at the clock and Frank kissed her head. "I hope it doesn't go to trial. I don't know how much more Phoebe can take."

He sat and began folding his laundry. "Well, I suppose the least I can do is pick up my shit, so here you go," he said with a grin.

"Thank you, darling," Cassandra said with a smile as she started to undress for the shower. She walked into the bathroom, turned on the water in the shower and waited for it to heat up. "For now, Phoebe's safe. I need to get to work on keeping it that way."

"Well, Counselor, I'll try to get something done around the house today and go to the store. Maybe Cat will come and help me. The fridge looked pretty bare last time I checked." Frank watched the steam rise from the shower. "Now get your sweet soul out to your client's!"

•••

After she had finished getting ready, Cassandra slipped into Catherine's bedroom and sat next to her daughter. Catherine's blonde hair spread out like a messy fan on her pillow, and Cassandra looked around the room and suppressed a giggle. At some point over the summer, Cat had torn down her posters of high-pitched male pop singers and in their place had taped up pictures of Joan Benoit Samuelson, the famous runner "Pre" and several modern American athletes. Cassandra almost missed the airbrushed teen idols. *Almost.* Now, a couple of her own icons were staring back at her from her daughter's Wall of Fame, and the thought that her offspring would draw strength from this familiar well filled her with pride. These had been her heroes, too.

But more than pride swelled in her heart as she sat in silence next to her easygoing, sweet-natured child. Nothing about Catherine's pregnancy had come easily. Cassandra had been alone for all of the ob-gyn appointments. Overworked, angry and too often drunk, Tim had disengaged from her during the pregnancy. No one had sat next to her during her sonograms, trying to detect arms and legs and other body parts. No one had fetched her ice cream at midnight; no one had rubbed her sore feet in the third trimester. Even when she had given birth, Tim had not been there to hold her hand and place ice cubes in her mouth as she pushed. Yet through it all, Cassandra had clung to the daughter inside of her, praying that this baby would make her stronger. Praying that the baby would bring Tim back from the precipice and change him from the monster he was becoming. *If only*, she had repeated over and over again, *if only I can hang on and stay strong.* But now, she knew that had been all wrong. Being strong wasn't staying and sticking it out. She should have left him a lot earlier than she did.

Cassandra watched the sheets rising and falling with each breath Catherine took, and she thought back to the times when she had checked in on her newborn baby in the middle of the night. How often had she watched her daughter sleep? Every day or night for seventeen years made for a lot of private moments, all of them different, but all of them united by a mother's love. Cassandra smiled at her sleeping daughter. *I love you so very much. Always.* Catherine's eyes fluttered and opened. *Was I thinking so loud she heard me?*

"Hi, Mom," Catherine murmured. Then, smiling, she turned on her side toward Cassandra and fell back asleep.

CHAPTER 30

Phoebe smelled the hay and the manure as soon as she opened the front door and began trudging outside in the pre-dawn darkness. She wore lined breeches, a long-sleeved t-shirt, a sweatshirt and a thin barn coat that flexed when she moved her shoulders. She wasn't even sure where all the perfectly-fitting clothes had come from. *Probably Anne.* The edge of her long boots scuffed the porch steps, but she stretched her arms out, feeling her muscles flex and contract, and caught herself from falling. For some reason she thought of Anne walking down the same steps and envisioned her scuffing her black boots in the same place and not catching herself before she smashed into the hard earth. Anne was aging. She was getting old, maybe too old to ride soon.

Phoebe tightened her jaw and pushed thoughts of falling out of her mind, and yet she could not stop the spark of tenderness in her heart from igniting. She had only known Anne for a day, but already she was missing her before she was gone.

I am afraid of losing her. She is old and I want her to be around for me. Will she be there or will she leave, too? What if I love her and she leaves too soon? Is it ever time for someone we love to leave us?

Phoebe shook off her thoughts and threaded her way down the grassy path that led through the gathering of pines to the stables.

A barn door clicked, and Phoebe heard the squeak of hinges and the whinny of a horse carrying through the heavy air. The stars stood out in the indigo sky and the girl paused before she opened the outer fence gate. With both hands on the uneven wood, she closed her eyes and took a deep breath. She felt anxious and excited, but desperate to drink in the moment as though it were the last early morning she would have. She nodded as if hearing someone whispering in her ear.

It is the only time I will feel this now, this first time training with Anne, and I want to hold on and not let go of it. Why must moments, good moments, pass? And why do the bad moments have to linger?

A horse whinnied again. Phoebe opened her eyes and realized that the moment, that moment that she could not freeze, had already changed. The first delicate ribbon of light had emerged far off in the distance. In fifteen minutes, the sun would rise with its orange-purple brilliance. Another day, this day, would begin.

With an easy athletic move, Phoebe skipped the gate door and hopped the fence. When she landed, she swung her arms and grinned. At McClintock, both the field hockey and the lacrosse coaches had tried to recruit Phoebe; but as she had explained with a dismissive shrug, she had bigger and better goals than helping teams win state titles. Those coaches, like so many of Phoebe's classmates, had thought her arrogant and had quickly written her off as not being a team player. Phoebe shook free of these thoughts and tried to focus on the day ahead of her as a stern voice called out from inside the barn.

"Phoebe?"

"I'm in here." Phoebe felt lightness in her heart and walked toward the voice. "Morning, Anne—er, Mrs. McCaffrey," she stuttered. "Gosh, what should I call you?"

Anne handed a pitchfork to Phoebe and nodded in the direction of Lusitania. "Come on this way. Let's get some of that crap cleared up before we check shoes and saddles."

Phoebe giggled. "Do you always call it 'horse shit' or is this a test to see if I am serious enough?"

Anne held the door open long enough for Phoebe to grab it with her right hand. "Good Lord, child, I am too old for tests and games. I'm just calling it 'horse shit' because that is what it is.

And shoveling horse shit is good, honest work. It's the sort of work that you have got to learn to love if you're going to ride at the highest levels." Anne paused and her tone grew serious. "As far as what you should call me, I don't care; but your mom does, and it's important to me that you respect her wishes."

"What does it matter what she says?" Phoebe's voice had a hard edge to it.

"This isn't so much about her, Phoebe. It's more about what's best for you. And I think that showing your mom respect is good for you."

Phoebe reflected on Anne's words as they stood side by side in the stall. For several minutes they worked in silence, with only an occasional whinny or the movement of tree branches to distract them from their work. Every so often Lusitania flicked his tail and caught Phoebe in the shoulder with it. Phoebe felt as though the horse meant to hit her, and finally she looked up with annoyance. "Enough, Lusitania! I feel you." Phoebe patted Lusitania's neck and then asked, "Why is it best for me, the whole call-you-by-your-last-name thing? How is that showing you respect if you don't want me to call you Ms. or Mrs. or whatever?"

"I'm not talking about showing *me* respect. You show me respect by showing up here every day and following my instructions to a T. I will not tolerate anything less. And I want to be clear about that right from the start," Anne added seriously. "No questions. No smirks. No eye rolls. And if you have any questions or don't want to do what I tell you, then you save it for after practice. When you're in the stirrups, I expect complete and total obedience."

Phoebe gripped the pitchfork a lot tighter. She felt torn between an involuntary reflex to scream and an even scarier reaction: relief. For years she had outperformed anyone else within earshot of her in the ring and on the trails, and as much as it had stroked her young ego, it also made her feel stagnant and oddly unsettled. Her ambition, so great, thirsted for something more. She sighed. Ambition warred with her inner rebel. To buy time, she replied tersely, "Those are the terms you give everyone you train?"

With starch in her voice, Anne said, "These are my terms, yes. Do you accept?"

"I'm not an idiot."

Anne continued to shovel horse manure.

"Just one thing that bugs me," Phoebe drawled, and she waited for Anne to look up.

Anne stopped shoveling and flexed her hand. "What's that?"

"Your name is too long! What if I am trying to get your attention mid-canter and you don't hear me yelling the first time?"

"Would you be yelling around a horse?"

"Exactly. Can't I call you something shorter, like Coach? It's still respectful, right? But it isn't so darn long."

"Okay," Anne proclaimed. "We have a deal. You can call me Coach as long as—"

"I obey you unconditionally and don't give you any shit," Phoebe interrupted.

"Um, right, and I was going to tell you to stop using that word, but the fact is that around here there is a lot of shit. We ride in it, through it and among it," Anne chuckled.

"And we smell it everywhere, even in our sleep," Phoebe cracked.

"Golly, I hope not." Anne cleared her throat and walked past Phoebe.

The light bulb in the barn no longer created a contrast between the dark early-morning sky and the inside of the building. The sun had risen above the horizon and sunbeams flickered in through the windows. Within each beam danced tiny dust particles, and Phoebe observed them and felt sad. The bits of dust reminded her of a crowd of strangers thrown together for an unknown cause, and she remembered all the days she had spent working alone in a barn, with just the dust in the air to keep her company.

"Coach?" Phoebe's voice wavered a little bit.

"Yes, my dear?"

Phoebe squirmed and looked down at the hay.

"Spill it," Anne ordered.

What Phoebe really wanted to ask was whether Anne thought her mom would come down to watch practice, but instead she tried to smile and change the subject. "Do you really think I have a chance if I do everything you tell me?"

Anne observed Phoebe and then, with a curt nod, replied, "There are no guarantees of anything in life. I don't like making promises that aren't up to me to keep. Do I think you have a chance? Yes. Otherwise I wouldn't spend time working with you. I promise I'll do my best by you. I promise that there is hope, and not just for the future. There is hope now. There's always hope."

•••

Helen awoke from a fitful sleep and rolled over, hoping to catch a glimpse of her watch. She shook her head in confusion and tried to remember why she wasn't wearing her watch, and then she remembered where she was, and the realization of it all, this inner jail, this heck she was in, lit her brain with fear and sadness and regret. No, she realized, it went much deeper than that. She felt waves of grief, or maybe it was guilt, and the sheer intensity of it all overwhelmed her. For years she had felt next to nothing, but now it seemed she could accomplish little besides feeling.

Pulling on a pair of slippers Mimi had given her, Helen wandered out of bed and tried to find her laptop. After she powered it up, she sat in an upholstered antique chair and imagined the seconds ticking past while the computer loaded her firm's intranet web page. It used to take four minutes and thirty seconds to load, back when Phoebe was five; now, it loaded in forty-two seconds.

Helen clicked over to her e-mail and groaned. Four hundred messages. She really couldn't contemplate sorting through them all. *Oh no*, Helen thought, *if I don't go through them and we have a Monday filing . . . no way. I'll check it later.*   With a sigh, Helen shut her computer and waded into the shower, trying not to think about what Phoebe had said to her at dinner. She couldn't bear to focus on it for too long because in her heart she knew that everything Phoebe had said to her was right. The last ten years of her life had passed in a whirl; she'd been sleepwalking through the pages of her daughter's days. The guilt pressed harder and harder in on her like a vice, and before she knew the wave was coming, grief again engulfed her. Helen crouched in the shower and cried and hoped the water would wash away more than her tears.

•••

Helen checked her laptop one last time after she got out of the shower. *I really should return some of these messages,* she thought, but she was just too tired, *so tired.* Instead, she absentmindedly began flipping through the back pages of an equestrian magazine Phoebe had left lying around in Helen's bedroom. She circled a few ads and made notes in the margins, but with a groan quickly realized that she knew next to nothing about horses. She had a lot of catching up to do.

Fifteen minutes later, Helen walked through the kitchen, stopping long enough to pour a cup of coffee. She didn't run into Mimi and she was relieved. Right now, she only wanted to watch Phoebe ride.

•••

Anne fixed her steady gray eyes on her charge. "What do you say we get to work?"

Their boots pounded the wood floors as they brought their horses outside into the early autumn sun. Phoebe wanted to ask why Anne was holding a rope instead of leading Lusitania, but she knew better than to question her new teacher.

Anne faced Phoebe and Phoebe squinted as the equestrian lectured her. "First, Phoebe, I want to get a thorough assessment of what you can and cannot do on a horse. Usually I will start the morning off with lunge lessons or work creating your seat—you do know what lunge lessons are, right?"

Phoebe hesitated, and Anne gave her an encouraging smile. "No harm in not knowing something, Phoebe. I'll tell you what. I am going to guide you through the lesson, so if you would kindly take hold on this line," she ordered. "And help me tie it to the ring on the lunging cavesson, and then we can get started." Phoebe watched Anne place what always reminded her of a dog's halter on Ginger's head and secure it so that the rings were situated just in front of the horse's mouth.

Anne gestured at Phoebe for the flat line and quickly secured it to the rings. "It is time to mount your horse, please. Often for lunge lessons I will get you on an older, steadier horse, but we're going to just hit the basics with the lunge and warm up with some gentle walking, trotting and cantering. Later we might segue into some jumping. But we must make sure we get Ginger warmed up, which is essential before she executes any jumps.

Please remember that the whole point of this exercise is getting you to focus on creating your seat."

Phoebe swung her leg over Ginger's saddle and breathed in the early morning dew. She felt like smiling, but her mouth didn't move.

"Please remember that Ginger has a sensitive mouth. Especially when you jump, you need to be mindful of how you yank the bit and grip the reins."

Phoebe nodded, and Anne began what at first felt like a boring park promenade. Anne remained in the center of a twenty-yard circle and led Ginger around it. After a few minutes the older equestrian began giving Phoebe more complicated instructions. Holding onto the reins as evenly and gently as possible, Phoebe bicycled and scissor-kicked her legs, she touched her feet over the neck and rump of her horse, she rode with her feet out of the stirrups and she posted without stirrups. The girl continued to perform everything Anne asked her to do. For the most part her facial expression barely changed; and though occasionally a tinge of consternation, a slight suggestion of frustration, crossed her brow, it never lasted more than a few moments.

Anne spoke in a level tone as Phoebe made another lap. "You need to ride in your own plane, Phoebe. Pretend you're sitting in a geometrical plane, and no matter what your horse is doing below you, stay in your plane."

Phoebe grunted softly.

"And your finger just tapped the reins again. Stillness. Ginger can feel every ounce of pressure, and it will affect her movement."

For more than a half-hour they worked through the lunge lessons. Finally Anne called out, "Good, Phoebe, bring her in to the center now."

Anne made the most minimal of remarks while explaining the sort of jumps Phoebe would be attempting. Phoebe, for her part, concentrated on remaining still in her seat the entire way through each jump, and after a few jumps she felt as though she had been jumping Ginger for years. Phoebe took a deep breath and relaxed just a little. She noticed that the leaves on a tree branch in the distance were turning orange, and she wished that she could slow it down, the moments, the minutes, these minutes, just a little bit.

She lined Ginger up and headed into her next jump. They moved fast, but a controlled fast, and Phoebe foresaw the angle she needed to take. Then out of the corner of her eye, she sensed motion. She tried to wait until she had completed the jump to shift her attention, but something about the figure moving in the distance felt too familiar. It was her mother, and for a split second Phoebe thought that now, finally, she had a chance to show her mother what she could do. *I will make her proud.*

And in that split second of inattention, a tiny brown rabbit popped out of the ground just a few yards from Ginger, and Ginger startled and bucked and broke from the approach mid-stride. That was all it took to break the connection between horse and rider. Looking back, Phoebe could never pinpoint the exact cause or even the exact moment when she no longer was upright.

One moment Phoebe sat tall in her seat, in control. In the next, she was flying or falling through the air, and she had no idea what she had done wrong. All she could think about was getting her feet free. By the time Phoebe had yanked her feet out of the stirrups, she could smell the thick Virginia clay and the horse manure mixed into it. She tried to get her arms out in front of her, but the ground hit her right wrist sideways. At first she felt nothing, then pain and fear. *Where is Ginger?* Phoebe closed her eyes, waiting for the worst.

•••

From up on the hill, Helen watched her daughter fall. Before Phoebe even hit the ground, Helen was running faster than she had ever run. She threw her coffee mug over her shoulder and raced to the fence, clambering over it like a much younger woman and sprinting to her daughter's side. Helen's fancy black shoes got stuck in the reddish-brown clay and the horse manure before she reached Phoebe, and she felt the cold, mud-like clay rising from her feet all the way up to her ankle bones. The tight bun holding her hair in place slipped, and her thick auburn hair tumbled in front of her face. Helen reached Phoebe and threw herself into the clay and the manure and covered her daughter from the approaching horse.

Ginger came to a total stop. Perhaps she had noticed Helen running across the ring; perhaps seeing another human, a grown human, had interrupted her sense of panic. Breathless, Anne jogged over and took hold of Ginger's reins.

Helen thought about the blood buried under the red clay battlefields. Her heart beat too fast as she looked at her daughter, who was vacantly staring up at the sky, unmoving. Helen held onto her and waited, and finally Phoebe moved her head toward her mother and raised an eyebrow. "Mom, your shoes are covered in horse shit. Does that mean we get to go shopping after we go to the hospital?"

CHAPTER 31

It only took Helen and Phoebe three hours to drive to the emergency room and obtain an x-ray and a soft cast for the girl's fractured left arm. Helen had refused to listen to Mimi and Miranda's warnings about the security risk of leaving the Bryson House. In the parking lot, Helen opened the door for Phoebe and helped her into the passenger seat.

"Hey, Mom?" Phoebe grimaced as she glanced at her seat belt.

Before Helen inserted the key into the ignition, she leaned over and tugged on Phoebe's belt. As she clicked it and double-checked to make sure it had locked, she felt someone's eyes on her; but when she looked around, all she saw was the back of a blue sedan heading toward the rear of her car. Startled, she hit the horn just in time and shook her head as the car peeled out of the parking lot with a screech of Goodyears on asphalt.

"Good grief. Teenagers." Helen looked over at Phoebe, but her daughter's eyes were closed. *Stop being paranoid. But shoot, I shouldn't have left without someone else with us.*

On the ride back to the Bryson House, Phoebe's eyes flew open when they passed a sign for the Equestrian Outfitters store in Warrenton, located between Fairfax and Middleburg. "Mom? Let's stop here, okay? Get you geared up?" Phoebe gestured toward the sign for the store. After a glance in her rearview mirror, Helen tapped her finger on the steering wheel.

Maybe now would be a good time to figure out if someone is following us. Before I get to an abandoned country ride. After all, a few of Richard's friends are still out there.

She might be crazy, but it seemed like a blue car was trailing a few cars behind her. *Don't be paranoid, Helen,* she thought, but she couldn't help adding to herself, *Don't be stupid, either.*

With a show of reluctance, Helen pulled the BMW into a parking lot filled with pickup trucks, SUVs and horse trailers. Inside the store, Phoebe walked right over to racks of boots and stared, rapt, at a pair that looked just like Anne's. Helen stopped in her tracks and took in the array of saddles, bridles, stirrups and other tack. In another part of the store she saw horse supplies and stable supplies, but she couldn't even figure out what most of it was for, so she kept walking until she came to the riding apparel section.

Phoebe sidled up to Helen, dragging a cart loaded with duplicate pairs of breeches, a five hundred-dollar navy show coat, chaps, gloves and helmets. "There, Mom, that should get us both started."

As Phoebe walked away, gesturing to her mother to follow, Helen tried to slow her down. "Why two pairs?"

"Come this way, Mom." Phoebe fidgeted with her soft cast. "We need boots, too. I found a perfect pair that looks just like Anne's, and I saw a pair for you in burgundy that look more like Ms. White's boots." Phoebe glanced over her shoulder. "Oh. Two pairs because I grew since you bought my last set and I can't be wearing secondhand crap, now can I?" She winked at her mother and flipped her hair.

Helen caught up to her daughter and gasped when she saw the boots Phoebe had picked out. Accustomed to shelling out five hundred dollars for dress shoes, Helen didn't care about the price. She was captivated by the fine detail and craftsmanship on the leather, and without a word she lifted the boots and smelled them. "Mmm," she murmured. "Yes, these will do."

Phoebe pointed at long, lustrous black dressage boots. "So," the girl said, looking up from under her eyelashes as she knelt on the dusty floor, "what do you think of these boots?"

"Aside from the price tag, you mean?"

Phoebe grasped the boots. "Yeah, aside from the price tag. I mean, can I please have them? Please?"

Helen nodded. Out of the corner of her eye she glimpsed a familiar blue car make a U-turn in front of the Equestrian Outfitters store and pull into the gas station to the right of the building. With an odd foreboding, she snapped, "Phoebe! We have to get going. Please grab me a few pairs of jeans over there, size six, and catch up to me. I'm going to start checking out."

Accustomed to doing what Helen told her, and still wanting to ingratiate herself before Helen could change her mind about the boots, Phoebe moved quickly. Five minutes later, Helen had popped open the trunk and thrown the purchases inside and was guiding her daughter to the passenger seat. As she fastened her own belt, Helen found herself craning her neck to see if the blue car was still at the gas station. It was gone. *Stop being paranoid, Helen.*

•••

When Helen and Phoebe returned to the Bryson House, the sound of tractors droned in the distance. Cassandra waved from the front porch as Zander bounded down the steps and skidded to a stop a few feet from Phoebe. But before Phoebe had a chance to acknowledge him, the boy had caught sight of a horse trotting in the ring and was running back to yell about horses to his mother. Phoebe hesitated. "Mom, can I go talk to my coach?"

"Of course. Please thank her for splinting your arm so professionally. And come on back to the house at one o'clock. Sascha is coming after lunch, and if your arm starts to hurt . . ."

"I know, Mom, I know," Phoebe interrupted with a smile that started at the corners of her eyes. She began ambling off down the path, but then turned and walked back to Helen. She looked over her mother's shoulder and then down at her mother's new boots.

"Um? I um, I am . . ." Phoebe fumbled around for words. Then she set her shoulders. "I'm really sorry."

"Phoebe!" Helen brought her hand up to her neck. "I am the one who owes you an apology. This is something that will haunt me for the rest of my days. I should have been home more. I am so sorry, and it's so good, so right, that Mrs. McCaffrey calls you a child of light, because that is why I named you Phoebe." Helen reached over and smoothed her daughter's long brown hair. "I had another name picked out, you know," she said. "And then I held you for the first time and a beam of sunshine fell on you, and I just knew. And it all looks dark now, and I bear so much of the responsibility, and I know that. But I vow with all that I am and ever will be that I will do everything in my power to make it right. To get you the help you need, and to be a better mother. And not just now, but always."

Phoebe reached out with her right arm and grabbed Helen's hand, and Helen gave up trying to hold back tears. Phoebe stared into her mother's eyes as if searching for something. Finally she squeezed Helen's hand and whispered, "It hurts so much."

"I know, darling." Helen moved to rest her chin atop her daughter's head. She could smell shampoo and the scent of tack and hay, and she inhaled. *This is my daughter. I will remember this smell, this moment, for the rest of my days.*

As she watched Phoebe head off toward the stables, Helen wiped her eyes on her sleeve with a tired smile and decided to ignore the message light blinking on her iPhone. Whoever it was could wait for a few more minutes. She had recorded a message advising her clients to contact Carl in the case of an emergency; right now it was time to focus on Phoebe and on her own case. Helen glanced at her new boots and allowed herself an admiring smile as she pocketed her phone. She could get used to this country life in a hurry.

•••

"Sorry I'm late," she said to Cassandra. "I hope you didn't have to wait too long for us to get back from the hospital."

Cassandra tried not to stare at Helen's disheveled appearance. "Oh no, not at all," she said lamely. "Are those boots new? It almost looks like you were out riding this morning?"

Helen was covered in reddish-brown clay and manure. Her dry-clean-only slacks and merino wool sweater were smeared and muddied; for the first time in years, Helen was a mess. Helen shrugged at Cassandra and started walking away. "I will see you back here in a few minutes, Cass, after I change into something . . . clean."

On the way to the hospital, Helen had telephoned Cassandra and filled her in on Phoebe's fall. She had requested that they meet outdoors and talk and walk rather than sit all day cramped up in the study. Cassandra liked this idea. One of the reasons she had started up her own law firm more than a decade ago was so that she could stop worrying about appearances. Then, too, if they walked the grounds for part of the interview, Zander would remain in her orbit and she wouldn't feel so guilty about missing a Saturday with him.

When Helen returned wearing jeans and a blue and black flannel shirt that they'd bought at the Outfitters, Cassandra smiled. Helen looked like a different woman. She had let her hair down in more ways than one. Cassandra almost said something, but thought better of it. She could hear her internal deadline clock ticking; they had a lot of testimony to prepare before the meeting on Monday.

"Ready?" Cassandra spoke in a businesslike tone.

Her hands behind her back, Helen nodded. "Yes. I even left my iPhone inside so that I could concentrate better. It won't stop blinking and I can't understand why the world needs to stop just because I'm away for a little while. It's strange, Cass. I have been unplugged for the last twenty-four hours, but instead of worrying about my clients or the darn home office, I almost feel calmer knowing that I'm not first chair right now."

"So that great associate of yours has an eye on all your cases?"

Helen squinted off into the distance and pulled her large Dior sunglasses over her eyes before responding. "I hope so. If he doesn't, all hell could break loose."

Helen laughed tersely, and Cassandra remained quiet for a few moments. She thought back to the first law firm she'd worked for, and about the old adage that an attorney owes her first and last duty to her client. *Only a man could have come up with that simple-sounding nonsense*, thought Cassandra. *A mother owes her first and last duty to her children, is more like it.* "I'm sure your cases are in good hands," she reassured Helen. "Speaking of cases, let's get started. We have a lot of material to go over."

•••

While Helen paced the grounds at Cassandra's side, Phoebe was following the path that led from the main house to Anne's chalet, which was situated a half-mile away. She caught sight of Zander hop-walking behind a slightly harried-looking

Jamie, and she suppressed a giggle. Zander reminded her of Sascha's little brother, and she imagined the two boys torturing Jamie. The thought pleased her far too much.

Built within the last decade, Anne's chalet looked as if it belonged on a ski slope rather than on the edge of a dense forest in the Virginia countryside. The chalet, squared off and built so that the front windows overlooked the stables, rose from its walk-out basement to a front door that opened onto the apex of a grassy hill. A flimsy screen door remained shut, but it blocked neither light nor wind, and the heavy, unpainted front door was open as though welcoming visitors.

Phoebe knocked on the wood panel flanking the screen door. Even before she could pull back her right hand to rap a second time, Anne's voice called out, "Come right in, Phoebe. But take your boots off! No matter how many times you wipe them on the front mat, there is no removing all of that red clay."

Anne gave Phoebe's arm a concerned frown, but before she could ask after it, Phoebe spoke. "Why do you keep calling it clay? I thought it was just plain brown mud?"

"Unless it was brought in from out of state, the ground here is known for its red clay. But you're right. It's not really red; it's more of a brown-red. Nonetheless, it is clay, not mud." Anne waved her hand. "Anyway, enough about clay."

Anne guided Phoebe past a mahogany gun cabinet. Phoebe gaped; it was partially opened and revealed more guns than Phoebe had ever seen stacked in one place. "Those all yours?"

"Yes. One thing I learned long ago was to handle a firearm. Maybe when that arm gets better, I'll take you out to the range."

Anne led Phoebe into the kitchen and turned on the stove to heat up the teakettle. With a gracious wave of her hand, she asked the girl to seat herself while she made them a cup of tea. "Did you ever eat breakfast this morning? I imagine you may have lost track of eating at the hospital."

Phoebe rested her head on her hand for a moment, then looked more animated. "No, you're right. I wasn't hungry, especially after the doctor read my x-ray and told me I might need surgery."

Anne set teabags into ornate blue and white teacups and reached over to grab a loaf of bread. "I'm so sorry. I feared from the way you fell that you might have banged that arm pretty badly. Shall I slice you a piece of homemade bread?"

"Yes, please. I think I'm starving and didn't even realize it."

Anne poured the tea, sliced the bread and set butter, strawberry jam and a couple of plates on the table. For a few minutes, Phoebe struggled to butter her bread in silence while Anne sat tall in her chair, silent and too respectful to try to help Phoebe. Then the equestrian broke the silence. "I once broke my collarbone in two places six weeks before the Olympics. I wasn't supposed to ride for eight weeks, but after four, I realized that it might be my last chance for Olympic gold. So I got back on the saddle and gritted my teeth through the pain."

"Did you get it?"

Anne shook her head and sipped from her teacup. "No, I placed fourth. So I took home no medal. But I gave it my all. No regrets."

A look of awe entered Phoebe's eyes. "Were you in pain when you rode?"

"Yes, I was."

"But it was worth it, right?"

"I suppose so. The Olympics are special. It's all for the marbles, so to speak: honor and country and all that. But I will guarantee one thing."

"What?" Phoebe gingerly held her teacup, which almost seemed too small for her fingers.

"You will not get back on a horse until that cast is off your arm, and until the doctor gives me written clearance."

Phoebe's shoulders slumped and she looked deflated. "Does that mean I won't be getting better until I get my cast off? Because that makes me feel like heck."

Anne reached over and took a piece of bread. "Not at all. As soon as you get a hard cast properly set, which I expect will happen on Monday or Tuesday if you don't need surgery, then we will get started on seat drills and core work. We will drill you a few hours a day and you will have abs of steel by the time I am done with you."

Phoebe contemplated what Anne said and gave a happy sigh. "I've never done core work before. Why's it so important? I don't mind doing the work of course." Phoebe looked proud and fierce for a moment. "I'm just curious."

Anne nodded and crossed her arms, her legs extended in front of her. "The core is essential for all riders because the core is what you use to influence the tempo of the horse, and also to encourage the horse's back to come up rather than hollow out. In the simplest terms, you use your core to lessen the impact of your weight in the saddle. You can't just bounce around up there and expect the horse will want to raise his back to meet that abuse. Does that make sense?"

Phoebe took another swallow of tea. "I suppose so, yes. And you said seat work. What is that?"

Anne gave a rueful chuckle. "Maybe I should have called it simulated riding."

Phoebe groaned with a good-natured smile. "Oh my God, you mean riding while I sit in a chair? That sounds boring!"

"It can be," Anne said. "But it will make you a better rider."

Phoebe relaxed and looked around Anne's small, neat kitchen. She liked the way it smelled of fresh-cut wood and orange spices and home-baked bread, and she felt a sudden wish to spend more time there. She'd never sipped tea out of a formal teacup or shared a loaf of bread with another woman. The whole thing made her feel wistful and almost a little tearful.

"Well," Anne said, "I have some work to do, and I always take Sundays off, but as soon as you get your hard cast on I'd like to meet with you at dawn in the stables so we can start our training. In the meantime, please visit me anytime. It gets a little too quiet here in the house sometimes."

•••

As Phoebe loped across the pasture that abutted the outer show ring, she spotted Jamie painting a fence post. As Jamie bent over, a tattoo became partially visible on the back of her neck. Jamie was wearing tattered jeans, and with the tattoo it was a cool sort of look, almost badass, but Phoebe could barely contain a sneer. Real riders wore breeches, not jeans. Still, the girl was intrigued enough to wander over for a closer look.

Before she could formulate a question, Jamie sighed and set down her paintbrush. Phoebe could smell the acrid, chemical odor of the paint. Wiping her forehead with her wrist, Jamie mumbled, "Hey, how's it going?"

Phoebe tried not to stare at Jamie's tattoo, but she didn't want to meet Jamie's eyes, either. Phoebe crossed her arms and examined the fence. "Do you have to paint all of the fences by yourself?"

Jamie swatted a fly off her neck, exposing more of the tattoo. It looked like a bird was flying through fire; Phoebe could make out the words, "Reborn again."

"Yeah, why?" Jamie chuckled suddenly. "Wanna help me paint?"

Her eyes still on the tattoo, Phoebe shook her head. "Oh God, no." She smiled faintly and, after a moment's hesitation, said, "Cool tattoo."

"Yep. Thanks."

"What's it mean?"

For a few seconds, the woman was silent. Then she fixed her eyes on Phoebe. "I was brutally assaulted a few years ago. He left me to die. I didn't die. It took months of rehab, painful rehab, but I got back to the point where I could ride again, thanks in large part to Auntie A."

"Auntie A?"

Jamie nodded, her black eyes fixed on Phoebe's with a glowing intensity. "Anne McCaffrey is my aunt. I was ten when my mom died, and Auntie A took me in. She trained me. Before the assault, I competed pretty seriously, but the damage to my brain means I can never jump again, and that's what I loved, so . . ." Jamie trailed off and reflected for a moment. "Well, anyway," she continued with a shrug, "Auntie A got me through all of the rehab, and she also got me started on working with the kids in the riding program."

Phoebe stared at Jamie. "How long ago was that?"

"Ten years, five months, three days. And not a moment goes by, you know, that I don't thank God for the days I've lived since."

"Even after the—"

"—the rape? Yes, Phoebe. It sucked. There's no getting around it. But I'm alive. And I have found peace. Here, with the horses and the kids and Auntie A. And in my own mind. So this tattoo is of a dove, actually. Doves symbolize peace, and I wanted to mix in some phoenix imagery; so the fire. The point is that I searched real hard for peace as a result of what I went through."

Phoebe tried to think of what to say, but her arm suddenly throbbed and she clutched at it.

Jamie glanced at Phoebe's arm. Her voice betrayed a smidge of sympathy as she asked, "Your arm okay? I heard you had a rough fall this morning. Something about a rabbit freaking out your horse, right?"

Phoebe tried to push the pain out of her mind. "I suppose Coach told you?"

"Yep." Jamie shoved her hand in her pocket. "We usually have breakfast together Saturday mornings, and Auntie A is a great cook." Jamie rose and shaded her eyes, looking off into the distance as if searching for something.

"What are you looking for?"

"Oh, nothing," Jamie shrugged. She had lost sight of Zander for a moment. Jamie wasn't irresponsible, but she had been busy with her weekend chores. One moment she was answering a barrage of questions from an adorable wreck of a little boy clutching a stuffed yellow chicken and a matchbox car. Then she bent over to open a can of primer, and as she wiped the thick paintbrush on the top of the can to make sure none of the paint spilled on the grass, she realized that Zander was no longer hopping at her side.

"Well, Zander ran off somewhere. I'll chase him down in a couple of minutes. He's a wild little guy." Jamie wiped her hands on her jeans and seemed to withdraw back into herself.

Phoebe grimaced and started to head toward the main house. She paused and looked back. "Thank you for telling me that."

"Yep. Sure, Pheebes." The use of the nickname made Phoebe feel like she belonged, and one side of her mouth turned up slightly.

"Hey, Pheebes," Jamie added, "if you spot Zander by the barn, will you please walk him back to me? I'm going to make sure he's not trying to catch goldfish out of Auntie A's pond."

Phoebe grunted in amusement and tried to wave, but her darn arm hurt too much.

•••

The rustic red barn was not locked; in fact, the door could be opened by a gentle push from a small child. Inside, a ladder led from the inside wall of the barn up to a push-through door that resembled a lid or the top to a trash can; once pushed, a small adult or a child could easily fit through the narrow space and access the roof. Until now, this ladder had not presented a problem or been a cause for concern.

•••

At first Zander raced off to search for four-leaf clovers. Then he spotted the red barn. Zander liked red barns. His Chickie liked red barns. His Chickie was born in a red barn and wanted to see if his Mama Chickie still lived in a red barn, so Zander ran across the pasture, pushed the barn door open and wandered inside. Zander paused. "Hey, Chickie, let's go look for your mama!"

Then he saw a ladder and he forgot all about Mama Chickie. Zander almost hopped with excitement. He really liked ladders. "Let's go, Chickie," he whispered, and shoved his car and Chickie into his pocket. Humming, Zander clambered up the ladder until he got to the top. He frowned at the lid until he remembered how he sometimes hid inside trash cans while playing hide-and-seek. All he had to do was push on the lid and he could climb out of the trash can, so he pushed on the weathered door. It opened. He saw sunlight.

"Roof," he murmured. "Is this the roof?" He grinned with excitement. "Roof!" Zander climbed up the last two steps and pulled himself through the opening, stumbling onto the roof. He looked around and saw big birds flying overhead and thought about his Chickie and grinned. It was time to free Chickie from captivity.

•••

From a few hundred yards away, Phoebe spotted Zander dancing around on the rooftop, and immediately she forgot about her throbbing arm. She could not see anyone else on the roof with Zander; the whole thing didn't make any sense. She trotted across the field, thinking briefly of Sascha and hoping her friend would be on time. The thick stalks of yellow grass made each footfall hurt a little, but she didn't falter or slow down until she reached the barn. The bright autumn sun beat down on her, and by the time she reached the door a layer of sweat had soaked through the back of her shirt. Her eyes burned from the blooming ragweed.

Phoebe grimaced when the barn door grazed her left shoulder on the backswing and gritted her teeth as she climbed the rickety ladder. No matter how she held her arm, the soft cast did very little to lessen the shock effects of anything that touched the left side of her upper body. She grunted and heaved herself up over the last step and onto the tar-colored roof.

Despite her pain, Phoebe laughed when she saw Zander crouching in the center of the roof, pretending to give his Chickie a ride on her matchbox car. "Hey, how is it going?" she asked in the same tone she used to guide a horse into a stall.

Zander mumbled something unintelligible. He was studying his Chickie and sucking his thumb. Phoebe knelt on the warm, grooved surface of the roof and waited patiently for Zander to repeat himself.

"Wanna see my Chickie fly?" he demanded, sounding almost angry as he spoke, his body lurching to the side.

Phoebe tried not to move suddenly, but inched toward him. The only problem was that he was heading closer to the edge. A few more feet, a sudden movement . . . Phoebe breathed in the roof tar and thought about a wild colt. That's what she was dealing with.

"No. You cannot go any closer to the edge. If you do, you could get hurt, and so could I." Phoebe shook her head strictly and inched still closer to the little boy.

Zander's hair stood up more on one side of his head and his pants were falling down, which made the flash of annoyance in his eyes look innocuous, even funny.

"And you could get in trouble. We could both get in trouble," she added.

"Why?" His voice sounded like a crow's, urgent and demanding.

Phoebe tried to stall for time as she carefully moved closer. "Why what?"

"Why would you get in trouble?"

"For the same reason that you will get in trouble if Chickie gets hurt while you're supposed to be taking care of him. Jamie told me to find you, so I am going to wait with you until she returns."

Zander nodded, seeming satisfied with Phoebe's explanation, and turned his attention back to his blue matchbox car. He asked Phoebe if she wanted to watch his car fly.

At that moment Phoebe realized that she liked Cassandra. This kid of hers was fearless, and it took a special kind of mom to raise someone like that. She filed this away. "No, don't send your car off the edge of the roof," she said. She was only a few feet away from him now.

●●●

Meanwhile, at exactly one in the afternoon, Carol Meincraft, Sascha and Sascha's little brother Ted stepped out of the minivan and waved at Helen, who waved back and walked in their direction. Carol quickly greeted Helen and then exclaimed, almost in stereo with Helen, "Look at the barn!"

Cassandra turned and gasped. "Is that Zander? Please tell me that is someone else's child," she murmured, covering the distance to the barn with long strides. Carol's children fanned behind them.

Helen laughed ruefully. "I'm afraid it is your son and my daughter up there. Hopefully she will wait for us before she tries to get him off the roof. I don't know how she managed to get up there with that arm. Pretty remarkable, actually—both of them."

While they headed down the hill and through the stand of pines, Helen introduced Carol and Cassandra. Carol, a mixture of amusement and concern on her face, replied, "I think our sons will get along swimmingly. I'm so glad Phoebe made it up there and is watching over him. She's such a good kid, Helen. And you mentioned she hurt her arm this morning?"

As Helen recounted the trip to the emergency room, Sascha climbed over the fence and called Phoebe's name. The two friends greeted one another, and Sascha said, "Need help?"

"Just climb on up the ladder inside the barn and we'll get this Chickie off the roof," Phoebe said.

Sascha climbed up to the top step of the ladder and waited for Phoebe to lead Zander to the edge. "Zander, that's my good friend, Sascha. How about if I hold your Chickie while she carries you down the stairs?" Phoebe smirked at Sascha and her smirk turned into a big, welcoming smile. She mouthed the words, "Thank you" to Sascha, and her friend's light-blue eyes sparkled in response.

At the foot of the ladder, Zander leapt out of Sascha's arms and ran to Cassandra, wrapping himself around his mother's leg and sucking his thumb. Cassandra hugged him back with a mixture of a smile and a frustrated frown.

Zander, meanwhile, peered out at the youngest Meincraft until curiosity got the better of him. After he introduced himself, Zander asked, "Will you be my friend?"

Jamie appeared without fanfare, stopping in front of Cassandra. Her jeans looked a few tears more tattered than the last time Cassandra or Helen had seen her, and yet she held herself with a grace and dignity that contrasted with her clothing. As she mopped her brow with the back of her wrist, Jamie apologized for losing track of Zander. "Let me make it up to you, please, Ms. White?"

"Make what up? Losing track of my kid?"

Jamie searched Cassandra's face and hesitated.

Cassandra, now laughing, moved over and patted Jamie on the arm. "Believe me, Jamie, this could have happened to anyone." Cassandra's smirk turned into a more dignified grin. "By all means, I think he'd love a ride, and maybe," Cassandra turned toward Carol and Helen. "maybe your son would like to take a few rides, too?" The boys ran off with Jamie, shouting about horses and chickens.

Phoebe glanced at Helen, who smiled at her and Sascha. "You two probably have a lot of catching up to do, right?"

With a grateful look in her eyes, Phoebe nodded. "Come on, Sascha. Let me show you my new digs."

CHAPTER 32

Cassandra woke up on Monday morning to an alarm clock blinking red and blaring "Livin' on a Prayer." She swung out of bed with a groan, pulled on her running shorts and headed out the door for a forty-five minute run along the creek behind her home. The wet weather made her reminisce about her children, and she imagined pulling on rain boots and splashing in the water with Catherine. She had always been that mom, the one who tossed footballs at tree trunks and sledded down hills and splashed in muddy water hip to hip with her offspring. Soon she would initiate Zander into the messy world of "creeking," as his sister called it.

Once Cassandra had warmed up the tight muscles in what she jokingly called her "old lady legs," she increased her pace and settled into a steady, almost automatic 8:15 per mile slow run. The cold autumn air entered her lungs through her nose. She pushed out of mind the tinge of colors ringing the transition from predawn to early morning, and with her gaze focused several yards ahead to scan for branches or rocks, she tried to mentally enter a worry-free work zone. She had a lot of preparation to do before she and Helen met with the Commonwealth's Attorney later that morning.

On the other hand, she knew that no matter how much time she spent preparing, much of the outcome lay outside her control. It was her job to narrow the possible results and consequences as much as she could. As she ran, she analyzed her tactics one last time before she would have to make her first call of the morning to set up the meeting.

•••

Almost an hour's drive to the west, Helen woke up without an alarm clock. The first thing she grabbed was her laptop. Over the din of the morning birds cawing and screeching, she heard the creaks of floorboards and she shook off the annoyance of noises that brought back childhood memories of her parents' summer home in Maine. She had no time to indulge in the memories of dilapidated clapboard images and sounds clamoring for her attention. She wished she'd taken Phoebe there before . . . *Well, shoot. Before it—before this life I thought we had, or that I had even forgotten I wanted to have—fell to pieces.*

Helen shook her head and tried to forget about the faded red lake home as she stared at the white laptop in her hands. After she logged in, she scanned her work e-mail and groaned. Eight hundred e-mails remained unopened.

Helen realized that if she didn't get a handle on her workload, some case somewhere was going to "circle the drain," as her first boss used to say. Helen ran her hand through her hair. She flew through all the possible uses of her next fifteen minutes, and a succession of images flipped one after the other like a high-speed visual Rolodex.

The way her brain entered some sort of turbo drive was never something she could explain to anyone else.

It's like right before you're about to smash your car into something, and then time slows down, and it seems like your brain can calculate everything so much faster than anyone else can. But this happens to me all the time. It's great, and I love it, but it's so unbelievably lonely. It's lonely being smart.

Helen finished scrolling. *Ah, that's it: I'll read only e-mails from clients.* With a roll of her eyes, she ignored a couple of curt messages from the head of the DC office, asking her why she had missed Friday's conference call with the other partners. A tap on Helen's door startled her right before she could click on a message from her old mentor at the firm. Helen set her laptop to her right and replied, "Come in."

Phoebe ducked into Helen's room and squinted at her mother across the nearly dark room. "Turn on some light in here, will you?" The girl swung around and, without thinking, hit the light switch with her left hand and bent over immediately in pain. "Darn!" she muttered.

Helen jumped out of bed and knelt next to Phoebe. "Hey," she said. "You okay?"

Phoebe opened her eyes and, still wincing, smiled at her mother.

Her dimple almost showed for the first time since it . . . this . . . stop. "Come sit down next to me." Helen perched on the edge of the bed and fingered the bedspread. It felt cool to the touch and reminded her of the quilts her grandmother used to crochet, but this one had a modern flourish. "We need to get that looked at by an orthopedist today, hopefully, so that you can get back to training with Ms. McCaffrey." Helen waited for Phoebe to respond, but the girl's eyes were following the doorframe to the shadows cast on the wall by the trees moving outside the upstairs windows.

Helen knew Phoebe was seeing something else because her daughter caught her breath and tried not to gasp. "Phoebe, you're right here with me, with Mom. What are you seeing?" She felt goosebumps rise on the back of her neck. *Dear God, what did he do to her?*

After a few moments, Phoebe startled out of her trance and shivered once. "Huh?"

Helen could feel her daughter's fear from a distance as if watching a scene in a horror movie play out, and she felt a need to see the ending, even though she knew she couldn't bear it. Her voice trembled a little. "I was trying to talk about getting you in to see the doctor today, but then you went away somewhere scary, didn't you?"

Phoebe nodded, and Helen realized that goosebumps were raging like an uncontrolled rash across her daughter's arms. She pulled her pale child to her bosom, covered her with a blanket and hugged her tightly, as tightly as she would have had she been in that room with the shadows and the ghost of her dead husband alive again, lurking, hurting, *oh God what did he do to her?*

"Do you want to talk about it?" Helen waited. When Helen had asked Cary one time too many how she could help Phoebe, Cary had cautioned her that Phoebe needed to know that her mother would listen without feeling pressured to answer any questions. But it was almost impossible not to ask. Helen wanted, no, needed to know what lay hidden under those shadows, so dark, so much pain, *oh dear God, what did he do to her?*

Phoebe shook her head and Helen tried to let it go. She stroked her daughter's hand and instead of shadows, Helen summoned that safe, faded clapboard summer home. Her mind again flying through images, she searched until she found one of the lake, with geese flying overhead. A light breeze blew off the water and rustled the trees, and she and Phoebe were feeling it as they sat side by side on the screened-in porch. It was the breeze that was making the goosebumps run up and down her entire body now, but it was just a chill. It would pass as soon as the sun rose higher in the morning sky.

"I love you no matter what." Helen leaned against her daughter and continued, "You don't have to say a word; I don't expect to hear anything from you or from Cary. In fact, Cary is not supposed to tell me anything you tell her unless she's worried about your safety. I just want you to know that you can talk or not talk to me whenever you want. Okay?"

Phoebe nodded.

Helen paused and gulped. She hadn't spoken about God much these last few years and she regretted it. The words just felt, she felt . . . inadequate. With another gulp, she tried to smile at her daughter. "And I'm . . . praying. I know it's going to be okay. I think, and it sounds so inadequate, but I think that maybe He's got this."

Phoebe looked like she was steeling herself so that she could tell her mom something momentous, and Helen prepared herself mentally. She closed her eyes and remembered the smell of the musty outdoor fireplace that smoldered with an almost burnt-out log. *Those Maine summers could kill you once you turned fifty*, she mused.

Instead, Phoebe shifted closer to her mother. "Okay. So, about that orthopedist's visit. How are you going to get me there if you need to see the Commonwealth's Attorney today?"

Helen gulped and glared at her laptop, as if that were the problem. And in a way it was, because it reminded her that she wasn't sitting on the screened-in porch in that summer house in Maine. But the laptop was an even more vicious reminder of her failure as Phoebe's mother. For just this once, it wasn't work that was interfering with her responsibilities as a mom; and yet work, and too much of it, had gotten her into this mess. *Crap!* Helen shook her head and tried to push it away, the guilt that sat on her heart like a log on top of a breaking dam. "I did think of what we could do if the appointments overlapped, but I wanted to talk with you about it first."

"As long as it doesn't include rescheduling your thing with the prosecutor, I'm cool with whatever you wanna do."

A chord of pride struck Helen's heart. Something in Phoebe's iron stare reminded Helen of herself. And yet, the dam. . . she shook her head at the thought and looked into Phoebe's brown eyes. "I feel like I shouldn't miss your visit to the orthopedist."

Phoebe lifted her shoulder, but not dismissively. "I don't know all the details of your case, but aren't you meeting with the prosecutor to stay out of jail, more or less?"

Helen thought about it. "I appreciate how mature you're trying to be, Pheebes. But don't you want to hear my plan for what to do if I can't make both appointments before you tell me what you're comfortable with?"

Phoebe tried to scratch underneath her cast and didn't respond, and Helen tried not to think too hard about what Phoebe might be thinking. "Well, I talked with Anne last night, and—"

"Oh," Phoebe interrupted. "So she will take me if you can't?"

The dam moved a little further away from Helen's heart. Her daughter surprised the heck out of her sometimes. *Then again,* thought Helen, *she is my daughter.*

"Right. As long as you don't mind bumping along in an old pickup truck—her words, not mine—she will drive you if I cannot. And that way the two of you can plot your training program for the next few weeks."

"Works for me," Phoebe said, pushing back from her mother's bed to an upright position. "I'm going to go get dressed."

•••

After Phoebe had left, Helen picked up her laptop and tried to figure out how to respond to her mentor, one of the most distinguished men who had ever litigated in federal court. In her early years as an attorney, Helen had learned much of what she needed to know from Gary Creedley. Gary had blazed the way a generation ahead of Helen at her law firm, and then he'd taught Helen how to "swim with sharks," as he would say in his gruff voice. She owed Gary a debt she could never fully repay.

Gary was a Brooklyn guy. A graduate from one of New York's state universities, he had blasted his way through Columbia Law School and had talked himself into a clerkship for a federal judge. And though he was the only lawyer to ever make partner in five years, he was one of the few partners at Baker Pitts who was still married to his first wife. Aging and arguably past his prime, he was wiry and could throw a nasty left cross, or so he always said, and there was almost no securities defense attorney more respected and even feared by federal prosecutors. Helen smiled. She could picture Gary prowling around his corner office, fingers underneath his suspenders, tie in a tight Windsor knot that was perfectly dimpled. In his office there was a massive painting of the Brooklyn Bridge, and on the opposite wall a set of windows overlooked Freedom Park.

Before she could get lost in further reflection, Helen remembered what she needed to say to Gary: She needed to tell him no. Gary had asked her to host an important client dinner on Tuesday night. She had never told him no before. *And I'm scared. I'm scared of what he'll say and even more, I'm scared of what I've become.*

•••

October, 1983

They were sitting in first class on a Delta flight from DC to Houston, and as usual, Gary was talking a little bit too loudly. Helen was preparing for her first jury trial, just second chair, and Gary was thinking about giving her a witness or two to handle on direct. Then he caught her eyes searching the clouds floating past at thirty thousand feet, and he stopped mid-sentence as if waiting for her to realize that she'd allowed her attention to waver.

Her eyes wandered from the clouds. She started to say, "Sorry, Gary, what was that?"

Before she could finish apologizing, though, he snapped, "I need you here, Helen. Not back in bed with your husband or sipping a beer with your best friend or wherever your mind just went."

Helen rubbed her finger against her thumb. She had been thinking about her father, who was lying in a hospital bed in Maine fighting pneumonia, and an edge came into her voice. "My father is sick."

Gary leaned over and patted Helen on the knee, but his hand didn't linger. That was one of the great things about Gary; he never made Helen feel uncomfortable, and he never talked about any woman other than his beloved wife. "I'm sorry about your dad, Counselor."

He nodded and she started to respond, but he held up a hand and she paused, waiting. She knew she had done something wrong, or not exactly right, but she kept envisioning her father wrapped in a thick white sweater or bundled up with a wool blanket in the rocking chair on the porch. Maybe Gary was going to talk about his own father, she thought.

Instead, in a voice as gentle as she had ever heard him use, he said, "If you want to rise to the top of our peculiar profession, kiddo, your clients must all believe that all you ever think about is them—their case, their problems, their best interests, heck, their golf game, if necessary. You're going to miss soccer practices and ballet performances and parent-teacher conferences, and it's going to be harder for you than it was for me. You see, my Bessie covers it all. She never misses anything involving the children, and right or wrong, that's how I manage it. Maybe I don't even miss it. Maybe I wasn't cracked out to be that dad, the one who coaches all his kids' sports teams. Heck, we can't all be those dads. The nine to five fathers. The world needs 'em. But the world needs this man," and Gary pointed to his chest, "just as much. And to be the man the world needs, I've made some sacrifices."

Gary paused and took a sip of soda from his plastic airplane cup. Helen was thirsty too, but she didn't want to admit it. She sat still and waited for him to continue.

"I don't mind the sacrifices I've made, not really. I hope my kids understand it when they're older. This is the life I've chosen, and I have no regrets. No regrets." Gary picked up his cup again and wrapped both his hands around it. "I'm sorry about your father, Helen, I really am. But if this is the life you want, if you really want to follow in my footsteps, you're going to have to think, dream, eat and drink nothing but Baker Pitts. That's your choice, and I'll understand if you decide to follow the baby track like so many lovely women your age. I'll even honor and respect that decision. But if you want something different, if you want something more, well, you don't have time to make castles in the sky."

Helen nodded. She was flying in the opposite direction of her dying father, but that was exactly what he would have wanted; the one thing her father had always told her was to use her talents. She could almost hear him saying it: "You have to do as much as you can with your gifts. You weren't born just to make beds and cook brownies. You were born to be excellent. Don't waste a moment looking back." A sense of calm filled Helen. She turned toward Gary. "Thank you for the reminder. This will not happen again."

•••

Helen shook her head in confusion. Excellence may not be about making beds and cooking brownies, but excellence was about more than rising to the top of your profession. She'd messed up. She hadn't meant to. She really hadn't meant to hurt her daughter, but she had. Her own excellence had been achieved by sacrificing her family, and now she was paying the price for it. No, now Phoebe was paying the price for it, she realized, and she winced. Quickly Helen typed a reply:

I am sorry Gary, but I simply cannot. I will explain later.

She hit Send and then she exhaled. She hadn't even realized she was holding her breath. *Now to wait for Gary to call.*

Helen's phone rang a moment later. She froze at first, though it wasn't Gary, but Cassandra. "You're awake, Helen? I wanted to call real quick before my house turned too loud."

Helen smiled into the phone. They had agreed to talk at half past six, which was her favorite time to hold meetings at the office. It scared the heck out of young associates, but sometimes they needed to be heck-scared into working hard. It had never made sense to her to pay a first-year attorney $150,000 coming out of law school, and it probably never would. All too often, the young attorney took the pay for granted. The early morning meetings either toughened them up or weeded out the weak.

"I've been awake since five. Trying to catch up on e-mails, but . . . I'm a little flummoxed." Helen rolled her neck, stretching as she switched the receiver to her other ear. "I have no idea how to keep up with office politics. Worse, I don't know what the other partners will say when they read today's press release."

Helen and Cassandra had worked on drafting a brief press release to go out first thing Monday morning, and the older attorney was more than a little worried about the repercussions. She and Cassandra were trying to be proactive by controlling the flow of information, but once all this came out, well, it would be out of their control. It would be like trying a case; she could control just about everything, right up until the moment the judge issued his instructions to the jury and sent them off to decide her client's fate.

"As I was saying," Cassandra began.

"Ah, I—"

"No, no matter. You've got a lot on your mind."

Helen almost smiled. Cassandra didn't sound annoyed, but Helen found herself wondering how she would have reacted if she were in Cassandra's shoes.

"Remember, okay, that first you are asking everyone to respect your family's privacy. Your firm will respect that. Well, they should respect it. Second, you are taking a leave of absence, so what happens at the firm in your absence is not, legally at least, your responsibility. And if anyone asks you any questions about Richard's death, you demur. No comment. And if the press contacts you, refer them to me. Got it?"

Helen did not answer right away. She was envisioning the imprint the golf club had made on Richard's scalp, and suddenly bile rose to her throat.

"Helen, what's wrong?"

Cassandra's voice hammered into Helen's senses and she shook her head and realized that she had moaned. "Oh, I'm sorry. I really need to talk some of this through with Troy, I think. I am meeting with him tomorrow morning. I keep seeing the murder—"

Cassandra interrupted her forcefully. "It was *not* a murder. You had better not call it that or even think of it as a murder. *Ever.* You got that?"

Helen gulped. Shadows flickering on the walls and golf clubs arcing through the air, and this was all so, so . . . *So hard.* "Yes. Sorry. I need to talk through Richard's death with Troy and get some help. It's pretty overwhelming. All of this."

Cassandra's voice came across on the line with four parts steel to one part silk. "You need to put that stuff aside today. I need you focused. You can cry. You can break down. But you can't lose it and unravel during this interview. Are you with me, woman?"

Helen nodded gratefully. Any other client would probably have been outraged or upset or even hurt if Cassandra had spoken in that way, but Helen knew that the younger attorney was saying what she needed to hear. "Thank you, Counselor. I got it. I need a shower and a pot of coffee, and then I will be ready for you." Helen felt a lump in her throat. She had no idea why she felt so grateful to someone who was yelling at her, and yet as she hung up the phone, she smiled.

•••

An hour later, Cassandra heard the slam of the front door and paused by her bedroom window to catch a glimpse of Cat walking to the bus stop. Just out of the shower, she had missed hugging her daughter goodbye, which unsettled her a little. She tapped on her bedroom window until Cat froze, and then, with a grin, turned to see her mother blowing kisses. For a moment Cassandra got lost in time, remembering a tiny Catherine waving to her from a school bus window. She pulled her bathrobe tighter; and with a hand on her throat she smiled with great tenderness as her almost-grown daughter blew kisses right back to her.

Cassandra wandered into her large closet to locate a sober blue business suit. A weird sense of déjà vu tugged at her memory, but she didn't have time to sort it out. She had a job to do. The smell of coffee brought Cassandra back to the present. To-go mug of black coffee in hand, she herded Zander into the SUV and headed on her way.

Like most trial attorneys, Cassandra lived by the clock. As always, she was five minutes early dropping off Zander; it was almost eight in the morning, and she had a very important phone call to make. Cassandra kissed her son goodbye and then climbed into her seat and dialed the phone number for the lead prosecutor for Fairfax County.

As the phone began to ring, she remained in the parking lot and tried not to clutch her pen too tightly. Tendrils of irrelevant thoughts tried to gain purchase, but she pushed them out of her mind and focused on selling her client's story to Elizabeth Baldwin, who picked up on the second ring.

After Elizabeth had introduced herself, Cassandra launched right into it. She knew from past cases she had worked as defense counsel on the other side of the courtroom that Elizabeth hated small talk. "Elizabeth, I have an urgent matter to discuss with you in person."

"Come on, Cassandra, I need more than that. I am right in the middle of trial prep." Elizabeth's voice sounded pleasant yet firm, with a slight touch of a southern accent.

So far, so good, Cassandra thought. She hadn't said no. Cassandra tapped her pen on her yellow legal pad and continued, "I am calling on behalf of Helen Thompson, whose husband, Judge Richard Thompson, died on Friday at his home."

The prosecutor clicked her phone off speaker and picked up the receiver. "I hadn't heard about that. Um, go on." Elizabeth spoke with a note of interest in her voice. "Quickly, please."

"My client is willing to proffer information about two different matters. The first is what I need to see you about urgently, because she and her daughter have had to take refuge in a safe house. Her husband—Judge Thompson, that is—was participating in and planning unspeakable sexual acts involving their daughter and individuals from out of state. He created pornographic films in which he raped his daughter, and he sent these films to individuals who were provided with his daughter's location. She is not safe at this time. I need your help getting these sick bastards off the streets."

Elizabeth did not speak for more than ten seconds, and Cassandra forced herself to remain quiet.

One of the most important tricks in a lawyer's negotiating arsenal is silence. When you're sitting across the table from opposing counsel and you put an offer on the table, shut up and wait. Let the offer stand, and while it stands, don't knock the legs out from under it by attaching to it conditions that will weaken it. Say nothing. It's the hardest thing in the world for many of us, because we are taught to talk and argue and act. No one teaches you in law school or in college to let things be, to speak and then bask in silence as the other person weighs and considers what she has heard.

"Well," said Elizabeth finally, "I presume you have proof?"

Cassandra made a fist. *I've got her!* "Yes. We have the video he made, as well as a binder containing copies of screenshots taken from his computer. I am handing you a neatly wrapped case. And if you're not ready to move, I will call the Feds."

"No, don't call them," Elizabeth replied quickly before Cassandra had completed her sentence. "We have jurisdiction, anyway, over sex crimes that occurred in Fairfax County." Cassandra smiled under her breath. Elizabeth was territorial because far too often, the Feds would sit on a case and do nothing with it just to keep it out of a state prosecutor's hands.

"I can clear my plate for a lunchtime meeting." Elizabeth was talking faster now. "Please bring the evidence." The prosecutor started to hang up, and then in a suspicious tone, she asked, "What was that second issue?"

"It's about Judge Thompson's death," Cassandra replied languidly, and then added, "Elizabeth, I've got a judge calling me on the other line. We'll talk in a few hours, okay?" Cassandra thanked the prosecutor and hung up the phone. It was time to start talking to the press, off the record, of course.

•••

The press release hit Helen's inbox before the wheels of Cassandra's SUV turned into the gravel driveway leading up to the Bryson House. Helen reviewed it, and as she was reading the final sentence, her cell phone rang. Helen glanced at it and saw that it was the managing partner at Baker Pitts. She thought about ignoring the call, but instead answered the phone and listened as Scott Abrams' secretary promised to patch the call through. Helen's neck throbbed as she tried to calm down. She hated when men asked their secretaries to dial the phone for them. *Such a relic, like an idiot who plays golf at an all-male club,* she thought, twirling her pen.

Scott got on the phone without even offering a cursory greeting. "Helen? Do you plan on telling the firm what the heck is going on? We've already got media outlets calling us."

Helen stopped trying to calm her temper and snapped, "What? How about we start this conversation over? How about if you say to me, oh I don't know, 'Helen, I am sorry for your loss?' Really, Scott, is that so fucking hard to say?"

Scott and Helen had been at loggerheads for over a decade. Helen thought he had wined and dined his way to the managing partner position and that he was an intellectual lightweight; in turn, he complained that she wasn't a team player. Scott's biggest complaint about Helen was that if she really cared about the firm's best interests, she would have taken on the role of Head of the Litigation Department years ago. Helen's response had always been to raise the back of her hand and walk out of his office, in a hurry to attend her next meeting.

"Oh, come on. Don't tell me that your feelings are hurt. That's idiotic. Everyone knew that you and Richard were on the rocks as a couple."

"Fuck you, Scott. You have no right to say anything about my marriage. And if you're calling about the press release that my personal lawyer just issued, I think it's pretty clear that this is a family matter. If you're calling about my caseload, I have clearly delegated everything to Carl, and I've already relayed that information to my clients."

"To Carl? He's not even a partner! What are our clients going to say?"

"*My* clients, Scott. *My* clients all know Carl and are perfectly comfortable with him in charge. And he better damn well be a partner by the end of this year. We already agreed to that at the last partners' meeting." Helen's voice dropped and then in a measured tone, she added, "And you were there, Scott."

Scott didn't answer right away. Helen imagined that he was holding his baseball, which had even been an affected mannerism twenty years ago. Now it just looked absurd. "That wasn't our official end-of-year meeting, Helen."

A cold sensation ran down Helen's spine. *So that's how this is going to play out.* She clenched her fists. They weren't going to hijack her into working. "It *was* an official partners' meeting. I read the list of rising partners in the meeting minutes. Listen, I don't have time to discuss this around anymore. If any of my cases require legal attention, Carl is in charge, and he's already on all the pleadings. I'm taking a leave of absence until I square things away. I have an important meeting to prepare for, so I must be going."

Helen hung up the phone before Scott could fit in another word. The thought of losing what she had spent years building made her feel tingly all over. She couldn't tell if her racing pulse represented fear or rage or a possessive determination to hold what she owned, but she knew she wouldn't let go of the foundation she had created without a fight.

Helen set her cell phone down on the bed and tried to ignore the voicemail icon. The vent from the heating unit made a ticking sound, and she caught her mind searching for the source of the noise. For some reason the ticking sound reminded her of her home with Richard. *I will never live in that house again*, she thought, and she felt an odd lightness. She shook her head and called the orthopedist's office, then tossed her phone on her bed. That darn thing had been her boss for too long.

CHAPTER 33

Cassandra stepped out of her Volvo barefoot. Not wanting her dress shoes encrusted with reddish-brown clay, she carried them in her hand and walked toward the front door without a second thought. Unlike many of the battle-ax female lawyers from her generation, Cassandra eschewed hose, and the combination of her beautifully cut blue suit and her unshod feet gave her the appearance of a much younger woman. Before Cassandra could turn the brass handle, the door swung open and she almost collided with Phoebe.

"Good morning, Phoebe. How is your arm feeling?"

For a few seconds Phoebe scanned Cassandra's outfit, and then she nodded, more relieved than smug. Her mom needed the best, most kickass attorney. Cassandra looked the part, except for the bare feet, of course. The fabric on her suit was expensive and expertly stitched. With her collar and her cuffs folded back just so, Cassandra looked unstoppable.

Phoebe tried not to gape. "Um, it's fine, thanks. Let me get my mom and tell her you're here, Ms. White."

Cassandra thanked Phoebe and walked into the study to wait for her client. Her cell phone buzzed while she waited for Helen, and with a sense of foreboding, she recognized the number from Zander's preschool at McClintock. *Gah.* Just as she reached to answer the phone, she saw Helen cross the front hallway.

Cassandra held up her hand to wave her greeting. Helen nodded and held up her coffee mug as Cassandra dialed Frank's direct line.

"Frank, Zander's school called. You need to call them back, please, okay?" She heard her husband exhale. "Frank," Cassandra snapped, "you promised that you would take point with the children this week. I know you have meetings, but I have absolutely urgent client needs today." Cassandra imagined Frank sitting at his desk, one hand scrolling through his e-mail, and she shook away the image. She could not afford to think about anything that was unrelated to the case. Cassandra heard papers rustling and then Frank's voice.

"Hey, gorgeous. I'll call the school and if there is anything wrong, I'll take care of it. You focus on your case."

Cassandra relaxed her tight neck muscles and clicked the phone off just as Helen strode into the room. "Kids?"

Cassandra managed a half-smile. "Kids. Always something." She waved her hand to dismiss the concern. "So, how are you doing today?" She moved over to the conference table and sat in a chair with her back facing a panel of windows.

Helen took the chair and slammed her cell phone down. "Darn it." She raked her hands through her auburn hair. "It won't stop ringing. I can't handle all of this crap from my firm."

Cassandra put her leather satchel on top of the table and searched through it while she listened to Helen. Frank had given her the bag many years ago, and like her favorite pair of boots, it had an expensive, well-worn look to it. Removing a thick black binder, she asked, "Why, what's going on with the firm? I thought you were taking a leave of absence and had Carl covering your cases."

Cassandra's eyes remained focused on the contents of her bag as she searched for a pen and a highlighter. Out of the corner of her eye, she spotted a tube of red lipstick. *"Mama, I like it when you wear red lips."* Cassandra half-smiled and stared at the lipstick.

"I thought so too, but they're giving me grief about taking a leave of absence, and I haven't even been gone for a full week yet. And the managing partner called me this morning, and instead of expressing his condolences, he went straight for my jugular."

Cassandra looked up. "What do you mean?"

Helen summarized her conversation with Scott, twirling a pen as she spoke.

Cassandra rested her chin on her right hand. "That doesn't sound good, Helen. Do you have allies on the retention committee?"

Helen's firm, like Cassandra's prior employer, promoted associates to partnership only after a retention committee had signed off on the promotion, but Helen appeared astonished by Cassandra's words. "Allies? Why in the heck would I need allies? I have a $50 million book. I never had the time to play office senator. It never stopped me before. The attorneys that serve on all those committees generally have small books and they leech off the high producers." Helen sounded more bemused than concerned or worried. She could have been describing the state of a mismanaged corporation's budget.

Perhaps, Cassandra imagined, *Helen isn't worried about her position at the firm because in her mind there is no rational reason for the firm to attack one of their highest billers*. Cassandra remembered, however, just how irrationally prestigious firms behaved when spooked by the possibility of scandal.

Law firms were like the stock market: They responded too easily to rumors, lies and misconceptions. Her first firm had pushed her out the door after word of her "scandal" had leaked from the boardroom to a big oil and gas client. "You know what happened to me, right?"

Helen studied the backs of her hands. "Besides what you told me? Yes. I've heard a few things, yes."

"Exactly!" Cassandra exclaimed with scorn, putting an edge into her voice. "Something about a drinking scandal, yes?"

Helen nodded.

Cassandra tossed her head back and looked at her shadow on the ceiling, framed by the morning light. "The thing is, it wasn't a drinking scandal. I was raped." Cassandra let her words hover in the air, a twin to the ceiling shadows. "Not to belabor the point, but I drank too much at an office party. So you think drinking scandal, right?" Cassandra did not wait for Helen to respond. "Well, the rapist was a client. So they had to choose between a mid-level associate and a billion-dollar corporation. Who do you think they chose?"

Helen's eyes switched from compassion to indignation. "That's criminal. Did you bring charges?"

Cassandra shook her head. "For a long time, my memory wasn't clear. It was only after I ran into him at the client's office and smelled his aftershave that I put it all together. And I just lost it on him." Cassandra shook her head ruefully. "The irony of it all? That client went down hard about ten years ago. And the man who raped me: He ended up in the slammer for his role in the fraud." Cassandra folded her arms and leaned back in her chair with a Cheshire cat grin. "So he got his."

"Good."

"Exactly," Cassandra said. "And that brings me back to the advice I am giving you." She paused and gave Helen a probing look. "You don't mind a bit of non-legal advice, do you?"

Helen shook her head and motioned for Cassandra to keep talking. "No. By all means, please do."

"Watch your back. Get your ducks in order. Get an exit strategy. Start talking to your clients about the future. Pretend that you are trying to win them over again, like you did the first time."

Helen took a deep breath. "If you don't mind my asking, how do I go about doing that? I am on a leave of absence and I swore I would put Phoebe first."

"Okay, yeah," Cassandra conceded. "Your family comes first. You. Your daughter. This case. But that still leaves an hour or two a day to call a client or two and schmooze, right?"

Helen groaned a little. The thought of it exhausted her, but she set her jaw and nodded. "Yes. I can do that. What should I tell them?"

"This is going to sound scary. You ready?" Cassandra spoke very slowly, with emphasis. "The truth. You tell them the truth. Remember, we're playing this out in the media in a very nuanced way. We're not going on a full court press offensive so to speak, but your clients will already know about it. We shall not shrink. Okay? You did nothing wrong."

"Are you sure?" Helen shook her head with a disbelieving glance at her lawyer. "I murdered my husband!"

"No!" Cassandra's arm jerked, as if she were going to slam the table in frustration, but she folded her arms and glared at Helen instead. "I've already told you to stop saying you murdered him. You defended yourself when he tried to kill you."

Cassandra held eye contact with Helen for a few seconds and then added, "When we're finished explaining it, people will say you're a heroine, Helen."

Helen's eyes grew wide. "Are you sure about this strategy? Really, really sure?"

Cassandra put a gentle hand on her client's wrist. "Taking this case to the press will put a lot of pressure on the state to prosecute the sex crimes because the media will sense a story. We're rolling the dice for sure, but the prosecutor will know that if they don't move to prosecute the sex crimes, then this goes viral in more ways than one. The Commonwealth's Attorney doesn't want to be depicted as soft on sex crimes, especially those involving children. And since this involves a state judge, the prosecutors must appear to be taking these crimes seriously or else risk looking like they're covering something up. Believe me. The press will be all over this, and it will deflect attention from *how* Richard died to *why* he died."   Helen   hesitated   and drummed her fingers on the table, and Cassandra tried not to notice how Helen's hand shook a little.

"If they prosecute me, I'll end up in jail?"

"Yes, at the beginning." Cassandra felt the muscles in her back tighten. "That's the idea of taking it to them with the sex case and playing it out in the press. We will go on the offensive, and hopefully this will put them on the defensive while we use the power of the press to make them not want to prosecute you."

Helen closed her eyes in what started out as a blink and then evolved into a sort of systemic reboot. When Helen opened her eyes after a long silence, she leaned forward and grabbed Cassandra's sturdy hand with her left hand.   "Cass?"   Helen shivered and her eyes glistened. "I'm scared of losing everything. My career. It took me years of work to build it."

Cassandra nodded. There was nothing she could say. She had lost everything, or what seemed like everything, and she thought it was pretty likely that Helen's career was going to crater. Helen would land on her feet, but there was no way to explain that to her now.

"And I am scared I am going to go to jail. I can't even imagine what that would be like!" Helen's voice rose and she buttoned and unbuttoned the sleeve on her white blouse nervously. "I am terrified of losing the person I love most in this world. What is going to happen to my daughter?"

Cassandra squeezed Helen's hand and sat with her client quietly. She didn't want to promise that things were going to be okay when she really didn't know; besides, she figured that Helen wasn't looking for meaningless reassurances. "I promise you I will do everything in my power to protect your interests. To keep you safe. It's not going to be an easy case or a simple process, but together we can navigate our way through this."

Perhaps, Cassandra mused, it was her speech; or maybe Helen's legal training had kicked in at that exact moment. The older attorney's face changed, and to Cassandra it seemed as though Helen had put on a mask or protective armor.

Just in time, Cassandra thought. It was almost time to face the press.

•••

Before Helen and Cassandra drove into the younger attorney's office in Fairfax, Helen spoke with her daughter privately. "Phoebe, Cary and Cassandra both agree that we need to protect you from the prosecutors for as long as possible."

Phoebe gave her mom a strange look. "Sure," she said easily, flicking a bug off her sleeve. "I trust Cass. I mean, Ms. White. You know why, Mom?"

Helen shook her head.

"Because I like Zander, her little boy. He has no fear. None. A child isn't fearless like that if his mom isn't the same way. So if Ms. White says to hold me off in reserve, that's what we'll do, right? As long as you're sure you don't need me?"

Helen placed her hand under her daughter's chin. Phoebe looked so old and yet so young, like a colt that could gallop but could not carry too much weight. She smoothed her daughter's brown hair. "Not yet, sweetie. Cary was adamant. And I am going to listen to Cary when your welfare is at issue."

Phoebe grasped the wall with her left hand. "But Mom, why can't I come, in case it doesn't go well?"

"We're not going to talk about this more today. You meet with Cary later this week and we can see what she says. My answer is not going to change until Cary says it should."

When Phoebe tried to interrupt again, Helen held up her hand and repeated, "Not another word. But if you need me, please text me. I will have the ringer off when I meet with the prosecutor."

Phoebe smirked with a mix of insolence and naughtiness. "Yeah right, Mom. Like you're going to text me back at what, one word per minute?"

Helen ignored the jibe; she bent over and kissed her daughter's cheek and whispered, "Sun, moon, stars," which was what her own mother had said to her the last time they spoke.

Phoebe's smirk turned into a smile replete with sweet recognition. She knew the story; it had been her favorite way to say goodnight as a small child. "Sun, moon, stars," Phoebe said. Her heart felt full.

•••

Cassandra and Helen barely spoke to one another during the entire ride from the Bryson House into Fairfax. Cassandra's Bluetooth blared several times. Her office kept forwarding calls from the press, and to each one Cassandra murmured, "Thank you, but no comment." Even though the press conference had been officially set for 10:45, members of the media all wanted to seize an advantage over their competitors and get an early scoop.

Like many trial attorneys, Cassandra maintained an office within a five-minute walk of the courthouse. Fairfax had changed a great deal in the decade since she had moved her offices. A few years earlier, the county had built a new courthouse and transformed the old building, which dated from the sixties, into a jail. The new courthouse was built in a discordant mix of postmodern and pseudo-colonial styles, and its mixed shades of fake red brick offered a veritable rainbow of color in contrast to the old gray building. Still, despite its somber, almost East European architectural influence, Cassandra preferred the old courthouse.

In the parking garage, Cassandra kept a wary eye on the columns that connected the ceiling to the floor like thick pencils stuck between two flat gray boards. As the younger attorney concentrated on backing into a corner space, Helen tried to make a joke about how much easier it was to park in the wider spaces of the suburbs. Cassandra didn't answer. Prior to the scandal, she had worked at a prestigious downtown address on K Street, and Helen's words stung a bit: a reminder of what had happened to Cassandra's career so many years before. She hoped Helen wouldn't notice the water spots left on the ceiling by one of the dripping HVAC units.

Cassandra felt a touch of self-consciousness as she led Helen toward the basement's bank of elevators, which weren't as well kept as the central bank of elevators they were avoiding because of the press. Her office was the best-decorated in all of Fairfax, but it wasn't DC. She worried that Helen would be contrasting the more modest, smaller-town atmosphere of Cassandra's firm with Baker Pitts, but if that was what Helen was thinking about, she did an excellent job of hiding any disdain.

As though she was sensing Cassandra's unease, Helen made a gracious remark. "Do you live near here, Cass? I imagine this would make for a dream of a commute."

Cassandra walked with her head up and her leather bag swinging off her shoulder, feeling suddenly proud and comfortable in her work environment. "Yes. It *is* a dream commute, especially after making the drive into DC all of those years. I am grateful, especially now that I have children, to work ten minutes away from home." Sure, she wished the dropped ceilings and lighting fixtures lining the basement and the hallway to the bank of elevators showed less grime and more light. Her office building was not as well designed or aesthetically pleasing as the one she used to work in, but the building did not decide the quality of the lawyer.

Cassandra led the way into her office, and as soon as she opened the door, noise assaulted them. She grinned. Directly in front of her sat a receptionist wearing a headpiece; Sally could work twenty incoming lines more deftly than an old-fashioned telephone operator, and she nodded at Cassandra and Helen while speaking into the receiver. Cassandra waved and guided Helen past the brown leather sofas in the waiting room into a conference room, where Nadia and Carl were bent over a pile of papers. The oval mahogany table shone and glittered in the soft light overhead.

Helen was so shocked to see Carl that she collided into Cassandra, then tripped and almost fell into the doorframe.

Cassandra put a steadying hand on her client and shot Nadia a questioning look. Nadia was still deep in conversation with Carl. Cassandra dropped her briefcase on the table and Helen cleared her throat. Carl, startled, looked up suddenly to see his boss. They grinned at one another with an additional layer of affection that had never before existed between them.

"Carl, I am so happy to see you!" Helen paused. "But what are you doing here and not downtown?"

Carl opened his mouth to answer, and then Helen chuckled and blushed. "Oh forgive me. Carl Hansen, please meet Cassandra White." She paused. "I see you have met Nadia."

Cassandra sat down in the corner chair closest to Nadia and took a deep breath. Her brown leather office chairs looked fine but felt heavenly, and she liked being back at her home base, even if she would only be here for a short while. She glanced at her dress watch. Fifteen more minutes.

Helen took the chair next to Carl and asked, "Why aren't you in the office?"

"It's a zoo. Apparently the PR Department is furious that you called a press conference and released a statement that they didn't write; even more 'disturbing,' as one partner said in the kitchen, is that you're holding a press conference here. They want to control what information gets out to the media. It looks like you're putting yourself first over the firm. I swear I heard someone complain that you're not a team player." Carl made a face and then continued, "The office line won't stop ringing. And when it does stop ringing, everyone keeps knocking on my door." He held his empty hands up in the air. "And the e-mails? My desktop pings every five seconds. My cell phone rings nonstop. And you know what's worse? Apparently Scott's secretary keeps calling mine and asking where I am and what I am working on, and when she isn't calling, Reed Anderson keeps sending his junior associate around to ask me for things." Anderson, to whom Helen reported, was the Head of Litigation, but everyone at Baker, Pitts, Kenzey & Moore knew who held the power in the litigation department.

"So you left your suit jacket on your chair, your computer running, and ducked out for a cup of coffee, Carl?" Helen and Cassandra grinned at each other.

Nadia uncharacteristically interrupted the conversation. "I worked with a guy who pulled that trick all the time, and darned if he didn't make partner."

Carl ran his hands through his thick, dark hair and leaned back in his chair to stretch. Then he bounced forward with a boyish grin. "Helen, I got something over the weekend." He showed Helen his brand-new white laptop.

Helen made a fist. "Good, Carl, wise move. This way you can work off-site until the dust settles back at the firm."

"Actually, if you want," Cassandra interjected, "we have an empty office that you are more than welcome to use."

Helen and Carl thanked Cassandra at the same time, and then Carl shot Helen an appraising stare. He folded his arms across his chest. "I was thinking, Helen, that maybe Nadia and I can come with you to the meeting with the Commonwealth's Attorney. I bet they pack the room with at least three prosecutors and maybe an investigator from the FBI or at least a detective, and we don't want to seem undermanned or, um, understaffed, as it were."

"Yes, Carl, great idea." Then Helen looked at her own attorney. "Cass, I'm sorry, I should defer to your judgment. It's odd not being in charge of the team assembled here." Helen gestured around the room. "But you're in charge, I know that."

Cassandra checked her watch again; seven more minutes until it was time to head down into the main atrium. "No, Helen, Carl made a great suggestion. I very much would like to march a large posse into the prosecutor's office for our meeting. So if you're comfortable with them riding with us, then so am I." Cassandra stood up mid-sentence and continued talking over her shoulder. "Nadia, follow me, please. Be back in five minutes, Helen. Then it will be show time."

Nadia trailed behind Cassandra and waited outside the bathroom. She knew the drill; Cassandra vomited right before most court appearances, and the normal stress of court was multiplied exponentially this morning. Despite years of experience appearing before judges and juries, Cassandra found the press terrifying. A minute later, Nadia tapped on the bathroom door and handed Cassandra a tube of Colgate and a white plastic toothbrush holder. "Thanks," Cassandra said, and

Nadia brushed a stray hair off her boss's suit jacket before she left Cassandra alone again.

Cassandra blotted her face with a damp paper towel and squared her shoulders as she surveyed herself in the mirror. She frowned as an image of her younger self, drunk and lying on the floor, edged into her mind. Gripping the sink, she summoned something different: herself racing at full speed around a banked red track. She could almost feel the wind in her hair and the flow of blood to her leg muscles. She felt fierce and strong as she glared with pride at her reflection.

Now. It was time.

CHAPTER 34

The main atrium of Cassandra's Fairfax office building crackled with activity. Halogen lights made the two-story open area appear even brighter than usual, and the late-morning sun reflecting off the black marble floors made the entire area feel like Virginia in August. Cassandra silently thanked her partner for recommending that she stop buying suits off the rack and invest more in her wardrobe. She rarely wore her most special suits, saving them for court appearances, depositions or funerals, but when she needed to dress to kill, she could. The fabric her tailor had used was durable but of a material that breathed well, which she considered a distinct advantage. Cassandra labored when she tried cases and she couldn't afford to let her body betray her. Even a single bead of sweat on her upper lip could give opposing counsel an advantage, and Cassandra didn't want to surrender anything today.

Carl and Nadia stood behind Cassandra, leaning against black colonnades that made the first floor of the building look like a maze. A few feet away from the colonnades was a wall of dark, tinted windows that led into the National Sunshine Bank. A small corridor for bank customers had been roped off with red velvet rope so that customers could squeeze between the windows and the colonnades on their way into the bank's first-floor lobby.

Cassandra heard Carl whisper to Nadia, "There are at least seventy-five members of the media here. Perhaps a hundred."

By the time we meet with Elizabeth Baldwin, Cassandra thought, *the press will be tracking the prosecutors like bloodhounds.* If Cassandra had calculated right, Elizabeth would be inundated with phone calls and media requests, and she would fast-track the police investigation into Richard's death. So long as Helen's story matched the evidence they found on the scene, they would be in a good position to lean on the prosecution and deflect their inquiries.

Cassandra saw Helen twisting her empty ring finger. She leaned over to her client, putting one hand on her back and whispering, "I am so sorry for the pain you're in. Don't be afraid to stand here and cry the entire time. It's okay to show the world that you are hurting. Let me worry about our case and about the press."

She patted Helen once on the back and took in the scene. A throng of reporters jockeyed for position. A group of men and women wearing suits and smiles stood in the middle of the room. These were the local anchors trying to land a headshot or a fifteen-second sound bite at the end of the press conference. Cassandra also spotted society reporters wearing bright colors and fashionable dresses. *Not surprising,* she thought. After all, the Thompsons were one of the wealthiest couples in northern Virginia. On the fringes of the throng stood several more studious-looking reporters; *They must report on the legal news,* thought Cassandra. Her eyes then fell upon several women, whose posture, serious demeanor and determined collective air made Cassandra realize that they must be the women's rights activists.

It is time.

With a theatrical gesture, Cassandra held her hands out and spoke into the microphone: "Ladies and Gentlemen of the press, thank you for being here. My client, Helen Thompson, issued a statement this morning regarding the untimely death of her husband, Judge Richard Thompson, and she has been overwhelmed by the response. She called this press conference to ask that the press respect her family's privacy during this difficult time. Because a number of people, including members of the press, have been contacting my client, she is concerned that members of the media would get wind of this and try to contact her daughter. In particular, requests have already been issued for comment to her daughter's school. Please, folks, I think we can all agree that a fifteen-year-old is off-limits to media inquiries."

Cassandra spoke in a loud, deep voice so polished that as she paused, the only sound in the room was a pen hitting the floor. She took her time as she spoke and made eye contact with as many members of the press as possible, especially the female activists. "At this time," Cassandra continued, "Ms. Thompson will be taking a leave of absence from her position at the law firm of Baker, Pitts, Kenzey and Moore to get her family's affairs in order. She is working closely with the prosecutors in the state court of Fairfax County."

Cassandra paused and looked around the atrium. Reporters scribbled. Cameras clicked and flashed. She had their rapt attention, but she couldn't say any more without getting sanctioned by the state bar. As it was, she was darn close to the line; one thing she wasn't supposed to do was to try cases in the press. Then again, she thought to herself, this wasn't a case yet, and her client had every right to request privacy. "At this time, Ms. Thompson has nothing further to say. She asks that in lieu of flowers, people send charitable contributions to the Rape and Incest Survivors' Association in her husband's honor."

Several reporters raised their hands at once, and Cassandra felt Helen lean slightly toward her. The older attorney looked the part of a grieving but dignified widow in her black suit. *This is going well,* Cassandra thought. She nodded at a black-haired woman from the *Fairfax County Legal Journal.*

"Ms. White, why is your client working with the state court of Fairfax County?"

"No comment," Cassandra replied, and pointed at another reporter she recognized from the *Washington Herald*'s Metro section.

"Ms. White, what were the circumstances of Judge Thompson's death?"

Helen shivered and Cassandra put an arm on her client's shoulder. "I'm not at liberty to discuss that at this time, Harry, but thank you for asking."

A reporter she didn't know raised his hand and Cassandra nodded at him. "Come on, Ms. White, can't you give us some indication of what you're working on with the DA's Office?"

Cassandra smiled genially and shook her head. "I'm sorry, I didn't catch your name?"

"Matt Briny, *DC Sun-Times*."

"Thank you, Matt. The Commonwealth Attorney's Office. And no, of course I can't discuss the status or the details of any ongoing investigation."

Cassandra suddenly became aware of the oppressive heat in the room. She glanced at Helen, who had gone completely white and stood twisting her nonexistent wedding ring with a blank expression on her face. Cassandra knew she needed to get Helen out of there. She thanked everyone for coming and gently led the older attorney toward the elevator. Carl and Nadia sprang forward to block several reporters who tried to push against them to ask Helen questions.

•••

In the elevator, Helen's iPhone buzzed and she reached for it before her mind could impose restraint. She glanced at the notification and saw that Phoebe had sent her a text:

On way 2 doc with Anne. Will u buy me a truck?
This thing is a monster. Miss u. Sun moon stars.
Meant 2 say that 2 u.

The lines in Helen's face grew looser, and in that moment she knew that even if she lost everything else, she would still have more than enough if she could just keep hold of Phoebe. Wordlessly Helen followed Cassandra through the double wooden doors, tapping a reply text message to her daughter.

I miss you, darling. The press conference is over.
Please don't answer your phone. No one should
be calling you. I will be back in time for dinner.
NO truck. Not safe! I will get you a horse, maybe
a used SUV. Deal?

After Helen hit Send, she stumbled on a loose piece of thick carpet and yet again bumped into Cassandra. "Gosh, I've completely lost my wits and my balance," she chuckled.

Cassandra shook her head. "Not at all. I have days where I trip on strands of hair." She led the way as the four attorneys filed back into Conference Room Two to begin discussing their strategy for their upcoming meeting with Elizabeth Baldwin.

•••

The sharp clicking of leather shoes beat a strange harmony as eight feet walked in unison down a sloped road on a warm autumn afternoon. They walked down the two-lane road and over the raised crosswalk that led to the prosecutor's office, which was nestled inside the new courthouse. Cassandra took one last deep breath and tried to take in the blanket-like white clouds hanging thousands of feet above them, but the case weighed too heavily for her to tune into the surroundings. She cared about one thing and one thing only as she pushed through the revolving doors and into the foyer: her client's welfare and her role in protecting it.

Mondays were busy days at the courthouse. Most trials started on Mondays, which meant that a large pool of jurors appeared for *voir dire*. In addition, the district court presided every day of the week over traffic and misdemeanors, and Fairfax County ran an efficient yet chaotic district court docket. Cassandra removed her briefcase from her shoulder and handed it to the uniformed guard, a burly, overweight black man with a gun in his holster. He grunted at Cassandra and she walked through the metal detector and tried to keep her pulse low and steady.

As they walked along the busy entryway, Cassandra saw everything through Helen's eyes as if for the first time. When Cassandra went to court for her own custody hearing, she had felt like a hybrid, stuck somewhere between her role as a lawyer and her role as a client. She wondered what Helen thought about the snatches of conversation they overheard between worried defendants and their attorneys. Cassandra heard more than one client ask if everything was going to be okay, but a good attorney could never promise that. And yet as Cassandra stood and watched the silver elevator door close and the faux old-fashioned needle above the door indicate the floors as the elevator rose, she suspected that all anyone ever wanted to know at this moment, at any moment, was an answer to that simple question: *Am I going to be okay?*

She sighed as the elevator dinged and the door opened onto the seventh floor. No matter how powerful a lawyer she might be, the outcome of Helen's case depended on matters outside Cassandra White's control.

A janitor in blue overalls passed, and Cassandra winked and called out to him, "Working hard, Jesse?"

Jesse had a beer gut and waddled along, his eyes cast downward until he caught sight of Cassandra. At the attorney's words, he stood up a little taller and his face softened. In the days before 9/11, he would have let her through the locked doors without a second thought; but this courthouse, like so many across the country, followed security protocols that were detailed and prudent. Helen, for one, had seen the Pentagon burn.

Elizabeth Baldwin approached the door and didn't exactly smile warmly. Cassandra scanned the brown-skinned woman and noticed that everything about the prosecutor shouted classic femininity: polished fingernails, pearl stud earrings, a tan suit and a black shirt that was unbuttoned an inch further than necessary. The bottoms of her heels clicked as she walked, and Cassandra pictured Elizabeth stalking a basketball court.

Elizabeth towered above Cassandra and Helen and prowled the corridor with leonine grace. Years ago the prosecutor had attended McClintock, where she still held the record for points scored in a varsity basketball game. After prep school, Elizabeth had attended Vanderbilt and then Duke Law School, where she had graduated Order of the Coif and matriculated to a federal clerkship in Virginia. Always a grinder in school, she brought the same tenacity and discipline to her role as Commonwealth's Attorney. Cassandra had always liked working with Elizabeth, and the two women had never exchanged harsh words.

Yet Cassandra felt the tension in the room increase as soon as Elizabeth shut the glass door and gestured for Helen's team to take a seat on the other side of the table. Already slouching at the table was a detective, and Cassandra eyed him with distaste. Bob Parkings wore a short-sleeved dress shirt with a tie that was too short. He was also the detective who had once called her a "little lady" when she had cross-examined him during a murder trial.

Before Cassandra could withdraw her black evidence binders, Elizabeth brought her own file folders down onto the glass table. The prosecutor's voice reverberated through the room. "What in the heck do you think you're doing, Cassandra? That stunt you pulled this morning—and make no mistake, it was a stunt—turned legal ethics on its head. You'll be lucky if the state bar doesn't sanction you."

Elizabeth leaned forward in her chair, her arms arranged aggressively, but something in her eyes undercut her anger.

Cassandra took a gamble. "Good to see you too, Elizabeth. How is your husband? And isn't Darren wrestling with the varsity this year?" Cassandra nodded at the rest of Elizabeth's team and waited for the Commonwealth's Attorney to finish opening and closing her mouth.

"Cass," Elizabeth continued in a calmer tone, "seriously, what was that about this morning?"

At this point, Helen spoke up in a stiff voice. "I called the press conference, Mrs. Baldwin. And you're also a McClintock alum? Good to know." Helen looked resplendent in her black suit and green scarf, and the attorneys on the other side of the table leaned backward as she spoke. "Because a number of people were contacting me, I worried that the press would get wind of this and try to contact my daughter. And given my status at Baker Pitts, not to mention my late husband's reputation, it seemed prudent and respectful to let the public know about his passing directly."

Cassandra suspected that no one in the room believed that Helen meant any of this, but what could anyone say in response? Even if she hadn't meant it, Helen's argument held together just well enough. *I hope*, Cassandra thought.

Elizabeth stared at Helen for a full five seconds. Her hands gripped the table and her eyes narrowed. Finally she released her grip and replied, "Okay. I don't know what to say to that, but I will say, Ms. Thompson, I am very sorry for your loss. Please accept my sympathy."

A sincere kindness flashed across Elizabeth's mien. She inspected Helen for a moment longer and then turned to Cassandra. "At the press conference you said that you would be working with us. What did you mean?"

Cassandra took a deep breath. She knew she only had one shot to get this right. "We have information concerning Judge Thompson's participation in a sex ring involving minors, including his daughter." Cassandra read a look of horror on Elizabeth's face, so she continued firmly, "Richard died in front of my client. We're here to proffer information as to how he died."

Elizabeth glanced over at Detective Parkings. "Bob, has the report come back from the medical examiner?"

The detective shook his head.

Elizabeth paused, then turned to her female associate. "Please grab a tape recorder, Sandy. Is that okay with you, Cassandra? If we record what your client tells us?"

"It's fine. We consent. My client has nothing to hide," Cassandra said. "I will begin by telling you that Richard Thompson died after he strangled his wife and she used a golf club to protect herself, and I can assure you that the scene has been left unmolested by my client and it will confirm my client's story."

Detective Parkings wrote something down on his notepad.

As Sandy set the tape recorder going, Cassandra nodded at Helen. "Go ahead," she said, and Helen began to describe what had happened that morning.

Elizabeth interrupted the story quickly when Helen described the aroma of marijuana. "Do you smoke marijuana?"

"No."

"So how do you know what it smells like?"

"I've been to concerts, lots of concerts." Helen stroked her finger against her absent wedding ring and kept her voice neutral.

Elizabeth followed Helen's finger and raised an eyebrow. "If your husband was unfaithful, why didn't you file for divorce?"

She folded her arms while Helen replied, her mouth drawn into a tight line, "I wanted to stay married for my daughter's sake."

"I don't understand your testimony about finding evidence of adultery on Judge Thompson's computer." Elizabeth leaned over and spoke with animation into the tape recorder, her eyes wide. "Why were you touching his computer? Wasn't that his work computer with all his court cases? Would he ever touch your work computer?"

Helen's voice rose as she tried to explain her thought process. "I wanted to find out *immediately* if Richard had brought another woman into the house in front of our daughter," she said, enunciating her words angrily. As Helen's green eyes turned almost black, she shot a look at Cassandra, and at this point Cassandra knew she needed to intercede.

"Really, Elizabeth," Cassandra interrupted, "is there any reason why you are turning this adversarial so soon? Do you want to hear my client's story or do you want to browbeat her into silence? If you want the former, I suggest you let her finish answering each question and let her tell you the whole story herself; if it is the latter, then we will mosey on over to the Eastern District of Virginia and pull in the federal prosecutors."

Like most trial attorneys, Elizabeth felt compelled to dig into the foundations of any story she heard. On the other hand, her office needed the publicity, and she could only push so hard to uncover the truth in a proffer session. Anything Helen revealed would have to be confirmed by the evidence at the scene of the crime.

Elizabeth pushed her chair back a few inches from the table and studied Helen closely, as if weighing and measuring her. Then she exchanged a glance with her counterpart and held her hands together so that only the tips of the fingers touched. "All right, then. I will reserve my questions for the end."

When Helen had finished speaking, Cassandra removed the DVD from her case. "Elizabeth?" she said in a quiet but commanding tone.

"Yes?" The prosecutor held out her hand for the DVD.

"Is it necessary for my client to view this video again? Would it be okay if she stepped out of the room along with my associate after she confirms that it is Phoebe in the video?" Cassandra put down her legal pad and re-crossed her legs. "As I am sure you can imagine, this has been a lot for my client to take in, and I see no reason for her to go through this again."

Before Elizabeth could begin to argue, Helen interrupted. "Thank you, Cass, but I can do this. I've seen it twice now and

I've seen it in my head a hundred more times. Seeing it here again cannot compare to the pain of watching it on replay over and over in my mind."

Helen's voice was strained by the end of her sentence, and Cassandra felt goosebumps rise on her arms. If anything, it was good that Elizabeth would see Helen struggle to hold herself together while watching the rape, but she couldn't imagine how hard this must be for a mother. She pushed away the image of her own daughter rounding the homestretch on the track. *Not my daughter. How could it be anyone's daughter?*

The DVD slid into the slot and Sandy dimmed the lights as it began to play. Cassandra found it difficult to focus on the man and the little girl, so she looked away to inspect the reactions of everyone else in the room. Carl was gritting his teeth and had put a hand on Helen's shoulder. Helen reached her hand back to hold Carl's. Tears ran down Helen's face, but she didn't bother to wipe them away.

Cassandra turned her focus to the Commonwealth's Attorney. Normally Elizabeth was about as cold and rational as women come. Cassandra knew she had a daughter who was about Phoebe's age, but what she did not realize was that Phoebe and Shelby Sue Baldwin were friends. Helen, so long disconnected from the daily routine of Phoebe's life, did not know Elizabeth or Shelby Sue, but Elizabeth recoiled as if she recognized the girl on the bed. The prosecutor held a hand to her temple and the muscles around her eyes looked strained. Seeing Elizabeth's ashen countenance made Cassandra want the video to end, but the process was one she needed to endure.

Detective Parkings murmured, "Do we know about chain of custody?"

Elizabeth held her hand up and Parkings looked away as the video kept rolling.

When the movie ended, the image remained on the screen. Elizabeth brought both her hands to her throat and croaked, "You may turn that off now, if you don't mind." She paused and removed her glasses. "Let the record reflect that we watched a video of a man raping a girl. For the record, Ms. Thompson, can you identify the man in the video?"

"Yes."

"And who is that man?" Elizabeth spoke in the smooth voice that almost all trial attorneys used when asking a string of questions.

"That man is my husband, the now deceased Judge Richard Thompson."

Cassandra let Elizabeth's questions flow like a slow-falling waterfall. She sensed the prosecutor had turned into an ally, but how best to use that to their advantage?

Before anything could crystallize in Cassandra's mind, Elizabeth asked, "Ms. Thompson, can you identify the female who appears in the video?"

"Yes, I can," replied Helen in a voice that had turned deep and throaty. "She is Phoebe Thompson, my daughter." Helen answered these questions while tears still fell down her cheeks. Cassandra silently passed her client a box of tissues that she had packed in her briefcase.

Elizabeth ran her left hand over the bun on top of her head and rubbed her eyes. She looked ten years older. "Bob? Do you have any questions?"

Detective Parkings set his pen down on his notepad. His hairline had long since receded and left behind a fingernail-shaped portion of closely-cropped hair. "We'll need to get some computer experts involved to establish chain of custody of the video," he said, leaning back in his chair. "When can we talk with the girl? It seems important to confirm her identity on that video."

"Phoebe will not be put through an interview, particularly an adversarial one, until she has received sufficient psychological treatment," Cassandra said tightly. She didn't take her eyes off Elizabeth.

Detective Parkings rubbed his stomach, which lapped over his wide black belt. "And who defines sufficient?"

Before Cassandra or Elizabeth could respond, Helen spoke in a cool tone. "I define it."

"Seems kind of presumptuous to let a murderer define anything."

Elizabeth bobbed her head and her neck swiveled dramatically. She put her glasses back on and gazed at Parkings. "I don't know that 'murderer' is an appropriate term to use here, Bob."

The detective shrugged. He scribbled something else in his notepad and grimaced, but he said nothing further after that. He seemed to be avoiding eye contact with Elizabeth; in fact, he didn't look at anyone.

Elizabeth wrote a few notes down on her yellow legal pad. As she wrote, Cassandra tried to read her cursive upside down, but like most attorneys, Elizabeth wrote with minimal legibility. The only phrase Cassandra could make out was "ME Report."

Cassandra decided to go on the offensive. "We prepared this binder for you, Elizabeth. All of the information we could access via MySpace and through Richard's home computer is included in here, but there may be additional evidence available on his work computer. It appears as if three other men were included in the conspiracy to victimize Phoebe Thompson. My client and her daughter must remain in a safe house until these people are put behind bars."

Elizabeth rose and shook hands with a firm grip. "Thanks, Cass. We'll be in touch."

Cassandra willed herself to relax as they headed back to the office. Now all they could do was wait.

CHAPTER 35

He sucked on his ballpoint pen and tapped his fingers on his laptop. Maybe he didn't need the slap-on after all, though it was still a great backup source. Maybe things were just meant to be. He had pretty much hit the lottery. If he could get her over to Cassie's office, then he wouldn't have to deal with the guards. Not that he minded. He was a man taking care of business.

Bob groaned as the sun came through the clouds. He'd gotten a stash of Oxies, but they weren't doing the trick. Not on a sunny day, and now not even on a cloudy one. He really needed to make an appointment, but first . . . brown eyes. Before he got to brown eyes, he needed to fix Richard's mess. Used his home computer and left the IP addresses all there, in one place. Damn it. Too soft. Got beaten by a woman? With a golf club? And now this mess. First things first, though. Cassie. Old vodka girl. *Slip some in her drink, next time they meet.* He'd learned how to neutralize obstacles.

CHAPTER 36

Phoebe closed her eyes and took in the night air, and while her eyes were still closed she took a drag from a cigarette. It felt so good and yet so bad as the nicotine entered her brain. It wasn't like her mind slowed down exactly. It hurt so good, and the hurt, more hurting, felt right in some inchoate way she could never explain, and darn, she didn't care if it was all about the pain of forgetting or the burden of remembering.

She'd almost argued about it with Sascha the last time they'd talked on the phone, her voice hushed as the grandfather clock ticked away loudly in the kitchen. She'd laughed and bragged about chain-smoking and how much she missed her dad's red wine. Darn it, why did she have to be such an idiot, talking like that to this kind, normal kid who'd never smoked or drank or even kissed a man, for that matter?

Just the thought of arguing with the only real friend she had left in this world made her want to smoke something a lot stronger than a Marlboro, but she shrugged and opened her eyes. Man, she missed Sascha. The moon looked so much bigger out here in the country, and as she flicked away an ash, she could feel him wrapping his arms around her again, and—

No God, no! She just wanted it to stop, and she had no way, no way of not feeling it when she stood outside and felt his arms, his chest, *oh God, no!*

Phoebe inhaled so hard that the cigarette vanished in three minutes, *or maybe it was four minutes*, she thought as she stared at the display on her cell phone and lit another cigarette with the butt of her old one. It was 11:34 P.M., and it was probably too late to call Sascha, but she dialed the familiar number anyway.

She held her breath and waited while the call went through. Sascha answered on the second ring.

"Hey."

Phoebe was mid-inhale and didn't want to be caught smoking. *This is so stupid*, she thought. She exhaled, took a deep breath and then started talking. "Sasch? I'm so sorry, but I can't stop thinking about it and I gotta talk to somebody before I lose my mind, and I'm sorry I'm smoking but I swear I'll quit, I will, before it—"

"Shh. Pheebes. Listen to me. You listening?"

Phoebe leaned against the fence, her back grinding into it hard to push away the feeling of her father pressing in behind her. *He's dead, so why do I keep feeling him?*

"What do you mean you keep feeling him?"

Phoebe gasped. She didn't realize she'd said it aloud, and now, now it was too late to hide it. "Um, what were you going to say?" she hedged.

"That I'm here. No matter what. No matter what, okay?"

"But how could you, if you knew what I'd done?" Phoebe inhaled again and wished she had a beer in hand, just a cold American beer, something to mix with the cigarette and keep her throat from feeling dry. Or maybe some red wine.

"Because you're my best friend." Sascha's words rolled out slowly, like honey dripping from a plastic jar, and Phoebe couldn't think of what to say. "And hey," her friend went on. "Listen to me. I love you, no matter what. I swear it. You're like my sister. Always."

"But I was with . . ." Phoebe's voice cracked and she started to cry silently, but even as she cried, she kept smoking. "My father. Sascha. My own father. Are you sure you still love me, Sasch? I mean, how could anyone love me?"

"Yes. I love you. No matter what happened. Is that why your mom killed him? Is that why you're on the run?"

Phoebe nodded. A teardrop fell onto her cigarette and she tried to inhale before it stopped burning, but the flame extinguished. She flipped open her metal lighter and lit another as fast as she could. "You love me even if I'm chain-smoking crappy cigarettes?" she whispered, her voice hoarse.

"I love you even if you chain-smoke cigarettes and drink too much, and I even love you if you take your eye off what you're doing and fall off your horse and break your arm, yes, yes, I love you."

Phoebe smiled wanly. She could hear Sascha murmur, "Sorry, Mom, I'm talking to Phoebe," and then Sascha paused. "Okay, Mom. I will. Pheebes, Mom says to tell you she loves you, too."

And then Phoebe was crying so hard she couldn't even inhale the cigarette. Her best friend loved her and her best friend's mom loved her and it made no sense, but she didn't feel her father pressing in against her anymore. The cigarette was gone and the dark was gone, and through it all she saw nothing and heard nothing except for Sascha, and she could tell that her best friend was crying, too.

•••

The buzzing of the little old-fashioned analog alarm clock woke Phoebe. She rubbed her teeth with her tongue and groaned. Nothing felt worse than the day after chain-smoking cigarettes, except for when a hangover mixed with the post-nicotine haze. With her eyes still closed, she pulled on her riding breeches and crept down the circular stairs toward the kitchen.

As she tiptoed through the hallway, she almost ran into her mother. "Hey, Pheebes, you up already?" Helen put a hand on her daughter's shoulder and wrinkled her nose.

Phoebe froze. For sure her mom must smell the cigarettes on her; she hadn't even showered. She nodded and kept her eyes on the boots she still held in her right hand.

To her surprise, Helen gripped Phoebe's shoulder and in a louder voice asked, "Have time for a cup of coffee before you go over to Anne's?" Every morning since she had gotten her arm in the cast, Phoebe had headed over to her trainer's chalet for seat work.

Phoebe hesitated, then forced herself to make eye contact. "You going to say anything about the way I smell, Mom?"

Helen narrowed her eyes. She didn't answer right away. First she sipped on her coffee, and only then did she pull Phoebe close. "No, I don't think I'm gonna say anything about it. Not unless you want me to." She looked at her daughter. "So, how about that cup of coffee?"

Phoebe took a deep breath and then leaned against her mom. "Okay. I'm sorry, Mom. I know I shouldn't."

Helen led her daughter into the kitchen and grabbed a mug from the wire rack hanging above the coffee pot. "Then make it so. But let's not get into that."

"You sure?"

"Yep." Helen leaned against the counter. "So. We gotta get your schoolwork figured out. I'm going to talk with your headmaster and see about that while you're working with Anne."

Phoebe tried to hide a smile. She hadn't realized how bored and lonely she'd been these last few days. "I guess it's good I don't need surgery." She swallowed more coffee and wondered if Sascha was awake yet. She missed Sascha. She missed the horses at school. She even missed AP Chemistry.

"How is the arm feeling today?"

Phoebe looked down at her arm and realized that it hadn't hurt for at least ten minutes. "Not bad, now that you mention it. And you know what else? I haven't thought of him—" Phoebe tried to pull up, but the words tumbled out. "I haven't thought of him since I got up this morning."

The muscles around her mom's left eye contracted almost violently, but Helen didn't cry. Nor did she say anything. She just reached over and put a hand on top of Phoebe's hand, and together they sat for a few minutes, sipping coffee and listening to the sound of the grandfather clock.

•••

After Phoebe had headed off to Anne's chalet, Helen sat in the kitchen reading *The Financial News* on her laptop until Mimi joined her at the table.

"So, Mimi," began Helen. She closed the lid of her laptop. "I was wondering if Phoebe can take classes virtually."

Mimi set aside her spatula, wiped her hands on a bright, flowery apron and took a seat. "You mean on the computer? What's that called, anyway? Wi-free?"

Soundless as usual, Miranda coasted in behind Mimi and chuckled. "Oh come on, Mimi. Wi-Fi, and no, it's not free."

Mimi waved a hand and laughed. "Oh, right, yes. Yes, the Wi-not-free-Fi sounds lovely. And if that Wi-Fi is what enables Phoebe to learn, why then of course, Helen, she can learn virtually." Mimi winked at Helen and then roared, "Now ladies, I must get to work."

After Miranda glided away with a diffident nod, Helen took her coffee out on the screened-in porch that overlooked the mountains. She glanced at the clock. It was 7:30 A.M. She checked McClintock's website and then dialed the Dean's office. Early morning was the best time to reach the big players in any profession.

"Dean Harper, it's Helen Thompson."

She heard a clicking sound, as if the Dean were leaning forward in his chair.

"Ms. Thompson, please accept the school community's condolences. We're uh, so very sorry—"

"Thank you."

"I was about to call you, Ms. Thompson, er, but first, if there is anything we can do, we're a tight-knit community here."

Helen imagined the trim Dean folding his hands below his chin and trying to look sincere, and she tried not to sound as dubious as she felt. "Thank you. And yes, there is something you can do to help. Phoebe needs to take her classes virtually, and I'd appreciate if you could get that arranged as soon as possible."

She waited for him to speak. Whoever talked first was going to lose, and she sensed that he didn't want to say yes but couldn't exactly say no.

"I'm not certain that would be wise, Ms. Thompson. We're doing all we can to protect the privacy of the students, but the sheer mass of media interest is presenting a challenge."

"Oh, really?" Helen twirled her pen and smiled. "How would virtual streaming present a privacy challenge? How about if I drive Phoebe to school this morning?"

Dean Harper cleared his throat. "Now, Ms. Thompson, that shouldn't be necessary. How about if I have my assistant call you back next week, after the media calms down a little bit, and then we can talk this through further?"

Helen's tone turned icy. "I don't know that it's in my daughter's best interests to wait for that." She twirled her pen again. "Maybe I need to give the Alumni President a call and meet her for a cup of coffee. We can talk about next year's athletic budget, among other things. Because you know, Dean, we go way back."

"Now that you mention it, Ms. Thompson," he replied smoothly, as if the conversation were just now starting, "I'll get with the computer department head and we'll have that remote access arranged by noon. Will that be soon enough?"

"That should work." Helen looked out over the veranda and tuned out the Dean's complaints about the media. She had no interest in what the other parents thought about her. She didn't even care what her colleagues thought of her—for the most part, anyways, she thought as she began to punch in the number for the general counsel at Sintab. That was one client she needed to keep.

CHAPTER 37

Bob rubbed his eyes. The eye strain was killing him, and the street lights and headlights made his head throb even worse. He'd driven past that Bryson House again, and the ride back through the sticks was grueling. He used to make these late-night drives without any problem. He just needed to focus now. Stop letting the pain slow him down and make his plans fuzzy.

I should be able to get in there and interview the mom. And my girl should be there, too. Maybe I can get her alone. And I need to switch the batteries in the slap-on. Check the guards out again.

If he had to shoot his way in there, and he didn't want to, he really didn't, he couldn't afford to make any mistakes. One shot kills. They were old. Lazy with their radios. Decent firepower—he needed to double-check that.

Obviously civilians. Not like him. No mistakes, as long as he could stay focused. And he'd get his brown eyed girl.

CHAPTER 38

Helen cocked her head and tried to figure out what sort of car door was slamming. Squinting into the autumn sunlight, she raised one hand above her head and scanned to see if it was just Anne clomping around in her old pickup truck. *Darned if Phoebe is getting a pickup*, she thought, and she wasn't sure if that made her want to laugh or cry. For the last couple of hours Helen had been walking the grounds, her long boots sinking into the red clay, and thinking about what she would say to Troy when she met with him later. But now, she realized with a glance at the sky, it was later. Troy had probably just arrived.

As she trudged up the hill, Helen realized that she had no idea what it was like to talk with a therapist. At least she already knew Troy, or she knew what he sounded like on the phone. Something about his voice soothed her. The back of her neck turned a little warm in embarrassment. She wondered what he must think of her after that rambling long-distance call the day she killed Richard. *Not murdered. Killed.* Helen set her jaw. This was yet another situation she couldn't control: therapy.

But when she spotted Troy, she smiled. Standing in his expensive khaki slacks and pink Oxford shirt with a blue tie, he somehow managed to pull off the outfit with élan.

"Hello, Helen, you're looking well." Troy greeted Helen with a genuine smile and a social kiss. After that, his tone shifted and he took charge. He guided her through the main door and, with an expansive wave, led her into the study. *Cary must have prepped him, right?* Still chatting about the fall weather, they sat down in the same study Cassandra had used to interview Helen. She welcomed the familiar feel of the fireplace and the bookshelves. Like Phoebe, she was out of her environment and lacking control, but at least she felt a little bit more comfortable surrounded by books.

It took Troy thirty minutes of gentle questioning before Helen could answer fully. She wanted to open up to Troy, but the words would not come easily. Troy eventually leaned back in his chair and asked, "Did you know he was raping her, Helen?"

Helen's emotional system was flooding like a computer trying to process new data without enough storage or speed. She tightened her hands into fists at her sides and yelled, "No! I had no idea!"

Troy remained calm. "What would you have done if you had known?"

"Probably the same darn thing I did, Troy. Not that I would tell anyone that. The awful truth is that I wanted to kill him. I thought about killing him."

"When?"

"When I watched the video." Helen spoke in a whisper. "It flashed through my head, seeing him die in my hands."

Troy nodded. "Most mothers would feel like that. Is that why you're feeling guilty?"

Helen fought back the urge to argue. A part of her wanted to say she wasn't guilty and that it wasn't her fault, but she knew it must be otherwise. She sat up a little straighter and looked Troy in the eye. "No. I think I am okay with what I did after I found out Richard was . . ."

"Raping your daughter?"

Helen nodded, cringing.

"Then why are you guilty?"

"I already told Cary," Helen snapped.

"Tell me, please."

Helen tried to keep her feelings in check; she held on so hard that she could barely speak. "I was never home. Always working and traveling. I failed her. Completely failed. I sucked as a mother."

Troy waited a few minutes for Helen to realize what she had said. "Okay, so now what?"

Helen shifted around in her seat a little. "So you don't think I failed my daughter?"

"Where does that get us?" Troy leaned forward and put one hand on his knee. "Your daughter was raped. You killed your husband, in self-defense in part and maybe in retribution in part, or at least Phoebe probably views it that way. She's looking to you to set the tone."

"But she told me it was my fault." Helen came as close to whining as she had in decades. She heard her voice and gritted her teeth. "Not only did I fail, but now I am whining like a teenager!" Helen clasped and unclasped her hands and looked out the window. A lone heron glided from one spot on the marsh to another, her long wings illuminated by a ray of sun that slipped between the gray-blue clouds. Helen's throat caught as she watched the bird until it vanished from view.

"Helen?" Troy's voice had lost its mellifluous roll and had taken an authoritative edge. "This perfectionism, this hatred of failure, it served you well in school. It served you well as an attorney. But it is not serving you well now. And it is not serving Phoebe well either, is it?"

"Come again?" Helen's voice wavered. She heard it wobble and roll through a pitch, up to a higher register and back down again, and the harder she struggled for her usual steady tone, the more out-of-tune she sounded.

"What point, what purpose does it serve to use the words 'I failed'? I'm not saying you failed," Troy added as he saw her chin retract and the muscles in her throat flex. "But Helen, listen to me. How does this help you? How does it make you a better mother?"

Helen sat very still. She didn't want to move because the act of moving reminded her that every cell in her body ached. She knew the ache hadn't come from exercise or even from tension. It was pain, pure pain, and each time she moved—each time she even took a deep breath—she felt it surge through her. "Her . . . my . . . it hurts. He . . . we . . . I." Helen's words made little sense. She held her hands up and stopped trying to explain.

Troy leaned closer. "Helen, may I hold your hand?" She nodded, and he held her hand in his and closed his eyes. "Listen to me. You set the tone. The future, your future, Phoebe's future, is in your hands now. Take the reins when you can, until she can ride the wind on her own. Until you both can."

Helen closed her eyes and dared to breathe. She forced images of Richard and Phoebe out of her mind and instead envisioned a white horse riding along a craggy path. A large bird flew in and out of view, and on the wings of that bird sat Phoebe. Helen opened her eyes and out of the corner of her eye she noticed the fire shimmering in the fireplace, and then she understood what Troy meant. She squeezed his hand and gave him a half-smile.

•••

Cassandra perched on the arm of her dark brown leather sofa and listened to Nadia rehearsing her closing argument for the medical malpractice case they had going to trial later that week. Cassandra noted, with a sense of professional appreciation, that Nadia sounded strong and forceful but spoke with just enough compassion for the deceased. When the associate paused and pretended to look each and every member of the jury in the eye, Cassandra smiled. *Good, Nadia, so good.* In a few years she would make partner—three years, tops—and then Cassandra would hire another associate or two. Maybe this time she would try to hire a man—

The phone made a burbling sound that indicated it came from an internal number, and Cassandra hit the speaker button. "Yes, Janice?"

"Cass?" Janice's voice sounded strained, perhaps even nervous, and Cassandra couldn't remember the last time her experienced secretary had sounded unsure of herself.

"Is something wrong, Janice?" Cassandra leaned over and lifted the receiver to her ear.

"Detective Parkings is in the waiting area."

"Seriously? For real?" Cassandra's voice was rock-hard. Janice couldn't say much, so the attorney asked a series of questions to try to elicit details.

"Did he call first?"

"Yes."

"You told him I was in a meeting?"

"Yes."

"He still showed up?"

"Yes."

"Okay, Janice, Nadia, here's what we're going to do. Nadia: grab Carl. Glad he's still camping out or in hiding or whatever, because we need him." Cassandra paused for a split second and nodded, her blue-gray eyes taking on a deeper tint. "Janice, escort Parkings to the conference room. I will be in as soon as I call the Commonwealth's Attorney. While you're waiting with him, Nadia, you and Carl ask him about football. Keep him talking. I think he's a big Redskins fan. Do not, under any circumstances, talk about anything legal."

Nadia stood up and her curls bounced a few times and settled down on the collar of her suit jacket. Cassandra hung up the phone and crossed the room until she stood beside Nadia. Then she rested a hand on Nadia's shoulder and gave it a light squeeze. "It will just be a few minutes, and Carl will be there. And we will get right back to trial prep. Your trial on Friday is still our first priority." Nadia straightened her shoulders and swung around and out the door without saying anything, but her body language expressed confidence. Cassandra knew she could handle it.

Cassandra flexed her fingers and rummaged through her desk drawer for Motrin. Her head throbbed; she had skipped lunch again. *No time.* She swallowed three orange pills and washed them down with a bottle of red Gatorade from her compact fridge. From the back of her office door she removed her emergency suit, and she shook her head with a grim smile. Her ex, Tim, had taught her to keep a suit at the ready at all times. *Darn him.* Just the thought of Tim made her head hurt worse. Cassandra cleared her mind of the past as if running a bulldozer across a beach. Then she snatched up her phone and dialed Elizabeth Baldwin.

"Elizabeth?" Cassandra spoke even before the prosecutor got her full name out. "Detective Parkings is here. In my office. Do you know anything about this, Ellie?" Cassandra used a nickname that few, if any, attorneys dared use, and Elizabeth laughed in recognition without objecting. "He's there in your darn office? Well, I'll be darned!" A rolling laugh followed on the line and Cassandra joined in. This was in fact more absurd than threatening. *I hope.*

"Okay, so I can toss him out and tell him to call you and he won't try to do something crazy like arrest my client?"

"Roger that. By the way, can you please tell me where your client is staying? I need it for the file."

Cassandra hesitated. She didn't want to alienate Elizabeth, but . . . *no*. "I can't. Until all of those sick, sick men are locked away, I just cannot reveal that information. I hope you understand the position I'm in."

Before Cassandra could finish her sentence, Elizabeth interrupted her, "Is it the Bryson House?"

"Excuse me?" Cassandra tried to buy time and think her way through this.

"Is it the Bryson House?" Elizabeth's voice came across steadily. The hair on the back of Cassandra's neck stood up. She was angry and more than a little concerned. *No one, no one was supposed to know.*

"Elizabeth, I have to know how you know about the Bryson House." Cassandra gripped the phone and felt the muscles in her hand protest.

"Ask Detective Parkings. He told me."

Parkings? "You realize that place is protected by a small militia? And I assume you would never get him a search warrant? There is absolutely no reason for him to go there. I need your word that if you need to bring Helen Thompson into custody, you will make arrangements with me. The Bryson House is and must be off-limits."

"This is an irregular request." Elizabeth used a gentle tone so that her words did not sound clipped and cold.

"I know it is, Ellie, but this is an irregular case. And I give you my word that if you ask me to produce my client, I will, no questions asked." Cassandra almost added that it would be a bloodbath if anyone, police included, tried to force his way into the Bryson House, but it wasn't necessary. Elizabeth agreed and Cassandra took a deep breath after she hung up the phone.

•••

"Detective Parkings. What a lovely surprise," Cassandra said in a droll voice. She surveyed the small conference room. Carl sat next to the detective, whose face was flushed or sunburned, and Cassandra heard him mumble something unintelligible about football. "How the heck are you? Did you make it out to FedEx Field for the game on Sunday?"

Parkings leaned forward but did not take Cassandra's hand. Instead he grabbed his notepad and pen and grunted, "Yeah. Damn fairy defense. Back in the day, we never let the bastards knock us in the teeth like that."

Carl fought the urge to kick the detective, or so it appeared to Cassandra; instead he murmured, "I don't know about that. The 49ers used to throw the ball all over the Redskins' secondary."

Cassandra cleared her throat and glared at Carl, who added, "Sorry. I grew up on the West Coast."

"So, how can we help you today?" Cassandra made a show of glancing at her watch, but she didn't see the numbers.

Detective Parkings did not answer right away. He continued to search for something, pausing only to lick his two fingers as he flipped through the scribbled-on pages of his palm-sized notebook. Finally, with a dramatic flip of a page, he glanced up and grunted. "It appears that your client's fingerprints are all over the murder weapon."

"This was not a murder, Detective. It was self-defense. And I am pretty damn sure that the deceased's medical examination will show my client's DNA under his fingertips from where he wrapped his fingers around her neck and tried to strangle her."

Detective Parkings raised an eyebrow. "So, what would that show? They were married. For all we know, they engaged in some marital, you know, before she whacked him with the golf club."

Cassandra shook her head and counted to five. Then she spoke without urgency, enunciating her words with great care. "We've been over this. We have cooperated with the Commonwealth's Attorney and made my client available for questioning. I am confident that the evidence at the scene will corroborate my client's version of events." Cassandra's voice took on a biting tone. "So, how is the sex crimes investigation going? Until you arrest the perps, my client and her daughter must put their lives on hold."

Cassandra thought about the Bryson House and the barn and Zander. What would it be like to live there? She pictured the circular staircase and the way the burnished wood felt on her hand when she leaned on the banister; then she envisioned Zander flying down the banister head first, and just as she imagined moving to catch him, Detective Parkings started to talk in a braying tone that pushed the banister out of her mind.

"I need to see Ms. Thompson and take a DNA sample." With an awkward grunt, he reached into his pocket and flashed his badge.

Cassandra waved at it with a dismissive flutter of her fingers. "Yes, Detective, I do accept that you work for the FCPD. And we can make those arrangements in the next day or so."

"No, not soon enough. I need to meet you out at the Bryson House this evening." Detective Parkings chewed on the end of his pen and Cassandra held her contempt and disgust at bay. The pen cap likely was covered in the detective's DNA, and she knew that he could remove Helen's DNA easily enough from one of her hairbrushes. But this wasn't about molecules on a brush. It was about her client's safety and the sanctity of a home that existed for one reason: to protect women in peril.

Without answering, Cassandra leaned over and dialed Elizabeth's direct line. She had a knack for remembering phone numbers, and yet in all her years of trial work she had never used this skill. *I never needed it until now, when I have to make an impression on a fucking douchebag,* she thought. *Perfect.*

Elizabeth picked up on the third ring. Cassandra identified all of the attorneys in the room and realized that Carl's role, while unspecified, made a great deal of sense. That in and of itself was odd. He didn't work for Cassandra, he wasn't related to Helen and he wasn't even licensed to practice law in Virginia; and yet here he sat as if he were a member of the firm. *Some things don't need to make sense,* she mused. Carl would be an asset to any firm.

"Ellic," Cassandra began, deliberately using the Commonwealth Attorney's nickname, "Detective Parkings showed up at my office for an impromptu meeting. While he is here I needed to clear up something with you—need to make sure we're all on the same page, so to speak."

"Sure. What is it, Cass?"

Cassandra put her hands on the edge of the conference table and felt the sturdy wood under her fingers. She stood up straight, but with her upper body at a slight angle to the table, and half-closed her eyes. She was taking the temperature of the room; it felt just right to her well-honed lawyer's intuition. "Detective Parkings wants to interview my client. And I have no problem with that, so long as I am present and we conduct the interview either at my office, at the police station or at your office. I'm reasonable and willing to accommodate your schedules."

Cassandra paused and waited for Elizabeth to reply.

"Okay, that makes sense."

Cassandra opened her eyes much wider and nodded at Carl, who sat with one hand resting on his chin. "But Detective Parkings here said something about going to my client's safe house, and under no circumstances can that happen. Not now and not ever." Cassandra switched her gaze to Parkings, but he shifted his eyes and looked away. "Ellie? The very integrity of the Bryson House hinges on its remaining secret. Women go there seeking sanctuary. Unless the police are investigating a crime that occurred there, or in the Detective's case, investigating a witness who will not cooperate, they have no business, absolutely no business showing up there."

Parkings shook his head and scoffed at Cassandra. "Are you telling me I can't investigate a crime?"

"No crime happened at the Bryson House. The only crime that occurred took place at my client's home, and—"

Parkings tapped his fingers on his notepad. "Yeah, she killed her husband with a golf club."

"That wasn't the crime I was talking about, Detective. The crime was when the deceased raped his daughter and then viciously attacked my client. That was the crime. And at no point have you identified my client as a person of interest."

At this point, Elizabeth interrupted the conversation. "Here's how I see it. Ms. White has offered to make her client available for questioning. If there is going to be any more interviewing, I want to be in on it, so we can schedule it here at the courthouse. In the meantime, Detective, the Bryson House— leave it alone. There is nothing there that pertains to the investigation, and both Cassandra and Ms. Thompson have given their word."

Parkings glared at his notepad and then exploded with a string of expletives. "That's outrageous, Elizabeth. I don't care if the goddamn Pope is staying at that ovary farm. I have an investigation to run and you can't limit where I conduct it."

"Yes, I can. You cannot get into the Bryson House, or past their armed guards, unless you bear a search warrant. And I can promise you something else."

"What's that, Counselor?" Detective Parkings leaned forward and angled his head toward the phone. "Are you going to block me from getting a warrant or some chickenshit thing like that?"

"Yes. That is exactly what I will do if you ask another Commonwealth's Attorney to get you a warrant."

"You can't stop me from conducting an investigation, Liz."

Cassandra imagined Elizabeth's jaw tightening. She hated that nickname.

"You're not investigating anything at the Bryson House, *Bobby*." Cassandra peeked at Parkings and watched his ears turn scarlet. She clenched her facial muscles and knew that Carl was doing the same.

Elizabeth continued coldly, "You have no business there. Ms. Thompson is not a person of interest. All of the evidence you need is either in your possession or at the Thompson residence or accessible via counsel for Ms. Thompson. We're not in the business of hounding people or creating collateral damage, and that is exactly what would happen if you entered the grounds at the Bryson House." Elizabeth paused with purpose. "Am I clear, *Bobby*?"

Parkings had turned almost purple, and now splotchy marks broke out all over his face. Cassandra found herself thinking of a dying lizard whose skin couldn't figure out if it needed to look like green leaves or brown leaves.

The detective licked his lips, mumbled something under his breath, and pushed his chair back with a clatter. As he strode toward the door, he waved his hand. "No need to escort me out.

I can find the elevator myself." Cassandra nodded at Carl and he followed Parkings out to the reception area.

Cassandra then directed her gaze at Nadia. "Okay, we have thirty minutes and then I got to head off to practice. Between now and then, we'll iron out the kinks. Ready?"

Nadia's eyes burned and she spluttered, "How did you do that, Cass? Do you think he'll listen to Elizabeth?"

Cassandra turned, one hand on the brass door handle, and reflected for a moment. "Sometimes, with the right people in place, a legal system can be just. Sometimes. As far as Parkings, he had better listen. He may think he's above the law, but he's not." A thought passed in and out of her mind, but she lost it before she could really hold onto it. After all, Parkings might be rude, but he was just doing his job. Cassandra shook her head. *This was no time to be imagining stuff.*

CHAPTER 39

Phoebe sprawled on the bed in Helen's room and tried to follow the screen on her mother's laptop as her chemistry professor strutted from one side of the chalkboard to the other. The camcorder did not show the sturdy wooden desks or any of the students, but if Phoebe closed her eyes and concentrated really hard, she could picture her bespectacled lab partner, David, sitting in the far right corner. She knew his textbook was open, and she imagined him scribbling equations with his black technical pencil. Her eyes still closed, Phoebe relaxed. *Sascha passed her a note. Phoebe read it, giggled and wrote a response, which she sent back while Mr. Brown's back was turned.*

Phoebe startled to attention. She was not sure if she had fallen asleep or just gotten lost in the maze-like trail of numbers appearing on the blackboard. Rubbing her eyes, she checked the time and smiled. A minute, no more, had passed, but in that minute she had felt like she belonged in a familiar place. In Mr. Brown's chemistry classroom, Phoebe had always felt safe and comfortable and a little bored. *Always a little bored*, she thought, *but feeling a little bored is a good thing.*

The girl ran her hands along the bedspread and flattened out the folds in the material. In the background Mr. Brown droned on. Phoebe tried to copy down every word and every number he uttered, but her mind buzzed and her attention wandered as the minutes trickled past. A bell rang onscreen, sounding strange, as if it were ringing underwater. "Don't forget, ladies and gentlemen," her teacher said as her classmates made for the door. "We have a test on chapters six through ten on Friday. Open book."

No one asked Phoebe for lunch. She wasn't there. She tapped the image on the screen until it receded, and then slammed her notebook shut and looked down at the stables from her mom's window. She was sick of it all. She wanted to break the computer screen. There wasn't anyone young to talk to, and even Anne had annoyed her in the morning. All Anne ever wanted to do was more drills, and while Phoebe worked hard, Anne talked an endless stream about philosophy and the quality of dirt and religion.

As if God made us and left us to rot in this stuff. Why did God make me? For whose sake? Why has he forsaken me? I hate God. He is not he, or is he? Is God Dad? That's what Dad joked the first time. The first time.

Phoebe covered her ears, hearing her father's words. *No! Stop!*

She didn't hear Helen open the door. "Sweetheart? Were you talking to someone? Are you okay?"

Phoebe looked down at her right fist, which gripped the window rod, and then she realized her left arm ached. "Do I look all right?" Phoebe snapped. And then something caught in her throat. Helen's left eye twitched and Phoebe read sadness and concern in her mother's face. She felt herself relax. "Mom?"

Helen nodded and tried to smile but gave up quickly.

"Did they burn Dad?"

Helen put her arms out and Phoebe rested her throbbing head on Helen's shoulder.

"Yes, sweetie." Helen's chin sank into Phoebe's hair, and it felt safe; almost like her mom was protecting her from seeing or feeling it. Without moving away, her mother added, "The cremation happened yesterday. If you want me to tell you more about it, I will, love."

Phoebe held her head still. She could feel her pulse beating and she could hear her mom's heart thumping, strong, steady and slow. Did she want to know more about it? She was too tired to think.

And so, even though it felt weird, this holding-hug, they held onto one another. Phoebe didn't know what to say. She needed her mother's reassurance right then, and yet words danced out of reach. All that remained was touch.

"I'm sorry I was mean, Mom," Phoebe murmured.

Helen put her hand on the back of Phoebe's head and caressed her daughter's hair. Then she pulled Phoebe away and kissed her cheek. "I know. It's okay. And I want to ask you something, but it's a hard thing to talk about."

Phoebe couldn't help giggling at her mother. "Come on, Mom. As you always used to say to me when I was a little girl, 'Out with it.'"

Helen sat down on the window seat. "Your father's ashes . . ." She took a deep breath and tapped her middle finger against her thumb. "When all of this is over and we're free to leave, do you want to spread them somewhere?" Helen raised her hand and covered her mouth. She could see Richard the first time he'd kissed her. She willed her mind back to the present.

Phoebe winced. She could read the pain in her mother's voice. "Mom? I'm sorry. I really am."

Helen swallowed. "No, no, you're not the one who should be sorry."

Phoebe moved her head so that it nestled in her mother's hand. "We can do that. Someday. But right now I don't want to talk about it. My arm hurts, and when I think about Dad it makes everything hurt even worse."

Helen was first chair, all alone on this case that was her daughter. There was no one else. *I'll have to be enough. I'll have to be. And I don't need to get it all figured out right now. I just need to make her feel better.*

Nothing else mattered. Not now. Right now, Phoebe's arm hurt; that was the issue. That alone needed fixing.

"Let's go downstairs and get you some more Motrin and maybe some lunch. Are you hungry?"

Phoebe almost replied that she didn't want to eat, but then the odor of homemade bread wafted from the kitchen below. Her stomach growled.

•••

A half-hour later, Phoebe pushed back from the strawberry preserves and warm bread. She took in the soft glow of the light oak kitchen table and murmured, "See you at dinner,

Mom." Helen watched her daughter, clad in jeans and a forest-green Henley shirt with one sleeve pulled up over her cast, walk out of the kitchen. She craned her neck and caught sight of Phoebe through the window as the girl curled around the back side of the house.

Before Helen could feel lonely, Mimi came in and sat down beside her. "I don't know if you've spoken with Cass yet, but Miranda and I wanted to let you know that the Bryson House is defended. Well. The grounds are patrolled at night. You're safe here."

Helen's heart beat faster and she felt a sudden rush of adrenaline. "Mimi, please tell me you have this talk with all of the women who stay here." Helen's effort at a half-smile fell short. She gave up on it and let her fear show. "Did something happen? I haven't had my phone turned on. I have been trying to be present and only check in on work for a couple of hours a day."

Mimi sipped from her thick-handled tea mug and waited to see if Helen was going to say more. When she didn't, Mimi set her mug down and put her warm hand on top of Helen's. "Well, I am pretty sure she called you, so I will let you call her back, but I wanted to reassure you that the Bryson House is practically impregnable, and . . ." Mimi prattled on, but Helen barely heard the rest of Mimi's answer. She was already dialing Cassandra.

Mimi made polite noises and managed to exit the kitchen before Helen's call connected, and once again the two old legal horses wasted no time on niceties. In a few succinct sentences, Cassandra explained what had happened with Detective Parkings, and Helen sounded deferential in response. Helen was trying hard to quell a rising feeling of irritability. To her own ears she sounded querulous and weak.

She clicked off the call and checked the elapsed time. Four minutes, give or take a second or two. She wished all of her client interactions could proceed at that rate of speed. She wished that someone else could be the client. Helen stood up and carried her dishes to the sink and returned the strawberry preserves to the side shelf of the stainless steel refrigerator. She wished there were no case.

•••

Cassandra tapped the Bluetooth's End Call button on her steering wheel and surveyed the undulating hills that framed her ride to McClintock School. She thought about calling Elizabeth one more time to press the issue raised by Parkings, until she realized that she would sound like she needed and wanted something that wasn't Elizabeth's to give. Instead, she dialed Frank's work number and smiled into the phone when he answered on the first ring. "Is it true we're having a date night tomorrow night?"

"Yeah, Cass. Looking forward to it, hon."

Cassandra frowned. He sounded businesslike and a little distant. "Someone in there with you, darling?" She imagined the crease of one of his gray suit pants, wishing she could run her hands up his leg, and then she shook her head at how young he made her feel.

"I am in the middle of a meeting, my dear, but to answer your question, yes, everything has been taken care of. Babysitter engaged. I'm so looking forward to a night out, just us."

Frank's voice warmed her like a familiar blanket. Cassandra smiled. "Well, I am picking Zander up from school and taking him with me to practice," she said. "So we will be home before six and I'll toss the lasagna in the oven, or something like that." Before Frank could answer, the Bluetooth beeped and announced Helen's phone number. The second time in an hour.

"Gotta bolt, hon." Cassandra switched calls. "Helen? I'm in the car now, and we might get cut off because I'm near a dead spot." Cassandra spoke in a level tone, almost devoid of inflection.

Helen didn't respond to this. She sounded angry. "Isn't there any way you can guarantee that asshole detective will stay away from us?"

Cassandra took a deep breath before she answered. While Helen was a high-powered downtown litigator, she was also Cassandra's client. Cassandra knew that fear, not disrespect, had fed this outburst; and reassurance, not rebuke, would quell it. "Helen, I hear you. And I think we have the situation under control."

Cassandra described the meeting with Parkings with a broad brush and then, as she wound up the driveway to McClintock, she added, "I don't have time to tell you the whole story now, but if you ask Mimi, I'll bet she'll tell you about the guards at the Bryson House. It's quite a story."

"Thank you for explaining that. I should've known you had it well in hand. I didn't mean to jump on you like this." Helen sounded apologetic. "Before you hang up, give me a hint about the armed guards."

Cassandra pulled up in front of Zander's preschool and let the engine idle while she finished her conversation. "Well, like I said, those guards are top-notch. They all retain foreign citizenship, which in certain circumstances might make them a little bit more reckless. I reckon they will go to extraordinary measures to keep you safe."

Helen laughed, a little breathless. "Like what?"

Cassandra touched the handle of her duffle bag. "I got to run, Helen. Just trust me on this. Those guards will keep the two of you safe."

Cassandra saw Zander before he saw her, and a feeling she had long since stopped trying to describe flooded through her. It wasn't that she loved him more than she loved Catherine, but she worried about him more. There was no getting around the hue of his skin . . . and yet it was a different world now. A better world. She hoped.

Before she could reach her arms out and lift her little creature into the air, the grim and gray middle-aged preschool headmistress approached, frowning. "Zander had another tough day today. He kept jumping off the playhouse, and then several of his classmates followed him. We talked about the class rules and he sat in the office with me during lunch."

Cassandra tried not to chuckle. She knew what the headmistress wanted her to say, but the last thing she wanted to do after a long day apart from Zander was to correct him. She directed a diffident nod at the woman and called out to her son, "Zander! I missed you!"

Zander squealed and body-slammed his mother. After she picked him up and nuzzled his cheek, he put one thumb in his mouth, rested his curly locks on his mother's shoulder and patted her back almost as if he wanted to reassure her. But what he really wanted was for her to comfort him, and so she did.

"Tough day?" she whispered in his ear. "We'll do better tomorrow." Changing her voice to a louder volume she added, "Now let's go get dressed for practice."

Zander's eyes popped open and he squirmed out of her arms and grinned. "Cat, Cat, never fat," he chanted, dimple showing, and Cassandra smiled and frowned at the same time. So many things to teach her son; so little time.

When she and Zander reached the stadium, Cassandra strolled in with an easy, athletic confidence and rubbed her son's head. "Go ahead, Zander." He glanced at her, clinging to her leg with a sad look in his eyes, so she knelt down in front of him. His lower lip trembled. "What's wrong, sweetie?"

He leaned into her and waited for his mother to hug him. As she stroked his head again, she said, "You can stay with me if you want to, darling. Is that what you want?"

His lips straightened into a crooked smile. "Yes, Mama. I lonely."

"You're lonely, hmm?" She hugged him and tried to sound stern and gentle at once. "Just stay on my six the whole time, 'kay?" Zander knew that this meant to stay right behind his mother, as if connected to her by an invisible string. She shook her head. Thank God she wasn't the coach anymore.

As Cassandra finished talking, Catherine crept up behind Zander, and with a wink at their mother, covered her brother's eyes. "Guess who, buddy?" she whispered.

While Zander hugged his sister and pulled on her ponytail, Catherine shot Cassandra a glare and her mother shrugged and held her hands up in response. She knew Catherine wanted her full attention and was used to receiving it. The track and the trails represented, in Catherine's mind, sacrosanct time with her mother, and Zander's presence made her feel slighted. *Some things are unavoidable*, Cassandra thought. Rather than apologize, she arched an eyebrow and stood up as straight as she could." How was school, darling?"

Catherine rolled her eyes. The cold war was on.

So be it, Cassandra mused. "Hopefully I can run a few laps with you, Cat."

Before Cat could flip her hair, Zander piped up, "Cat Cat! Kit Kat?"

Cat grinned as her brother broke the tension. "Okay, Mom, that would be great if you could." The side of Catherine's mouth twitched. "Is he sick or something?"

Cassandra's mind shifted into a higher gear. Her daughter saw what she should have seen: Zander got clingy whenever he was coming down with something. She felt her shoulders slump; really, how could she run if he was sick? She rustled Zander's hair and kissed his cheek, shifting her body away from the gaggle of teenagers while she tried to think about, or justify, going running anyway.

Cassandra flexed her arms and brought them together behind her back. The scapular muscles in her upper back were knotted up and she knew her body was reacting to inner tension. Was she angry at Zander? She felt something akin to anger; and yet she knew it wasn't his fault that her date nights with Frank always got cut short or canceled altogether. She glanced at Catherine, who was stretching her upper legs in a dynamic motion, and she realized that it wasn't Zander's fault or Catherine's fault. It was not even her fault. Sometimes Zander needed her more; sometimes Catherine's needs came first. And all too often Cassandra's needs got squeezed out of the equation. She couldn't please everyone all of the time or even most of the time.

Somewhere there was a lesson in all of this, but Cassandra was tired of worrying about it. She longed for a quiet moment with the man she loved, and absent that, she longed for a moment of physical freedom. In running she could set her worries, her burdens, down.

"Mama?" Zander leaned against Cassandra's leg, waiting for her to wrap an arm around his shoulders. She gazed off into the distance at the wispy feathers of white moving across the afternoon autumn sky. A football coach's whistle echoed in the almost-empty stadium, and the ghost of a halfback from three decades past flashed once into her memory and then fluttered away, replaced by another image, in the modern day, of a powerful black quarterback sprinting up the sideline and stepping out of bounds with delicate, prancing steps. She wanted to watch the football players practice from the shifting vantage point of a runner circling the track.

"Yeah, buddy?" She gave an inaudible sigh and rubbed her son's head again. His almost bristly curls moved between her fingers, and the feeling of the rough edges brought her back to the present. She was here, with her only son. And someday, all too soon, he would be leaving. *Wonder if he'll play football someday?*

"Who are they?"

"You mean the guys wearing helmets and running on the grass?" Cassandra tried to use words he already knew as she answered his questions.

Zander scarcely waited for her answers before he asked more. "Are they playing tag?"

"No, they're playing football."

"What's football?" Zander persisted. Cassandra held her son's hand and led him to the top of the bleachers, where a mesh metal fence rose several feet above the railing. *It's safe here. I could leave him alone and let him play here, but he looks so sweet and lost and vulnerable today. He needs me right here.* "Football is the name of the game they're playing, hon." Cassandra contemplated how hard it was to explain a sport like football to a little boy. *Where to start?*

Zander grasped Cassandra's hand and brought it up to his eyes, almost as if trying to memorize the lines that crisscrossed her palm. "Hey, Mama?" His voice was muffled by her palm.

She nodded and pulled him in front of her as she sat down on the gray bleacher seat. "Yep?"

Zander turned her hand and rubbed her knuckles with a wide-eyed curiosity. "Can I run with Cat? *Puh-leeze*, Mama?"

Cassandra began to answer no reflexively, but she caught herself. For all of the years she had been a mother, she had never sat in the stands and watched one of her children play a sport. She had helped coach all of Cat's teams, and when she wasn't on the sidelines as a coach she always ended up pacing behind her daughter's bench. Cassandra did not really know how to watch her children. She was an active participant in their lives, in part because sitting still was anathema to her hard-driving personality. She could not say yes today. But she couldn't bear to confine herself to the sideline just yet, so she hugged Zander tight and pointed to the quarterback. "See? He drifts back in the pocket to throw . . ."

"He has pockets, Mama?" Zander swiveled his hips. "I have seven pockets today!"

"Well, seven pockets is a lot of pockets, but they use the word in a different way in football."

Zander grunted and kept chattering about pockets. A breeze ruffled the leaves off in the distance, almost past the horizon, and Cassandra watched Catherine race around the backstretch. She bobbed her head and stood up. "YEAH! MOVE IT, CAT!" she bellowed.

"Mama!" Zander giggled. "Is that an inside voice?"

The smell of fall hung in the afternoon air. The football players chanted in unison, in voices unnaturally deep for their adolescent bodies: "Five, four, three, two. Hit—hit—blast them blue!" as they sprinted up and down the field. Cassandra itched to move; yet she forced her legs to be still while she observed her daughter's world.

She felt a knot of pride and a vague sense of loss watching her not-so-little girl glide over the track with the effortless grace of youth. Cassandra remembered when she was able to move like that, free from care, free from pain. Here she paused, a woman entering the autumn of her own life. She leaned closer to Zander, his small, warm body sheltering her from the sharp cold of the metal bench.

•••

Cassandra rubbed her eyes and set aside Catherine's English paper. For the life of her, she couldn't understand why her daughter couldn't get through a single writing project without comparing something in the book she was writing about to running. This time it was Faulkner's *The Bear*, and somehow, chuckled Cassandra with a rueful laugh, it bore a close relationship to Joan Benoit Samuelson's epic win in the 1984 LA Olympics. Before she could summon her daughter, Catherine sidled up next to her.

"Too much on Joannie?" Catherine rested one hand on her mom's shoulder and then set her chin on top of her hand.

Cassandra wrestled with what to say. She couldn't write the papers for her kid, and it wasn't like Catherine wasn't trying.

It was just . . . how could Cat make it in life if everything came down to splits and finishing kicks? Then again, marathoners matured late, and if Cat got into Oregon there was a chance she could go as far as her legs would carry her. A chance. *Aw, shoot. So she's not going to be a lawyer, and she might not even crack a 3.0, but she loves one thing, and I'm not going to get in her way.*

"It's not bad, not bad at all." Cassandra turned her head sideways so that Catherine could see that she was smiling. She didn't want to sound harsh; that never had worked with Catherine. "But Cat. Your teacher told you not to write about running so much, right? Are you sure this is the way you're going here?"

Catherine grabbed her mother's hand and used it to launch from a slouch until she was facing her in an athletic stance. She made a chopping motion with her hand. "I'm slashing right to the heart of the story, Mom!" She giggled as Cassandra shook her head. "And, like, Mr. Mahon didn't say I couldn't write about running. Just not so much, ya know?" Catherine waved her hand expressively. "Besides, I'm just rolling with it, letting inspiration take me where it gets me."

"But—"

Catherine snatched the paper from her mom and a gleeful smirk tugged the sides of her mouth. "Anyway, Joannie wasn't scared when she ran in '84. So why should I be afraid of getting marked down for doing exactly what we're supposed to do: Connect the story to something else in life?"

"Joannie was coming back from being injured, Cat. That's different."

Catherine's shoulders slumped, and Cassandra recognized her own body language in her child. It was time to stop arguing. "Listen, Cat. It's fine. It's good. Actually, I think you made a good connection here. I worry about your grades, that's all."

Catherine's jaw tightened. "I'm doing my best."

"I know." Cassandra took off her reading glasses and set them on the end table next to the leather sofa. "And you're doing just fine. For real." Cassandra gulped. It almost killed her that "just fine" was a C+, and she left unspoken what she was thinking.

Catherine blurted it out for both of them. "I'm not getting into Oregon based on grades, Mom." She bounced on her toes and then shifted into a dynamic stretch. *Her flexibility is outstanding*, thought Cassandra, unable to stop feeling proud.

•••

Cassandra tried to talk with Jen every Thursday night, a tradition that they had mostly kept up since their bar-hopping days in law school. She felt a wave of sadness hit her as she remembered the years they did not talk every Thursday night. Those were the drunk years. But before she could wallow in it, something hit her above the eye and she yelped in pain. "Darn it, who hit me with that darn dart?"

At the moment, Frank was tucking Zander into bed; more often than not, this meant they were shooting Nerf guns. Cassandra grabbed the dart, threw it on the landing and slammed the study door. "Aw crap, Jen, I just got shot in the eye with a freakin' dart gun!"

Jen's bubbling laugh cascaded on the other end of the line. "I hope it wasn't a real dart!"

Cassandra laughed with Jen, but after she hung up the phone she opened the study door and slammed it again with a glare at Frank, who came bounding around the corner chasing Zander. Cassandra tried to tune out the pitter-patter of Zander's feet on the landing above her head while she called her backup babysitter. Then she spent more than an hour on the computer and on the phone with Nadia as they fleshed out the predictably messy list of last-minute emergencies before Friday's trial.

At ten o'clock, after Zander had finally fallen asleep, Cassandra waded into the kitchen to survey Frank's handiwork. He had picked up dinner from Milano's: a Caesar salad that Cassandra and Catherine liked and pizza for "the men," as he had said with a sideways wink at Zander. He had done the dishes. Sort of. Truth be told, he had thought about doing the dishes and forgotten to clear the table. He had taken care of the laundry by tossing a load of Cassandra's "Wash in Cold Water Only" blouses from the dryer onto the floor of his office, which meant that Cassandra would be up until midnight ironing her clothing for tomorrow's trial.

After listening for a few moments, she took a deep breath. She was pretty sure that Frank had finally settled Zander down because she couldn't hear any squeals or thumps and wall-thwacks.

She threw her hands up in disgust and flicked on the gas stove to make tea. When she put her hand on the cupboard handle to bring out the tea chest, green slime oozed from the bottom of the brass handle, and she jerked her hand back so fast that a splinter stuck in her index finger.

"Ouch!" she muttered, and just then Frank drifted alongside her. She smelled his cologne and her body flew toward his like a magnet to metal, and yet . . . "Darn you, Frank!" she exclaimed. "What in the world is this green slime?"

She felt his hand dance along the ridge of her neck and then his lush lips brushing against her collarbone. "No way, not that easily," she murmured, but mid-sentence her growl turned into something sultry as an electric current surged through her.

On the way up the stairs they were absolutely quiet so as not to awaken the children. Frank pulled the door shut behind him and Cassandra checked to make sure the lock clicked; and when she turned toward Frank, she covered her mouth to stifle her laughter. Frank stood in front of her, naked.

She grinned up at him. "Well, hon, waste no time."

Afterward, Frank held her tightly. She rested her head on his broad chest and listened to his heart race. Like a fast, steady drum it beat, and as the seconds wound down it slowed and she sighed, content. But even as she registered that she was content, she started to worry about her blouse and the trial and all the things she had to do in the morning. She stirred and intended to shower and take care of a long list of items in her mental to-do list, but his arms tightened around her.

"Shh," he whispered in a voice that made her feel safe and comforted. "Don't worry about the blouse. I'll get it for you in the morning." She tried to argue with him, but he rubbed his fingers through her hair and she stopped moving. *Just one more minute*, she thought, *and I will get up*, but the minute became five minutes and her breathing slowed down and matched Frank's. And then she stopped checking the time or counting the rate of their beating hearts, and let sleep overtake her.

CHAPTER 40

Cassandra rolled over and felt for Frank. Instead of the familiar scent of his body, musky with a hint of aftershave, the smell of coffee wafted up the stairs. She heard Zander coughing. Cassandra groaned and padded downstairs.

Frank was singing along to an old Aretha Franklin song he was blasting on his monstrous basement speakers. With a mug of steaming coffee in her hand, Cassandra grabbed the rickety banister and headed down to see if he had finished his workout. He lifted weights every other morning in their basement, which he had turned into a small gym.

But Frank wasn't lifting weights. Instead he swayed back and forth, holding the iron a few inches away from his chin as he cheerfully belted out the chorus from "Respect." Cassandra set her mug down and leaned against him.

"Aw, babe," she murmured after the song ended. "Are you ironing my blouse for me? Are you really doing that for me?"

Frank's eyes twinkled. Still holding the iron, he put a hand on her hip and whispered, "Hey Gorgeous." A burble rose in her throat and at that moment the tapping of Zander's feet announced his arrival with enough time for Cassandra to extricate herself from Frank.

"Mama!" He rubbed his red-rimmed eyes. "I slept bad last night. Can I have a blue popsicle for breakfast?"

"No," Frank snapped.

"Mama? Gimme popsicle? I'm sick. So I eat popsicle."

Cassandra shrugged. "Well, I do usually let you eat popsicles when you're sick, but it's up to your dad. Hey, Frank, how about if I finish the ironing while you get Zander sorted?" Frank and Zander both grumbled, but Cassandra was already gone, a mental switch flicked in her mind. She would be in court in three hours and she felt more nervous for Nadia than she ever felt for her own court appearances. Except of course when she was on the witness stand.

Cassandra pushed Tim out of her mind. *He has no control over me now.* She picked up the iron, and the hot steam rose and swirled to the ceiling as she completed the job her man had started. With her blouse in her hand, she turned the corner and climbed the basement steps.

At the top of the stairs she smiled at her almost-grown daughter, born of Tim but raised by Frank, the only father the girl had ever really known. Cassandra reached her hand out and cupped the side of her daughter's suntanned cheek, and she felt like crying or smiling or maybe both. In her mind's eye she held her tiny daughter's hand as they walked down the steps leading away from the Bryson House and began their long journey to a new life together.

"What are you thinking, Mom?" Catherine asked, and a sob caught in Cassandra's throat.

"To be honest, Cat, the case I am working on has me spending a lot of time back at the Bryson House, and I was ironing my blouse downstairs and I got to thinking about it all again. I could see you as a baby girl, and it was so hard, leaving your birth father and starting over again. Mimi and Miranda helped me grow strong enough. And when I felt like I couldn't make it, I would hold you and think about the life I wanted you to have. And every night for weeks I would hold you close to me and sing a song to you."

While Cassandra paused to wipe her eyes, Catherine handed her a tissue. "Mom, was it *'Que sera sera'*?" Cassandra nodded.

Zander careened around the corner and ran into Catherine. "What's that mean?"

Cassandra, with one arm now wrapped around Catherine, rubbed her son's dark, curly locks. "It means 'Whatever will be, will be.' It's a song." Cassandra swayed back and forth for a moment, then added, "Come here, Zander, and Catherine and I will sing it for you."

Cassandra helped Zander climb up on the chair next to them, and with his thumb in his mouth he listened to them as if spellbound.

Cassandra looked over at Catherine and saw a young woman with a strong jaw and an athletic confidence: a younger Cassandra, but with a full lifetime ahead of her. And beside her perched a beautiful brown boy with the clearest set of blue-gray eyes she'd ever seen.

"Gosh, Mom, I remember that song well," exclaimed Catherine, and then, before Cassandra could answer, she added tenderly, "Are you coming to my cross-country meet tomorrow?"

Cassandra gazed at her children and clung to the doorjamb before she left for the day. "I wouldn't miss it for the world."

•••

Miranda walked into the kitchen and gasped. "Mimi! For the love of Pete, what in the heck are you doing with that thing inside the house?" Mimi was cradling a handgun in her lap, and Miranda suddenly thought of all the babies Mimi had held while sitting in the same comfortable, food-stained armchair that her partner insisted on leaving in her otherwise pristine kitchen.

Innocently, but with a hint of crazy, Mimi stated, "Anne is taking me to the shooting range. She said I needed to get comfortable sitting with the gun first, so I have been, um, you know, sitting with it."

"Aw, now come on, Mimi. You remember what happened the last time you fired a shotgun." Miranda glared across the room.

Mimi blinked and continued to polish the handgun. "Anne took me to Bud's Gun Store. Check it out. It's a nine-millimeter stainless steel Ruger, and I love this synthetic black handle. It fits just right in my hand and won't slip in an emergency."

"Mimi?" Miranda chided her. "You do remember what happened the last time you shot a gun, right?"

Mimi blinked again and Miranda gritted her teeth and waited impatiently for Mimi's response. But underneath her annoyance was the smallest seed of amusement, and she knew Mimi sensed it.

Mimi smiled. "Do you want to hold it? It shoots fifteen rounds! If you like the way it feels, I bet Anne will buy one for you, too."

"What? You almost shot a man's foot off! And Anne! Wait until I talk with her about this. I cannot believe she would buy *you* a gun."

Mimi waited for Miranda to take a breath, and with another theatrical blink thrown in she drawled, "But Miranda, that was a shotgun and this is just a wee little nine-millimeter. Now check out the way you load the magazine. It's as easy as pie!" Mimi exclaimed.

"Is it . . . *loaded?*" Miranda's voice cracked.

Mimi waved her arm expansively. "Oh heavens, no. The magazine is empty. Anne said I could practice with it before we hit the range." Mimi's voice trailed off as she picked at the magazine in the bottom of the Ruger's grip. She shrugged with a helpless half-smile. "Oh sugar, it seems to be stuck. Miranda, be a dear and see if you can get it unstuck."

Miranda sighed and, against her better judgment, took hold of the Ruger. With a practiced motion she clicked the release and caught the clip as it slid free from the pistol. She surreptitiously checked the chamber as Mimi looked away.

"Anyway, that unpleasant gentleman had it coming to him. He was lucky he only lost two toes." Mimi wiped her hands on her apron and slipped on her reading glasses. "Here, you keep hold of the gun and I'll write out the shopping list you've been pestering me for."

Miranda didn't answer, and for a few minutes the two women stood in a companionable silence. When Mimi had finished writing her list, she let her reading glasses hang back off the silver chain that dangled from her neck. She glanced over at Miranda, who was fiddling with the Ruger with an expert hand.

"Miranda?" Mimi spoke in an undertone so that no one else could hear them.

Miranda tilted her chin toward her old friend.

"I'm scared. I got the gun because the detective on this case is relentless. And he gives me a bad feeling."

Miranda's eyes widened. Mimi's intuitive ability to read danger in men was legendary.

"It's probably nothing," Mimi added.

Miranda knew Mimi wasn't convinced, but she didn't say it aloud.

"But he's hounding Helen and Cassandra," Mimi added. "It just feels wrong."

Miranda nodded, but before she could ask another question, the front door slammed and Anne's boots clicked on the wood floors. Miranda glided across the kitchen and raised her eyebrow at Anne, who leaned over, grimacing, as she removed her boots and chuckled apologetically to hide her discomfort.

"How's your hip today, Anne dear?"

Anne rocked her hands back and forth and up and down clapping them together once for emphasis. "No use complaining, eh?"

"No more use complaining about your hip than me complaining about your boots, my friend."

"Aw, sorry, I forgot." Anne flashed a good-natured smile that made her look twenty years younger. "Now are you ready to go to the range? I figure we can fit an hour or two of shooting in before lunch."

Mimi grabbed her purse and zipped the Ruger into its quilted case. Miranda checked her watch. "Wait. I'm coming, too. How can I miss Mimi shooting something she means to hit?" Anne's eyes glinted with amusement as she followed Mimi and Miranda out the back door to Mimi's SUV.

•••

When their trial went into recess after *voir dire* and opening statements, Cassandra checked her messages at the office. The only urgent one was from Elizabeth, and Cassandra didn't need to return the call directly. Waving at Nadia, she took the stairs two at a time on the way to the fifth floor.   Before she pushed the door that led into the foyer, Cassandra marveled at the light-filled staircase. The architects had built windows and skylights, which had transformed what was usually the darkest and scariest part of a building into a calming and placid respite from the bustling courthouse traffic.

Elizabeth escorted Cassandra back to her office and asked her about Catherine's cross-country meet. The two women sounded like any other set of McClintock School mothers. All of that changed when Elizabeth shut her office door behind them. Even their posture became more rigid, and any attempt to exchange pleasantries gave way to fast-paced dialogue.

"You called?"

"Yes, Cass." Elizabeth tapped her computer screen and squinted at her inbox as she spoke. "I got a call from Detective Parkings. First, some good news. He got a lead on two of Richard Thompson's conspirators, and he should be bringing one of them into custody sometime today." Elizabeth fixed her black eyes on Cassandra. "You might even have time to call one of your media contacts. Just don't say how you got the information."

Cassandra nodded and tried not to look smug or too interested. "Thank you. How about the second one? And how did he get these leads so fast?"

The phone rang, and Elizabeth picked it up on the second ring. "Bob? You bringing him in?" Elizabeth listened and hung up after scribbling a few words on her super-sized desk calendar. "Sorry, Cass, that was Detective Parkings. He should be bringing the first perp into custody around five o'clock." She folded one leg across the other and continued, "Where were we? Oh, right. The second perp lives in Maryland, so we need to bring in the Feds. But it shouldn't be a problem."

Cassandra didn't say anything. She needed to call her friend Murphy, who was a crime reporter for the *Washington Herald Tribune*. Cat's practice started at half past three. Nadia needed to handle direct and cross without handholding. *Helen.* She needed to call Helen and get her up to speed, but first she needed all of the details herself.

Cassandra pushed all of this aside and tried to ignore the distracting pings from Elizabeth's computer. Like Cassandra, Elizabeth received hundreds of e-mails each day, and staying on top of both a busy caseload and her entire family's schedule would have posed an insurmountable hurdle to a lesser woman.

"How did Detective Parkings get hold of the perps so fast?"

Elizabeth flexed her right hand and then lifted a sheet of paper off one of the many stacks of documents on her desk. After perusing it for a moment, she set it back down and held eye contact with Cassandra as she explained, "Well, believe it or not, he lifted their Internet protocol addresses off their social media posts. They didn't go to any real lengths to conceal their identities."

Elizabeth's fingernails glistened a dark red shade of nail polish that matched her suit and high heels. Her gimlet eyes focused on a point somewhere off in the distance, and Cassandra braced for whatever was coming next. The Commonwealth's attorney seemed stiff and uneasy. It felt like a South Side chill had blown through the HVAC and dropped the temperature in the room by several degrees, and yet beads of sweat glistened on Elizabeth's forehead. She tapped her pen once on a file folder, making a thwacking sound. "Now the bad news." This was the worst part of Elizabeth's job, but she was too professional, too loyal of a public servant, to admit as much out loud. Part of her job included broaching the hard subjects.

"What is it? Is it about Helen?" Cassandra spoke with little inflection but in a deeper tone than usual. It was the same tone she took with Catherine before her daughter handed her a note from a teacher: concerned, but trying to hide it.

"To avoid sending this case to the grand jury, I am afraid we need Phoebe to identify the man in the video."

"Come on, Ellie!" Cassandra exclaimed, her cheeks flushing. "You realize what you're asking, right?"

"Yes. And if there were another way—"

"But Helen identified Richard. And even you know it is Richard in the picture." Cassandra's voice rose to punctuate her sentence. She fought to keep a queasy feeling in her stomach at bay. She despised what the legal system did to victims, and at that moment, indignation for all that she too had been through almost overcame her.

Elizabeth sighed.

Cassandra had to argue these points, but she knew she would lose. *Shoot*, she thought, *they both knew it.*

Elizabeth didn't betray any resentment. "Cass, you know this is the way it has to go down. His face could have been Photoshopped."

"Come on. That's ridiculous."

"It has happened before. Helen is hardly competent to testify on the matter of the rapist's identity. Not after she killed Richard. You know this. We need the victim—"

"Phoebe Thompson, a fifteen-year-old girl who was raped by her own father," interrupted Cassandra abruptly.

"Yes," agreed Elizabeth, her eyes still fixed on Cassandra's. "A girl, brutally raped by a man, must testify that the man in the video was in fact her father before the Commonwealth will accept that as a dispositive fact."

Cassandra crossed her arms and glared at Elizabeth's computer. Inside there was an e-mail from some bastard bigshot, and there wasn't a darn thing she could do about the situation. Cassandra knew that she had pushed Elizabeth as far as she could; that she had possibly pushed this particular Commonwealth's Attorney more than prudence dictated. If she argued any more, it would look like posturing, and it might even anger her old friend. Tight-lipped, Cassandra chose her words carefully and kept her tone level.

"This is nonnegotiable?"

Elizabeth nodded. Her eyes gave nothing away.

Cassandra frowned. "How soon does this need to happen?"

Elizabeth moved a stack of papers around and flipped through a second, smaller calendar. Most trial attorneys keep backup calendars, which seems excessive right up until a filing deadline is blown. "Cass, it's gotta be soon. Like next week." Elizabeth lowered her voice. "It's a high-profile case and next year is an election year." Both women sighed. Prosecutors earned exponentially less than partners earned downtown, but they lusted after power the same way big firm partners lusted after money.

Cassandra folded her hands together and tried not to think of Phoebe, but she couldn't stop thinking about how the girl had broken down when she interviewed her. Cassandra had not been gentle or sensitive enough with Helen's daughter, but she had tried. Elizabeth could not worry about being gentle, not when it was her job to cut straight through to the truth. She needed to set some limits, things she could negotiate ahead of time, to protect her client's interests; in this case, that meant preventing as much harm to Phoebe as possible.

The next fifteen minutes passed in a blur of offer and counteroffer as the two women argued back and forth without rancor. Cassandra inclined her head at Elizabeth and stood up in a brisk motion. "All right, Ellie. Friday at eleven, here in the conference room, right?"

Cassandra pushed the heavy door to the stairwell and let her shoulders slump as she raced across the landing to the window sill and leaned against it. Her heart was pounding too fast. She needed help. She needed to breathe again. She should call Helen right away, but Helen would ask questions that Cassandra didn't feel up to answering. How do you tell a mother that her daughter must identify her father as her rapist in public?

Instead of fumbling her way through a conversation with Helen, Cassandra dug out Cary's business card and dialed her therapist's emergency number. To Cassandra's relief, Cary picked up immediately.

"Cass, you never call me here. Is everything okay?"

"Can you talk?" Cassandra whispered. "It's about Phoebe and the case." Cassandra tried to breathe, but she felt like she was drowning in humid, pre-thunderstorm air. She managed to explain that Phoebe needed to testify in a week.

Cary's voice took on a bit of an edge. "I assume that Helen and I will be in the room for the interview?" In an earlier conversation with Cassandra, Cary had suggested this provision.

"Yeah, done."

"Well, okay, Cass. You do your job, okay? And I will do mine." Cassandra winced and her body stiffened. This felt like a slap to her face. "Come on. How about a little support?"

Cary chuckled. "Counselor, I will be right there with you the whole way. You're going to be okay. But for now we got a job to do, and I have complete confidence that you will handle your end of it. Right?"

Cassandra wasn't sure if she wanted to cry or smile or both. Cary never coddled her, and sometimes it made her angry; yet somehow it worked. It always worked. Her voice cracked a little as she replied, "Yeah. Thank you. Let me get off the phone and make the call to Helen."

Cassandra's call to Helen lasted less than a minute.

"It is what it is. You did all you could." It wasn't exactly a question, but it wasn't quite a vote of confidence, either.

Cassandra sighed. This client, this case, was a hard one, but she wasn't going to admit it. "Yes, I really did." Cassandra breathed in the fresh-smelling paint. "Any other questions?"

"No."

Dealing with a hard-ass has its advantages, Cassandra thought. She clicked off the phone, re-buttoned her blazer and headed back to Courtroom Two.

CHAPTER 41

They'd embarrassed him. It would never happen again. It was all coming clear to him.

Those bitches and their fag boy pushed me too far. I know where they all are, and when that bitch attorney is also at the house, I'm going to show them how a man takes care of business.

That was the thing. He'd been working within the constraints of an ancient system, one that balanced hunter and his prey, as if one had more rights than the other.

This wasn't about rights. He'd seen it over and over again—the victims turned victimizer. Criminals or victims? Law . . . justice . . . judges like Richard, issuing edicts, controlling access, above it all, but right smack-dab in the middle, in the middle linebacker . . . damn it. *Middle linebacker? Focus, Bob. That's just your awesome sense of humor. You're fine.* But now he had to focus.

Airplane tickets, passport, cash. *And one last fuck. I gotta have my brown-eyed girl.*

CHAPTER 42

"Scott, I don't have time to argue this." Helen stalked up and down the study, her leather boots punctuating each word with an echoing bang on the wooden floor beneath her. "Listen, yes, Carl's on top of this. And no, he doesn't need to be in the office just to prove he's on top of it. The motion has already been filed." Pausing before one of the windows, Helen twirled her blue pen.

"Is it really true that he's working out of Cassie White's office?"

"Where he's working is irrelevant. He's billing more than his usual crazy hours, and he can't get any work done at the main office right now."

"Whose fault is that? You're the one who—"

"I'm not arguing this with you right now." Helen pressed so hard on her pen that it almost snapped in half. "I have a meeting in two minutes, Scott."

"Bull. You're on leave, remember?"

Helen imagined Scott holding his signed Barry Bonds baseball. The image made her feel almost violent. "Yeah, Scott. I'm on leave, but I do have a few matters that require my urgent attention."

"Rumor is you hit him with his driver, Helen."

She broke the pen in half, and the shards splintered into her hand. "You're such a jerk, Scott." She slammed the phone down and stared out the window.

•••

"So, we need to prep for the meeting with the prosecutor."

"Unfortunately. What can you do to protect her?"

Cary put a hand on Helen's elbow and held it there. "I wish it didn't come to this. I feel like we're pushing her, but I think she can handle this."

"But she's just a kid!"

"I know. But to help her heal, I need to go over some incredibly tough stuff with her as it is. She was treated as an adult. Adult things, brutal adult things, were done to her, and to an extent, in order to help her I must treat her as more of an adult. At least on the topic of the rape and the sexual acts." Cary took a deep breath and studied the auburn-haired lawyer to try to detect any reluctance, but Helen's shield was engaged.

Helen gave a brusque nod. Her voice sounded even more clipped than usual, almost New Englandish: "Yes. Adult. Brutal. Healing. That gets to the gist of it." Helen started to twist her ring and lifted her fingers, almost as if the absent ring burned her. "You must do what you think is appropriate to treat my daughter." She looked around the room as if searching for something. "You need my permission to go over the video that the prosecutors want her to watch?"

Cary hesitated. "I don't think they will need her to watch the video, but they will need her to review still frames of it to identify the participants. That said, I think it might be best for her to watch at least the beginning part of it."

Helen's eyes rested on a stray ballpoint pen. She reached over and started to twirl it, then dropped it. "Okay. So, well, okay. I should best be going." Without another word, Helen stood up, inclined her head and marched out of the room. Cary suspected that Helen wanted to leave the room before Phoebe walked in because Helen was about to cry.

Cary smoothed down her billowing paisley skirt as Miranda waved at her from the doorway. The therapist's face creased into a smile. A minute passed. Then another.

Phoebe tapped on the doorframe with her cast, and it made a thwacking sound. Cary tried not to laugh at the teenager's brash greeting as she invited Phoebe to sit down in the leather chair closest to her. Phoebe had a way of making noise wherever she went. It wasn't clumsiness, but more of an inherent confidence; Cary could envision an older, brasher, even fearless

Phoebe entering an arena and grinning before taking hold of the reins and riding off. Someday.

•••

"Your skirt is bright." Phoebe's first sentence indicated that she was intent on getting a reaction from Cary. She tried to fold her arms and gave up with a grouchy shrug of her shoulder when her injured arm wouldn't tuck into its usual spot.

Cary tapped her pen against her leather folio. "Good afternoon, Phoebe. And yes, my skirt is bright and interesting, and maybe it clashes with my hair, but you know what? It makes me chuckle, and some days that's more than enough reason to wear it."

She wasn't looking angry, Phoebe thought. She grappled with an instinctive urge to rebel and argue with Cary, but she was fast losing the energy. "Paisley? I guess it is an interesting pattern." Now her voice was not cutting so much as curious.

"Your mom talked to you, right? About what we need to prepare for?"

Phoebe squirmed and watched light blue and magenta colors swirling in Cary's skirt and reflecting off the bank of windows. Things took on a kaleidoscopic glow as the energy in the room transformed, almost as if Cary had willed Phoebe to relax just by wearing that skirt. *Whoa, that's weird.* "Yeah. I gotta meet the state prosecutors." Suddenly Phoebe couldn't breathe.

"I will be with you next week. So will your mother and her attorney."

"Yeah." Phoebe tried to swallow. "Mom told me."

Cary nodded again. Phoebe tried not to stare at her. Cary nodded a lot, and Phoebe was worried that Cary had Parkinson's and was going to die soon. The only person she had ever seen with Parkinson's was Michael J. Fox. She was addicted to that old TV show from the '80s, whatever it was called.

All I know is that I don't want to be here, and my therapist, is she dying, too? Will she be gone, like Anne will be gone, and everyone will be gone? No one lasts long, anyway. I never said goodbye to him.

"Phoebe?" Cary gazed at the teenager.

"I never got to say goodbye to him, and now I have to look at him, don't I? Do I have to watch him . . ." Phoebe gasped and then went on, "With me all over again?" Phoebe's eyes widened with fear.

The show was called Family Ties. *And I can hear his voice and his parents hardly ever argued, just like my parents didn't really argue. Dad laughed when Mom yelled at him, and then he went and played golf. Oh my God, no, not my father, please no, not him. Stop!*

Cary put her folio on the delicate side table next to her. "Phoebe?"

From far away, Phoebe heard Cary calling her name, but she didn't want to come back. She was stuck, not in the moment and not quite nestled in another moment. She did not exist in the video he had made, but she wasn't here, in the study, not now, not all of her. She was in pieces, fragments, disconnected, broken. *I am floating, floating like I did when . . . oh God, no, no, not like when . . . I can't get away from him.*

"I can't get away from him," Phoebe blurted out. "I close my eyes and he is there. But I am not there. I am floating overhead watching, cut off somehow, but I can't feel it because I am not there, and my eyes can't see if I close them."

Cary took a deep breath, slow and steady. "Open your eyes, Phoebe."

Eyes still shut, Phoebe felt like a little girl sitting there in the chair. She *was* a little girl, tiny again, and he was there behind her, explaining how she could put one foot in the stirrup and pull herself up into the saddle without any help this time. Phoebe opened her eyes. A big white cast flanked her on one side, and then she moved and realized she hurt all over. He was there, his hand on her back, *no, Dad, no, not here. Not that you ever cared.* She drew her leather boots up to her chest to protect herself from the images that played in her mind. Phoebe didn't need to see the video to know what it really looked like and felt like, and yet a part of her still lived in the darkness because she didn't want to know that it was true. It was easier if she were a stranger watching from afar.

"I keep wishing it's just a dream. You know how when you're a little kid and you're not sure if something is real or imaginary, this world we live in? Is this the stuff that dreams are made of? Who said that? Shakespeare?"

Cary held eye contact and tipped her head. "I believe so. But that stuff you endured was real. You were not dreaming. Some lives exist as if unspooling in a nightmare, but Phoebe, please know that it is over. The worst has already happened. You are safe now."

Phoebe shivered. "How do you know I am safe? How can you protect me? How can anyone ever protect me?"

"That is a good point. There are no promises in life, but I can promise you that I will do everything I can to keep you safe, both now and at the interview next week."

Cary got up from her chair and pulled over one of the smaller wood chairs that matched the table. With one hand, she pulled it over beside Phoebe and sat down again. In the other hand she clutched her laptop, and with the cover still closed, Cary explained that she had saved several photos of the scene as still frames. "I want you to breathe while we look at these five photos. That is all. No more."

Phoebe sounded like a little girl. "Is that all I have to look at next week?" she asked. "Because if it is, I can do that." She got choked up and she almost reached out to hold Cary's hand, but she couldn't. Like a magnet drawn to its opposite pole, her arm stuck to the side of her chair and would not rise.   Phoebe noticed Cary's fingernails as she typed painstakingly on the keyboard. *Cary is a dinosaur, just like my mother. Why can't they learn to type? As smart as they are, and yet they can't even type. Oh no. Am I talking out loud again?* Phoebe couldn't be sure of anything anymore, and her thoughts moved too fast. *I need to get a grip. I've been so rude. She is going to hate me. It doesn't matter. She's going to die anyway. And how could anyone ever love me?*

The sound of Cary's nails still clicking on the keyboard brought Phoebe out of her reverie. A series of unfamiliar faces showed up on the photo library, and before Phoebe could stop pretending she wasn't curious, Cary had already clicked on the folder marked "Phoebe." With the gentlest of gestures, Cary placed the laptop on the side table, which she had pulled so that it sat in front of Phoebe almost like a TV tray. "Go ahead and review the pictures when you are ready." The therapist sat back down, crossed her hands on her lap and waited.

Phoebe leaned forward in spite of herself, and then she saw him. His hair was slathered across his forehead. The next image flashed on the screen. It was her leg with its familiar birthmark. He wasn't touching it, but he would be soon, and suddenly the room was spinning.

Cary grabbed the wastebasket just in time for Phoebe to vomit into the white plastic bag. The therapist did not speak, but nor did she wince or look disgusted when Phoebe groaned and lifted her head from the wastebasket. She merely smoothed Phoebe's hair out of the way and, one hand still on the girl's head, waited for her. The look in her eyes was oddly familiar.

Phoebe had seen that look once before when she was at a riding event, watching, not riding, that afternoon. A horse had slammed into a rock wall at the wrong angle. When the horse landed, its foreleg shattered; the rider had jumped off the horse and tried to hold the broken leg off the ground, but it was too late. While the audience waited for a veterinarian to arrive, Phoebe had crept up behind the wall and watched as the trainer gazed into the horse's eyes and whispered, "You'll be feeling better soon; it's going to be okay." As the trainer stroked the horse's head, a look of pure compassion had shone in his eyes. Five minutes later, the vet had arrived and had injected the horse with a syringe, but Phoebe could not stop staring at the trainer. It was the saddest thing she had ever seen, but it made her feel unbearably happy, too.

She was that broken horse, she knew. She wanted to believe that Cary could help her get her legs working again, and she knew she needed Cary's help. *She will never be my friend, but she will take care of me. No,* she corrected herself, *she is already taking care of me.* Phoebe wanted to shrug off that need, but she couldn't. Her body shook and she felt like crying, but it was a different emotion, and it hurt. She wanted to whisper "Thank you," but it hurt too much to feel gratitude because that meant she needed someone. Needing anyone meant she would get hurt by them.

•••

Phoebe stepped outside and tried to breathe in the smell of fall. It was always her favorite time of year, but now she couldn't take any more fall. No, she couldn't take any more of *this* fall. *No. No.* She couldn't take any more of anything. *It hurts too much.* The pain ripped too deep. She couldn't even smell the leaves or follow the flight of the geese overhead. Her vision kept shifting and her eyes hurt, as if someone were squeezing her temples.

She wanted to scream and run as fast as she had ever run, and fall down in the leaves. Climb into a deep hole and never have to worry about flickering lights or shadows, like on the film Dad had made. Her sins would be buried, saved by the darkness from discovery. Who would know if she left? Would the film matter anymore? *Yes. It would.* They needed her to testify, or else her mother would go to jail. *What have I become, and what will I become if I am no more? I love her and I need her, but it all hurts too much. It hurt to love and it hurt to be loved, and what is love anyway?*

She was sobbing hard now, and she couldn't breathe. She needed to slow everything down—the sounds, the words, the questions, the images—and she needed it all to stop hurting. A drink. A cigarette. Some of her father's good drugs. *No, no.* She didn't know. She didn't want any of his crap. It was all a sin, everything that he was and everything that he represented and everything that he did to her and with her—it was all a sin.

Except for one thing. Phoebe rubbed her arm. It itched under the cast. There was one thing and he would not, no, not ever, take it from her. *Not a sin and not his. Mine. Mine alone. The horses are mine.* She stopped worrying. Anne said she shouldn't ride, but there was only one way out of this pain. She would ride straight through it.

As Phoebe made her way down the hill, her senses began working again. First she smelled the pine needles. Then she could focus her vision on the geese flying in a V-formation overhead. She heard the sound of something motorized whirring away in the distance. Lawn mower? Blower? No, a chain saw, she concluded. A light breeze ruffled the leaves and raised goosebumps on her upper arms. Suddenly she was sprinting, and as she spread her arms out from her sides, she felt she could almost fly if the wind caught her just right.

Phoebe slowed to a trot as she came to the outer fence that surrounded the riding ring. She moved as if to climb over it, but then frowned at her cast and flicked open the lock, pausing to fasten the gate and recheck it to make sure it was secured. Anne said she could not ride until she got the arm looked at, but she didn't say anything about riding in a cast—did she? Even if she did forbid her to ride, Phoebe reasoned, she and that loud woman who cooked and her quiet partner were out running errands. *No one has to know.*

From a distance Phoebe spied the barn door, and she groaned. It looked like bacon, cooked just right, not burnt, not flecked with spots of charred black gristle, just good old medium-brown bacon. And if the barn door looked like bacon, then she must be crazy. Phoebe sighed and wondered what the heck was wrong with her. She didn't smell bacon. She smelled tack and hay and manure and burnt leaves and leather soap and something unfamiliar. Maybe it was the industrial-strength soap she had used to shower with the night before. But it wasn't bacon.

After she rubbed her eyes with the back of her right hand, Phoebe sighed and cracked a tired smile. She was standing right in front of the barn door now, and it didn't even look like bacon anymore. It just looked like a darn barn door. Still, something about it made her pause. She shook her head at her own foolishness. It was just a cracked, medium-brown barn door without a handle, and when she pushed against it with her fingertips it creaked and opened a few inches.

Then she remembered another barn door, on another farm, and she heard her father's voice, husky, deep and authoritative. She pushed harder with her shoulder against the door, a strange and unsettling mix of fear and nostalgia and hope overwhelming her.

Suddenly the barn door made a groaning sound and opened wide, and Phoebe winced as a splinter cut through her index finger. It hurt and it was bleeding, but the absence of his voice and the confused memory of what he had been to her pained her much more than a darn brown barn door ever could. Phoebe shook her hand and braced her shoulders against the darkness as she walked into the dim, dusty barn. The door slammed shut against the frame behind her.

It took her eyes a few moments to readjust to the dark, and while she stood waiting, she heard whinnying and the thwack of a horse's tail against the side of one of the stalls. Instinctively Phoebe made a clicking sound in the back of her voice and moved purposefully toward where Ginger was pawing at the hay. She rubbed Ginger's neck and spoke in a tone that almost carried a melody. The Iberian nuzzled Phoebe's hand and reached over as if to nibble at Phoebe's plaid shirt, and the girl smiled at the familiar, safe touch.

She knew better, but now there was no turning back. The urge to ride hit her like a waterfall that overflowed from a melting spring snow. Saddling up wasn't easy, and though it took her more than twice as long as usual, her broken arm wasn't entirely useless. She leaned against the saddle to hold it in place as she brought the brown leather straps underneath Ginger and pulled the girth tight. She continued to prop the cast against the saddle to keep it from shifting as she buckled it. A spare helmet was lying by the tack; this she snapped on without difficulty.

Now she needed to figure out how she could get on her horse without scaring Ginger or falling off and reinjuring her arm. Anne's mounting step? That would work. It took what seemed an interminable block of time to carry the unfinished mounting step outside, return to the stall, walk Ginger outside and mount safely.

Phoebe chuckled to herself and tried to remember how to ride one-handed. A cowboy lassoing a colt came to mind, and she nodded. Thumb on top, reins pulled between pinky and ring finger; and she could leave her broken arm in position, as if holding the reins, so that she didn't knock her posture too far out of balance. She nudged Ginger forward.

And then all of the science fell away. Years of lessons and all of the silent reminders and rules, all were released. She couldn't ride like she normally rode, and that was okay. She felt free. She felt loose. Liberated from constraints, she just rode.

For a moment Phoebe closed her eyes, letting Ginger clop through the reddish-brown clay, and she envisioned a thin dirt trail winding up a mountainside. Moss and a thick covering of leaves bordered the dirt, and small rocks and roots made it a technical ride. When she opened her eyes, she was back on the farm, with its clay and tall grass and manure (or horse shit, as

Anne would say), and the land was flat. All the same, she was riding; and while she rode, all of her pain fell behind.

Phoebe circled the ring a few times and hummed an old hymn under her breath. Sometimes Helen took her to church when her dad was out of town or playing golf, but it had been almost a year since they had last gone on Christmas Eve. She couldn't remember where her dad had been that night. Probably at a party, drinking and getting all red-faced, which was funny, because her friends called it getting shit-faced, but shit was brown, not red like her dad's face when he drank too much. *No, not Dad, not now*, she whispered, and so she pictured her mother sitting beside her in the pew, and together they were humming "Silent Night." Very softly, Phoebe sang the chorus alone until she ran out of words.

In the background she heard a few doors slamming. *They must be back from wherever they all went*, she thought, and she knew she had better get back to the barn before Anne caught her riding. *How am I going to dismount?* she wondered, and then she realized she could toss the reins over a fence post and climb down without ending up ass over teakettle. She couldn't help smiling. That was something Anne might say.

Phoebe pulled up a couple of feet away from the fence, and without thinking it through, she threw the reins over the post. But she missed the post. A childlike urge to giggle gave way to annoyance: at herself, at the flies zinging her ears and at the cast that itched and made it impossible for to use her left arm. She shifted in her saddle, tried to grasp the reins and almost fell out of her saddle, and just then she heard the crackling of twigs and looked up to see her mother, wearing new boots, heading toward her.

Helen leaned against the fence post and surveyed the situation. Her mouth moved a little, more than a twitch, but not exactly a frown.

Phoebe braced herself, anticipating her mother's criticism. Instead Helen cracked, "You're in a little bit of a pickle, aren't you, dumpling?"

Phoebe stared at Helen and tried not to admit how much she liked it when her mom called her a dumpling. It was such a babyish word, and yet, oh no, she couldn't help it.

Helen scuffed the back of one of her boots against the fence post and grimaced. "Is it always this muddy down here?"

"You going to get on me about riding, or what?" Phoebe's retort ended in an eye roll.

Not missing a beat, Helen let go of the fence and started walking toward the gate. "As long as you don't fall off that horse, I won't say a thing."

Helen approached Ginger from the side. Phoebe nodded in silent approval. Then in a firm voice, she directed her mother to hold the reins steady as she dismounted. When she landed she grunted something that sounded too unintelligible to count as gratitude, but Helen smiled as Phoebe continued, "Follow me and hold the reins nice and steady, Mom, and talk to her a little bit as she walks. Just tell her it's going to be okay, or tell her about the law of perpetuities or whatever else you would say to calm someone down."

"Aye aye, dumpling." Helen directed her words to Ginger, and in a solemn voice intoned, "You are a life in being whose life will remain unvested until—"

"Oh my Gawd, Mom, I was joking about the law of perpetuities!"

Phoebe clubbed the door open with her left arm and winced a little. She hadn't felt any pain while she rode, but now her shoulder ached and it felt like a shock wave of sharp splinters was entering her broken arm. She should not have ridden Ginger. She really shouldn't have. It wasn't so much the riding that was wrong, but worse was the fact that she was too tired to take care of her chores and do her share of the work after riding.

With her eyes focused on the hay under her feet, Phoebe trudged into the barn and entered Ginger's stall. She knew she should talk more to her mother, but she couldn't muster up the energy to say more than what was absolutely necessary. She needed to clean the tack and she needed to remove the saddle and muck the stalls. What she really needed was to sit down and rest, but there was work to be done. Phoebe stopped thinking and rested her head against Ginger's neck and let her lips brush against the soft but bristly hair.

"It looks like she is nuzzling you," murmured Helen.

Phoebe tried to smile, but only her eyes moved.

"Do you need help, Phoebe? You look exhausted, and I know you have chores you need to get done."

Phoebe tried to formulate an answer. What would happen if she said she needed help and then Helen got a phone call she had to take? That used to happen all the time, before Helen stopped pretending she cared what Phoebe did at night. Phoebe shot her mother a challenging look. "If you start helping me and then have to leave to take a call, that is worse than not helping me in the first place." Her words sounded harsher than Phoebe had intended, but Helen did not seem to notice her daughter's tone.

"I don't even have my cell phone on me." Helen touched Ginger's saddle and ran her hand down the side of it. "Is this the girth, this strap that runs underneath?"

"Yes. The girth."

"Okay," Helen continued. "How about if I undo the strap, and then you can tell me what to do next?" Helen kept asking her daughter questions, as if taking a client through a direct examination, and Phoebe was able to guide her mom through the dismounting process while saying the fewest possible words. Helen helped Phoebe remove the saddle and the reins and even unbuckled Phoebe's helmet, and, with her daughter issuing directions, she stored all of the equipment.

Phoebe nearly collapsed on the wooden bench in the tack room. "Mom," she whispered, "I really need to muck the stalls. But I am so, so tired."

"Do you want me to help with it?" Without waiting for an answer, Helen reached out her hand, yanked Phoebe to her feet and grabbed two pitchforks. "Okay, Phoebe, show me how it's done and we'll get it shipshape here in no time."

Phoebe took the pitchfork her mother had passed to her and tried to use it until she had to confess her weakness. "Mom, I don't think I can do any more. My arm is killing me and I am so tired." Phoebe's voice trailed off and she let her eyes show the pain and exhaustion she was feeling. A mixture of concern and fierce maternal love crossed Helen's face. She put her arm around her daughter, guided her back to the bench and ordered her to wait.

A half-hour later, Helen tapped Phoebe on the shoulder and woke her from a light sleep. "Come on, dumpling."

Phoebe lifted her head from the bench where she had fallen asleep. As she stood, she moved closer to her mother and rested her head on her mother's neck for just a moment. Helen patted her exhausted daughter on the back three times before she realized that Phoebe was nuzzling her. They stood together for one extra-long beat, and then they walked up the hill and into the main house without speaking, but without needing to speak.

CHAPTER 43

She also has a daughter. That damn Cassie. I like them young.

CHAPTER 44

"Thanks, Gary. I'll keep in touch." After Helen had hung up the phone, she shook her head and tried not to think about Scott Abrams and the upcoming partners' meeting. Absentmindedly she rubbed her index finger against her thumb. There was nothing else she could do, except for call a few more partners. Later.

It was Saturday morning, and this was usually when she caught up on her reading. As the sun rose, she sat at the dining room table and put a hand on Friday's *Wall Street Journal*. Helen hadn't been able to transfer her newspaper and business magazine subscriptions to the Bryson House, but last night her favorite periodicals had appeared. Helen suspected that Anne had had something to do with it. After all, Anne was everywhere, or at least everything seemed touched by her.

Anne clomped by, wearing her spurs. Helen stifled a smile as Miranda called from the study, "Anne! Boots! Spurs? Off, please!" Anne groaned and sat down in the wooden chair with the tapestry fabric on the back and set down a magazine next to Helen's carefully stacked pile of newspapers. "I got something for you yesterday."

Miranda appeared in the foyer, calling over her shoulder, "Yes, thanks, Mimi." She chuckled. "It was about the only target you acquired yesterday."

Helen shot Miranda a quizzical look and then realized Miranda was talking about the firing range. "Do you go out there a lot?"

Miranda made eye contact with Anne and quipped over her shoulder, "Yes. We're still trying to teach Mimi to fire straight. Anne is a crack shot with a rifle."

Helen's eyes moved to Anne. "How interesting."

Anne's crisp nod ended all firing range discussion like a door slamming shut. "I picked this up for you."

"What is it, Coach?" asked Phoebe, who had just sauntered downstairs for breakfast. Before Helen could move her hand, Phoebe had swooped over and starting flipping through a *Properties for Sale* magazine.

"Mom, look at this one!" she cried. "It has stables!"

Helen tried to view the property over Phoebe's shoulder and frowned with disdain. "Good God, Phoebe. The house is a dump."

"But Mom, you said we're going to have to downsize. Remember?"

Helen's position at the firm was growing less stable by the day. She could see that her future there was over, but somehow, at least this morning with the sun shining on her daughter through the window, she felt a certain peace with however things were going to turn out. As her mother would have said, "What is, will be." Helen had felt a weight lifting from her shoulders the longer she remained out of the office, and yet it bothered her. She wasn't essential. Or was she? Besides, she could rebuild her client base. *I hope.*

The attorney chuckled. "I did. The house will sell for a lot." Both mother and daughter had agreed, without ever discussing it, that they could never go back to their old home. "But we cannot afford several acres, along with a house that doesn't look like a dump. Oh, and a horse. "

Phoebe blinked at her mother. "So we're going to get a mansion, Mom? Wait," Phoebe paused to execute a hair flip. "A McMansion."

Helen snapped the newspaper shut with an exaggerated motion. "No. I don't want a McMansion or any sort of mansion, for that matter. Now pass that over to me and please go say something nice to the little kids in the sunroom."

Phoebe's mouth dropped open for a moment. Helen raised an eyebrow before it turned into a pout, and her daughter closed her mouth. She had grown accustomed to lounging around the Bryson House almost as if it were her own, and the idea of sharing it with anyone new irritated or maybe even scared her. Helen caught Phoebe's hesitation and put a reassuring arm around her daughter. "Come on. I am going to grab another cup of coffee and take it out there to drink. I can introduce you to the kids, and maybe you can get them to run with you down to the stables."

With Phoebe at her side, Helen sat down at the circular table and surveyed the Latino woman sitting across from her. The woman looked like heck. She was leaning her head on one hand and had barely moved when Helen and Phoebe had stepped inside. The skin around her eye was a deep shade of indigo, with a greenish hue on the outer ring of the deep blue bruise. Her black hair, limp and greasy, was plastered against her skull. Helen waved and greeted her stiffly.

With the barest of smiles, the other woman murmured, "Hello" and extended her right hand formally. After shaking Helen's hand with a soft grip, she gestured at a little girl and her even littler brother. "I am Sylvia Martinez, and these are my children, Carlos and Isabel." Sylvia seemed too tired to talk after these introductions, so Helen sat without speaking and took in this new woman and her two children.

Unlike Helen, who was attired in her country-chic, still expensive clothing, and Phoebe, who wore comfortable but well-heeled riding attire, the Martinez family wore discount store clothing and hand-me-downs on their third or fourth cycle. Carlos carried around a stuffed zebra and stared at the painted cement floor, while Isabel, in a tattered yellow sundress a size too small for her, lay on her stomach, carefully drawing with crayons in a coloring book.

Helen felt self-conscious. The juxtaposition between her family's wealth and the Martinez's poverty would have brought disdain or condemnation to mind even a month ago. This morning, though, she felt something else; and yet it wasn't guilt. She had worked hard for every cent she earned, and the only people injured in the process were well represented and wealthy. *What am I feeling? She has a massive bruise on her face, so she let some pig beat her up in front of her children. What kind of woman lets a man do that to her?*

Helen felt the blood draining from her hands, and she gripped her coffee mug even tighter. Steam swirled and obscured her vision of the battered woman sitting a few feet away from her. And in Helen's mind, as if on a fast-moving projector, scrolled a single word: *Cass. That's who. That was the sort of woman who let a man beat her in front of a child.*

But how could she square it? Cassandra was the strongest woman she had ever met. She had held sway like an imperial ruler at the press conference. She had handled the meeting with the Commonwealth's Attorney like a seasoned professional. She had even stood up to Helen at their first meeting.

Helen had always been the strongest one. But now she wasn't feeling so strong. She was a mess. And Cassandra had been a mess. A loser. But that didn't make any sense. It wasn't Cass's fault her husband hit her. Cass had been pregnant, but had lost the baby. How could that have been her fault? And the rape? Not her fault. Well, she had been drinking. But Phoebe had been, too, and it wasn't her fault that Richard . . . *oh God. Here I've been judging her and not even knowing it. What a presumptuous idiot I've been.*

Helen thought about the times she had gone to church and seen a single mother herding three or four well-dressed children like a mother goose directing goslings. At least one of the children would scream out of turn, and the mother would stare down with a combination of exasperation, frustration and . . . what? *Love.* It was love. Yes. And hope, too. Helen's disapproving frown slowly transformed into a smile. What was the feeling in her heart, then? A slice, a thin wedge, of compassion, perhaps imbued with admiration. That was it. It was admiration that she felt when she gazed at this battered Latino woman who hunched over her cup of coffee, staring vacantly into the mountains with her thousand-mile stare.

The truth was, Helen felt like she was swimming and couldn't see the shore. She couldn't make up for all the years she had closeted her mind in ignorance, but right now, at this moment, she could still tap into her better nature. Helen leaned over and whispered into Phoebe's ear, "Those kids could use a little distracting if you're up to it," and she squeezed her daughter's slim shoulder.

Despite her hesitance, Phoebe pushed back from the table and walked over to sit beside the children. Sylvia waved her hand, her gaze still fixed on the distant horizon. Helen rubbed her index finger and her thumb together and tried to think of something to say. *What can you say to a woman who just got the crap beaten out of her?*

"Sylvia?"

With effort, Sylvia turned her head and briefly made eye contact. Helen tried not to stare at the devastation etched on Sylvia's face. She sat very still, and in as gentle of a tone as her clipped accent could muster, she started to speak. "I guess you just got in last night."

Sylvia bobbed her head. She seemed bored, but Helen wasn't sure. Usually she would leave someone like Sylvia alone. This morning, she kept talking. "I've been here for a while now. My husband is dead."

"Uh, Mom." Phoebe tapped Helen on the elbow. "Can I maybe take the kids down to look at the horses?"

Helen put her arm around Phoebe. "Sylvia Martinez, I'd like for you to meet my daughter, Phoebe. She is an expert rider, even with a broken wrist." Phoebe's smile lit up the sunroom as she extended her hand to shake Sylvia's. It was a little awkward, but something about Phoebe made her seem to Helen like a proud bird with a broken wing: endearing, but in need of fixing. Sylvia held Phoebe's hand and her eye that wasn't bruised hinted of a smile.

"It's a pleasure." Sylvia reached out to hug her children, who had trailed behind Phoebe like little ducklings. Helen noticed that Carlos clung to Sylvia while the little girl hung back, uncertain. She and Phoebe exchanged a significant glance, and Phoebe bent down and whispered something to the child.

Isabel's eyes lit up and she clasped her hands together. "Mama! Ponies! Yes!"

Helen waited for the children to walk a little ways down the hill before she offered her next words. "Sylvia, I was a mess when I came here. The first night, I collapsed on the floor when my daughter told me it was all my fault."

Sylvia's eyes widened. "Why did your daughter blame you?" She accentuated the first syllable of "daughter," and it felt harsh to Helen, as if Sylvia blamed her for not taking care of Phoebe. *I'm being paranoid again.*

"Because I worked too much and wasn't home to protect her from her father."

"He hit her?"

Helen touched her ring finger. The indentation would never go away. "No, he didn't hit her."

Sylvia was silent, locked inside her own memories. For a moment Helen wanted to tell Sylvia what Richard had done, and then she realized she didn't need to tell everyone the whole story. Or maybe, thought Helen as she caught a glimmer of fear in Sylvia's eyes, she shouldn't tell this woman. Because Sylvia, who was watching the autumn leaves dancing on the broad trees, already could bear no more. She didn't need Helen's pain on top of her own.

Helen really had no idea what to say. She shook her head and imagined a movie she had once seen where two women talked over a cup of tea. One woman talked and started to sob. Her friend listened and made comforting noises, a box of tissues on the ready, and seemed unfazed by the tears and the excessive emotional display.

"Your children are safe here." Helen took another sip of coffee. Her head hurt from trying to figure out what to say. "It's going to get better. The first couple of days are the hardest. Would you like me to get you a cup of coffee? I need to refill mine."

"Thank you. That would be a nice thing. I appreciate your kindness." Sylvia's tone was formal, but she relaxed the muscles around her mouth a little while she spoke.

Helen returned with two steaming mugs of coffee and a few more newspapers. In a businesslike, almost brusque way, she took the Money sections from two New York papers and pushed the rest of the stack toward the other Bryson House guest. Sylvia seemed confused at first, and then she picked up the Lifestyle section from the Washington newspaper and thumbed through it, licking her thumb each time she turned a page. The women sat side by side for almost an hour in companionable silence.

When Phoebe returned with Isabel and Carlos, they all wore smiles and smelled of the outdoors. Carlos ran over to his mother, and she tried to smile back at him. Isabel waved at Phoebe and returned to her coloring books. "Thank you, Miss Phoebe."

Sylvia inclined her head and turned her eyes back to the distant horizon, as if waiting for something.

•••

Saturday morning hit early for Cassandra. She had set her alarm for 4:55 A.M., but rolled out of bed and was out the door for her morning six-miler fifteen minutes earlier. By half past six, she was showered and stretching out over a cup of coffee when Catherine popped her head into her mother's room. "Mom, can I borrow a hair tie?"

Cassandra gestured toward her nightstand. "If you can find one, take it. And if you find two, give me one." Cassandra winced as she stretched her hamstrings with her foam roller. The regional cross-country meet was at nine, and Catherine was expected to place in at least the top ten. She had an outside chance to win it all, but Cassandra didn't want her daughter to know that. *Of course, maybe she already knows.*

Once in the car and waiting for Catherine to gather all of her gear, Cassandra reflected on racing. She had a love-hate relationship with it. She hated the tension before the starting gun went off. Her stomach would turn sour and she would end up in the bathroom vomiting, just like she did before a trial. And yet a few miles into the run, all of that would melt away, and she would be left with the road, her feet and a sense of elation. Surging legs; strangers in the crowd cheering; splits unfolding, even negative splits on a perfect day—

The door slammed and Catherine jumped into the passenger seat. "Ready, Mom? We gotta be there by quarter of eight at the latest." Cassandra ignored the edge in Catherine's tone. Harnessing all of that adrenaline wasn't easy, and her daughter, as respectful and easygoing as she was, was still just a teenager with a race to run.

While Cat checked and rechecked her duffel bag, Cassandra reached into her console and grabbed her iPod. She hooked it into the auxiliary volt outlet and touched her playlist titled "'80s Power Anthems." By the second song Catherine had stopped rolling her eyes and sighing, and she began singing Joan Jett's "I Hate Myself for Loving You" along with her mother. Cassandra rolled the windows down and let the wind wash over them. She loved these moments alone with her daughter, and she appreciated them even more, knowing how much more rare they would soon become.

More than an hour later, a kaleidoscopic wave of color rushed past Cassandra. The wave resembled birds flying in a V-formation, with the front runners rushing from their assigned starting positions to the tip of the V. Since the race was held off-road, it started in a green field with ankle-high grass that would be trampled by a thousand churning feet.

The October sun shone with a golden hue that only changing seasons could bring. A breeze turned the leaves up, and wide brown leaves fluttered and fell to the ground; but the yellow, orange and red leaves stuck to their branches, where they would remain a few weeks more. No wonder she loved fall, Cassandra thought. The temperature, fifty degrees, and the contrast of blue sky with green grass and multicolored leaves created a perfect setting for her favorite sport.

Catherine appeared in view, sprinting to the front of the pack. She was clearly in pursuit of a few runners from the elite public schools. Cassandra fretted a little. Catherine needed to surge from the right side to the front within the first tenth of a mile to avoid the elbows and high-stepping knees flying in the middle of the pack. To trip or fall like Mary Decker Slaney at the 1984 Olympics, even at the beginning of the Regional Cross-Country Meet, could prove fatal to her chances to place in the top five. And Catherine was a front runner, like her hero Prefontaine—or "Pre," as she always called him.

Catherine was leading the V by the quarter-mile mark. Cassandra wasn't surprised, but she still worried a little. At every practice she had attended, she had cautioned her stubborn daughter to "leave a little in the tank." Catherine never listened, and her intervals had gotten faster and faster most practices, but at times she sputtered and faded toward the end of a series of sprints. On the other hand, she had never won a race from behind. In fact, Catherine had lost a few races to opponents who drafted off her the entire race and then outkicked her in the last quarter-mile. Cassandra sighed. The coach in her knew it probably wasn't going to end well, but the mother she had come to be hoped otherwise.

The course followed an oval pattern, starting and ending in the middle, which enabled Cassandra to follow her daughter at different points in the 5K run. At the one-mile mark and the halfway mark, Catherine was leading a pack of several elite runners. Two of them, wearing the same jersey, were taking turns tucking in on Catherine's left shoulder. Yet all the same, her daughter looked strong, her long stride slicing across the grass like machine-powered scissors cutting paper.

She needed to let someone else lead the V or create some space between her shoulder and the girls using her body to block the wind, Cassandra thought to herself. But she knew she wouldn't.

She's going to learn this one the hard way, or like her hero, Pre, never learn it. After all, there are worse things in life than losing after giving your all from starting gun to finish line. God knows I never learned the easy way, and I didn't win every race I ran either, even if I had the most wicked finishing kick in the state.

Cassandra jogged to the two and a half-mile mark and stripped off her blue button-down Oxford shirt. She stood, legs spread and eyes focused with the intensity of an eagle, glaring, almost angry, proud as heck of her daughter. Under her shirt she had been wearing a green Oregon tee. Cassandra had never worn this shirt to any of her daughter's races. It was a nod to Pre, and every runner would understand the message, but only one runner would think it was directed at her.

Even from a quarter of a mile away, Cassandra spotted her daughter's stride, clicking along at 180 beats per minute. The young runner was still holding off the two runners stacked within a yard of her hip, and she did not seem to be laboring up the steep hill. Unfortunately, the maroon-clad teammates were also running tall and holding their heads high.

Cassandra didn't yell. She held up a fist as her daughter charged past, not flagging, but not extending her lead. Her daughter was unable to acknowledge her mother with more than the briefest eye contact, but Cassandra knew she understood. Catherine's jaw tightened and Cassandra hoped that it would be enough.

On this day, though, it proved to be insufficient. The two girls who had used Catherine as a windshield to block up to ten percent of the wind resistance broke down her last reserves and passed her within 200 meters of the finish line. Catherine had given her all and more, but she still had finished in third place. Cassandra had tears in her eyes. It had been a brave race. A very brave race.

Cassandra hurried to the finish line corral and caught her collapsing child just in time. "You did *so* well, dear Cat, so, so well," Cassandra whispered. A chill ran up and down her arms. She could hear an announcer from a 1970s Prefontaine race yelling, "He ran a brave race, a very brave race," and now she held her own child, and she had run as heroic a race as any of her running idols. She had lost, and yet Cassandra knew she had won so much.

Catherine leaned on her mother's sturdy arms and shook hands with the two girls who had outkicked her. Instead of shaking her hand, the taller of the girls reached out and hugged her, and when Catherine turned to walk away, her eyes widened. A trim, fit man with salt-and-pepper hair shook hands with the winners and then stopped in front of her.

He wore the famous forest-green colors, with "University of Oregon" written in white across the front of his shirt. As he approached, he glanced at his stopwatch and at his clipboard. Then he held out his hand, his eyes sweeping over Catherine and Cassandra.

"Catherine White? From McClintock, yes?"

Catherine tried to stand unassisted, but her legs gave way, and before Cassandra could get a hand out to steady her, the man had put his hand on Catherine's shoulder. "I am Coach Carter, and that was a great race you ran. You front-ran the entire way with two teammates riding you. It was gutsy. You obviously left it all out there. We can make you faster at Oregon. But we can't teach guts. My people will be getting in touch with you next week. If you want to run for us, we'd love to have you."

Catherine could not speak, so Cassandra stepped forward, one arm wrapped around her daughter's sweat-soaked waist. In a crisp tone, she greeted the Oregon coach, "Cassandra White, Coach Carter. Catherine's mom."

Carter stared back at Cassandra with a straightforward sincerity. "Nice shirt." He paused and met her gaze. "And if I am correct, you wore these colors, and you wore them well, but you went by 'Cassie' back then."

Cassandra's eyes welled up with tears. Her years at Oregon had been some of the best days of her life, and yet it had ended, her serious running career, after a disastrous injury her junior year. That was when she had started drinking. And standing there, on the green fields of her daughter's nascent running dream, the full extent of her own loss overwhelmed her as though she was missing something that had never been.

Cassandra, hiding her emotions behind her dark sunglasses, turned Carter over to Coach J.T. and focused on her daughter. With the expertise of a five-time marathoner and cross-country coach, she laid Cat out horizontal, grabbed bananas, bagels and red Gatorade, and helped her front runner pull on her blue and gold McClintock sweats. For more than an hour they sat side by side, replaying the race, watching the other runners and chatting about the next weekend's state finals. Catherine would be there. And this time, she'd win it.

CHAPTER 45

Bob slammed his laptop shut and took another swallow of Bud to wash down three more pills. *Just a few more days.*

He'd checked and re-checked the guards' schedule. He'd fixed the Internet protocol address. Just removed one. Not something they'd likely notice.

He looked down at his hands with one eye shut. No shaking, no tremor. *Good.* But he had this weird sense that he was forgetting something. *No way.* He'd been over it, and it was going to be fine.

She looked so much like his precious Janie. Whatever had happened to her after high school? He rubbed his temple. It wasn't right to think about Janie. Not with his girl waiting for him.

She was going to be his.

Soon.

CHAPTER 46

After she had thrown her sweats on the laundry room floor and slammed down two plates of food, Catherine headed straight upstairs to take a shower. Later, curled up in her pajamas, she watched an old DVD of *Pre* in the family room.

With a laundry basket balanced on her hip, Cassandra paused in the foyer as a scene between Pre and his coach played on the flatscreen TV mounted on the wall. She had watched *Pre* so often that she could recite many of the scenes. In this one, his coach upbraided Pre for front-running. Pre never listened to his coach. It was part of what made him famous: his stubborn refusal to change the way he ran. He left it all out on the track or on the field, and usually he won, but not at the 1972 Olympics. Cassandra sighed and bit her tongue. Maybe Pre would have changed tactics and won the gold medal at the next Olympics had he not wrecked his car.

Cassandra hated watching the car accident, and yet she couldn't stay away. She set her laundry basket down and sat cross-legged on the floor next to her daughter. It was as if she could see Pre alive one last time and bid him farewell in the next instant, and this made no sense. It was a film. Pre had died more than thirty years earlier. She sighed as she watched him leave the party and drive off into the night, never to be seen alive again.

Catherine sniffled into a tissue.

Cassandra shook her head. "He made a mistake. A terrible mistake, and he died for no reason. And that, my sweet, is why you don't get behind the wheel with someone who's been drinking."

Catherine twirled her hair. "Yeah, I know. I wouldn't. I promise." Cat stared at the screen again as the credits rolled. "Mom, I've got things to do. Races to win. So that isn't my thing, the whole scene. You know?"

Cassandra glanced at the credits. An image of the real Pre flashed before her and she felt an aching loss for what he could have been. It made it hard to hear what her daughter was saying, but she tried. She wanted to hear her. She wanted to know her daughter's story would turn out better.

"Mom?" Catherine stood up and began carrying her empty plate and glass over to the sink. Her back was turned. "Um, is it okay if I go over to Darcy's house tonight? We thought we might go out and see a movie."

Cassandra almost snapped a reflexive no, but she stopped. She couldn't keep her daughter safe from everything. It not only made no sense, but it was also poor mothering. It wasn't Cat's fault she was in a funk about bad choices and ruined collegiate running careers. That had been Cassandra's fate, but Cat's fate was whatever she made of it.

•••

Later that night Cassandra and Frank were snuggled on the loveseat outside, talking and listening to jazz music. They had tucked in Zander, who was already back to his usual healthy, skidding-across-the-room self, at half past eight, and now they were enjoying a quiet evening together. It wasn't exactly a date night, but it was something close; almost like taking a vacation without leaving the house.

Cassandra took in the smell of the outdoors. It was humid but not hot, with an ever-deepening bite in the air as the middle of October approached. She glanced up at the sky above and spotted the Big Dipper. So many eons ago, another man, with thick wrists and legs like oak trees, had showed her where to find it. Somehow it almost felt like a betrayal to stare at what she still saw as Tim's constellation.

We lie next to one another. It is the last time. He holds me against his chest and I feel his heart rise and fall and I cannot bear to let him go. The ceiling fan ticks as it whirls and I shiver and pull the sheet tighter. His body is warm and I know every mole it holds.

Helpless, I turn away. I watch the lines on the digital clock form patterns and I count how many little lines make up each number. Number one: two lines; number three: five lines; number seven: three lines. When he is close, I cannot turn from his embrace; and so I wait. He closes his eyes and the Vicodin takes him far away.

Just one more thing she couldn't explain to Frank. It made her feel a little alone. She put her hand on Frank's hand, and when he asked her what she was thinking, she pulled his hand to her mouth and kissed it. She knew what that would lead to and she wanted it. She wanted to stop remembering.

And then the phone rang. Cassandra frowned when she saw the caller ID. It was Cat's cell phone, and it was just after eleven o'clock. Late-night calls from children were never a good thing. *Not that I've ever gotten one,* Cassandra mused.

"Mom?" Catherine's voice cracked. In the background Cassandra could hear loud music and the sound of high-pitched laughter.

"Where are you, Cat?" Cassandra demanded. Her voice cut through the deep bass beat.

"Paul's house."

"You told me you were going to Darcy's house." Cassandra switched the phone to her left hand, and when she stood up she slammed her shin into the hammock. "Ouch!" she cried, and then realized she hadn't heard Catherine's answer. Annoyed, she added, "And how did you get to Paul's house, Cat?"

Catherine didn't answer right away. *She's twirling her hair right now,* Cassandra thought, *and she's afraid to answer my questions.*

Except that she wasn't afraid, and she did answer. "Mom, Jason drove me."

Cassandra frowned and bit back a curse word. Frank shot her a questioning look, but she held up her right hand and paced up and down the wood deck.

"Why did Jason drive you? Come on, Cat! I told you not to ride with him, what, two weeks ago? I forbade you. And you did it anyway? What in the heck were you thinking?" Cassandra's questions piled on top of one another, admitting no room for a response, until she ran out of breath. Then she felt like heck, like a lawyer instead of a mother.

"Cat?" She spoke in a softer voice now. "What happened? Please tell me, and I will stop yelling. I'm done. I think." She chuckled and leaned against the back railing.

"Darcy left. She and Mike left and they . . . you know, they left. And she told me she'd be right back, and then . . . like, she sent me a text message and she wasn't coming back. She was waiting for me at Paul's house. And . . ."

"So Jason came with Mike, and Darcy drove you, so she left you no way to get home?" Cassandra bit her lip and tried to keep her voice down.

"Yes."

"Why didn't you call me then, Cat?"

Her daughter didn't say anything, and Cassandra reflected back on all the stupid mistakes she had made when she was seventeen. She realized she was gripping the phone as tightly as the pain of remembering that encircled her chest.

Cassandra took a deep breath and tried to relax. "Okay, Cat, stay put outside, a few feet off his property in case the police come, and I'll be there. And tell your friends the cops *are* coming, because if I see any alcohol when I get there, the cops will show up right on my tail. Got that?" After she hung up the phone, Cassandra shook her head at Frank. He tried to hug her, but she shrugged him off with an anger that found no direction. She felt like she would burn anyone or anything that came too close.

Ten minutes later, Cassandra wheeled up a wide residential street lit every fifty yards by fancy streetlamps. This upper-class neighborhood dripped nouveau-riche, with its McMansions and tiny lots with carefully landscaped yards. With a tight smile, she watched people with adult bodies but teenaged brains piling into their cars. She also spotted her daughter handing something to Jason's parents. Jason looked chastised.

Cat climbed into the passenger seat and slammed the door shut behind her. Cassandra checked her rearview mirror and pulled out onto the street. "What did you hand Jason's parents?"

"His car keys. I snagged them when he wasn't looking." Catherine paused.

"Was he drunk?"

Catherine drummed the dashboard for a moment. "Yes."

"How about you, Cat? You have one chance to answer me honestly. And the state meet is at risk if you lie to me."

"Mom, it is not my fault you drank a lot. You don't trust me, and if you think I was drinking and don't believe what I tell you, then don't believe me. Shame on you, Mom." Angry tears streamed down Catherine's face. She rushed on, "Darcy ditched me. So I did a stupid thing. I got a ride with Jason, 'kay? Stupid. I'm sorry if that matters. But I did nothing wrong. Nothing else, at least. I didn't drink. I took one look at the beer and the noise, and then I saw Jason drinking, and . . . and . . . I thought about Pre. So I took his keys and I stepped outside and did what I was supposed to. It is so unfair that I have to pay for your mistakes. You are the one who got in trouble. *You* screwed up in college. Not me." Cat stopped yelling when she realized that her mother was crying, too.

Shaking, Cassandra spotted an all-night diner and pulled into the lot. Once they were seated in a booth, she folded her hands on the table and fingered the coffee cup in front of her. Catherine sipped a glass of orange juice and waited for her mom to talk. She was caught between anger and the excitement of being at an all-night diner in the middle of the night, but the anger faded as soon as her mother began to talk.

"Cat, you're right. I'm sorry for not trusting you. I'm sorry for letting my mistakes color how I mother you. You deserve better." Cassandra sipped her coffee and glimpsed her reflection in the window. Maybe she still had it, but her joints were done. She could never again run like she used to, and the realization of it was killing her.

But that wasn't why she was being so hard on her only daughter. It was time to tell her. "You know about my drinking. You might even know I drank away my senior year of running at Oregon, and if you don't know, I might as well be the one to tell you. I could have run that last year. My ankle healed in time. But I was too darn busy partying every night." Cassandra wiped away her tears, took a deep breath and continued.

"But that isn't the worst of it. I drank with your birth father. And I kept drinking right up until the night that almost sank my career." Cassandra looked at Catherine and fixed her gaze on her daughter while she completed her thought. "That was the night I drank until I passed out. That was the night I was raped in the bathroom at work. And that was the last night I drank. I am so sorry, Cat, that I've been projecting my own failures on you. I will not do it again. You are a daughter that any mother would be proud to call her own. And make no mistake. I am proud of you."

Catherine had reached out to hold her mother's hand, but now she sat there in shock. With her thumb she rubbed the top of Cassandra's hand. Her eyes crinkled up at the edges and she held on even tighter, not saying a word, until the tears had stopped falling down her mother's cheeks.

CHAPTER 47

A few days later, Carl got into his office downtown at seven o'clock. With a cup of coffee still steaming in his hand, he glared at the documents on his desk. Two of the perpetrators had been brought in. Those two had insisted that there was a third perp, but the subpoenas from the Commonwealth's Attorney had brought back no fresh leads. Luv2Watch had been a promising lead. He'd checked out as a maker of dirty videos, but not a part of the conspiracy to rape Phoebe. Besides, he lived in Nashville.

Though it was early, Carl picked up the phone and left a message for Nadia. Then he surveyed the list again.

Carl double-checked his list and tried to make sure that the IP addresses all matched up to a physical location. Deep in concentration, he startled when the phone rang. It was Scott Abrams' direct line. Carl sighed. He couldn't avoid this call. He should have stayed at Cassandra's office today.

"Morning, Scott—"

"Carl? I need to talk to you in my office right away," Scott snapped.

Carl looked around at the neatly-stacked piles of paperwork and sighed.

•••

Helen flicked her pen one last time before she hung up the phone. "Thank you, Gary. I know you did as much as you could. I'll call you later."

She pushed away from her chair and stood up to stretch. She could feel the pulse in her temple pounding in perfect rhythm, but all the muscles in her neck were drawn tight in spasm. She winced as she imagined Gary prowling in front of a jury box. They had represented a major oil company in a case where the government had brought insider trading charges, and Gary had chipped away at the government's witnesses bit by bit until it was time to knit all the threads for the defense together in a mosaic of words and gestures and subtle intonations.

He stopped mid-sentence and froze, as if a thought had just occurred to him, and then, before he delivered the last few paragraphs of his closing statement, he stared at the members of the jury. After each one looked away, he nodded. With a sideways smile at opposing counsel and a slight twitch of his right eye in the client's direction, he continued talking, voice rising to a crescendo and then falling to a gentle "We ask you to find for the defendant."

It had been a magical performance, one of many Helen had witnessed. The jury had come in with their verdict in favor of the defendant in record time, and the entire defense team had gone out for drinks at a famous bar overlooking the bay.

Those were the old days, when Gary was in his prime. He had been a titan of the legal industry, but this was a profession that prized the appearance of strength. Although Gary was a young sixty-five, his power had faded a bit. His time had passed and he could do very little to save his best and brightest lawyer.

•••

Carl strolled through the hallways, and after he nodded to the Head Partner's secretary, he tapped on the outside of Scott's door. Scott's back was to Carl. Still gazing out the window of his twelfth-floor corner office, he motioned for Carl to sit down on the burgundy leather sofa.

Carl sank into it and felt swallowed up by its pillows. "I see you're in early, too . . ."

Scott flipped a baseball around in his hand and set it back on the window sill, seating himself a few feet from Carl. Rearranging the folds of his gray suit pants, Scott placed one foot on top of the other. He ignored Carl's attempt at small talk; instead, he seemed to study him like a cat assessing a bunny stuck in a briar bush. "Carl, I don't want to waste your time. The partners met last night to go over some personnel matters." Scott's eyes gleamed and he rubbed his hands together. "None of this is your fault, of course. But when you ride someone's coattails, no matter how well you ride, Carl, and in truth you are one of our most skilled senior associates . . . well, you picked a sinking ship. And for God's sake man, I don't care who you're sleeping with, but getting engaged? Really? Bad move, son. You should have waited until you made partner." Scott shook his head and held up his hands helplessly. "Once some of the older partners got wind of that, your sails were stripped, old boy. Heck, you burned the masthead."

Carl could have sworn Scott was grinning, but a shadow had fallen over his face. *Black magic.* Carl's head was spinning. And darn it all, there was some truth to what Scott had said. He had no idea how Scott had found out about Troy. Someone must have seen them together near their Adam's Morgan apartment. Not the bars; they were too old for that. It had been years.

He sighed. Whatever had happened had already played out. Besides, he was sick of hiding his personal life. And to be fair, he had barely been in the office for the last month; for the sake of appearances, it obviously did matter. He had to leave before he laughed, or cried, or told Scott to go to heck.

As he pushed up from the sofa, Carl laughed. He felt free of it all. "You'll need to pay me six months' severance, Scott, if you don't want the rats eating your own ship. This is the 21st century, and in case you haven't checked the newspapers, a majority of Americans support gay marriage."

Scott also stood up and waved his hand to dismiss Carl. "My secretary has already put the check in the mail. You have one hour to clear out all your personal effects from this office. Best of luck to you, Carl. We will provide excellent references for you, and the firm is confident you will land on your feet and experience tremendous success in your professional life."

Carl tried not to feel ashamed on his way back to his office. He gathered up his law books, photos and diplomas, then saved all of his documents on a zip drive and carried a single box downstairs to the garage. This morning he was glad that his man was a licensed therapist.

Before half past nine, Carl was on Route 395 South, heading toward Virginia. The sun bore down on the back of his neck and he touched the button that raised the roof on his hardtop Mercedes convertible. The first phone call he made was to Helen's cell phone. He needed to tell her in person, or at least that was his intention. But she already knew.

"Scott blindsided you, Carl?"

Carl summarized the conversation as he raced down the interstate in the opposite direction of the typical Wednesday morning traffic. He waited for Helen to interrupt or comment, but she maintained a judicious silence until he repeated what Scott had said. Helen chuckled suddenly, and as Carl imagined Helen's auburn hair glinting in the golden sunshine, he considered what Helen was going through and had a moment of clarity. No one had been killed. Jobs end. People move on. But everything was going to be all right.

"Carl, I'm sorry about all of this. Gary called me about an hour ago."

Carl's mouth dropped open. "Why didn't you warn me? I was at the office early."

"By the time I got done with Gary and called a few of our most loyal clients, it was too late."

Carl didn't know what to say. He gripped the wheel and tried to think.

"We will lose most of our clients. I'm sorry, Carl. I'm sorry for everything. You've been—" Her voice caught.

"It's okay. Not your fault."

"Well, yeah, it kind of was, but it's done." Her voice lightened. "But we'll keep a few of 'em. Like Sintab. They're in the bag."

Carl noticed that she was using the word "We," and he smiled. "Do you have a plan, Helen? And do you want me to work on your case over at the Bryson House today? I was in the middle of trying to puzzle out the third perp when Scott called me in." Carl pulled his hand through his hair and exited onto I-495, heading toward I-66 West.

"I don't think you need to work here, actually. You've been working at Cassandra's offices, correct? For most of the last two weeks?"

Carl tried not to sound rueful. "Yes. That was my first mistake."

"No, it wasn't," she replied right away. "They smelled weakness. Sharks. They would have let you go no matter what.

And they wouldn't have left you alone; they would have played you and plied you for information. You got a lot more work done for our clients and you gave me time to work the phones. None of this was your fault. That was the one thing Scott said that was correct."

Carl nodded at the speaker. "Okay, so you want me to work at Cassandra's offices? I needed to talk to Nadia anyway."

"Yes. And while you're there, Carl, would you do me a favor?" Helen had lowered her voice a little bit.

"Anything . . ."

"Get a sense for her practice." Helen was strategizing. "See if you fit in. If *we* fit in."

Carl pressed two fingers to his forehead. "That's your plan?"

"Assuming I don't go to jail, I have a plan. Maybe it's a Hail Mary. Certainly it is a long shot, but I still am carrying a multi-million dollar book, and so is she. And she doesn't care what anyone else thinks."

"Okay, Helen. I see where you're going with this. Because you don't care, either."

"Exactly."

Carl slammed the accelerator down. It felt like he was speeding into uncertainty.

CHAPTER 48

Today.
Today I ride with my brown-eyed girl.

CHAPTER 49

Carl parked his Mercedes in the garage beneath Brickman & White. It was easier to park in her Fairfax office than in his old office downtown because of the wider spaces, he thought. After he removed a leather briefcase containing all of the case files from his trunk, he locked his car and almost crashed into Cassandra, who was walking from the other end of the garage toward the elevator banks. She only realized it was him after she had already stridden past.

"Oh, Carl, you're back! Good to see you." When Carl didn't respond right away, she waited and then added, "How are you doing?" She studied his solemn face and checked her watch. It was almost eleven. "Tell you what. I need a cup of coffee, and I have a few questions to ask you. How about if you walk down the street with me? We can catch up a bit."

Carl nodded and turned around to pop the trunk on his convertible. "Just give me a moment to lock up my briefcase."

Carl still didn't say much while they walked down the street to the Starbucks on the corner opposite the public library. Downtown Fairfax contained a quixotic mix of very old, middle-aged and brand-new buildings; what had once been quaint now appeared more and more like any other bustling modern main street, replete with heavy traffic, chain restaurants and small stores facing leases they could barely pay each month.

After Cassandra paid for their coffees, she motioned to a black plastic table outdoors. "You feel like talking, Carl?"

He sat on a shaky plastic chair, and then the words tumbled out before he could stop them. "They fired me this morning. I was trying to match up the names of the sickos with their IPAs, and something, something was forming, making sense. And then Scott called me."

"Scott?"

Carl shooed a fly off the table. "Scott is the Head Alpha. Helen hates him. They've been fighting for years." He checked Cassandra's face, and when she nodded, he went on, "So he said that I picked the wrong coattails, and something about rats on a ship, and insulted my sexuality." Carl played with his cup of coffee, but he didn't take a sip.

"He sounds lovely." Cassandra squinted at Carl and then shook her head.

"Yeah."

"What happened next?"

"Well, there's not much else to tell. I'm a touch— overwhelmed, that's all. A few weeks ago I'm looking at making partner. Now I don't know what I'm looking at, you know?"

"I'm so sorry." Cassandra cocked her head and let her eyes crinkle, and she sat like that for a moment as if holding a part of his pain in her own mind. "Having worked with those sharks, well, I know what this feels like. It's a shock, like you've been kicked in the man-parts, right?"

Carl shook his head and chuckled. "About that, yeah."

"How's Helen holding up?" Cassandra tried to keep her voice low. A few attorneys from another Fairfax firm were sitting a few tables over, and one of the men had shot a few furtive looks in their direction. The entire town knew that Cassandra was on the case.

"Well, that's the thing. She already knew about it. I was worried about Helen, but she already knew." Carl paused as a white SUV went speeding past, horn blaring. "It sounds like she has a plan to hold onto a few of her clients. She comforted me, actually, if that makes any sense? And she's the one who has it all to lose."

Cassandra's fingers tapped her coffee cup. In her mind she sketched the name Brickman, White & Thompson. Then she scratched it out because Helen would have the biggest book, but Brickman was older. How about Brickman, Thompson & White? She felt like a young woman trying on her boyfriend's last name.

Maybe that's how the best partnerships start? Cassandra shook off the thought, but not without filing it away.

She wanted to give Carl a hug, but he didn't seem like the hugging type. "Of course Helen has a plan. The best litigators never get caught unawares." She paused. "Now let's hear your theory."

Carl nodded and leaned forward. It had seemed to him, as he had scanned the documents, that there was an IP address missing. If they could find out whose number was missing, maybe they would find the third perp. Left unanswered, he added, was why there was a number missing from the stack.

"You'd better figure out why the number's missing as soon as you can," Cassandra said. "Until we figure that out, Helen and Phoebe are in danger."

•••

Cassandra held the list at arm's length and studied it, squinting. Then she took her left hand and shook the paper. "It's gotta be this Park-it guy," she exclaimed.

Nadia made a face. "ParkMyLittleBob? What does he mean by that? Is his first name Bob?"

Carl wasn't listening. He leaned forward. "Here's what I want to know. I gave the files over to that detective, what's his name?"

"Parkings. Bob. Bob Parkings."

"Right, Nadia." Cassandra snapped her fingers. "Yet another Bob."

"But here's the thing," continued Carl. "The prosecution didn't get our original files, remember? So maybe when we printed this off, he omitted one of the files."

Cassandra looked doubtful.

"Listen, Cass, that would be on me—"

"No, Carl, it would be on me," interrupted Nadia.

"Oh come on, you two, it doesn't matter. Carl, do you have the original files stored on your laptop?"

"I do. And listen, Nadia, one thing Helen taught me is that blamestorming is a wasteful exercise. If a mistake was made and we submitted an incomplete case file, then so be it. Let's get it fixed, right?"

Nadia nodded. Cassandra stood up and headed out of the conference room. "I have a few calls to make, okay? As soon as you learn something, please let me know."

It only took Carl five minutes to turn on his computer and scan the original list of the members of Richard's MySpace group. He called the names out loud and Nadia counted:

"Okay, Nadia, how many is that?"

She reviewed her list. "Twenty-five."

There were twenty-four Internet protocol addresses. Carl thought for a moment. "Okay, match them up, and then I will read them back to you."

They matched the Internet addresses with twenty-four names. That left one name: perp number ten. ParkMyLittleBob.

Carl leaned toward Nadia and pointed to another number on the file. It was an IP address, not from one of the perps, but on the file jacket itself. There wasn't anything unusual about it, but for some reason something seemed . . . Carl snapped his fingers.

"Look at this Internet address. It's got a weird number. I think." Carl scanned the numbers on his screen. "Listen. It says FCPD. Nadia, do you have any idea what that means?"

Nadia studied Carl's face. "Fairfax County Police Department?"

Carl snapped his fingers. "Exactly. And listen. The prosecutor—that detective—"

"Bob Parkings?"

"Right, Parkings had the original files. Okay, so maybe he wasn't dumb enough to watch porn at the office. Maybe he . . . " Carl looked at the final IP address. "It's not that this is the same IP address as the missing one. It's just, I don't know. I got a feeling. You still following me?"

Nadia started to nod, and then shook her head. "Okay, but . . ."

"So he's been sitting on this." Carl squinted at the wall for a moment. "Why? Who is he protecting?"

Nadia shifted one shoulder. "Do you think Parkings knows who did it?"

"He knows something. That's for damn sure." Carl ran his fingers through his dark hair, and his eyes widened. "Nadia,

Bob Parkings. The name of the missing perp has Park and Bob in it."

Nadia's jaw dropped. She ran out of the conference room and burst into Cassandra's office.

•••

At the Bryson House, Helen and Phoebe continued their usual routine-in-waiting Wednesday. Phoebe had been uncharacteristically silent most of the week. She didn't speak to anyone at meals and she spent more and more time pacing the grounds and riding Ginger, often with an assist from Helen, whenever Anne left the grounds.

Helen, on the other hand, felt an odd comfort at the Bryson House. She spent her mornings reading the newspaper and scanning the local real estate listings or staring off into the color-crested mountains. In the afternoons, she usually worked the phone.

This morning, however, was different. Helen hung up after talking to Carl and called Gary one last time. "You know what I need to ask you," she began.

"Yes." Gary's voice was softer than usual. "And if I could, I would leave and start up a new firm." Gary paused and the line sounded so quiet, it made Helen feel cold. It wasn't possible. They both knew it. Gary was turning sixty-six in November, and that was a few years too old to start over.

"I know. You've done so much for me, and now it's ending. And I'm at peace with all of that, Gary, but I wish I could thank you better than leaving a mess behind."

"The best way you can thank me is to keep your head up, take your clients and Carl and show those sharks, especially Scott, how a firm should be built."

Through the tears that were forming, Helen managed to smile and say goodbye without crying. Someday she'd invite Gary to her new offices, and in the meantime she'd start making some calls. She'd lined up Sintab, and there were three other major clients she had placed calls to; and as she thought of each one her mind raced with possibilities. Those corporations' legal departments were run by three of her old law school friends, people who would follow her no matter where she ended up.

Even better, Baker Pitts would be unable to enforce a non-competition agreement against her.

She could build a smaller but still exceptional litigation boutique and work fewer hours. A vision was forming in her mind: this new practice, a country home in the mountains, a horse and stables and a reduced caseload that would allow her to spend time being a mom. No wonder she hadn't slept in days.

•••

At first light, Phoebe ambled over to Anne's chalet and opened the door after knocking on the panel to the left of the doorknob. The teakettle screamed and Phoebe rushed into the kitchen and lifted the shaking kettle off the burner. Anne emerged around the corner with a wry grin on her face. "Morning, child of light. You realize you're becoming a morning bird, don't you?"

Phoebe rolled her eyes. "It's not that much earlier. I make sure I get my beauty sleep."

Anne poured tea into white and red porcelain teacups and set the cups on the cozy kitchen table, along with milk and sugar. "Sheesh, the morning bird . . ."

Phoebe laughed and interrupted. "What? Catches the best worms? Drinks the morning dew? The night owl is overrated. Wise and one of your favorite adjectives, Coach: reticent."

"Precocious child," exclaimed Anne as she stirred sugar into her tea. "You are learning!" With a wink, Anne added, "Be careful this afternoon. I will be in a meeting with Miranda and the accountants from two until four. I am certain you wouldn't take advantage of my absence to do the rider's version of swimming in a neighbor's pool at midnight."

Phoebe's mouth dropped open. She couldn't think of a response.

•••

After she finished talking to Cassandra, Elizabeth walked as fast as she could from her office to the side of the building that housed the Fairfax County Police Department. Her high heels left loud echoes on the marble floors as she wove through the corridors. The Commonwealth's Attorney wore high heels that matched her suit and nail polish. With her four-inch heels, Elizabeth rose to well over six feet in height. Even if she had not been boiling with anger, she would have cut an imposing figure. Now, with eyes flashing and legs swallowing several feet with each pair of strides, she resembled a speeding freight train.

She eyed Lieutenant Patrick Stockman's nameplate and threw the door open without knocking. Stockman, a trim but aging black man with white hair, glanced at Elizabeth and motioned for her to shut the door. "It must be pretty important for you to honor me with a personal visit, Ellie." He clicked his computer screen off and swiveled around in his chair.

Elizabeth shut the door behind her and leaned against it. "As much as I'd love to visit with you, Stockman, we have a situation and not much time to fix it."

"Election year, is it?" Stockman had been in the force a long time. He wasn't intimidated by Commonwealth's Attorneys.

When Elizabeth responded by shaking the paper in her hand, Stockman sat up straighter. "Is this about the missing GPS units?"

Stockman was referring to "slap-on" GPS units that police departments could affix to a suspect's vehicle with tamper-resistant magnets. The Supreme Court had ruled slap-on GPS units unconstitutional, but many police officers and detectives had ignored the federal government's directives to return them. The units had saved many victims' lives.

The vast majority of police officers who held onto their units had used them as they were intended, even if this violated the Constitution, but a few dirty cops had recently affixed the slap-on GPS units to the vehicles of suspicious Muslim scholars. On Monday morning the Governor, in response to pressure from civil rights groups, had sent letters to police departments statewide, and the FCPD had spent the last two days tracking down all the missing units. One remained at large.

"Stockman, you realize the Governor asked for these back two days ago? And you get that your men are not allowed to use them, right?"

Stockman formed a triangle out of his hands and exhaled. Elizabeth couldn't tell if he was annoyed or overworked, but she didn't care. When he didn't answer right away, she rushed on. "I need you to tell me who has that GPS unit immediately, and while you're getting me the name, I need to discuss something else with you."

Stockman nodded and dialed his sergeant. He barked a few words into the phone, hung up and faced Elizabeth. "What else?"

"The Thompson case—the one that Detective Parkings is working, you know what I am talking about?"

Stockman grunted. "We've brought in two of the perps. We've given you all we learned from the house where the judge died, and now you're determining whether you should charge the person of interest, the judge's wife—right?"

Elizabeth clenched her teeth. "That's what the Detective has told you?"

Stockman nodded again. "Yes. And he is one of our best men. Why?"

"I have reason to suspect that he is protecting someone here in the department, and damn it, if I find out you're involved in this too, I will burn the entire department to the ground."

The expression on Stockman's face changed from skepticism and annoyance to bald curiosity. Stockman was an old-fashioned detective, but he almost never took anything personally when he worked cases. "Protecting someone? What do you mean?"

Elizabeth summarized her conversation with Cassandra.

"May I see the printout with the IP address?" Stockman's brow furrowed. Perusing the sheet of paper Elizabeth handed him, he picked up the black receiver on his phone and dialed Parkings' phone number. He left a terse voicemail and then turned back to Elizabeth. "You said you were concerned that he was protecting someone. Any idea who?"

Just then there was a knock on the door, and a frazzled sergeant appeared. "Billings, come in."

"Lieutenant, I have the name of the detective who last checked out the slap-on GPS." The sergeant hesitated, but Stockman directed him to continue. "Detective Parkings checked it out."

Elizabeth watched Stockman's deep brown eyes turn even darker. "Run a tracer on the GPS unit and let me know if it shows Parkings' address."

Billings, a middle-aged white man, turned on his heels. Elizabeth smiled; he looked like he was ex-military, like so many cops in Stockman's department.

"You know, Elizabeth," the Lieutenant said, "I don't want to be caught with our hand in the proverbial cookie jar. As long as it returns his home address, we can rest a little easier, right?" He leaned back in his chair. "Anyway, how are your kids? Has your son heard back from any colleges?"

Elizabeth sat down in the faux-leather chair in front of Stockman's desk, but Billings returned before they could begin.

Stockman cleared his throat. "Yes, Sarge?"

"We got an address, but it wasn't his home address." Billings studied the small green notepad clasped between his long fingers.

"What is the address, Billings?"

"It's somewhere out in Middleburg, Virginia."

Elizabeth leaned forward. "Middleburg. Hmm."

"Yes. The owner is a Bryson—"

"Oh my God!" Elizabeth gasped.

"What is that, Ellie?"

"That's where Helen Thompson is staying. Do you think that Parkings could have—" Elizabeth's voice faltered and she felt a vague fear in the pit of her stomach.

"Damn it, I don't know what to think," Stockman snapped. "Maybe you're right, Ellie, maybe he is protecting someone."

Elizabeth gazed at the Lieutenant. Then she spoke in a voice just above a whisper. "What if he is protecting himself?"

Stockman's eyes narrowed. "Well, we need to get to the bottom of this ASAP." He turned to the sergeant. "Billings, ping his cell phone."

"But sir," Billings hesitated, "don't we need a warrant to do that?"

Elizabeth shook her head. "If he is trying to hide something or is somehow involved in this, we don't need a warrant to protect her."

"Billings—go now." Stockman folded his arms across his chest. "Do it. I'll fill out the paperwork later." The Lieutenant and prosecutor waited in silence until the sergeant reappeared at the door, frowning.

"What is it, Billings?"

Shaking his head, Billings looked at his notepad. "This is the weird thing, sir. His location is the same as the GPS unit we traced."

Elizabeth sucked in her breath. "He's not supposed to be there!"

Stockman slammed his hand against the desk. His department did not have jurisdiction in Middleburg. "Billings, call the state police. Apprise them of the situation and tell them we have a rogue cop." He turned to Elizabeth and spoke tersely. "Do you have the phone number for the Bryson House? Or at least for Helen Thompson? We need to give them a heads-up."

Elizabeth shook her head. "No, but I will give Ms. Thompson's attorney a call. From what I gathered, she is actually meeting with her client at the Bryson House as we speak." Elizabeth took her BlackBerry out of her red leather purse and scrolled down until she came to Cassandra White's name. The call went straight to voicemail.

CHAPTER 50

Even though he'd planned it all out, and hopefully his escape plan was solid, he wasn't so sure he cared what happened to him after he'd taken her. Had her. Every inch. . . of her. He'd waited. He'd waited and planned and suffered for this. Now he'd have her. All of her. And when he finished with her, he would have that fine mother of hers, too. It wasn't so much a question of right or wrong, because doing right too often felt so wrong. He'd done the right thing for so long, but Richard had promised and then not followed through. He couldn't take it any longer.

As far as Richard went, he had been weak. A pretty boy with soft hands. Liked hunting only with a semiautomatic. Never a bow and arrow, and never ate what he killed. Richard was more hunted than hunter, wasn't he? And that big-mouthed, hard-boiled wife of his, she thought she could go into hiding and keep his brown-eyed girl away from him? She had no idea how a real man hunted. Couldn't take Bob the Hunter down with a bit of titanium driver, now could you?

Bob Parkings looked outside the windshield of his white Jeep Grand Cherokee and winced at the bright sunshine reflecting into his eyes. He stroked himself atop his jeans. Then he pulled on his aviator sunglasses. They were his magic lodestone, those glasses; all the women found him irresistible when he wore them. They all begged for it. She would, too. And now, now he could take her without having to worry about that blinding headache coming on.

Light. Goddamn it, why couldn't it be dark out? He wished it were nighttime, but he knew that wouldn't work. The best way—the only way in would be to drive straight up to the guardhouse at three in the afternoon.

He fingered his mini-Uzi and set it next to his Glock 22 forty-caliber Smith & Wesson pistol. After he used the mini-Uzi on the guard, his Smith & Wesson, with fifteen rounds per clip and three extra clips, would give him plenty of ammo to take out any remaining obstructions between him and his brown-eyed girl.

The gravel driveway to the Bryson House appeared to his right as he pulled into the entrance road. He'd been taking the pulse of his target and all its inhabitants for weeks, and he was ready. He didn't like shooting people. The blood would leak out and a pool would form, and maybe the brain's gray matter would flow all over into a big gory puddle. It wasn't enjoyable, but sometimes it was necessary. *Hunters hunt.* And even if the side of someone's head broke off, just like JFK's had, he'd fall back on his training.

Bob took a deep breath. Getting his hands bloody might be necessary, and it wouldn't be the first time. Probably not the last time, either. *Hunters hunt.*

He slowed down as he approached the guardhouse. Fifty yards, then twenty. Then five. He could count the black shingles on the roof. The broad-shouldered guard with salt-and-pepper hair held a notepad and tapped on the window.

Bob rolled his window down, but before the guard could get a word out, the detective picked up the black mini-Uzi and shot him right between the eyes. He caught a flash of movement from behind the guardhouse and jumped out of the Grand Cherokee, his finger on the Uzi and his legs spread wide, his body shielded by the steel frame of his SUV.

Bob tried not to breathe too deeply. *Wait, wait, wait, he's coming.* He cleared his brain of everything else until the remaining guard was just an obstruction, even a paper target, with a black shirt and a white hand moving. The guard was moving fast, but not fast enough. As he raced around the edge of the guardhouse and tried to draw his gun, it was too late. Bob took aim and hit his target in the forehead, just above the eyes. The man reached his arm out as if to scratch his head. That was the last move he ever made.

Bob tried not to inhale as he checked his perimeter. It reeked. He had to get moving. The smell of blood revolted him and the taste of bile rose in his throat until he remembered the girl. Her body. How he had wanted her for so long. He squared his shoulders, wiped his mouth with his sleeve and popped a piece of gum into his mouth. He'd smell good for her, at least.

As he moved forward, a sunbeam got between the frame of his sunglasses and his left eye. For a split second, he clutched his head. *Be strong.* He couldn't let the damn sun stop him. This was his day. *Focus, Bob.* A few more minutes. He got back in his SUV and drove. *Time to find her.*

He'd given years to hunting the hunters. Damn good years. This was another hunt, and he was . . . Bob shook his head. Didn't matter. Above his pay grade to figure it out. He needed this; he was done waiting. He'd been waiting too long.

Out of the corner of his eye, he caught sight of a girl on a ginger-colored horse. Could it be his brown-eyed girl? He'd been listening to that song over and over again the last few weeks. Reminded him of his Janie, this girl did. His brown-eyed girl was young again.

He could not believe it. *There she is.* He looked around to make sure no one else was nearby. This was his chance. With his handgun tucked into a side holster, he parked his vehicle behind the guardhouse and tracked her from the trees as she rode. She was riding toward the stables, so he cut across the far side of the field, unhurried, as if taking an afternoon stroll in the country. Now he was really hunting. As he walked, he hummed their song.

Bob was already leaning against the side of the barn when his girl pulled up. *Now.* She screwed up her face at him, seeming to study him, but continued speaking in a gentle voice to her horse. While she sat in her saddle, one hand on her horse's neck, patting it, Bob, always a gentleman, just like his mom had taught him, made a nice gesture and took hold of the reins. "Hello there, m'lady. It seems you suffered a mishap since the last time I saw you."

Phoebe rubbed the reins and, in a glum tone mumbled a greeting.

What, doesn't she recognize me? He tried not to frown. *I thought we'd had something back at the gas station.* "May I give you a hand?" He put his hand up to Phoebe, but with a look of annoyance she shook her head and swung her legs down all fancy, landing on the balls of her feet.

"I'm sorry, but have we met?" Phoebe reached out to take the reins, and Bob's body tensed as his hand brushed against hers.

As she led the horse toward the door, Bob moved to the barn door and pushed it in, ducking inside the entryway. He waited for her to lead the horse past him. "Don't you recognize me from the coffee shop? When I gave your mother a break on the ticket?"

She made a polite sound. "Ohh, I do remember. Are you here to talk to my mom?"

"Yes, m'lady. I was assigned to her case and I just had a few questions for her. They told me up at the house that she was out riding, and when I saw you from a distance, I thought she was you."

The girl seemed to freeze. "Is my mom in trouble?"

He walked closer to her and held open the horse's stall. The girl, his brown-eyed girl, turned around with a gorgeous, helpless look, and Bob felt himself growing hard in his pants.

"Aww, don't worry, m' lady, it is going to be okay. We got a call to come down and check, make sure everything was safe. I was just about to check the barn." He paused and tried not to smirk. He was so close to getting her inside. *Focus, Bob. Almost there.* "I'm sure this has been so hard on you. How about if I help you get that saddle off?"

Phoebe's shoulders sagged, and Bob relaxed. The hunted was now the prey. Then she shook her head. "No, how about if I take you up to the house."

•••

Up at the house Mimi sat in the kitchen, cleaning her handgun again. Folk music played in the background. She was alone; Cassandra and Helen were meeting in the library to prepare for Friday's meeting with the Commonwealth's Attorney, and Miranda and Anne were meeting with the accountant in the dining room. Occasionally Mimi could hear Anne teasing Miranda, who no doubt was ignoring her beloved friend.

Finished cleaning her Ruger, Mimi chuckled, and with a now-efficient motion she practiced loading. She hoped Anne and Miranda wouldn't walk into the kitchen at that moment. She wanted to surprise them at the gun range the next time they went.

And that was when she heard something. She thought it was a delivery truck backfiring, but no trucks were due today. Then she realized it was too clean of a noise. Streamlined. A chill ran down her spine. It wasn't quite deer hunting season. She grabbed the radio and called down to the guardhouse. No answer. She called their cell phones three times each. Nothing. It just didn't add up. She stood up and screamed, "Miranda! Helen! Where is Phoebe?"

Anne reached Mimi's side first. "She is taking Ginger out for a ride. Why?" Anne's eyes lingered over Mimi's right hand, which was wrapped around the Ruger. The other women ran into the kitchen.

"What's wrong, Mimi? You said Phoebe is out riding, Anne? She was supposed to be watching calculus."

"I heard gunshots. The guards didn't answer."

Helen's worry lines turned into panic.

Anne ran toward the front door. "Stables!" she cried. Mimi had already sprinted outside, and she was covering ground faster than she had ever thought possible.

•••

Parkings knew this was it. This was his chance. *Inside, right here, right now*, a voice inside him shouted. As soon as Phoebe stepped outside the stall, Parkings put his arms around her. "I've been waiting, Phoebe. I've been waiting so long for you." She kicked and flopped, pushing, pushing, but not screaming, and she landed a kick to his shins. He laughed. *Man, she was a wild lil' filly. Nothing like breaking a lil' mare.*

"Shh, now, lil' thing, my lil' thing, shh." Parkings walked Phoebe backward until she was up against the wall outside Ginger's stall. He could feel her heart racing faster and faster beneath his hand. *Just don't scream or yell. It's going to be all right.*"

•••

While Parkings fumbled with his belt strap, Phoebe's mind raced. This was what her father had left her? This stammering, sick old man? This was Dad's legacy?

It wasn't enough that he slept with—no, no—he raped me. Now he's sending this cop to get me? Haven't we already killed you, Dad? Isn't it enough? It's like some stupid horror show, this—this what? This life? Is this it? Is this all there is? That was hell and so is this. I wanted none of it. And I don't want this. He's going to have to kill me first.

The belt clicked as he put his hand on it as if to rest for a moment while he savored the thought of taking her. Her eyes followed his fingers as they connected with the steel belt buckle. The buckle glistened as it reflected a sunbeam. Phoebe tried to ignore the dancing dust particles. She couldn't move, couldn't scream. She couldn't even breathe. It was all happening so fast, and all she could do was stare at dust particles.

She thought about dying, and that would be better than this. *No, no, God, please kill me first.* Then she pictured her father. She'd never really liked it. She had said that to hurt her mother and even more, to hurt herself. To kill even more of the cancer he'd planted inside her. And in killing it all off, she had hurt her mom, and she was sorry. She was so sorry. And now she could never tell her; she couldn't tell Cary and she couldn't tell her mom how sorry she was for all the times she'd lain next to her father, waiting for her daddy to return.

It wasn't him; he'd been replaced, stolen, by a different man. He'd become someone, or more like something, that turned her love against itself. She was done with trying to forget. She could never forget. Some pain can never go away. It can only fade a little bit, the jagged edges worn smooth by the vague tapping of a second hand round and round the face of a massive grandfather clock that only God could reset.

Out of the corner of her eye, Phoebe caught the flickering of a shadow on the unfinished wooden beams overhead. But it wasn't the shadow of a TV on the ceiling. What she saw moving was a bird, a big blue bird flying across the sky, and it looked awkward but strong. Then Phoebe could smell the hay and the manure and Ginger. And while the big blue bird flew in her mind's eye, she could breathe again. She could feel. And then Phoebe knew. She knew she could fly.

But first, she had to get free. How would a horse break free? First they're bucking, all crazy and out of control, and then it seems like they've given up, so the rider relaxes her hands, maybe scratches the fly that lands on her nose or gets distracted by a drop of dew on a stray blade of grass. Then the horse puts every ounce of will and power into motion. Before the rider can tighten the reins, the horse is off and running. A horse could break free from a two hundred-pound rider, but a horse is bigger, so much bigger, than the rider.

She breathed in the smell of the horses. She had to channel their power. But first she had to pretend he'd broken her. He would like that. It was what Dad had really liked. He wanted to break her over and over again because when she broke, it made him feel like he had mastered someone, or something. *I was never broken. He was the broken one.*

She willed all of her muscles to relax, waiting until she heard the sound of a belt buckle being undone. *Now. Move now.* Springing up, she jumped out of his grasp and landed so that she was facing him. With her left arm still covered in a hard cast, she swung it as fast as she could and connected with his rib cage. He growled like a dog in pain and stepped back.

As Parkings reeled and staggered from the edge of Ginger's stall, Phoebe looked around the barn, frantic, seeking a way out. *The ladder.* She saw the ladder and bolted for it. She couldn't feel her feet but she knew she was moving because the ladder was getting closer. She knew she could climb it much faster than he could. All that one-handed riding, those moments of joy not so much stolen as borrowed, had been for something. Once on the roof, she would jump off it and run. He could shoot her then. She was going to die running, not cowering.

A horse neighed and Parkings bellowed. Ginger rose up on her back legs and landed a kick that broke open the stall door and sent Parkings slamming into another stall. He staggered and fell to one knee, and Phoebe reversed direction. She could see daylight. She vaulted over Parkings and, arms wheeling to keep her balance, she took three more steps. Now she was screaming, angry, not scared anymore, not scared because Ginger was not scared.

"You—" Parkings put his hand on his gun and stood up, and Phoebe could feel his eyes boring into her back. "I'm going to shoot your horse if you move another step."

Phoebe froze, and for a split second she wasn't sure. Ginger's nostrils were flaring and her ears were all the way back. *She'd die for me. I can't save her from him.* Phoebe's throat filled with bile. It was no choice. Her dad had always told her it was her choice, but it was never her choice. And yet she still couldn't move. She couldn't feel her feet. It was like an invisible band tied one foot, then the other, to the dirt floor beneath her.

"No!" Mimi burst through the barn door and pushed Phoebe behind her. Before Parkings could grab his Glock, the woman pointed and shot. Three rounds left the chamber. He fell backward as two bullets slammed into his right shoulder. The third bullet ricocheted off a wooden beam.

Parkings sagged onto a bale of hay, red soaking through his shirt.

Hands shaking, Mimi kept the gun pointed at Parkings. She kept her eyes fixed on him as she called out, "Detective Parkings, right?"

Parkings glared at Mimi. With one hand clasping his bleeding shoulder, he reached for his gun.

Anne strode through the barn door, and in one smooth motion she reached her right hand out and snatched the riding crop that hung on a hook on the wall. Somehow appearing unrushed, Anne slapped the whip once, just in time to stop Parkings from getting hold of his Glock. Wincing, Parkings grabbed his hand as the gun skidded across the barn floor. Phoebe could smell an acrid, burning smell, and she stared over at Parkings. She realized she was starting to shake all over, but she knew that she couldn't ask for help. She was so tired.

Then she let her eyes meet Parkings', and he gave her an imploring, almost pathetic look. Confused, she shook her head.

The detective shifted his gaze to Mimi. "You ol' hag! You got it coming to you!" Before he could try to move again, Mimi shook her finger. "Don't move. I have twelve rounds left and I'll fire every last one of them into your head."

The barn door banged shut again. Miranda sidled up beside Mimi. Anne immediately put her arm around Phoebe and stood beside her, not speaking, but covering Phoebe the way a protective goose would cover a gosling during an early spring thunderstorm.

"I'll take care of that for you," Miranda murmured, and took the Ruger out of her friend's hand. "Nice shot, my dear."

"Thank you. I told you I had a bad feeling about that detective." Mimi wiped her hands on her dress.

A look of shock followed by comprehension came over Miranda's face. "That—that's the detective that kept calling here?"

"That's about the size of it. How about if you and Anne keep an eye on him until the law arrives?"

At that instant, Helen crashed through the barn door and almost collided with Anne. She put a hand to her mouth as she took in the scene. Her eyes lit on Parkings. She opened and closed her fists and started to take a step toward him, but Anne put a hand out and whispered, "She's safe now." A little louder, Anne added, "Go ahead, we've got this."

After Phoebe and Helen were out of earshot, Anne stood next to Miranda and scratched at the ground with her boots. Manure went flying and slapped into Parkings' face, and there he remained, writhing on the dusty floor.

•••

Inside the Bryson House, Phoebe huddled up under a light blue fleece blanket and sipped hot chocolate from a white mug. The police and the ambulance had left over an hour earlier, but Phoebe was still silent, staring into the distance. Her eyes tracked the blue heron that had made a habit of flying over the red earth ever since the Thompsons had first come to the Bryson House.

Helen sat beside her daughter, flanked by Cassandra and Anne. Phoebe wasn't really listening to their conversation, until she heard Cassandra speak. "They will dismiss it, Helen. He destroyed and hid evidence. This is worse than any police misconduct I've ever seen."

Helen took a deep breath and the lines in her forehead faded from sight.

Phoebe put her mug down on the table. "Are we safe now, Mom?"

"Yes, Phoebe, we're safe."

Anne stood between Phoebe and Helen, staring at the girl while she spoke. "With all due respect, Helen, there are no guarantees of anything in life—least of all, safety. There will be hard days and there will be easier days. We will move on, like ripples follow a stone thrown in still water."

Anne paused and stroked Phoebe's cheek. "Remember, Phoebe, child of light, no matter how many times the phoenix falls, she always rises."

Phoebe glanced at the real estate brochures scattered on the kitchen table. "Can we go look at this house, Mom?" Squinting through the ray of sunshine that streamed in from the window, the girl looked at her mother. Then Phoebe pointed to the ramshackle house with the stables. "It looks like home."

About the Author

E.L. Phoenix is a truth explorer and a lay minister. She is an adventurer, a charismatic speaker, a lover of nature and animals, and a happy learner. From an early age, she has studied theology, archeology, history, philosophy, quantum physics and modern literature. Elaine is currently on sabbatical from her work as a lay minister to hunt for proof of prehistoric advanced civilizations on all seven continents; in other words, she's hunting for proof of God. She splits her time between Wyoming and Virginia and lives with her three children. El is the author of several books, including the award-winning and best-selling Ripple and I Run.

Along with Chance Stevens, Phoenix is building an interfaith ministry that will teach the deeper principles of spirituality. El views herself as a follower of The Way, which is what Jesus originally called his movement. She also embraces indigenous faith traditions as well as the scientific method. El honors Jesus and Muhammad, Buddha and Lao-Tze, Gandhi and MLK, Whitman and Jung in her work. She teaches in a fearless style that embraces all souls and all systems of thought.

El teaches from all holy scriptures, whether they are found in the New Testament, the Torah, the Qur'an, Rumi's Masnavi, the Mahabharata, or in modern works of such poets as Wordsworth, Keats, Shelley, Whitman, Byron, and Coleman Barks. When El speaks, she is almost as likely to quote from Plato as she is to bring up the lost gospels of Mark, the son of Jesus and Mary Magdalene. Like Rumi, El is neither Sufi Mystic nor Hindu; Christian nor New Age; Buddhist nor Jewish—she is all these faiths and believes that the Way Home can be found both inside as well as outside church doors.

If you would like to get an e-mail when E.L.'s next book is released, please visit:

http://strayswelcomeinterfaithministries.com and subscribe for updates, or to subscribe to her newsletter directly, please go here: http://eepurl.com/AGRb9.

Word-of-mouth is crucial for any author to succeed. If you enjoyed this book, please consider leaving a review where you purchased it, even if it's only a line or two; it would make all the difference and be very much appreciated:

http://tinyurl.com/RippleYAV.

And if you know anyone who has been sexually abused or has been the victim of domestic violence, please recommend they read Ripple.

Stop by and visit!

E.L. loves to talk, and she answers all her correspondence personally. Well, at least for now. She would love to see you, either on her Facebook Page, https://www.facebook.com/strayswelcomeinterfaithministries or via e-mail at farrisburke@me.com.

Thank you, and peace and love to all of you.

Support Resources

Crisis Support

Universal Emergency Number Nationwide: 911

National Hopeline: 1-800-656-HOPE (4673)

National Suicide Hotline: 1-800-273-TALK (8255)

Rape Abuse & Incest National Network (RAINN)

> Direct link to immediate online chat intervention
> http://online.rainn.org

> Direct link to search all local crisis centers in the US by
> state or zip code
> http://centers.rainn.org/

Survivor Support

About.com Post Traumatic Stress Disorder
http://ptsd.about.com/

After Silence
http://aftersilence.org

After The Rain
http://aftertherain.com

Arte Sana (English/Spanish)
http://arte-sana.com/arte_sana.htm

Dancing In The Darkness
http://dancinginthedarkness.com/

Healing Through Creativity

http://healingthroughcreativity.org/

Incest Survivors Anonymous
http://lafn.org/medical/isa/home.html

Let Go . . . Let Peace Come In Foundation
http://letgoletpeacecomein.org/

Lori's Song
http://lorissong.org/

Male Survivor (for male survivors)
http://malesurvivor.org/

1in6 (for male survivors)
http://1in6.org/men/

Pandora's Project
http://pandys.org/index.html

Project Unbreakable
http://projectunbreakable.tumblr.com/

Recovered Memory Project
http://blogs.brown.edu/recoveredmemory/

Sexual Abuse & Rape Survivor Links
http://aswaterspassingby.org/sexualabuse.html

Safe Horizon
http://safehorizon.org

Survivors Network of those Abused by Priests (SNAP)
http://snapnetwork.org/

Survivors of Incest Anonymous
http://siawso.org/

Witness Justice
http://witnessjustice.org/resources/hotline.cfm